# Stolen Splendor

"Sir, you are no gentleman."

"And you are no lady," Stefan replied easily, "to frequent lowly taverns for your . . . amusement."

Kassandra raised her arm to slap him, but he caught it and brought it to his lips, his burning gaze never leaving her face.

"So beautiful . . ." Stefan murmured, a rakish smile tugging at his lips.

The sound of his voice shattered the spell that held her captive. Kassandra drew herself up, meeting his gaze unflinchingly. "As I said before, my lord, we have never met. As for your strange talk of taverns, it appears the full moon has addled your senses. You are both mad . . . and a black-guard!"

She wrenched her arm from his grasp and forced herself to walk calmly away.

"Hardly mad, my lady," Stefan said softly under his breath. "Captivated."

# Stolen Splendor

## Miriam Minger

AVON BOOKS ◆ NEW YORK

*To Barbara—*
*A romantic spirit, dreamer, cherished friend.*

AVON BOOKS
A division of
The Hearst Corporation
105 Madison Avenue
New York, New York 10016

Copyright © 1989 by Miriam Minger
Inside cover author photograph by Priscilla E. M. Purnick
Published by arrangement with the author
Library of Congress Catalog Card Number: 89-91269
ISBN: 0-380-75862-8

First Avon Books Printing: November 1989

AVON TRADEMARK REG. U.S. PAT. OFF. AND IN OTHER COUNTRIES, MARCA REGISTRADA, HECHO EN U.S.A.

Printed in the U.S.A.

RA 10 9 8 7 6 5 4 3 2 1

# Chapter 1

*Vienna, Austria*
*November, 1716*

**"A**re you sure you won't accompany me, Kassandra?" Countess Isabel von Furstenberg ventured one last time as she twirled in front of the full-length mirror, admiring the shimmer of the morning sunlight as it played across the lilac watered silk of her gown. She loved beautiful clothes, especially wearing them to galas, and today she wasn't going to just any gala. She had been invited by Charles VI, emperor of Austria, and his wife, Empress Elisabeth, to the Favorita, their country palace.

Kassandra Wyndham turned abruptly from the window, her large amethyst eyes flashing with exasperation. She had already declined perhaps a dozen times. But the heated retort died on her lips at Isabel's hopeful expression.

Kassandra was truly fond of Isabel. After all, the countess and her father, Miles Wyndham, Earl of Harrington and ambassador to Austria, were planning to marry as soon as he returned from his diplomatic mission to King George's home court in Hanover, Germany.

But, much as she liked Isabel, their interests could be no further apart. She did not share Isabel's enthusiasm for court life and intrigue. On the contrary, the thought of spending the day at a stuffy gala surrounded by pompous aristocrats and their preening ladies—even in Isabel's charming and lively company—was more than she could bear. Still, there was no sense in trying to make Isabel understand. She would only be shocked if she knew where Kassandra's true interests lay.

"Thank you, Isabel, but no," she said firmly. "Perhaps another time."

Dismayed by the finality in Kassandra's voice, Isabel glanced over her shoulder at her younger companion. "But what will you do on such a lovely day as this, Kassandra? If you won't accompany me to the gala, at least promise me you won't hide yourself in the library. Surely there are other diversions than poring over those dusty books again."

"I think I'll . . . go for a ride today, and then write Father a letter," Kassandra replied quickly, turning back to the window. Her lie made her wince, especially in light of Isabel's kindness. But she had no choice. She pushed aside the lace curtains, her finger tracing a pattern on the cool glass. The sunny day outside seemed to beckon to her . . . crisp, clear, tinged with a promise of excitement and adventure. Soon, she breathed to herself. Soon.

Barely masking her disappointment, Isabel turned back to the mirror. She fussed a moment with the small lace cap set atop her glossy black curls, then attempted in vain to readjust the long lappets that cascaded down her back in a froth of cream lace and lilac ribbon. "Oh, Gisela . . ." she began in frustration to her maid, who stood nearby.

"Please, milady, if you will allow me," Gisela murmured. With expert fingers the spry middle-aged woman first smoothed the unruly lappets, then walked over to the dressing table and chose a delicately painted satin fan with an ivory stick for her mistress. Her footsteps were quick and light as she returned to Isabel's side. "Your fan, milady."

"Thank you, Gisela," Isabel said softly, her usual good spirits revived by her maid's thoughtful ministrations. "As ever, your taste is exquisite."

Gisela smiled at the warm compliment. "Will there be anything else, milady?"

"Only my velvet cape. If you would take it downstairs, I will put it on just before I leave."

Gisela nodded, gathered the cape trimmed with luxuriant blue fox from the bed, then, with a sideways glance at Kassandra, quietly left the room.

Absently thumping the fan against the palm of her hand, Isabel creased her forehead in thought as she studied Kassandra's reflection in her mirror. The tall young woman reminded her so much of Miles . . .

Dear Miles. How she missed him. She had met the newly appointed English ambassador and his nineteen-year-old daughter at a welcoming reception shortly after their arrival in Vienna in July. Isabel had fallen in love with him almost immediately, and to her delight, Miles had returned her devotion with equal fervor.

At twenty-five, Isabel had almost given up hope of ever marrying. It wasn't that she had lacked for suitors. There had been many a dashing aristocrat who had sought her hand, but she simply hadn't found the right man among them. It hadn't helped that her older brother, Stefan, had never approved of any of them, claiming they were interested only in her great wealth.

A faint smile touched Isabel's lips. At least Stefan had not objected to this match. It was true that there was a seventeen-year age difference between them, but Miles Wyndham was handsome, distinguished, with abundant wealth and land of his own in England. Most important, he truly loved her.

To her utter amazement, this time Stefan had finally trusted her judgment and had even given his consent to their marriage in a recent letter. She could hardly wait for them to meet each other.

Isabel sighed. That meeting would just have to wait. Though Stefan was due to return from the Turkish campaign any day now, Miles would be in Hanover for several months. Could it be only two weeks since he had left? It felt so much longer . . . an eternity.

At least Kassandra had accepted her invitation to stay at the von Furstenberg estate while her father was gone, Isabel consoled herself, glancing across the room. Her mood brightening once again, she whirled around to face Kassandra, a warm smile lighting her delicate features. "If you will not attend the gala with me, will you at least walk with me to the door?"

Kassandra felt a surge of relief as she turned from the window, grateful that the matter was put to rest—at least for now. She smiled in assent and followed the countess from her chamber. Together they walked the length of the long corridor, Isabel chattering excitedly about the outdoor gala, then down the massive marble staircase to the light-paneled foyer.

Waiting by the front entrance, Gisela watched as the two women gracefully descended the staircase. They were so different, yet both women were strikingly beautiful. Her mistress, Countess Isabel, was dark and petite, her curved figure unequaled in its delicate proportion, while Lady Kassandra, almost a full head taller, was slim and lithe, with flaming red-gold hair that reached to her waist, and stunning features.

Gisela elbowed the nearby footman, who was gaping appreciatively at the two women. She could hardly blame him, but he was forgetting his duties. "Open the door, man, and call for the carriage!"

While the red-faced footman hastened to obey, she hurried over to Isabel. "Your cape, milady." Deftly she draped it around her mistress's delicate shoulders, then smoothed the velvet folds.

"Gisela, as you know, Lady Kassandra will not be attending the gala today, so please see to it that her needs are well met while I am gone."

"Yes, milady."

Isabel and Kassandra stepped outside into the bright sunshine, and within a few moments a splendid lacquered carriage bearing the coat of arms of the von Furstenberg family pulled around the curved drive.

As Isabel was helped into her seat, Kassandra looked across the manicured lawns of the estate and breathed in the crisp autumn air. Only a short while longer, she thought excitedly, and she, too, would be summoning a carriage—but not to take her to a gala. No, she was going to spend her day far differently.

"Give Miles my fondest, fondest greetings in your letter, Kassandra," Isabel called out gaily, waving farewell as the carriage rumbled down the drive. Then it was gone, disappearing into the dense trees that bordered the lawn.

At last! Kassandra turned to the young footman and flashed him a dazzling smile. "Please have a carriage here for me within the half hour," she requested in her lightly accented German, trying to ignore the effect her smile seemed to have on the youth.

"W-will you be traveling far, Lady Kassandra?" the footman stammered. "I m-mean . . . not to pry, miss, but the coachman must know—"

"Just into the city and back," Kassandra tossed over her shoulder as she hurried back into the mansion. Then, as an afterthought, she turned around and added, "Is there a carriage without a coat of arms engraved upon the door?"

Puzzled, the footman nodded. "One, milady, though it's rarely used and not quite as fine as the others."

"I'm sure it will do nicely. Please have them bring it 'round." How perfect! Kassandra thought happily as the footman strode off toward the stables. Such a carriage was exactly what she needed.

She rushed past an astonished Gisela and, holding up the voluminous skirt of her morning gown, took the marble steps two at a time.

Kassandra could barely contain her excitement as she rushed down the corridor and into her chamber, closing and bolting the door behind her. She crossed to the armoire and flung open the bottom drawer, pushing aside the carefully folded camisoles and linen underclothes, then pulling out a bulky package wrapped in white tissue and secured with twine. It took her only a moment to tear open the package, revealing a simple cotton gown in a flowered print of the sort worn by a lady's maid, a petticoat, gray yarn stockings, and a small white cap modestly trimmed with blond lace.

Untying the wide sash at her waist and slipping the silk morning gown from her body, Kassandra plopped upon the bed wearing only her linen chemise and pulled the coarse stockings up her long, slender legs.

She dressed quickly. The homespun material of the gown scratched her skin, but she didn't care, for it was in this gown that Kassandra would explore the fascinating heart of Vienna by herself, a pastime she had enjoyed on several occasions before her father had left for Germany. She was endlessly intrigued by the city and its people; the infinite, everchanging parade of life was far more entertaining than any frivolous gala or court function. When she was dressed as a lady's maid she could pass for one of the common folk and lose herself in the crowd, unburdened by the affectations and trappings of her true station.

And today—thanks to the royal gala at the Favorita, which would occupy Isabel well into the evening—she had her first opportunity to wear the gown and venture out alone since she had come to stay at the von Furstenberg estate. During the past two weeks she had felt suffocated by Isabel's constant, albeit well-meaning, attentions. Kassandra was used to spending time alone and doing exactly what she pleased. Now at last she had her chance.

Kassandra quickly tied the laces of the demure bodice, then walked over to her dressing table. She coiled her thick mane into a heavy knot, pinned it at her nape, then set the small cap atop her head and secured it with two silver combs.

Perusing her image, she was pleased with her transformation. Lady Kassandra Wyndham, daughter of Lord Harrington, the English ambassador to Vienna, had suddenly become a prim and proper lady's maid. And the carriage without a coat of arms would add credence to her disguise. She wanted it to appear that she had simply hired the carriage to bring her into Vienna for a day's shopping.

A soft rap on the door made Kassandra start in surprise, her breath catching in her throat. Sweet Lord, what if Isabel had forgotten something and returned to the estate?

"Lady Kassandra," Gisela called to her from beyond the door. "Zoltan is waiting with the carriage."

Kassandra exhaled sharply. "I'll be ready in just a moment." She hurried over to her closet and pulled out a dark blue cloak. It, too, was simple in design, and well suited for the rest of her ensemble. She fastened the plain frogging on the front and wrapped the cloak around her body, then slipped on some low-heeled leather shoes, grabbed a cloth bag from a hook inside the door to hold her money, and she was ready.

As she unbolted and opened her door, she was not surprised to find Gisela waiting just outside. The maid's inquisitive hazel eyes were full of questions . . . questions Kassandra had no intention of answering.

"If Countess Isabel should return before me, please tell her I've gone into Vienna on some errands," Kassandra said as she hurried along the corridor and down the stairs. She could hear Gisela's footsteps following close behind, but she did not slow her pace.

"Milady, I have taken the liberty of arranging for two of the menservants to accompany you—"

"Oh, that won't be necessary, Gisela," Kassandra replied over her shoulder. "The coachman will be with me. That's enough for so short a journey."

"But, Lady Kassandra, surely you must realize it is highly unsuitable for you to travel without an escort. I'm certain Countess Isabel would be most unhappy."

Kassandra quickly made her way across the foyer and out the door, determined not to be swayed by the truth of Gisela's words. She knew haste was her only ally. Accepting the hand of the coachman, she swung up easily into the carriage and settled against the plush velvet seat.

"I'm in a great hurry, Zoltan," she murmured as he closed the door. "I have many errands to accomplish this day."

"Rest assured, milady, I'll get ye to the city in no time at all." The stout coachman winked kindly. The carriage shifted and creaked from his weight as he climbed up to his seat, then he cracked his whip above the heads of the two prancing horses. "On with ye, my girls!"

Gisela stepped closer to the carriage. "But, milady—"

"Gisela, you mustn't worry," Kassandra called from the window as the carriage jolted to a start. "I'm quite capable of taking care of myself!"

# Chapter 2

〜◯◯〜

As the carriage sped along, the unpaved, tree-lined avenues that wound past the stately white mansions on the outskirts of Vienna soon narrowed into the cobbled streets of the imperial city. Kassandra sat on the edge of the seat, her heart fluttering with excitement as she gazed out the carriage window at the busy streets and bustling market squares.

Everywhere she looked was a blur of color and motion: early afternoon shoppers with overloaded baskets dodging the open carts and fine carriages that choked the narrow streets; hawkers with their trays of trinkets vying with one another for space on the busiest corners; flower girls in bright, patterned aprons selling their garlands of autumn blooms to passersby.

"A lovely bouquet for yer mistress, dearie?" a buxom flower girl called out to her as the carriage inched its way along the crowded street.

Kassandra smiled, shaking her head. The girl merely shrugged and sauntered over to another carriage.

"Ah, now there's a fine gentleman to buy a posy for yer wife . . . or yer mistress, whichever she may be!"

Kassandra blushed as the flower girl's hearty laughter was lost in the raucous cacophony of the street. She wondered fleetingly what it must be like to be so bold . . . and so free.

Suddenly, with a loud crash, the carriage came to a jarring halt, accompanied by the frantic neighing of terrified horses, the sound of splintering wood, then furious oaths and curses. Kassandra was flung to the opposite side of the vehicle, her fall fortunately broken by the well-padded seat.

"Look to your horse, man, not your blasted cart!" Zoltan shouted at the top of his lungs, followed by a streak of coarse obscenities in his native Hungarian. Then he jumped from his seat to the ground and pulled open the carriage door. "Are ye all right, milady?" he asked, his swarthy face a mask of anxious concern.

"Yes . . . yes, I'm fine," Kassandra assured him shakily, righting herself in the seat. A rush of pity surged through her. The poor man, red-faced and sweating profusely despite the cool air, looked in a much worse state than she.

Kassandra smiled brightly at him, her tone reassuring. "Truly, you can see that I am unharmed, Zoltan. But what has happened?"

Zoltan shook his head grimly, wiping the perspiration from his brow with a massive hand. "Ah, it's an awful thing, milady. Two carts have collided just ahead, and a fine horse is down, its leg broken, looks like to me."

"How terrible!" Kassandra gasped, feeling a sick knot in her stomach at the thought of the stricken creature. She loved horses. Riding was like life to her.

"A pity it is, too, those damn fools. Rushing along the crowded street like that, their carts full of heavy water barrels. I'd like to take my whip to 'em both!"

"Is there anything we can do?" Kassandra asked, peering out the window at the curious crowd pressing in around the accident.

''No, milady. They'll see to it soon enough.''
Grunting his displeasure, Zoltan glanced over his
shoulder at the wreckage strewn about the street just
twenty feet away. ''It's fortunate we were no closer,
else we might have been caught in the middle. Now
we'll have to wait until the mess is cleared away . . .
hopefully no more than a half hour.''

Kassandra sat back against the seat at this news,
her mind racing. A half hour! That was far too much
precious time to waste sitting in this carriage.

No, she decided quickly, she would set out on her
own and meet Zoltan later in the afternoon. This
place was as good as any other to begin her stroll,
though she would have wished it had been under
different circumstances. But now she would not have
Zoltan dogging her every step with the carriage.

Gathering her cape around her, Kassandra held
out her hand to him. ''Please help me down, Zoltan.''

The coachman did as she requested, a puzzled
look on his face. ''Milady?''

''I have far too much to do this afternoon to spare
even a half hour,'' Kassandra said, stepping onto
the cobbled street. She quickly looked about her to
get her bearings, recognizing the name of the street
posted high on a corner sign. She was in the market
district. She turned back to Zoltan. ''I shall meet
you at four o'clock in the square in front of St. Stephen's Cathedral. That should give me enough time
to complete my errands.''

''Ye shall walk, milady?'' Zoltan asked, incredulous. These English! Why would she choose to walk
about the city when she had a fine carriage at her
beck and call? He shrugged. It was not for him to
say what the nobility could, or could not do.

''Yes,'' Kassandra murmured, reaching inside her
bag. She pulled out a few coins and handed them
to him. ''I know there must be taverns nearby where

you can find some refreshment, Zoltan. Now I must
be on my way."

"Thank ye, milady." Zoltan nodded, the coins
heavy in his hand, and flashed a toothy grin. The
promise of a frothy mug of beer or two and a hearty
lunch of sausage and fried potatoes cheered him
considerably, especially after the miserable disaster
he had witnessed. He tipped his cap to her. "St.
Stephen's Cathedral, then, at four o'clock."

Kassandra barely heard him as she hurried from
the carriage down a crowded side street, a sense of
exhilaration coursing through her. She was on her
own . . . at last! And with an entire afternoon to
spend exactly as she wished!

Such sights, sounds, and smells surrounded her
as she strolled up one twisting street and down another. Common people of many races—Germanic,
Latin, Slav—passed by her, their languages as di-
verse as the rustic costumes they wore. Street ur-
chins, most of them accomplished pickpockets,
careened through the crowds, preying lightheart-
edly on the nobility, the men clad in black velvet
coats lined with rose-colored satin over embroidered
gold waistcoats, with powdered periwigs, white silk
stockings, and red-heeled shoes; and their ladies
wrapped in capes trimmed with luxurious fur, or
edged with bright red satin and gold lace.

Kassandra had never before seen a city where the
aristocrats mixed so freely with the common people
. . . so unlike London. And it seemed the entire
town was composed of palaces, whether they be the
homes of the wealthy, middle-class, or the poor.
Three- and four-story buildings towered above the
shadowed streets, their gleaming white facades decorated with all manner of fine stucco ornamentation.

A wide variety of shops occupied the first floors
of these buildings, some with fine glass windows
through which passersby could watch the workers

inside—jewelers, leather-smiths, tailors, and dress-makers—busily plying their trade. Kassandra paused here and there to admire carefully arranged displays of fans, embroidered handkerchiefs, and comfit boxes, the finest adorned with delicate wreaths of jewels and pearls.

Luscious, mouth-watering aromas wafted into the street from pastry shops, bakeries, and sausage makers' shops. Kassandra's stomach soon growled hungrily, reminding her she had not eaten since early that morning. She stopped to buy a buttery roll filled with sweetened cream, then ate it as she walked along, reveling in her independence and contemplating life in all its diversity and richness. She had waited a long time for a day such as this!

Rounding a corner, Kassandra paused in the doorway of a coffeehouse and finished the last of her pastry. A rousing blare of trumpets and the thunderous beating of drums took her by surprise and she peered down the street, amazed at the great throng of people moving ever closer. Overcome by curiosity, she stepped from the doorway and walked toward the lively din. It appeared to be some sort of procession . . .

Two small boys brushed by her, their ruddy cheeks flushed with excitement as they jostled and pushed each other down the street.

"Wait!" Kassandra called after them. "Could you tell me what's going on?"

The boys stopped in their tracks and turned around. One lad, overcome by shyness, blushed awkwardly and shuffled his feet. But the other piped up, eager to share his important news. "It's the Hungarian oxen, miss. They've just arrived from the country and they're taking 'em down to the slaughterhouse." He bobbed his head to her, then sharply elbowed his friend, who did the same. Then they scurried on their way.

A cattle parade. Kassandra had heard of this strange custom from Isabel, who had told her the Viennese loved pageantry of any kind. The lamentable procession of oxen on their way to the slaughterhouse qualified as entertainment of the highest order, especially because it was free.

She watched in amazement as householders and shopkeepers left their homes and shops to throng in the street with their wives and children, all jockeying to get the best view. Shrieks of boisterous laughter rent the air, already charged with a carnival-like atmosphere.

Kassandra pressed her back up against a wall as the procession moved past her. The roar was deafening as the trumpeters and drummers marched by, followed by dragoons on horseback, their swords drawn and flashing in the sun, who encircled the frightened oxen and herded them onward. Young boys goaded the oxen with long, sharpened sticks—Kassandra gasped as she spied the two she had spoken with earlier diving into the fray—while mastiffs snapped at the beasts' legs and barked ferociously at any laggards.

Kassandra felt a wave of pity at the sight of the miserable creatures, clearly terrified by all the shouting and noise. Unable to watch such cruelty any longer, she turned away and began to struggle through the onlookers to a nearby side street.

Suddenly a great cry of alarm went up as a large black ox broke away from the herd and charged at the crowd, bellowing in rage. Whirling, Kassandra dodged just in time to escape the maddened animal's horns, only to find herself swept down the street in the midst of the screaming throng.

For a terrifying moment it seemed she would be dragged under and trampled, but, clawing and kicking, she managed to fight her way back to the side of the street. Spying a half-open door, she lunged for it and nearly tripped inside a large, dimly lit room. She slammed the door behind her and leaned on it for a moment, gasping for breath. The she stumbled to a nearby table and collapsed in a chair.

Burying her face in her hands, Kassandra listened dazedly as the screams of the crowd carried on down the street. Everything had happened so fast! Her breasts rose and fell rapidly beneath the bodice of her gown; her throat felt raw and parched. She struggled against the swamping sensation of dizziness that threatened to overwhelm her, fought back the hot tears that burned her eyes.

Sweet Lord, she could have been killed . . . A shuddering sigh escaped her at this numbing realization. Suddenly chilled, she reached behind her to draw her cloak around her body, only to find it was no longer there.

It must have been wrenched from her shoulders during her struggles, she thought, her mind reeling. She looked down at the skirt of her gown. The flowered fabric was grimy and torn, ripped on one side from the muddied hem almost to her thigh. With trembling fingers she touched her head, only to discover her lace cap was also missing. Her hair, tangled and snarled, had fallen from its pins to frame her face in riotous disarray. And her bag was gone, along with her money.

The dress and the money are no matter . . . At least you are unharmed, Kassandra chided herself, still astounded that she had so narrowly escaped death. Somewhat calmed, she gazed nervously about the large room. She was in some sort of a tavern, that much she knew.

The dense, smoke-filled air stung her eyes. Kassandra blinked, wiped them with the back of her hand, then looked up again . . . straight into the eyes of a stranger staring boldly at her from across the room.

# Chapter 3

Count Stefan von Furstenberg took a slow draft from his goblet, his gaze never leaving the flame-haired wench on the other side of the smoke-dimmed tavern. Damn, but she was tantalizing!

He had seen her only a moment ago, when he had stood up from the table to take leave of his men. A cavalry commander in the Imperial Austrian army, he and his soldiers had just returned to Vienna that morning from a victorious campaign led by their famous general, Prince Eugene of Savoy, against the Turks.

With their hard night ride behind them, the taverns of the city had been a welcome sight. He had not refused his officers' invitation to join them in a well-earned drink to victory, though they had been celebrating in this wine tavern, the Yellow Eagle, for the past few hours, far longer than he had intended to stay.

Now he was glad he had remained. To have missed such uncanny beauty as this wench possessed would have been a shame indeed. Perhaps his plan of surprising his sister Isabel before she received word that the Imperial army had arrived in Vienna would have to wait awhile longer, as well as a visit to his mistress, Sophia, whom he had not seen for the past six months.

17

Stefan chuckled to himself, a rakish grin tugging one corner of his mouth. Sophia. No doubt she had amused herself with countless lovers during his long absence and was probably even now in the arms of another man . . . perfecting her skills in the fine art of lovemaking, she would say wickedly, and without apology.

Ah, but Sophia was not here . . . only the tavern wench in all her tousled beauty, he considered, his eyes raking lustily over her. Surely a quick tumble with her would not hinder his plans overmuch. He would be on his way home to the von Furstenberg estate within the hour.

Stefan drained his goblet, the wine flooding his body with fiery warmth, and felt a surge of desire rip through him at the thought of possessing the long-limbed wench . . . intoxicating his blood far more than the wine. He quickly reached a decision. The devil knew he was no saint. He had not denied himself the pleasurable company of women during the campaign, but it had been many weeks since he had felt a woman writhe beneath him. He would wait no longer.

Setting his empty goblet upon the table with a thud, Stefan strode over to the proprietor of the tavern and drew him aside.

"Have you any rooms?"

"Ah yes, milord." The fat proprietor grinned, nodding his balding head eagerly. "I have several, but there is one, a corner room, that is quite well appointed, if I might say so." He paused, his eyes narrowing shrewdly. "Of course, it will cost a bit more than the others—"

"I'll take it," Stefan said, dropping some gold coins in the man's sweaty palm. "I trust this will cover the cost of the room and another barrel of wine for my men?"

The proprietor stared greedily at the coins. "Oh yes, milord! You are most generous!"

"Good. Now bring some wine to that table over there, the one by the door, and be quick about it."

"At once!" The man scurried off, the gold coins clinking in his pocket, anxious to please the formidable-looking officer. It was not every day he had such a guest in his tavern, a commander of the Imperial calvary no less . . . and a wealthy one!

Stefan glanced down at his uniform, dusty from the long ride the night before, and at his knee-length boots, streaked with mud and dirt. He longed for a hot bath and a shave, but there was not enough time. Besides, he doubted the wench would mind. If she plied her trade this close to the Danube Canal, she had probably lain with far worse.

He walked back to the table where some of his men were seated. They stood as he approached, raising their goblets in salute.

"Another draft of wine, Commander?" one young officer blurted drunkenly, sloshing the contents of his goblet down the front of his uniform and on to the floor.

"Aye, let's drink in fond memory of the Turks we blessed with the kiss of our swords, may they all rot in hell!" another shouted loudly.

Stefan shook his head, silencing the boisterous rabble with a single gesture. "Gentlemen, if you will excuse me, I must take my leave of you. Pleasures other than your fine company beckon to me."

With a gleam of laughter in his eyes, he turned from them and strode toward the front of the tavern, where the wench was sitting, ignoring his men's low whistles of approval and stamping feet.

Kassandra watched wide-eyed as the strikingly handsome officer approached her table, the same man who had been staring at her only moments before. He was tall and powerfully built, his shoulders very broad beneath his dark blue uniform. His hair was black, black as a raven's wing, she thought fleetingly, and pulled back into a short queue at his nape.

It was his eyes, flint gray with just a hint of blue, like a wild, storm-tossed sea, that caught and held her gaze. Deeply set beneath straight black brows, they seared her with a burning intensity that made her flush with a strange, stirring warmth.

Suddenly uncomfortable, Kassandra tore her gaze away. Surely he must be looking for someone else, she thought, her mind spinning. She turned and glanced behind her, but there was no one else seated anywhere near them. Turning back around, she started in surprise when he pulled out the only other chair at her table, the wooden legs scraping along the planked floor, and sat down beside her.

A fat, balding man suddenly crossed to them with two silver goblets filled to the brim with red wine, set them on the table, bowed, and hurried away.

What was going on? Kassandra wondered. She hadn't ordered a drink. She blushed hotly, embarrassed, as the officer's eyes raked over her, slowly, openly.

Stefan stared at Kassandra for a long moment without saying a word. Now that he was closer, it seemed his gutter waif had become a goddess. Either that or the wine had sorely affected his vision.

By God, she was stunning . . . an enchantress, he marveled, astounded by her disheveled beauty. Despite the smudges of dirt on her face, her skin was like the finest porcelain, her features a study in perfect symmetry—high, curved cheekbones, a straight nose that tipped slightly at the end, slim, arched brows that matched the fiery red-gold of her hair, and a lush curved mouth that was full and inviting.

Stefan was tempted to reach out and trace the exquisite line of her chin, a stubborn chin that bespoke strength and spirit. But studying her, he hesitated. She looked so tantalizingly innocent for a common tavern wench, like a fresh rose amidst flowers that had long ago lost their bloom..

Perhaps she was new to her trade, he considered. She looked young, barely seventeen. He noted now her large amethyst eyes studied him warily, dark violet pools opulently fringed by thick lashes tipped with gold. He could not help feeling that a man could easily drown in those luminous depths . . .

Enough! Stefan berated himself, shifting impatiently in his chair. Obviously he had been away from women far too long to become so easily besotted over a common tavern wench.

Gazing steadily into her eyes, Stefan raised his goblet to his lips and drank deeply, the heady liquid fanning his desire. But the girl did not follow his lead. He gestured to the cup before her. "The drink is for you," he murmured, his voice low, edged with roughness.

Kassandra stared at the goblet, then back at him. The man must have seen her plight and was offering wine to her out of kindness, she reasoned with a surge of relief. "Thank you," she replied softly.

Her hand trembled as she lifted the goblet to her lips and drank thirstily. It was a coarse vintage, and overly tart, but she did not mind. She felt a relaxing warmth wash over her as she drained the cup, her jangled nerves calmed at last.

Perhaps the soldier might call a carriage to take her to St. Stephen's, Kassandra thought hopefully. She doubted it was past two o'clock, but Zoltan might already be waiting for her in the cathedral square. She had experienced quite enough excitement for one day, and was more than ready to return to the von Furstenberg estate. She smiled warmly, gratefully, at the officer and leaned toward him.

Stefan's breath caught in his throat, his eyes falling upon the creamy swell of her breasts, firm and high, straining against the taut fabric of her bodice. He knew he could no longer restrain his mounting desire, burning like a raging inferno within him. "I have a room waiting upstairs," he said abruptly, rising from his chair. "Come."

Kassandra stared up at him, dumbstruck, as if she had not heard his words. Room upstairs? What could he possibly mean? she wondered wildly. Why was he looking at her so?

Then a flicker of fear flamed within her, and her gaze darted around the smoke-filled room. She noticed for the first time the other women present, their heavily rouged faces, easy smiles, and low-cut gowns blatant testimony to their calling. In a far corner one woman had even unlaced her bodice, and a sailor was suckling at her breast!

"If it's money that concerns you, wench," Stefan said wryly, "I will pay you well for your trouble." He held out his hand, the gesture a command. "Now walk with me, else I will be forced to carry you up the stairs."

Kassandra gasped, incredulous. Sweet Lord, he thought she was nothing more than a common harlot . . . a . . . a tavern whore!

She jumped up from her chair so suddenly that it crashed to the floor, her only thought to flee. But before she had taken two steps, a strong arm encircled her waist, and she was pitched unceremoniously over the officer's broad shoulder like a sack of wheat.

"Wh-what are you doing?" she sputtered indignantly, fighting to quell the terror filling her heart. "Let me down at once!"

Stefan chuckled deep in his throat and slapped her backside, his hand lingering there. "Enough, wench! You play the part of the innocent quite con-

vincingly . . . a captivating illusion . . . but I have
no time for games!" With long strides he carried her
toward the back of the tavern and up a flight of
creaking wooden stairs.

"No! Please, you are mistaken!" Kassandra cried
out, pounding her clenched fists against his rugged
back. But her desperate protests were of no avail,
drowned out by the crude laughter and ribald jests
that filled the tavern, resounding from the high
beams.

"The corner room is straight along the corridor
and to the left, milord," the proprietor shouted
above the din. He watched with no small amount of
envy as Stefan reached the top of the stairs and disappeared down the darkened corridor with his stunning load, a kicking, struggling vision of flaming hair
and flailing limbs.

Funny, he had never seen that wench at his tavern before, he thought, scratching his head. What a
tigress! Surely he would have remembered such a
beauty . . . and such a temper. He shrugged. Perhaps he might sample her charms when the gentleman was through with her. Licking his lips, he filled
some goblets from a newly opened barrel of wine
and hurried toward the crowded tables. "Here you
go, m'lads, more wine! Compliments of the commander."

Stefan reached the end of the corridor, turned left
down a short hallway, and kicked open the door of
the corner room. He glanced around, quickly noting
that the room was well appointed, just as the proprietor had said it would be.

A wide bed was set in the middle of the room not
far from the window, a luxurious spread of green
damask pulled back to reveal crisp linen sheets. A
thick oriental carpet covered the wooden floor, and
a richly upholstered chair was the only other furnishing, that and a small table beside the bed. Thick

tallow candles burned brightly from several polished wall sconces, for although there was a window, it was small, with the shade drawn, and the room would have been dark but for the warm glow of the candlelight.

Stefan walked over to the bed and dumped Kassandra upon it.

"Oh!" she gasped, the breath knocked from her body. She watched wide-eyed as he moved with lithe grace back to the door, and felt a sinking sensation in her stomach as he bolted it securely. Then he turned and faced her, his eyes blazing into her own, wild, turbulent, and laden with open desire.

"Take off your clothes, wench, or I shall have the pleasure of removing them myself," he murmured, his voice deep, commanding. He slid his sword from the scabbard belted to his waist and leaned it against the chair, then he stepped toward her, loosening his wide leather belt and dropping it to the floor. The ornately carved butt of his pistol hit the floor with a dull thud. "And believe me," he said softly, "I would relish the task."

# Chapter 4

Kassandra swallowed hard, her eyes never leaving his face as he kicked off his boots and stripped the clothing from his body. She forced herself to remain calm, vainly fighting the dizzying effects of the wine that clouded her mind.

Surely there must be some way to make him see reason, she thought wildly, edging to the far side of the bed. She knew she couldn't tell him the truth of her identity, that she was the daughter of Lord Harrington, the ambassador to Austria. There would be no end to the scandal—to the detriment of her father and his diplomatic mission to the Viennese court—if it became known that she was in such a place . . . and such a predicament. And even if she risked explaining who she was, would he believe her? She doubted it; the man had obviously been drinking. No, there had to be another way.

Kassandra groped behind her and felt only air. She knew she was at the edge of the mattress. In one quick movement she jumped from the bed and stood facing him, her hand clutching the carved corner post.

"Please, you don't understand," she began, her voice shaking. "I know what you're thinking, that I'm a tavern wh-whore"—she stumbled over the word, flushing heatedly—"but you're mistaken."

25

Stefan moved toward her, his powerful, sinewy body gleaming like burnished bronze in the candlelight. "No, wench, you do not know what I am thinking," he murmured, fascinated by the shimmering highlights in her hair, silken threads of dancing flame shot through with gold. A gossamer tendril lay curled at the base of her throat beside the rapid beat of her pulse, a tempting hollow that seemed to cry out for his kiss.

Kassandra backed away as he drew closer, and still closer, like a beast of the forest stalking its prey. His features were masked by flickering shadows cast by the sputtering candles, but she could feel his gaze, glittering, implacable, upon her.

Unwittingly, her gaze darted over him. She had never before seen a man completely unclothed. She stared with reluctant fascination at his bared body, sleek and handsomely proportioned. His rugged shoulders and chest were banded in rippling muscle, his stomach sculpted and flat, his hips tapered, his thighs powerfully knotted with muscle, and . . . and . . .

"Oh!" she gasped, a burning blush scorching her skin like wildfire as her eyes fell on his erect manhood.

Stefan chuckled deep in his throat. What a game she was playing, he thought wryly. Obviously, she feigned such innocence as an enticement, a seductive trick to earn an extra coin or two, and if he did not know better, he might have thought she had never seen a naked man before. He wondered fleetingly if she might even claim she was still a virgin . . .

"Come, wench," he said softly, his deep, rough-edged voice almost a whisper. "You play your clever game well, and I promise you will be rewarded. But enough. It's time to earn your wage." He reached out, his hands expertly untying the laces of her bodice, his fingers lightly grazing the lush curve of her breasts beneath the plain fabric.

Though he barely touched her, Kassandra jerked away from him as if she had been stung, her back hitting the wall behind her. Realizing she could go no farther, she drew herself up proudly and met the full force of his gaze, her eyes large and flashing with defiance.

"I-I'm a serving maid, sir, a lady's maid, and certainly not the harlot you imagine me to be," she blurted indignantly, her hands flying up and bracing against his massive chest as he once again drew closer, so close that his scent enveloped her senses and made her limbs feel strangely weak. "I stumbled into this tavern by mistake . . . My mistress is surely looking for me. If you will only let me go—"

Stefan captured her mouth with his own, silencing her vehement protests with the savagery of his kiss. When her hands curled into tightly clenched fists and pounded desperately against his chest, he caught them in his own, their fingers entwining, and forced them against the wall.

Kassandra could scarcely breathe, the rampant pounding of her heart a deafening roar in her ears, like the crashing waves of the ocean. Warmth coursed through her body as his mouth, warm and fragrant with wine, encompassed her own; his kiss, plundering and searching, was a sweet torture unlike anything she had ever known. His tongue flicked against her teeth, demanding entrance, then filled her mouth, tasting, savoring, making her forget . . .

Kassandra's eyes flew open as he released her hands and drew her closer, his powerful arms crushing her to him, the warmth of his body like a hot brand searing through her clothing to the tingling flesh beneath. No! her mind screamed, awful reality flooding back to her. She had to do something, anything to protect herself!

Suddenly she remembered his sword and pistol on the other side of the bed, and a glimmer of hope flared within her. They were her only chance, if she could just reach them. She had been taught enough of weaponry that she could fire a pistol with accuracy or strike a glancing blow with a sword. But his well-muscled arms were like a prisoner's bonds about her, the only barrier between her and the weapons that might save her.

If only she could think of a way to catch him off guard. Something that might make him loosen his iron grip . . .

She almost laughed in giddy relief at the idea that flashed through her mind. Instinctively, and with an innate sense of all that was seductively feminine, she wound her slender arms about his neck and returned his kiss with a fiery passion that took him totally by surprise.

Startled, Stefan tore his mouth away and looked down at her, mesmerized by the darkened amethyst pools of her eyes and the provocative smile curving her lips. A low rumble of triumph broke from his throat at her sudden acquiescence. So the wanton was revealed at last, he thought appreciatively. He sought her mouth again in a lingering kiss, his hands lightly caressing the curved line of her hips, then lifting ever so slowly the torn skirt of her gown.

Now . . . now! Kassandra's inner voice screamed. Steeling herself against the stirring power of his kiss, she summoned every ounce of her strength and shoved against him. He reeled backward, almost falling, but she paid him little heed. Her only thought was to reach his weapons on the other side of the room.

Desperately she lunged across the bed, scrambling and clawing over the damask spread, then hurled herself toward the leather belt lying on the floor, knocking the breath from her body. Her fingers touched the carved butt of the pistol just as two strong hands spanned her narrow waist and spun her into the air.

"What game is this, wench?" Stefan spat, his handsome face clouded with anger as he tossed her back onto the bed. In the next instant he was straddling her, his muscled thighs a heated vise around her hips. "First you seduce me with mock innocence, then you play the temptress," he said grittily, his gray eyes blazing into her own, "and now you seek to use my weapons—to rob me, perhaps? So now it is a bewitching thief who shares my bed."

Dazed and gasping for breath, Kassandra could only return his stare. The fury tinged with lusting desire she saw in his eyes, and the terrible heat of his thighs about her, filled her with despair. A sinking feeling told her she had lost the battle against him.

Stefan leaned over her, his breath warm against her flushed cheek. "Well, my beautiful thief, we shall play my game now." With practiced ease he slipped the gown from her shoulders and arms, catching her wrists above her head with one strong hand. He barely grazed her lips with his own, then trailed a fiery path down her throat.

Kassandra tensed beneath him, fighting shivers of sensation. She watched wide-eyed, unable to move, as he shifted his weight and lay down beside her, his hand still holding her wrists, his hard, sinewed length pressed against her.

With his other hand Stefan quickly slid the gown from her body and tossed it to the floor, along with her petticoat, shoes, and gray yarn stockings. The only clothing left to her was her linen chemise. A tearing sound rent the air as he ripped the flimsy undergarment from bodice to hem, baring her body to the scorching intensity of his gaze.

Stefan sharply sucked in his breath, his eyes savoring the trembling beauty lying beside him. Her body was slender and long-limbed, yet provocatively curved and lithe, the creamy porcelain of her skin tinged with palest rose. Her breasts rose and fell rapidly, taunting mounds tipped with hardened nipples, fashioned for a man's caress . . . tempting him, beckoning to him . . . Her belly was taut and firm, her hips gracefully curved, the downy juncture at her thighs a silky invitation, a promise of sensuous delight.

Kassandra arched her back, a low moan escaping unbidden from her throat as Stefan ran a calloused finger between her breasts. Sweet Lord, he was going to ravage her! And there was nothing she could do to escape him.

Suddenly Stefan released her wrists and drew her to him, his arms tightening like bands of rippling steel, his mouth coming down cruelly upon her own, the bold hardness of his desire pressing urgently against her thigh. In the fierceness of his embrace, Kassandra defiantly decided she could not, would not, allow herself to be taken by force in this, her first experience with a man . . .

Fate had thrown them inexplicably together, and it could not be altered. She had always faced life fearlessly, accepting whatever challenges were thrown in her path; she would now meet the blazing heat of his passion measure for measure, if only to spare herself the brutality that might come if she resisted. Perhaps a chance for revenge might come later . . .

Kassandra moaned again, conscious thought fleeing from her mind as his dark head bent over her breast, his tongue flicking against the taut, rose-tipped nub like a moist, taunting spear. She felt a strange tightening in her belly, a fluttering, that shook her to the depths of her being, eliciting a new-found hunger within her, surging, powerful, all-encompassing.

She gave free rein to the primal urge that seemed to demand its own awakening, its own driving ful-fillment.

Stefan lingered at her pouting breasts, first one and then the other, teasing, suckling, tasting the sweetness of her skin, until she took his head in her hands and drew him up to face her. She kissed him deeply, astounding him with the wanton desire re-flected in her eyes, her darting tongue exploring and savoring the textures and crevices of his mouth. Her long, tapered fingers loosened the band that held the short queue at his nape and entwined in his thick black hair.

Kassandra gave herself over to the new sensations coursing through her body, her flesh burning wher-ever he touched her. His fingers, his nails, his tongue, traced molten paths of flame about her breasts, down her belly, and between her thighs to the secret heart of her longing.

Then he was towering over her again, his eyes gleaming into hers, inflamed from wanting her. He parted her legs with his knee, plying the silken soft-ness between her legs first with his fingers then with the hot, insistent strength of his throbbing desire.

Suddenly he thrust himself into her, his raging desire a molten blade of fire. She gasped aloud and arched against him, tears stinging her eyes. The pain of her lost innocence blazed through her body with lightning speed.

Startled by her outcry, Stefan swore vehemently. So the wench *was* a virgin, he thought in disbelief, moving slowly within her. Then he thought no more as she began to writhe beneath him, an intoxicating vision of glistening skin, tangled hair, parted lips, and bewitching violet eyes, half-closed with passion.

Kassandra moaned anew, the piercing agony only a fleeting memory as he stroked her breasts, then cupped her buttocks with his strong hands, lifting her closer, filling her body with his pulsating strength.

She was on fire. A surging wave of ecstasy was drawing ever closer . . . closer . . . teasing her, enveloping her in a yearning more powerful, more exciting than anything she had ever sensed before.

At the seeming height of her pleasure she wrapped her arms around Stefan's neck, her long legs around his waist, her lips melding with his in passionate fusion, their ragged breath merging as one, higher, faster, and still higher . . . until she drove against him at the sizzling pinnacle of her passion, clinging to him, crying out as he groaned and exploded within her, a shattering release that whirled around them like a tempest unleashed, a maelstrom of blinding desire.

It was a fleeting moment . . . a spellbinding eternity, the sweetest rapture and the wildest fury . . . then she was drifting down, down . . .

Kassandra's eyes fluttered open, and she sank back upon the rumpled bed, spent and exhausted, her arms slipping from his neck to lie limply at her side. She could barely see him through the entangled web of her hair, the outline of his rugged shoulders sleek and glistening in the golden candlelight.

Then the powerful weight of his body was gone, collapsing onto the bed beside her, his sinewed arm wrapping about her and pulling her close, her back pressed against his chest. She did not think to fight him; her mind seemed dulled and sated as if from a potent drug. His breath was a shivering warmth on her nape, labored at first but easing gradually to a

slow, measured cadence. It lulled her, seduced her
. . . and, in moments, she slept.

Stefan inhaled the heady fragrance of her fire-gold
hair, wrapped like a mysterious veil of intrigue
around her creamy shoulders and rose-tipped
breasts, a silken fan half covering her face.

Was the wench a thief, temptress, or lady's maid,
as she had said? he wondered dazedly, the effects
of the wine, his long ride the night before, and the
wanton passion of the last moments finally taking
their toll. He closed his eyes, reveling in the feel of
her lithe body melded against his own.

She had been a virgin, that much he knew. And
as sleep stole over him, his last conscious thought
was that whatever she might be, he was not about
to let her go.

# Chapter 5

A candle sputtered and hissed in the silent room, its flame flaring brightly for a brief moment, then died into a curling whiff of smoke, the wick a glowing ember.

Awakened by the sound, Kassandra sighed contentedly, snuggling ever closer to the radiating warmth beside her. "Hmmm . . ." she murmured, her cheek brushing against crisp curls that tickled her nose. She smiled faintly, the steady rhythm of a strong heartbeat pulsing gently in her ear. It seems so real, she thought drowsily, so real . . .

Suddenly Kassandra's eyelids flickered open, burning memory flooding back into her dazed consciousness. She tried to sit up, but she was held fast.

"Oh—!" she gasped, biting her lip hard, tasting blood, her stifled cry echoing around the room. She froze, scarcely breathing, fearful that any further sound, any movement, any breath, however shallow, would surely waken the man who held her prisoner.

How long had she been lying there? Kassandra wondered frantically, glancing at the window. The opaque shade was drawn, completely covering the glass. She could not tell if it was day or night.

Rising panic gripped her throat, but she fought against it, willing herself to think clearly. She lifted

34

her head slowly, her gaze darting about the room. It was dark and filled with shadows except for a solitary candle still burning in a wall sconce near the door.

The door! Kassandra thought wildly. Her only means of escape, if she could only reach it. But her heart sank. First she had to free herself from the man who held her captive within his embrace, without waking him.

Forcing herself to stay calm, Kassandra took a deep breath and looked up at him, fearful that she might find him staring boldly back at her, his eyes laughing wickedly at her plight. But he was sound asleep, the even rise and fall of his chest a hopeful sign that he would not wake easily. His face was cloaked in shadow, yet even in the dark she was struck by the rugged masculinity of his features: black brows set against a wide forehead, commanding profile, chiseled lips, strong jawline, cleft chin . . .

Fool! Kassandra berated herself on a wave of furious indignation. He may be handsome to look upon, but do not forget the bastard has ravaged you, wantonly stolen what was yours alone to give. It's more likely he lies in a drunken stupor than a deep sleep.

The thought flooded Kassandra with giddy relief, giving her the courage she needed. Fueled by her growing outrage, she pushed gingerly against him, trying to free herself. She nearly choked, her heart banging against her chest, when he suddenly rolled over onto his back, sighing heavily, his arms falling to his sides.

She hesitated for the barest moment, motionless, her breath caught in her throat. God help her if he awoke! But he slept on, his breathing deep and steady.

Kassandra could hardly believe she was free of

him. Waiting no longer, she crept to the other end of the wide bed.

Damn! She cursed inwardly as the wooden bed frame creaked from her furtive movements. She was still not out of danger, she chided herself, swinging her long legs over the side of the mattress and stepping onto the floor.

At least the carpet would mask her footsteps. She looked around, her eyes adjusting to the darkness. Where were her clothes?

As she took a few steps from the bed, her foot fell on a linen garment lying crumpled on the floor. She picked it up, cold fury welling inside her as she surveyed what was left of her chemise.

Filthy bastard! Kassandra raged. Tears rolled down her flushed cheeks as the enormity of what had happened hit her with full force. She was ruined! She dropped the mangled garment, wiping the wet stains from her face with the palm of her hand.

Suddenly a glint of light near the bed caught her eye and she turned, inhaling sharply. Her gaze fell upon his sword, still propped up against the chair where he had left it, the polished blade brightly reflecting the candlelight.

Kassandra walked trancelike to the chair and picked up the weapon, testing it in her hand. It was fairly light, surely no heavier than the swords she had wielded in her fencing classes at Wyndham Court. She moved to the bed and stared coldly at the man sleeping there, his bronzed body in dark contrast with the white linen sheets.

It would be so easy to kill him now, to run him through with his own sword. Surely it would be a rightful revenge for what he had done to her. She pointed the sword at his chest, the blade steady even though she was trembling, the deadly tip aimed directly at his heart.

She stood for a long moment, her overwhelming

hate a bitter bile upon her tongue. He deserved to die . . .

Suddenly he groaned and rolled onto his side, his back to her, startling Kassandra from her deadly reverie. She dropped the sword upon the bed as if stung and backed away, fearful that at any moment he might wake and discover she was no longer beside him. All thoughts of revenge fled from her mind. Sweet Lord, she had to get out of there at once!

She fell to her knees, desperately groping on the floor and beneath the bed for her clothing. She dressed hurriedly, her hands shaking uncontrollably as she fumbled with the laces of her bodice. At last, after several agonizing moments, she was ready.

Money, you will need money to hire a carriage if Zoltan is no longer at the cathedral, she reminded herself. Spying the coat of his uniform tossed over the back of the chair, she quickly rummaged through the deep side pockets, her eyes lighting when she pulled out a small velvet bag filled with coins. She slipped the bag into her bodice; then, with a last glance over her shoulder, she stole silently to the door.

She turned the polished knob, her heart pounding in her ears. But the door held fast. The bolt! Open the bolt! Her fingers grasped the heavy iron lock and slid it back. Once again her hand tested the knob, twisting it slowly. She could have cried with relief as the door swung open, squeaking on its hinges.

Kassandra held her breath, cautiously peering into the short hallway that led to the main corridor. She could hear the low rumble of voices and outbursts of raucous laughter filtering up the stairs from the tavern below, but there was no sound coming from any of the adjacent rooms. Confident that she would not be seen, she opened the door just wide enough to squeeze through it, then closed it quietly behind her. She edged along the wall, stopping when she came to the darkened corridor.

" 'Ere we go, love, just up these steps," a woman's shrill voice called from the bottom of the stairway. "Now, mind ye, I take on only one at a time. Tell yer friend there to go have another draft of wine. He'll have to wait his turn just like the rest of 'em."

Kassandra's throat constricted in fear as heavy footsteps sounded from the stairs, the wooden steps creaking loudly under the weight of the woman and her companion, their drunken laughter echoing down the long corridor.

The noise will surely wake him! Kassandra thought wildly. Her worst fears were suddenly confirmed when a sharply uttered curse came from within the corner room, then what sounded like a chair crashing to the floor.

She waited no longer. She bolted into the corridor, determined to dash down the stairs and through the tavern to the street. But the stairway was blocked by the weaving, belching couple, a heavy-set blond woman and a rough-looking sailor.

"Heh, there, dearie, what's yer rush?" the woman yelled amiably. A bleary grin twisted her rouged face until her companion lunged at Kassandra, tripping over the doxy and knocking both onto the stairs. "Ye stinkin' swine, not enough woman for ye, eh?" she blurted angrily, cuffing him on the side of the head.

Kassandra whirled and fled the other way, trying the doorknobs to several rooms. A few were locked, while one opened into a small bedroom that was occupied, the scantily clad woman shouting out crude obscenities, much to the delight of her prone companion, until Kassandra quickly slammed the door shut.

There must be another way out of this tavern! her mind screamed, as she tried yet another doorknob.

This one turned easily in her hand, and she almost fell down a narrow flight of stairs in her haste to escape. Stumbling and groping in the dark, she lifted the latch on the wooden door at the bottom of the stairs and pushed with all her strength. The door swung open so suddenly that she fell to her knees on the ground, the late afternoon sun blinding her.

Momentarily stunned, Kassandra pushed her hair from her face and struggled to her feet. At least it was still daylight, she thought gratefully, noting her surroundings. She was now at the back of the tavern, the Danube Canal only thirty odd feet away. Several sailors loitering at a nearby wharf spied her and called out, gesturing for her to join them, their leering grins arousing sheer terror in her.

You must find your way back to St. Stephen's, Kassandra reasoned, fighting again to stay calm. Without another glance at the sailors, she turned and fled down the alley beside the tavern, their crude taunts ringing in her ears. Each breath tore at her throat, her chest heaving from exertion.

Will this nightmare ever end? she wondered wildly, reaching the cobbled road that wound in front of the tavern, the same street on which she had almost been trampled earlier that day.

She began walking hurriedly in what she hoped was the direction to the cathedral, dodging passersby, carriages, and sedan chairs with their scurrying footmen that clogged the street. Suddenly she spied an empty carriage in front of a coffeehouse, the stout driver leaning on the lacquered side as if waiting for someone. She ran toward him, startling his horses as she called out to him. The two spirited animals neighed and snorted, their hooves nervously pawing the cobblestones.

"Pl-please, sir, I need . . . a ride to . . . St. Stephen's . . ." she gasped breathlessly, slumping exhausted against the carriage.

"Eh, there, what do you think yer doing, wench, scaring the horses like that?" the driver shouted angrily, grabbing the bridle of the nearest horse and making clicking sounds with his tongue to calm them. But his tone softened as he noted her obvious distress.

"If it's the cathedral you want, miss, yer heading the wrong way," he said, pointing his thumb in the opposite direction. "And this carriage isn't for hire. I'm waiting on a fine gentleman inside, sorry to say, for I'd like to oblige ye."

Kassandra drew out the velvet bag from her bodice, ignoring the man's raised eyebrow. She opened it, her eyes widening at the bright gold coins tumbling into her open palm. She had stolen a small fortune! But she quickly recovered her composure, holding out three of the coins to the astonished driver.

"If you please, sir," she murmured, her gaze not leaving his face, "I will pay you three more as soon as we arrive at St. Stephen's."

The driver gaped at the coins in his hand, nodding his head, then quickly pocketed them. He fumbled for the door, opening it with a bow and a flourish, then gallantly held out his arm.

"My thanks," Kassandra said tersely, accepting his offer of assistance. She stepped into the carriage, relief surging through her. "I'm in a great hurry," she added. "You must get me to the cathedral as quickly as you can."

"Oh, aye, miss!" the driver blurted, shutting the door firmly. He jumped into his seat and snapped his whip above the heads of his horses.

"Hold there, man, I thought I paid you to wait," a rotund gentleman called out, hurrying from the coffeehouse. "What's going on—"

"Sorry, milord, but this lady here says she's in a

hurry,'' the driver shouted with a laugh as the carriage clattered down the street at a devil's pace.

Kassandra stared out anxiously from the window, unable to relax even as the cursed tavern was left farther and farther behind. Would Zoltan still be at the cathedral? she wondered. She could tell it was well past four o'clock. The streetlamps were already lit along the darkening streets.

Kassandra sighed heavily. She could only hope he had not yet returned to the estate and raised an alarm over her disappearance. There would be hell to pay for this misadventure if Isabel had already returned from the royal gala to find her missing.

If only she had not lost her cloak, Kassandra thought miserably. Then she might at least be able to hide her wretched appearance. She looked down at her gown, her fingers quickly working through the tangles in her hair. There really wasn't anything she could do about it, she told herself resignedly, except brush off some of the dirt. The jagged tear in the skirt was another matter. How would she ever explain it?

''Damn him,'' Kassandra muttered under her breath, her amethyst eyes flashing fire.

She shook her head fiercely. No, you will not think of him anymore! she vowed with defiance. You will put this whole experience from your mind and pretend it never happened. Yet even as she made her vow, her skin burned with the unwanted memory of his caress; her lips, bruised and swollen, ached from the savagery of his kiss.

Kassandra closed her eyes tightly and slammed her fist upon the velvet seat, willing the seething memories from her mind. But she could not forget the blazing heat of his eyes, flint gray with just a hint of blue. They were like a hot brand searing into her even now, a scorching reflection of his all-encompassing desire . . . forever etched upon her memory.

"We're almost there, milady." The carriage driver leaned to one side and shouted down to her.

Kassandra started, his voice jarring into her tormented thoughts, flushing her body with apprehension.

"Please, please let Zoltan still be waiting," she murmured fervently, peering out the window at the massive cathedral, its twin spires piercing the twilight sky.

"Whoa! Whoa, there," the driver commanded as the carriage rumbled to a stop.

Kassandra opened the door and stepped onto the street just as the driver jumped from his seat. "My thanks," she said, dropping the three gold coins into his hand and searching anxiously for the familiar carriage. She began to walk toward the main entrance of the cathedral, the driver forgotten.

He's gone back to the estate without me, Kassandra thought resignedly, her heart sinking as she surveyed the deserted cathedral square.

"Lady Kassandra!"

She whirled sharply, the sound of Zoltan's gruff voice filling her with elation. She spied the von Furstenberg carriage waiting by the side door of the cathedral and ran toward it.

"Milady, what kept ye?" Zoltan asked, his face etched with worry. His gaze moved over her, quickly taking in her bedraggled appearance. "It's almost six o'clock. I didn't know whether to leave and fetch help, else stay here and wait awhile longer."

Kassandra flushed at his frank perusal, inwardly cursing again the man who had so wantonly disrupted her life. "Please, Zoltan, I'm fine," she assured him, her mind racing. She wanted to avoid the question in his eyes, but she had to offer him some explanation for her tardiness. "I'm sorry I kept you waiting . . . but I—'' She stopped. She simply could not think of any plausible excuse.

No, Kassandra decided. It was better to say nothing. She looked steadily at the burly Hungarian, her eyes pleading for his understanding—and his silence. ''Please, Zoltan, I would like to return to the estate at once.''

Zoltan cleared his throat uncomfortably, shifting his feet, then slowly nodded. ''Aye, milady, as you wish.'' He whipped his great cloak from around his shoulders and wrapped it about her. ''You'll need this, milady. The night is growing cold.'' He looked away for a moment, embarrassed, then turned back to her. ''You may return it to me on the morrow.''

Kassandra smiled faintly, tears springing to her eyes. ''You have my thanks, Zoltan,'' she murmured, taking his proffered arm as he helped her into the carriage. She slumped against the seat, her body limp with exhaustion, wanting nothing more at that moment than to be safely back at the von Furstenberg estate.

# Chapter 6

Kassandra hurried up the winding marble steps of the grand staircase, Zoltan's great cloak swirling about her. So far she had been lucky. The only person she had seen since her arrival at the estate a few moment ago had been the footman. He had informed her that Countess Isabel had not yet returned from the gala, another stroke of good fortune.

She made her way quickly down the corridor to her chamber, clutching the cloak tightly under her chin. It dragged at least a foot upon the floor behind her, frustrating any illusion that it might belong to her, but at least she was almost to her door. She reached out, grasping the ornate doorknob.

"Lady Kassandra, I'm so glad to see that you have returned! I was growing concerned about you. Were you able to complete your errands?"

Kassandra's shoulders slumped, her hand falling from the knob. She turned around, forcing a smile to her lips. "Yes, Gisela, thank you," she said evenly, as Isabel's maid closed the distance between them. "Now if you will excuse me . . ."

Gisela's sharp gaze fell from Kassandra's face to the cloak she wore, a sudden frown creasing her forehead. "Milady, forgive me if I seem impertinent, but is that not the coachman's garb?"

44

"Ah . . . yes, it is," Kassandra answered, a story swiftly forming in her mind. She looked steadily at Gisela, forcing her voice to remain calm. "My cloak was caught under the wheel of a carriage earlier today and ripped from my shoulders. It was a shame, really, for it was completely ruined."

"How terrible!" Gisela interjected, her eyes wide with shock. "Surely you could have been hurt, milady."

"Yes, I suppose I was lucky," she lied. It seemed this entire day was composed of lies, she thought guiltily. "I simply left it where it fell in the mud. Zoltan kindly offered me the use of his cloak for the rest of the day."

Gisela clucked her tongue in sympathy. "Well, miss, at least you are unharmed. Is there anything I can do for you?"

Kassandra breathed an inner sigh of relief that her story had satisfied the inquisitive maid. "Yes, Gisela. A bath would be very nice. It has been a long day." Truly, she could hardly wait to bathe, to rid herself once and for all of the scent of that man! It clung to her, reminding her of him, when all she wanted to do was forget.

"Of course, milady. And I'll bring up a warm brandy for you to sip," Gisela offered kindly. She turned and bustled down the hallway.

Kassandra opened the door to her chamber, grateful to see the familiar turquoise and cream surroundings. She was safe at last. She pulled the heavy cloak from her shoulders and laid it over a chair, then quickly stripped the soiled gown from her body, along with her remaining clothing, kicked off her shoes, and rolled the gray stockings down her long legs. Hastily she folded everything together in one pile and hid it in a far corner of her closet, beneath a stack of oval hatboxes.

She would have to dispose of the gown later, she

thought with distaste. It was damaged beyond repair, and besides, she wanted no further reminders of this disastrous adventure.

Kassandra pinned up her thick hair, then donned a robe of blue satin, absently tying the sash. Her reflection in the full-length mirror caught her eye and she paused for a moment, gazing at herself.

Strange, you don't look any different, she mused grimly. Yet she knew she would never be the same. Her only consolation was that there was little chance she would ever see the soldier again. Vienna was a large city. People came and went like the wind, especially common soldiers, passing through the city on their way to the fighting in the East, or bound for their homes in faraway regions of the Hapsburg Empire.

"No, your secret is safe," Kassandra whispered to her reflection. Even if she could never forget what had happened that day, it would be a memory of stolen passion that would surely fade with time.

A sudden chilling thought struck her, her eyes darkening to a deep violet hue. What if there was a child? It was possible . . .

She turned abruptly from the mirror, her slender fingers rubbing her aching temples. No, she could not think of it!

A firm rap at the door broke into Kassandra's roiling thoughts. "Yes? What is it?" she snapped, her emotions at a near breaking point. Then she shook her head, drawing a deep breath. It would not do for her to appear overly upset, for that would only encourage more of Gisela's prying questions.

"It is only your bath, milady," Gisela responded stiffly, as if affronted by Kassandra's tone. But, observing the paleness of the young woman's features, she relented. "Please, Lady Kassandra, if you would sit and rest until your bath is ready," she murmured, gesturing toward the chair.

Kassandra nodded, following her suggestion. She watched silently as Gisela opened the door wide for several maidservants, who carried in steaming buckets of hot water. They returned again and again, pouring them into the large porcelain-lined tub set behind an oriental screen in a far corner of the room, until it was filled. Then Gisela liberally splashed some perfumed oil into the water, lastly unwrapping a fresh cake of hard-milled soap and setting it in a dish on a low table beside the tub.

Assured that all was in order, she hurried to the door. "I will return in a few moments with your brandy. Enjoy your bath, milady."

"There is no need to rush, Gisela," Kassandra murmured. She smiled her thanks as the maid closed the door behind her, then she tested the water with her toe, the robe slipping to the floor as she stepped gingerly into the tub.

"Hmmm . . ." Kassandra murmured contentedly. The warm water felt so wonderful. She lay her head against the tub, the tension gradually fading from her mind. After a few relaxing moments, she rubbed the soap in a soft cloth until it was thick with lather, then ran it along one slim arm, luxuriating in the heady jasmine fragrance.

A sudden commotion in the hallway just outside her chamber startled Kassandra. She sat bolt upright in the tub, the soapy cloth slipping from her hand into the water. "What!" she gasped in surprise as the door burst open and hit the wall behind it with a resounding thud.

"Kassandra, what is this I hear of you almost being killed?" Isabel cried, sweeping into the room in great agitation. She crossed the floor in a flurry, her velvet cape flaring behind her, her skirts swishing and swaying from her rapid movement. "Oh, forgive me," she murmured, blushing. "Gisela didn't say you were taking a bath." She moved to the other side of the screen, allowing Kassandra some privacy.

"I simply told Gisela—"

"I just met Gisela in the hall. She told me all about your terrible brush with death," Isabel rushed on, clearly horrified by what she had heard. She paced back and forth. "A carriage, you say. Did you see the driver, or the coat of arms, perhaps? We should report this to the authorities at once! Oh dear, what would Miles say if he knew such a thing had happened?"

Isabel paused for breath, glancing reproachfully in Kassandra's direction. "I thought you said you were going for a ride today, not into Vienna on errands. And Gisela said you refused an escort. Oh, Kassandra, I am simply stunned that you could go into the city by yourself! Especially with all the soldiers about, now that the Imperial army has returned."

Clearly exasperated, Isabel plopped into a nearby chair, a difficult task due to the stiff whalebone hoopskirt beneath her gown. She held her skirts down as best she could, her voice betraying her irritation. "This fashion is so impossible," she blurted.

Kassandra could have laughed out loud, a welcome urge after such a day. But the feeling quickly passed, a sense of irony gripping her in its place. Yes, there had been soldiers in the city, much to her misfortune.

"If you will give me just a moment, Isabel," she called out, rinsing the soap suds from her body. With a sigh, she rose out of the tub and grabbed the thick towel draped over the screen, quickly buffing herself dry. Then she snatched her satin robe from the floor and wrapped it about her. Stepping from behind the screen, she was struck by the color of Isabel's eyes, usually a lively blue but now so

clouded with concern that they appeared more gray
. . . flint gray.

That's odd, Kassandra thought, a chill coursing
through her. They were so much like . . . Then she
dismissed the unsettling coincidence. What she obviously needed was a good rest, as soon as she
appeased Isabel.

Kassandra sat down in the chair adjacent to Isabel's. "I don't know what Gisela told you, Isabel,
but the incident was really nothing. A slight scare,
that's all. I will simply have to be more careful in
crossing the streets."

Isabel shook her head, her dark curls bobbing
about. "But, Kassandra, venturing into Vienna by
yourself—"

"If it will make you feel better, Isabel, I promise I
won't go there again, at least not without an escort," Kassandra assured her, though she knew that
would be a hard promise to keep. Even after what
had happened that day, she was still not willing to
give up her independence. She deftly changed the
subject. "Now, enough talk about me. How was the
gala? Tell me."

Isabel's worried expression immediately brightened, a smile of pleasure curving her mouth. "Oh,
it was truly lovely, Kassandra. I wish you had chosen to go with me."

As do I, Kassandra thought ruefully. As do I.

"Their Majesties were so gracious and charming,
and the amusements they had arranged. The gala
was outdoors, and they had shooting games. All the
unmarried ladies present were given light guns to
shoot at the prettiest of targets—Cupid, Venus, Lady
Fortune—and those who had the highest points were
given prizes from the hand of Empress Elisabeth
herself. Why, look at this!" Isabel held out her right
hand, upon her forefinger a gold ring set round with
sparkling blue sapphires.

"It's lovely," breathed Kassandra.

"Yes, but most important of all," Isabel enthused, "we received wonderful news at the gala. Prince Eugene of Savoy has returned to Vienna at last from the campaign in Hungary. That means Stefan will soon be home! He is probably even now in the city."

Kassandra smiled. She had heard a great deal about Stefan von Furstenberg—his accomplishments, his bravery, his sense of fairness, and so much more—from Isabel, who clearly adored her older brother. "That is wonderful news, Isabel," she murmured, a wave of exhaustion suddenly assailing her. She would have loved to show more enthusiasm, but she was so tired.

"Oh, Kassandra, you must be exhausted," Isabel sympathized, noting the faint shadows beneath the younger woman's eyes. She had to admit she was disappointed at Kassandra's reaction to her news, especially after she had expressed such an interest in meeting her brother. It was probably her trying day, Isabel reasoned. After all, Kassandra had narrowly escaped serious harm. Perhaps a good night's rest would bring her round.

"Yes, I think I will go to bed early tonight," she replied sleepily.

"Very well, then," Isabel said, rising as Gisela entered the room.

"Your warm brandy, Lady Kassandra." She set it on the table near the bed. "Will there be anything else? A light supper, perhaps?"

"No, thank you, Gisela. I'm really not very hungry."

"As you wish, milady."

"Sleep well, Kassandra. We'll talk more in the morning," Isabel murmured. She followed Gisela from the room and closed the door carefully behind her. Yes, tomorrow she would tell Kassandra about the welcoming reception at the Hofburg to be held that evening for the victorious Prince Eugene and his officers. She only hoped that Kassandra would be more receptive to accompanying her this time—especially since Stefan would be there.

Kassandra took a sip of the brandy, the subtle warmth a soothing balm to her tormented thoughts. She walked around her chamber, snuffing out the candles, then climbed into bed.

Stefan von Furstenberg, she thought, a sudden thrill of anticipation coursing through her. If he was half the man Isabel had made him out to be, he was certainly someone she would enjoy meeting.

Kassandra unpinned her hair, the thick, burnished waves falling about her face and down her back. She yawned drowsily, laying her head down on the welcome softness of her pillows, and in only a few moments, fell fast asleep.

# Chapter 7

**K**assandra stepped from her room, somewhat embarrassed at the lateness of the hour. She was sure it was already well past midday. But each time she had opened her eyes that morning they had closed heavily once again, as if she had been drugged, and sleep had held her fast for another hour. At last, drowsy and dulled, she had forced herself from bed, and once up and about, she had begun to feel more like herself. After eating a thick slice of buttered bread with her favorite raspberry preserves and drinking strong hot tea, she would feel as good as new.

Kassandra moved down the corridor, laughing voices carrying up to her from the high-ceilinged foyer. She paused to listen. She could not make out the words, but she recognized Isabel's animated voice. The other, a man's, deep and resonant, was unfamiliar to her, at least from this distance. She heard footsteps crossing the polished floor and the sound of the heavy door at the front entrance closing firmly.

She walked to the staircase and looked down, but the foyer was now empty. Perhaps Isabel and her guest had stepped outside, she thought, holding the mahogany railing as she descended the stairs. The wild neighing of a horse startled her, then she heard the pounding of hooves upon the packed dirt of the drive. Curious, she moved to one of the tall windows flanking the front door and pushed aside the lace curtain.

Isabel was standing on the last step leading down to the curved drive, her hand uplifted in farewell, her gaze following the cloaked figure of a rider on a spirited black stallion as it disappeared into the trees bordering the lawn. She turned, smiling happily, and began to walk back into the house, suddenly spying Kassandra at the window before she could drop the curtain. Her lively blue eyes lightened with excitement and she swept through the door, her skirts rustling and swaying.

"Oh, Kassandra, did you see him?" she asked breathlessly.

Kassandra flushed bright pink, chagrined that she had been caught spying behind the curtain. If Isabel had another gentleman friend besides her father, well, that was none of her business.

She had discovered it was an accepted practice in Vienna for women to have both a husband and a lover—and husbands their mistresses in addition to a wife—a surprising arrangement that was openly encouraged. She had been shocked at first, but then had decided that at least it was not as hypocritical as the surreptitious affairs rumored to be so rampant in the English court.

Just because Isabel and her father weren't married yet did not mean the countess might not already have a handsome paramour to keep her company during her father's long absence in Germany, Kassandra considered, though in her heart she hoped this was not the case.

"I only saw a rider . . . I did not see his face—" she began, deeply flustered.

"It was Stefan," Isabel blurted gaily, noting the heightened color on Kassandra's cheeks and the way she was nervously twisting the silken fabric of her skirt. A look of feigned indignation crossed her delicate features. "Oh, Kassandra, really! My heart has room for only one man, despite Viennese customs, and that man is your father." She laughed merrily. "Come now, have you had anything to eat yet?"

Kassandra shook her head, astounded that Isabel had so clearly read her mind.

"No? Well, let's go into the dining room. I have so much to tell you." Isabel wound her arm through Kassandra's, and together they walked into the adjoining room. They had hardly sat down at the table before Isabel rushed on.

"I had hoped you might come downstairs before Stefan left for the city, but I decided it was best to let you sleep, especially after yesterday," Isabel said kindly.

"But when did he arrive?" Kassandra asked. She winced inwardly, Isabel's innocent remark an unsettling reminder of the events of the day before. No, it was done and in the past, she told herself defiantly, willing herself to think of more pleasant things.

Stefan. She felt a flicker of disappointment that she had so narrowly missed him. She nodded to the serving maid, who filled a cup with hot tea and set it on the table in front of her.

"Fetch some of that marvelous bread that the cook baked this morning, if you would, Berdine," Isabel murmured to the young girl, who bobbed her head and hurried from the dining room. She turned to Kassandra. "Gisela came to my door at three o'clock in the morning to tell me Stefan had just arrived at the estate. I barely had time to put on my robe before he was there in my chamber."

Isabel smiled happily. He had looked so handsome and dashing in his uniform, standing so tall in the threshold. She had flown into his arms, tears of joy streaking her face, relief that he had survived yet another military campaign flooding her body. He was all the family she had . . .

Isabel sighed. No, now was not the time to think of her dear parents or her sweet sister, Gretchen, only twelve years old when she had died in Vienna's plague of seven years ago. Besides, she thought, Stefan was home now, and she had Miles . . . and Kassandra. She looked at the young woman beside her, intent upon buttering and slathering with jam the warm bread that had just arrived from the kitchen.

She was so lovely, so spirited, Isabel mused. She would be the most wonderful stepdaughter, and hopefully . . . the perfect sister-in-law. That is, if Kassandra and Stefan took an interest in each other, as she was hoping they might. She could not think of a better match for her brother than the young Englishwoman.

Kassandra set the knife upon the table and took a bite of bread, savoring the tart flavor of the raspberry preserves. She could not believe how hungry she was. She smiled at Isabel, noting that the countess was studying her frankly. Again she was struck by the color of her eyes. She had seen such a color only once before . . .

"Now, Kassandra, I have more exciting news," Isabel began, her voice breaking into Kassandra's thoughts. "Tonight there is going to be a welcoming reception at the Hofburg for Prince Eugene and his officers, and it would please me so much if you would attend." She rushed on excitedly. "Stefan will be there. I have told him a great deal about you in my letters, and he is looking forward to meeting you." Isabel held her breath, as if gauging Kassandra's reaction to her news.

Kassandra swallowed the last of her bread, her gaze meeting Isabel's. She hated the thought of disappointing the countess—she looked so hopeful—yet she hated those damnable court functions even more. The stuffy protocol, the gossip, the awful intrigue, the self-serving lords and their haughty ladies. She shuddered to think of it.

So it had been ever since her first ball at the court of Queen Anne, when she was only fourteen. The malicious conversation she had overheard between two ladies-in-waiting about her mother, Lady Caroline, the mother who had died at her birth, the mother she had known only through the beautiful portrait hanging in the main hall at Wyndham Court, came back to haunt her as if it were only yesterday.

"So that is the harlot's child," a stout, heavily rouged lady had whispered to a friend, yet loud enough for Kassandra to hear.

"Yes, and see how she resembles her mother, with those eyes and that flaming red hair, a damning color to be sure. To think Lord Harrington would have married that woman, knowing who she was, that she had been a whore on the streets of London!"

"You had best guard your son well, and see that he doesn't dance with that harlot's spawn," the stout woman spat, a grin splitting her powdered face at Kassandra's stricken expression, knowing she had heard everything . . .

"Kassandra, are you listening? Please say you will go with me," Isabel pleaded with a hint of impatience.

Kassandra blinked, her thoughts dragged back to the present. "I-I don't think so, Isabel. Surely I can meet Stefan here. Will he be returning to the estate before the reception?"

Isabel shook her head, a look of exasperation flitting across her face. "No, he said he had to go back into the city for the rest of the afternoon, to look for someone, and that he would meet us at the Hofburg.''

No doubt he was looking for Sophia, she thought, annoyed. She loved her brother, but she had been sorely vexed ever since he had begun a dalliance with Archduchess Sophia von Starenberg, the wife to one of Charles VI's court ministers, over a year ago. She detested the woman and firmly believed Sophia was plotting to become Countess von Furstenberg after the death of her elderly husband, whether from natural or unnatural causes.

But not if I can prevent it, Isabel told herself determinedly. It was time for Stefan to choose a wife and start a family, perhaps even retire from the military and manage the estate in person, rather than through lengthy correspondence written to her from the battlefield. Lady Kassandra Wyndham was her best hope, and if she would not go to the reception tonight for the sake of meeting Stefan, perhaps there might be another way to persuade her . . .

''Kassandra, I must insist that you attend the reception with me, if only to represent your father at the court of their Imperial Majesties,'' Isabel said, hoping this new tack might convince her. ''It is an important occasion for Austria, to welcome its victorious army. Since Miles is not here, who could better stand in the ambassador's place than his daughter?''

Kassandra sighed. She knew Isabel was right. Her father would be pleased to learn she had gone in his place, even knowing her intense dislike of such occasions . . . and the reason behind it. Yet it was ironic that she would represent him at an event celebrating the Austrians' victory over the Turks. It was her father's diplomatic mission to dissuade them from any further campaigns against the Ottoman Empire to protect the trade interests of England.

''Very well, Isabel,'' she agreed halfheartedly.

"Good," Isabel said, a smile curving her lips. She glanced at the clock on the marble fireplace mantel. It was already half past two; the reception began at six o'clock. If she was to be ready in time, she would have to begin her toilette at once. Such an important occasion demanded that she look her very best.

She rose from her chair, laying her small hand on Kassandra's shoulder. "That lovely gown your father bought for you, the silver brocade, would be perfect, Kassandra," she enthused. "I shall send Gisela to your room by half past four to help you dress and arrange your hair." She swept happily from the room, her thoughts already on the difficult task of choosing her own gown.

Kassandra sat silently in her chair, absently toying with a knife.

Perhaps it will not be so bad, she tried to convince herself. The incident at Queen Anne's court had occurred long ago. Perhaps it was time she let go of that awful memory and learned to enjoy the diversions of the court.

Kassandra frowned. Well, if not enjoy them, at least tolerate them, she thought ruefully. Besides, Stefan would be there. She would have a chance to meet him at last, just as Isabel had said.

Kassandra took a sip of tea, wrinkling her nose. It had already grown tepid. She pushed away her plate and leaned back in the chair. Yes, Isabel had told her a great deal about Stefan over the past several months, so much so that she felt she already knew him very well.

She knew he was courageous and committed, preferring the life of a soldier to that of an aristocrat, that he was a man of honor, respected by his peers as well as by the men he commanded, and as intelligent as he was handsome.

Yet she also knew he was considered a rogue, a wickedly disarming trait that caused Isabel no small amount of concern. Kassandra was not so naive as to think that he had not had his share of women. One day Berdine, the young maid, had told her of Stefan's current paramour, Archduchess Sophia, in an animated outburst, then had clapped her hand over her mouth for fear she had said too much.

Kassandra smiled. Whether Stefan was a rogue or not, she was looking forward to meeting him. He sounded intriguing, and it seemed they had at least one thing in common. Isabel had told her that Stefan had chosen the life of a soldier because he disliked the idleness and selfish pursuits typical of the Viennese aristocracy. He was one of a handful of wealthy landowners who had decided not only to manage the affairs of his estate as his livelihood, but also to serve in the Imperial army as an officer.

And Kassandra, though a peeress by birth, raised amidst luxury and wealth at Wyndham Court in Sussex, England, had spent far more time in intellectual pursuits and attending to the needs of the common people who rented and worked her father's lands than in the feminine occupations more usual to her class: finely stitched needlework and acquiring a rich husband.

Kassandra stood abruptly and walked toward the stairs. Well, if she was to attend the reception, it was time she summoned a bath to her chamber. Perhaps, unlike the night before, she might have a chance to enjoy it.

And perhaps, if she was lucky, she thought, this reception might offer some diversion from the memories that continued to plague her. She could only hope . . .

# Chapter 8

❝ "**C**ountess Isabel von Furstenberg and Lady Kassandra Wyndham," the liveried footman announced at the entrance to the great ballroom, bowing courteously.

"Isn't this exciting?" Isabel whispered behind her fluttering fan as she and Kassandra swept into the throng of guests milling about the massive room. "And you look so beautiful, Kassandra," Isabel said approvingly.

Kassandra's voluminous gown, with an underskirt of rich brocade and a bodice and overskirt of shimmering silver satin, heightened the creamy porcelain of her skin and the fiery highlights in her hair, and set off to perfection her unusual amethyst eyes.

Isabel smiled behind her fan, recalling Kassandra's concern over the low-cut neckline of her gown just before they had left the estate that evening.

"But, Isabel, it's indecent," Kassandra had exclaimed, tugging irritably at the bodice. But it was of no use. She could do nothing to hide the provocative swell of her breasts, further enhanced by the stiff upper molding of her stays, which made her every movement startlingly revealing. "My other gowns have a bit of ruffle around the edge of the bodice, a tucker. Surely—"

"Oh, really, Kassandra," Isabel replied, laughing.

"The tucker is well out of fashion. But you needn't worry that you will stand out. All the ladies of the court wear such gowns."

Ah, but she does stand out, and ravishingly, Isabel thought, elated that she had convinced Kassandra to accompany her this evening. In her own rose-colored taffeta gown edged with delicate gold ribbon, she knew they made a stunning pair.

"I'm so happy you are here with me, Kassandra," Isabel enthused, raising her voice to be heard. The din that echoed off the high frescoed ceilings was almost deafening, laughter and conversation from bewigged gentlemen and their sumptuously dressed ladies vying with the festive melodies being played by court musicians beneath an arched alcove.

Kassandra forced a bright smile. Though she knew she could not match Isabel's enthusiasm, she was determined to give the evening half a chance. She stared around her, wide-eyed, at the gilded splendor of the Hapsburg court. Though her father had come here several times for audiences with Charles VI and his ministers, this was her first visit to the Hofburg. She had to admit she had never seen such a ballroom, not even at the royal palace in London.

Mirrored walls reflected the light from a long row of gleaming gilt chandeliers, each one holding hundreds of slender tapers that flickered brightly, their radiance casting a golden glow on the richly colored paintings on the ceiling and the polished parquet floor. High, arched windows looked onto the magnificent gardens, and pairs of liveried servants, resplendent in white powdered bob wigs and uniforms of blue brocade edged with silver threads, stood at attention beside tall, latticed doors that opened onto a curved terrace.

At one end of the ballroom tables had been set up for the banquet that would follow the formal reception, the fine Bruges lace tablecloths graced with gleaming silver candelabra and crystal wineglasses. The white chairs placed around the tables were upholstered in a plush red velvet brocade; white benches with gently curling legs and matching red cushions were set against the walls for guests who needed a respite from the constant standing.

"Kassandra," Isabel said reproachfully, though her eyes twinkled, "you're staring as if you've never seen a palace before." She slipped her arm through Kassandra's and guided her along. "Come, we must first be presented to Their Majesties and Prince Eugene of Savoy. Then we must find Stefan. I haven't seen him yet, but I'm sure he's arrived by now."

Kassandra felt her face grow hot at Isabel's teasing, but she quickly swallowed her embarrassment as they took their places in the winding receiving line. In no time at all she was standing in front of Their Imperial Majesties, Charles VI and his consort, Empress Elisabeth, who were seated on a raised dais at one end of the room. She curtsied deeply as she was introduced, her gown spreading out upon the floor in shimmering ripples of silvery satin.

"How lovely you are," the fair-haired empress murmured kindly, after Kassandra had kissed her hand and risen to her feet. She turned to her husband, who sat stiffly at her side.

"Charles, this is the daughter of Lord Harrington. If you recall, Countess Isabel von Furstenberg is betrothed to marry the good ambassador upon his return to Vienna."

As the emperor acknowledged her with a nod, Kassandra thought fleetingly how truly like a Hapsburg he looked, with his prominent chin and protruding lip. His somber black court dress was in striking contrast to the iridescent blue silk of his wife's gown and the richly colored fabrics worn by his courtiers. Isabel had told her that the emperor chose to follow the strict code of etiquette and dress adhered to in the Spanish court, where he had spent most of his youth.

"I had heard Lord Harrington had a daughter, and now I wonder where he has been hiding such a charming young woman these past months," Empress Elisabeth continued, glancing back at Kassandra. She smiled sweetly. "For I believe this is your first time at court, is it not?"

Kassandra nodded, blushing. "Yes, Your Majesty," she said.

"Well, now that you have graced our court, we hope to see much more of you during your stay in Vienna. I'm sure that we have many young gentlemen who would be most delighted to make your acquaintance."

Kassandra smiled weakly, her mind racing. Sweet Lord, now she would never be free of court functions! But she had no more time to think as Isabel took her elbow and steered her to where a rigidly erect officer was standing a short distance away. Instinctively she curtsied.

"It is a pleasure, Lady Kassandra," Prince Eugene of Savoy murmured in a heavily accented voice that affirmed his French heritage. Gallantly he held out his hand and helped Kassandra to arise, then turned to Isabel. "Ah, and Countess Isabel. Your brother, Stefan, has once again proven an invaluable asset in our latest campaign. His bravery is to be commended."

Kassandra stood at Isabel's side, barely listening as the countess and Prince Eugene discussed Stefan's valor in battle. She could hardly believe that this frail-looking man with his swarthy complexion and sunken cheeks could be the renowned commander of the Imperial army. She felt awkward, fairly towering over him, while Isabel, a woman of petite stature, was gazing at the famous general, the most hated and feared enemy of the Ottoman Empire, eye to eye.

"Countess Isabel tells me you have yet to meet her brother," Prince Eugene repeated, regarding her quizzically.

Kassandra started. "Ye-yes, that is true," she stammered, strangely flustered. She could not help but sense that the general had surmised her thoughts. His dark eyes, the liveliest feature about him, seemed faintly amused as he turned back to Isabel. Several other guests soon joined their group, pressing around the general to hear more news of his recent victories at Peterwardein and Temesvar in Hungary.

Oh, this was all going very badly, Kassandra chided herself. Suddenly she felt very warm, her tight stays an oppressive vise. What she would give for a breath of fresh air. She glanced over her shoulder, gratefully spying a set of nearby doors that led to the terrace. She grasped Isabel's arm and gently pulled her aside.

"Isabel, please excuse me, but I feel a bit lightheaded. The air in the room is so stuffy. I think I'll step onto the terrace for a while."

Concern touched Isabel's delicate features. "Would you like me to go with you—"

"No, I'll be fine." Kassandra stopped her, shaking her head. "Please make my excuses to the general. And don't worry, I'll be back in a few moments." She whirled on her heel and hurried across the room, nodding to the footmen standing on either side of the doors, who quickly opened them for her.

As she swept onto the curved terrace, Kassandra paused for a long, deep breath of the night air. She did not have her cape, but she doubted she would need it. So far it had been unusually warm for this time of year.

She felt refreshed immediately, the stirring breezes working like a tonic to cool her flushed face. The rapid beating of her heart gradually subsided, replaced by a feeling of calm as she looked over the moonlit tranquillity of the formal gardens.

It seemed almost a magical night, a haunting night. Thin banks of clouds hung across the sky, a fine gossamer netting against the backdrop of blues that arced from the lightest turquoise at the horizon to inky blue-black at the highest zenith. Myriad clusters of stars glittered like drops of dew through the translucent clouds, reminding Kassandra of a spider's web.

The late autumn breeze rustled through the trees, the crisp leaves that still clung to the half-naked branches shimmering and dancing like undulating ghosts in the pale moonlight. There was a hushed quality in the air, broken occasionally by bursts of soft, secretive laughter coming from guests strolling along the darkened paths. A few flickering torches lit the marble stairs leading to the gardens on each side of the terrace, glowing beacons that seemed to illuminate the entrance into a mysterious world of shadows and intrigue.

Kassandra moved slowly to the balustrade, her hand sliding along the smooth polished marble as she walked to the edge of the terrace. She hesitated for a moment at the top of the stairs, wavering uncertainly. She relished the idea of a walk in the garden, but it seemed so dark beyond the sputtering torchlight. Yet her only other alternative was to return to the stuffy ballroom.

That dreadful thought gave Kassandra the impetus she needed. She walked quickly down the stairs and onto a wide graveled path flanked by tall, manicured hedges. As she moved farther away from the lighted windows of the palace and her eyes adjusted to the darkness, she found that she could see quite well in the moon's veiled glow.

To her surprise, there were quite a few guests in the garden. Some strolled in thoughtful solitude, while others were seated on marble benches beside classical Greek statues that shone an eerie white in the moonlight. And then there were the pairs of lovers embracing fervently in secluded alcoves or walking arm in arm, their heads close together as they whispered in passionate conspiracy.

Kassandra walked quietly along the path, content to be alone. She did not stop until she had reached a far corner of the garden, then she leaned against a gnarled tree beside the entrance to a vine-covered alcove and gazed up at the night sky. It was all so peaceful, she thought dreamily, so peaceful . . .

"Oh . . . !" A ragged moan, breathless and panting, suddenly carried to her from deep within the alcove behind her, breaking the enchanted silence. Kassandra froze, her hands pressing painfully into the rough bark of the tree, scarcely daring to breathe.

"Ah, love me . . . love me," a woman's sultry voice, laden with the impassioned heat of approaching ecstasy, called out into the night, her cry lost to the sighing wind.

God in heaven, what had she stumbled into? Kassandra thought wildly.

Suddenly the woman gasped aloud, "Stef—" But her moans of delight were quickly stifled, and again all was quiet in the dark corner of the garden.

Kassandra's face flushed shamefully. She had unwittingly eavesdropped on a lovers' tryst! She gripped the tree, afraid to move even one step lest she be heard and found out. Then she stiffened in surprise as a man's voice, deep, and edged with roughness, spoke from within the alcove, cutting through her like a knife, twisting into her mind with cruel familiarity.

"Would you . . . flaunt your infidelity . . . to the world . . . ?'' the man queried, his labored breathing melding with the woman's husky laughter and whispered reply.

Kassandra blanched, her nails digging into her clenched hands. Could it be possible? She felt rooted to the ground, though every instinct cried out for her to flee. She barely heard the rustling of silken skirts and a sword belt being buckled for the thunderous pounding of blood in her ears. Surely she had imagined that voice!

"It is time you returned to the reception," the man murmured. "No doubt your husband has need of you.''

"His needs are none of my concern!" the woman snapped petulantly. "It is your needs that interest me, my love . . . yours alone—''

"And you have seen to them very well this night, as always,'' the man interrupted her, somewhat impatiently. "But go now. We have tarried overlong. I will follow in a few moments.''

"Oh, very well. But kiss me again . . . for good measure.''

Kassandra held her breath during the long silence that ensued, exhaling only when the woman spoke again.

"If I did not know better, my lord, I would say your mind has been elsewhere this night. But at least your lovemaking has not been lacking. You are, how shall I say . . . as magnificent as ever.''

Kassandra peeked from behind the tree, relief surging through her when the woman stepped from the alcove, but she could not see her face in the dark. The woman paused and smoothed her rippling silk gown, then she set off down the path toward the palace without a backward glance, her skirts swaying provocatively, her fading laughter low and throaty.

Kassandra watched breathlessly as the man, too, left the cover of the alcove and stood with his back to her, his tall silhouette etched against the moonlit sky. He had said he would follow in a few moments . . .

Her heart sank when the man lingered, apparently in no hurry. She closed her eyes and leaned against the tree, waiting . . . waiting, her body taut and tingling with tension.

Suddenly a twig snapped on the other side of the tree, only a few feet away.

"Oh!" Kassandra gasped, her eyes flying open as she fairly jumped through her skin. She clapped her hand over her mouth, but it was too late. She heard heavy footfalls, slow, deliberate . . . like a lithe, stalking animal, moving ever closer, around the massive gnarled trunk . . . Oh, God, toward her!

Kassandra waited no longer. In one swift movement she lifted her skirts and darted onto the path, straight into the man's open arms.

"Let me go!" Kassandra railed, struggling to free herself from his grip. She kept her head down, a terrible fear, an awful premonition, preventing her from looking at his face. But he held her fast, his arms tightening around her like muscled bands of iron, astonishingly powerful.

"It seems I have found a spy in this garden . . . perhaps a beautiful one," he murmured huskily. Holding her easily with one arm, he brought his other hand under her chin and forced her to meet his gaze.

Kassandra's eyes widened in shock, her throat constricting painfully as she stared up at the man she had thought she would never see again. His piercing gaze seemed to devour her in its gray depths, and she flushed with sudden warmth, her limbs strangely weak.

Perhaps he wouldn't recognize her . . . He had

been drunk, hadn't he? Perhaps he had no recollection of what had happened between them . . . Kassandra's agonized thoughts tumbled over themselves like nightmare phantoms, her desperate plea that he not remember like a silent scream upon her lips.

Stunned, Stefan gazed into the flashing amethyst pools that had haunted his every moment since he had first seen them the day before. Damn! He could hardly believe it! His eyes raked over the length of her, from the elegant coif of her fire-gold hair, the dazzling beauty of her features, the shimmering silver gown that accentuated the lushness of her form, to her slippered feet.

A far cry indeed from the disheveled waif in the tavern, he thought incredulously. Yet he could swear she was the same woman. He had not consumed so much drink that he would forget such exquisite beauty. And now, just when he had been tormented by thoughts of her, wondering if he would ever find her, suddenly she was in his arms!

He had been looking for her since he had awoken in the tavern to find her gone, along with his money. It was not the loss of his gold that had fueled his vow to scour the streets of Vienna until he found her. Never before had he met a woman who so fired his blood, who had so disrupted his life. She had become his obsession . . .

No, not even his wanton Sophia so perfectly matched him in passion, Stefan thought wryly. He knew that now, especially after their garden tryst. All the while he had been thinking of the flame-haired beauty who had filled his senses with a raging tempest of desire.

Yet he had almost despaired of finding her. No one had ever seen her before in the tavern, and no one had noticed her leave except a drunken woman and her sailor friend. All they could tell him was that a fiery-haired wench had dashed down the back stairs as if the devil was on her heels. And when he rushed into the street, she was nowhere to be seen. It was as if the earth had swallowed her whole, without a trace.

Even after he had gone home to his estate in the early morning, his search interrupted for a few hours rest, he had not been free of her. She had come to him in his tortured dreams, a mysterious woman of many guises . . . whore, thief, innocent, temptress . . .

Stefan started, searching her features in the moonlight. But this woman was none of those, he considered. She was dressed as a lady of the Imperial court, hardly a thief. He was not a man to doubt his instincts, but what if he was wrong, and she was not the woman he was seeking? Could there be two such women in Vienna, so alike in face and form?

Kassandra's blood ran cold at his sharp scrutiny, yet she did not miss the flicker of doubt in his rugged features. Sensing his confusion, she felt hope flare within her that her plea had been answered. It fanned her anger and gave her sudden courage.

"I demand that you let me go at—"

"Surely we have met before, my lady," Stefan interrupted.

Kassandra gulped, stunned, but she forced herself to think clearly. Do not give yourself away! her inner voice screamed. "You—you are mistaken, sir. I can assure you we have never met. As for calling me a spy, I was merely walking along this path and unwittingly came upon you and your lady . . . I mean, in the alcove . . . That is, I stood behind the tree for fear you might . . ." She blushed, unable to go on.

Stefan chuckled at her discomfort, not ready to give up so easily. "But I could swear we have—"

"Sir, you are no gentleman to hold me against my will," Kassandra snapped, her eyes flaring.

"And you are no lady," Stefan replied easily, "to spy on lovers and frequent lowly taverns for your . . . amusement."

Kassandra gasped, her mind racing wildly. He knows! He had recognized her! She raised her arm to slap him, but he caught it and brought it to his lips. He kissed her open palm, his burning gaze never leaving her face.

Kassandra jumped at the touch of his lips against her skin, a thrill of fire streaking to the core of her being, memories of shared, tempestuous passion flooding her mind and threatening to overwhelm her. She stared breathlessly at the unmistakable challenge in his eyes . . . It seemed she had given herself away without saying a word.

Damn him! Damn his kisses and damn his eyes! she raged, swept by a terrible storm of emotion that battled within her until she thought she might be torn apart. She hated this man. God, how she hated him . . . for what he had done to her, and for the awful predicament she now faced.

It was obvious from his attire, a rich brocade overcoat, waistcoat, and dark breeches, which he wore with casual flair, that he was a member of the aristocracy and not the common soldier she had thought. Would he cause a scandal?

But all thoughts fled as he once again kissed her palm, lingeringly, possessively, his warm breath making her shiver. Unconsciously she leaned against him, unaware of the smoldering desire reflected in the depths of her eyes, conscious only of the feel of his lips upon her skin and the wild beating of her heart within her breast . . .

"So beautiful . . ." Stefan murmured, a rakish smile tugging at his lips. The feel of her lithe body pressed against him was the sweetest torture; his blood raced hot through his veins. He could swear she was the woman he had been seeking.

Kassandra blinked at the sound of his voice, the taunting smile on his face shattering the spell that held her captive. She tore her hand from his grasp, her eyes glinting fire.

"How dare you," she whispered, steeling herself against trembling desire, a determined resolve forming in her dazed mind.

She would give him no further indication that she had ever seen him before, she vowed. And if he challenged her, whoever he was, soldier, aristocrat . . . yes, and most certainly a scoundrel, she would deny everything. He had no proof, other than her own admission, and that she would never give him.

Kassandra drew herself up, meeting his gaze unflinchingly. "As I said before, my lord, you are mistaken," she stated with icy reserve. "We have never met. And if we had, I am sure I would recall your brutish manners. As for spying on lovers and your strange talk of taverns"—she paused, drawing a deep breath—"it appears the full moon has addled your senses. Now release me at once."

Stefan gazed down at her, amazed by her sudden transformation. Damn! but she was a tantalizing mystery, one he felt compelled to pursue . . .

"If you truly wish it—"

"I do wish it." Kassandra cut him off curtly.

"Very well." Stefan released her so suddenly that she lost her balance. He caught her arm before she fell, steadying her, but she wrenched from his grasp. He merely smiled at her, a rogue's smile. "It has been a pleasure, my lady," he murmured with a gallant bow.

"You are both mad . . . and a blackguard!" Kassandra tossed over her shoulder as she forced herself to walk calmly along the path leading to the palace. Yet she was shaking uncontrollably, her foremost thought to leave the reception at once.

"Hardly mad, my lady," Stefan said softly under his breath. "Captivated." He waited for a few moments, then followed, determined not to let her out of his sight.

# Chapter 9

Kassandra swept into the ballroom, her chest rising and falling rapidly from her labored breath. She blinked in the sudden brightness, yet she was not so blinded that she did not catch the appraising glances of several gentlemen standing nearby, who stared blatantly at her breasts straining against the low-cut bodice.

Men! she cursed inwardly, ready to lash out at anything that wore breeches. She would never wear such a gown again! She fought to catch her breath, chiding herself for dashing up the stairs, but her stays were laced so tight she could scarcely breathe.

"There you are, Kassandra," Isabel exclaimed, rushing toward her from the window where she had been standing. "I was almost ready to organize a search for you. You've been gone so long."

Thank God she hadn't ventured into the garden, Kassandra thought grimly, imagining the expression on Isabel's face if she had found her in the arms of that, that . . . She shuddered, rubbing her temples with slender fingers. At least she didn't have to feign an excuse to leave the reception. Her head ached miserably.

"I-I'm sorry, Isabel," she barely managed without gasping. "But it seems . . . the stroll did me little

74

good—'' A rousing blare of trumpets startled her, drowning out her words.

''It's only the signal that the banquet will begin soon,'' Isabel explained with a laugh, noting Kassandra's unease. Why, she was practically shaking in her slippers!

Isabel's forehead creased in a frown as another thought struck her. If it was already time for the banquet, where could Stefan be? she wondered, her eyes darting around the crowded room. Her gaze fell on a statuesque, dark-haired woman standing beside an aged court minister, who was nodding off in his chair. The woman caught her look and smiled, yet the expression in her lustrous dark eyes was hardly friendly. Isabel smiled tightly in return before looking away.

At least he is not with Sophia, she thought, pleased. She turned back to Kassandra. ''Let's sit over there,'' she said, pointing with her fan to a nearby table.

''Isabel,'' Kassandra began again, wincing from the awful pounding in her head. Those damnable trumpets had only made it worse. ''I was trying to tell you that I'm not feeling very well. I'm sorry, but I think I will have to leave the reception at once.''

''Oh dear, you cannot mean that, Kassandra,'' Isabel blurted. ''We only just arrived an hour ago. Perhaps some food might cure whatever is ailing you. I was so looking forward to the music and dancing after the banquet . . .''

Isabel bit her lip, embarrassed color rising in her face. Perhaps that's why she is trembling so, she thought fleetingly. She took Kassandra's hand in her own. ''Forgive me, Kassandra, I'm being terribly selfish. If you're not well, I can hardly expect you to suffer through the rest of the evening on my behalf. I will call for our wraps and we'll leave immediately.''

"No, no, you must stay and enjoy yourself," Kassandra protested. "The driver can take me back to the estate and return in plenty of time to fetch you home."

"Are you sure?"

"Yes. I'll be fine," she insisted. She clasped Isabel's hand warmly. "You'll have a wonderful time tonight, whether I'm here or not—"

"Stefan!" Isabel suddenly exclaimed, her eyes moving from Kassandra to a point just beyond her. "It's Stefan, Kassandra! I was beginning to think he had missed the reception, but he's here at last. Oh, you must at least wait another moment to meet him." She waved her hand, calling gaily out to him. "Stefan!"

Perhaps there may yet be some hope for this evening, Kassandra thought, her headache momentarily forgotten in her anticipation. After all, she had awaited this meeting with Isabel's brother for a long time. But Stefan or no, she decided quickly, she would still only remain at the Hofburg for a few moments longer. She had no desire to risk another encounter with that blackguard, whoever he was! Smiling brightly, she whirled around.

"Isn't he handsome?" Isabel asked in an aside to Kassandra, watching proudly as Stefan strode toward them.

Kassandra stared in stunned surprise, her breath caught in her throat, the smile fading from her lips. If the world had stopped at that moment, she would have taken no notice. There was nothing but the fierce beat of her heart thundering against her breast, and the flint–gray gaze that seared boldly into her own.

"Kassandra, this is my brother, Stefan." Isabel's voice came to her as if from very far away, a whisper in a deafening maelstrom of emotion, one thought etched upon her mind.

Count Stefan von Furstenberg . . . the soldier at the tavern . . . the rogue in the garden . . . They were one and the same!

Kassandra felt suddenly faint, the awkwardness of her situation hitting her with physical force. She was living at the estate of the man who had ravaged her! But she was jolted from her dazed thoughts as he took her hand in his own and brought it to his lips, his kiss grazing her fingers.

"It is a pleasure to meet you at last, Lady Kassandra," Stefan murmured, masking well his initial astonishment. So the flame-haired temptress he had followed back to the palace was Lady Kassandra Wyndham, the daughter of Isabel's Lord Harrington. He studied her with frank appraisal, amusement lighting his eyes.

Damn, this intrigue seemed to have been fashioned by the hand of Fate herself, he mused, watching emotions flicker across her face. "Isabel has told me a great deal about you, and your father, in her letters."

Spurred by the taunting laughter in his eyes, Kassandra quickly regained her composure. Damn him, if he could play along, then so could she! And there was no sense in giving Isabel the impression that something was amiss, especially since they had only just been introduced. She smiled prettily.

"And I have heard much of you, Count von Furstenberg," she said simply.

"Why be so formal?" Isabel asked, looking from Kassandra to Stefan with mock exasperation. "We're soon to be family. I insist you call each other by your given names." She laughingly took Stefan's arm. "But where have you been this evening, Stefan?"

"I walked in the garden for a short while—"

"The garden? Why, Kassandra just returned from a long stroll as well. You must have just missed each other."

Kassandra looked down uncomfortably, not wishing to meet Stefan's eyes, which were surely laughing at her. Her head was pounding once again.

"Isabel, I really must be going," Kassandra began, raising her head, but avoiding Stefan's gaze. She was struck suddenly by how closely brother and sister resembled each other, with their hair as black as midnight and eyes of the same striking gray. Why had she not guessed it? she wondered, recalling her intuition the night before.

"Of course, Kassandra, forgive me. I had forgotten," Isabel said in a rush of apology. She looked up at her brother, who towered over her. "Perhaps you might accompany Kassandra back to the estate, Stefan. She's not feeling well and must leave the reception, but I dislike the thought of her traveling alone in a carriage, especially at night. Could you?"

"I'd be honored," Stefan responded before Kassandra could protest, smiling rakishly at her as he took her arm. He nodded to Isabel. "I'll return later in the evening for you."

Kassandra started at the pressure of his hand on her arm. She flushed with warmth, her plan to retreat suddenly gone awry. Just like everything else this evening, she thought, as they said their farewells to Isabel and began to walk to the front entrance of the ballroom.

"Stefan, are you leaving so soon?" a dark-haired woman called out as she moved toward them with provocative grace, her gold brocade gown catching the light from the chandeliers, her daring décolletage accentuating her alabaster shoulders and lush breasts.

Kassandra grimaced inwardly at her voice, recognizing it as the one she had heard in the garden. She watched as the woman laid a hand possessively on Stefan's arm, and strangely enough, felt him tense. The woman's eyes, the color of dusky topaz, narrowed visibly.

"Stefan," she murmured sweetly. "I have not had the pleasure of an introduction to this . . . lady."

"Archduchess Sophia von Starenberg, Lady Kassandra Wyndham," Stefan stated, his voice cool.

So this was Stefan's paramour, Kassandra considered appraisingly. She could not imagine the reason behind the odd change in his manner. The archduchess was probably one of the most beautiful women she had ever seen. She was uncommonly tall, like herself, yet where Kassandra was of slender proportion, Sophia von Starenberg's figure was voluptuously curved. Her luxuriant hair, piled high upon her head, was a deep mahogany that shone with burnished highlights. Her profile reminded Kassandra of a statue of a Greek goddess, singular in its beauty.

But her most startling feature was her eyes, tilted slightly upward at the outer corners, almost almond-shaped, and heavily fringed with thick lashes. They stared back at her, the dark depths glinting with so much angry jealousy that Kassandra longed to tell the archduchess her resentment was misplaced. She had no interest in Stefan von Furstenberg.

"Lady Kassandra is a guest of Isabel's, and myself, while her father is in Germany," Stefan continued. "Now, if you will excuse us, Sophia, she is not feeling well. I am escorting her home."

"How kind of you, Stefan," Sophia purred, leaning seductively against him. "Will you be returning?"

"Yes, later. Until then, Sophia."

Kassandra could feel Sophia glaring after them as they walked from the ballroom, the beautiful woman's gaze boring into her back as surely as if it had been poisoned daggers. But her mind quickly turned to the long carriage ride to the estate, a ride they would share . . . alone together.

"Your cape," Stefan murmured, taking the luxurious fur-lined garment from the footman and wrapping it around her. His fingers grazed her bare shoulder, and she drew back as if stung. But if he noticed, he made no mention of it, his features implacable as he hailed a carriage. It pulled around the magnificent entryway of the Hofburg, and in a moment she was seated beside him and he was shouting for the driver to be on his way.

"Good night, my lord," Kassandra said tersely, her back proud and straight as she walked up the stairs, a surge of relief overwhelming her.

She had thought the carriage ride might never end. But fortunately it had passed in relative silence, after her initial excuse that she felt too ill for any discourse. She had sat as far away from Stefan as possible, discouraging further conversation by keeping her eyes trained out the window as the carriage clattered through the darkened streets of Vienna.

Yet she could have been blind for all she had seen on the way back to the estate. She had sensed his unflinching gaze upon her the entire time, his unwanted presence arousing emotions she could not suppress.

"Sleep well, Kassandra."

His deep, rough voice carried from the foyer below, causing her to stiffen momentarily, clutching the banister. She quickened her pace up the rest of the stairs and down the corridor. She did not stop until she was in her chamber, did not feel safe until her trembling fingers had securely bolted the door. She was not about to take any chances with him in the same house.

Kassandra leaned on the door for a long moment,

her eyes closed, her heart pounding. She started when a soft knock broke the silence.

"Who is it?" she whispered, whirling around, her hand to her throat.

"Berdine, milady," the maid replied in a hushed voice. "Count Stefan said you had returned, so I've come to help you undress."

Kassandra relaxed and unbolted the door, opening it with a sigh. "Come in, Berdine," she murmured. She said little else as the maid went expertly about her business, and soon she was free of the gown and its ungodly stays. As Berdine hung everything in the closet, Kassandra donned her linen sleeping gown, then followed the maid to the door, thanked her, and bolted it once again.

At last she was alone. Kassandra ran to the bed and climbed in, pulling the thick covers under her chin. She gazed unseeing at the cream lace canopy above her, turbulent thoughts tumbling through her mind.

What was she to do? She wanted to ignore Stefan completely, but that might arouse Isabel's suspicions that something was wrong. And she couldn't leave the estate; she had nowhere else to go. Her father had given up their apartment in the city when she had agreed to stay with Isabel. No, she would have to remain at the von Furstenberg estate, however awkward it proved, until her father returned to Vienna.

Kassandra rolled onto her side, a hot tear trailing down her cheek. Her situation was so wretchedly impossible! she raged silently, stifling her sobs with her blanket as a torrent of tears streaked down her flushed face. She cried until she was spent, one determined thought ringing in her mind.

She would do just as she had vowed in the garden . . . give him no indication that she had ever seen him before this night. And if, God help her, he challenged her, she would deny everything. He had no proof!

Except for the tattered gown in the closet, she remembered with an awful start, and his velvet money bag. There was a chance he might not recognize the gown, but the bag was another matter. She would have to find a way to rid herself of the incriminating articles, perhaps find a place to bury them during her ride in the morning. She would be alone. Isabel trusted her prowess with horses enough not to require any escort to accompany her, as long as she remained on the estate grounds. Yes, that would be the perfect opportunity.

Closing her eyes, Kassandra prayed fervently that once that was done, she could lay her fears to rest.

Stefan entered the library just off the foyer and poured himself a brandy. He tossed it down, grimacing as the fiery liquid burned his throat, then stared into the blazing flames roaring in the fireplace, leaping red-gold flames that reminded him of the glistening waves of Kassandra's hair.

God, she was beautiful, far more so than he had remembered from the tavern, or even in his dreams. And she was here, in this house. What a twist of fate! Lady Kassandra Wyndham. He could swear she was the one he had been seeking, the woman who had given herself away on more than one occasion tonight, though she pretended—quite convincingly, he thought, with a hint of a smile—that they had just met.

Yet he had to be completely sure, Stefan considered, setting the crystal glass on the mantel. There had to be a way to draw her out, to confirm beyond any shadow of a doubt that she was the temptress who had ensnared him with her passion.

Stefan chuckled deep within his chest. He was a soldier. It would take time, yes, and patience . . .

like mounting a campaign. Somehow she would give herself away completely, perhaps with her own admission, possibly even with her kiss . . .

Stefan brought his fist down hard upon the mantel, the memory of her lips parted beneath his own almost more than he could bear. This woman had fired his blood and captured his imagination like no other! he thought, striding from the library and out the front door. He must know the truth—whether the woman he had possessed was a lowly tavern wench or a high-born woman of title and position.

Once outside, Stefan paused and gazed up at the ink-black sky, glittering with stars. These warm autumn nights enlivened his senses. He filled his lungs with the fresh air, his eyes drawn to the golden cast of a lighted window on the second floor. Kassandra's window . . .

A lithe form passed in front of the window, a tantalizing silhouette. Stefan's breath caught in his throat, a searing pang of desire ripping through his body. Then the light was extinguished, plunging the room into darkness.

"I will have you," he whispered fiercely, shaken by the intensity of his need for this one woman. He knew he was letting his desire get the better of him—he was behaving like a brute—but he couldn't help himself. Nothing could stop him . . . Abruptly he wheeled about and climbed into the waiting carriage.

"To the Hofburg, man," he shouted to the driver, the snorting horses leaping forward at the crack of the whip above their heads. As the carriage lurched into motion, Stefan leaned against the seat and closed his eyes.

Ah, but what of Sophia? Even now she was waiting for him at the palace, waiting to begin again nights of passion such as they had enjoyed before he left on the last military campaign.

There would be no more of those nights . . . at least not with Sophia. But she would understand. He had never led her to believe there was anything more between them than the erotic pleasures they had shared. She had always known it would end one day, for whatever reason.

Sophia would easily find another man to fill her bed, Stefan thought with wry humor. As for him, he could wait . . .

# Chapter 10

"**S**tefan, I have a favor to ask of you," Isabel murmured, closing the door to the library. She turned to find he had already seated himself in the leather chair near the fireplace, his long legs stretched in front of him, his boots crossed casually. A gentle smile played upon her mouth to see him in the room he loved so well, among his books and papers. It was so good to have him home again.

"Ask away, dear sister," Stefan replied, arching a black brow. What could Isabel wish to discuss so early in the morning, and in such secrecy? he wondered. She had interrupted his morning meal—one he sorely needed, he thought, his stomach growling loudly, since he had missed the banquet at the palace the night before. She had insisted they speak at once, before the rest of the household was awake, so he knew it had to be important. Isabel was not one to rise early.

Isabel sat down in the chair across from him, her morning gown falling in gentle folds. "It's about Kassandra," she murmured, her delicate fingers worrying at the lace flounces edging her sleeve.

Noting her nervous gesture, Stefan narrowed his eyes. Had Kassandra perhaps gone to Isabel's chamber late last night and told her of their exchange in the Hofburg gardens? Considering he was still not certain she was the woman from the tavern, he had to admit his behavior toward her had been brazen and ungentlemanly. Yet she had had a chance to mention it when they were introduced, and she had not . . .

"I'm worried about her, Stefan," Isabel began, interrupting his thoughts. She leaned forward, her voice a raised whisper. "Why, just the other day she was nearly killed when she went into Vienna by herself."

"What do you mean, killed?" Stefan queried tightly, tensing.

Isabel shook her head in consternation. "I invited her to attend a royal gala with me at the Favorita, but she insisted she'd rather remain at the estate . . . to write letters and perhaps go riding. Instead"—she paused briefly, taking a breath—"she had Zoltan take her into the city on errands. While she was there, a carriage nearly ran her down. She lost her cloak under its wheels. Oh, Stefan, it could have been a dreadful accident!"

Stefan's mind raced with this news. So Kassandra had been in the city the other day. Another clue to his tantalizing mystery. But if Zoltan had escorted her, she wouldn't have been alone. Or would she? He would have to speak with the carriage driver later and discover the truth.

Isabel rose and paced in agitation. "And if that wasn't enough"—she sighed heavily—"Kassandra refused an escort, even at Gisela's insistence. What would Miles say if he knew his daughter was roaming the streets of Vienna with only a carriage driver to protect her? It's not only unsuitable, but dangerous! There are so many soldiers in the city now, carousing, drinking, and whoring—"

"Isabel!"

"I'm no green girl, Stefan," Isabel countered, "and hardly ignorant of the ways of men, in this city of all places, where infidelity is encouraged. You can hardly blame the soldiers, really, after enduring another long campaign. But think of what might have happened, Stefan, if Kassandra had fallen into such ill company.''

Stefan nearly choked. Thank God Isabel could not read his mind! he thought, suddenly conscience-stricken. He rose from his chair, anxious to put an end to the discussion.

"So what is this favor you ask of me?'' he queried, rankled by his unease.

"If you could watch out for her, Stefan, at least until Miles returns from Hanover,'' Isabel replied. "I would rest easier knowing she was in your hands.'' A bright smile lit her face. "You could think of yourself as her warrior knight.''

Stefan exhaled sharply. If only she knew how far from Kassandra's savior he really was. But Isabel's request would give him an excuse to remain in Kassandra's company. And being near her might further unravel the mystery that spurred him on . . .

He nodded. "Agreed.''

"I knew you would!'' Isabel exclaimed, embracing him warmly. "You have my thanks, and Miles's as well.'' And it will give them a chance to become better acquainted, she thought, her hope that she could match them together flaring higher than ever.

"Now, Isabel, if you know me so well,'' Stefan said, "I'm sure you won't take offense if I return to the dining room and finish my meal—''

"Of course.'' Isabel laughed, walking with him to the door. She stopped suddenly and brought her finger to her lips. "Ssshhhh.''

"What is it?'' Stefan asked, perplexed. He heard light footsteps in the foyer, then the front door opening and closing.

Isabel only shook her head, motioning for him to look out one of the tall, arched windows. He drew

back the velvet curtain, his eyes widening as he
spied Kassandra, dressed in a form-fitting riding
habit and walking briskly across the lawn toward
the stable. Immediately he wanted to follow her, and
was chagrined by his own eagerness. Never before
had he had so little control where a woman was concerned . . .

"You agreed, Stefan," Isabel said, interrupting his
thoughts. "I'm afraid your meal will have to be
postponed." She shrugged, her eyes dancing. "The
lady awaits her protector." She held the door open
for him. "She's gone for a ride every morning since
she came here, without fail, except for yesterday. It
is her passion."

One of many passions, Stefan amended, the mere
thought of that afternoon in the tavern arousing his
desire.

"Very well, Isabel." He winked playfully. "As I
am a man of my word, a warrior knight should be
about his duties." His laughter echoed through the
hall as he whipped his black cloak over his broad
shoulders and stepped outside, closing the door
firmly behind him.

Kassandra veered off the path leading to the stable
and walked determinedly toward the carriage house,
Zoltan's woolen cloak draped over one arm while
under the other she clutched a tight roll of clothing.
The heavy cloak was slowing her down, much to her
irritation, but it was time she returned it to the burly
driver. It had looked out of place in her chamber,
another glaring reminder of a day she would rather
forget.

Her breath was becoming labored, hanging like a
fine mist upon the morning air, which was tinged
with the first cold snap of the season. At last she
neared the large outbuilding. The great wooden
doors were open, so she stepped inside, her eyes

adjusting quickly to the darkened interior. It smelled of horse dung and varnish, the sort used to lacquer the fine wood of the carriages.

"Zoltan?" she called out. "Are you here?" A burst of laughter startled her, then the carriage house fell silent again except for the low drone of masculine voices deep within the building. Hesitating, she shrugged and followed the sound past a line of well-kept carriages, almost stumbling into a group of drivers seated upon the hay-strewn ground. They all jumped to their feet, holding bowls of steaming porridge in their hands.

"Lady . . . Kassandra," Zoltan managed, hastily swallowing a hearty mouthful with a gulp.

"I-I'm sorry . . . Please, go back to your meals," Kassandra stammered, almost as surprised as the wide-eyed drivers. She stepped to the other side of the carriage and waited for Zoltan to set down his bowl and hurry to her side. She looked up at the huge Hungarian, gratitude shining in her eyes. His kindness the other day had touched her deeply.

"Here is your cloak, Zoltan," she murmured, holding it out to him. "Forgive me for not returning it yesterday. I rose late, and then there was the reception to prepare for—"

"It is no matter, milady," he replied, his deep-set eyes intent on her face. "Are ye all right, miss?" he asked, absently twisting the cloak with his huge, callused hands.

"Yes, I am fine," she replied. "And thank you for waiting for me at the cathedral the other day." She chewed her lip nervously. Could she ask him? she debated, then shook her head. She had to . . . "Zoltan?"

"Yes, milady?"

"There is something I must ask of you," she said softly, meeting his gaze. "If—if anyone should ask if we, I mean, if you followed me in the carriage during the day as I went about my errands"—she paused, gauging his reaction, but his swarthy features were devoid of expression—"would you tell them that you never lost sight of me?" She held her breath, waiting for his answer.

Surprised, Zoltan mulled over her unexpected request, yet in his heart he already knew his answer. God help him, she was so beautiful, he could hardly deny her plea. For he knew it was a plea, and a desperate one.

Something had happened to this young woman two days past—he was no fool; he had seen the anguish in her eyes when she had met him at the cathedral—something she wanted to keep hidden. Now she trusted him enough to ask him to lie for her, aye, to knowingly deceive whoever might ask any questions about that day. And, Zoltan decided firmly, he would not be the one to betray her trust.

"Aye, milady, I will," he answered gruffly, nodding his shaggy head.

A wide smile broke across Kassandra's face, but she had no time to thank him, for just then another voice called within the carriage house. "Zoltan!"

Kassandra tensed, her smile disappearing. Stefan! Clutching the roll of clothing to her breast, she brushed past the startled driver and, skirting his equally astonished companions, slipped through an open side door just beyond where they were seated.

She headed straight for the stable, her heart lurching. Was it a coincidence, or was he following her? She entered the low building and hurried to the stall where her favorite roan mare was quartered.

"I have her all ready for ye, milady, just like every day," a young stableboy piped up, his fair complexion reddened by the frosty morning air. An eager grin split his face. "Shall I walk her out for ye?"

"No, I'll manage, Hans, thank you," she murmured, taking the reins from his chapped hands. "Go and warm yourself."

"Aye, miss." He nodded and raced back to the small brazier in a far corner of the stable, where several other stableboys were huddled.

Kassandra walked the frisky mare into the stable yard, her only thought to be on her way as quickly as possible. She wanted to find a place far out in the woods surrounding the estate to bury the telltale roll of clothing—the tattered gown, petticoat, and stockings, and the velvet money bag that still contained several clinking coins. She was about to set her foot in the stirrup when, out of the corner of her eye, she spied Stefan striding toward her from the carriage house.

Dear God, what was she to do with the clothing? She flipped the reins over a nearby post, tethering the mare, then hurried back into the stable, her eyes darting about the shadowy recesses. Quickly she ran to the wall and buried the roll beneath a heaping pile of straw, then straightened and shook the dust from her skirt. Obviously she would have to wait for another time to rid herself of the offensive garments . . .

He must be following her, the bastard! Kassandra raged, forcing herself to walk calmly back outside into the bright sunlit morning. How could she possibly act civilly to this man, when at the very least she wanted to scratch out his eyes?

Ignoring him as he called to her, she again set her foot in the stirrup and hoisted herself into the sidesaddle. She clucked to the mare, digging her heel gently into its side, and they set off at a canter through the stable yard, then out onto the road that led away from the estate.

It seemed only a moment had passed when she heard the pounding of hooves not far behind, then the fierce snorting of Stefan's mighty black destrier as he reined in beside her. The mare tossed her head at the sudden intrusion, her hooves pawing the earth as she threatened to rear.

"A lovely morning to you, my lady," Stefan offered gallantly, reaching for the mare's bridle and steadying the frightened animal. "Whoa now," he murmured in soothing tones, until the mare had settled down. He laughed, a deep, husky sound that rang out in the surrounding woods. "Would you mind if I rode along?"

Kassandra bit her tongue against a bitter retort. Play the part, she admonished herself. Remember, there is nothing more between you than your recent acquaintance.

"Not at all," she replied, smiling brightly, her heart thumping against her breast as she was struck again by his dark good looks. He smiled back, his teeth a flash of white against his bronzed face.

"Good," Stefan said, matching his destrier's pace to that of the mare's as they set off at a walk. "I was hoping for a chance to offer an apology for my behavior last night at the reception."

Stunned by this statement, Kassandra felt her skin flush with sudden warmth. She kept her eyes trained on the winding road before them, fearful that he might see her discomfort. "An apology, my lord?"

"Yes, for what happened in the garden," Stefan replied easily. "I was certain I had seen you somewhere before, but of course, that's impossible. I'm only surprised you didn't mention to Isabel that we had already met, so to speak, in the garden."

Kassandra swallowed, her mouth suddenly gone dry. What game was he playing? she wondered. "I saw no need," she finally managed, glancing at him. "It was an error easily made in the dark, and certainly not worthy of mention. But I do accept your apology, Stefan." She turned away, flustered, and rubbed the coarse hairs along the mare's neck. Strange, that was the first time she had called him by his given name.

Stefan sat back in the saddle, studying her exquisite profile. It seemed he was getting no further in unraveling the mystery. First Zoltan had insisted that Kassandra had never been out of his sight during that day in the city, and now his apology had scarcely raised a slim eyebrow, let alone the indignant outburst he had expected. What could he possibly say . . .

"I wonder what you must think of me," he began, "after stumbling upon such a, well, such an indelicate situation in the garden—"

"Isabel told me you were something of a rogue, so I am not surprised you would choose such a place for a tryst," Kassandra cut him off flippantly, doing her best to conceal her true feelings. If he only knew what she really thought of him! "And from what I have heard of Viennese gentlemen, it seems discretion is not a valued trait." With that, she spurred her mare into a trot, then a fast gallop. "I thought you wanted to ride, my lord," she tossed over her shoulder.

Stefan's eyes gleamed with amusement, following Kassandra's lithe figure riding low on her mare as the animal raced across an open field. "You have won this match," he murmured to himself with admiration, undeterred that she had bested him once again. "But there will be others." After all, he thought fleetingly, the chase was nearly as exciting as the quarry . . .

Stefan dug his heel into the stallion's glistening flank and the mighty animal leaped forward, bolting from the road into the field.

# Chapter 11

Stefan tore up the perfumed letter, the second he had received by messenger that morning from Sophia, and tossed it into the bright orange flames blazing in the fireplace. He watched silently as the ivory paper curled and blackened at the edges, then was consumed in a puff of acrid smoke.

Fool! You should have told her by now, Stefan berated himself, running a hand through his thick hair. It had been going on like this for two weeks, ever since the day after the reception. Letters, some written in a furious pique, some seductively suggestive, some desperately pleading, had been arriving every day from Sophia, and all of them contained the same message. When, and where, could they meet?

Stefan turned from the fireplace in frustration. If only Sophia had been at the Hofburg when he had returned that night to fetch Isabel, instead of having left unexpectedly with her husband, the archduke, who'd suddenly taken ill. Then the matter would have been settled. Instead, she still had no inkling that their affair was over. He had been so busy catching up on matters concerning the estate, and with his much more pleasurable task of keeping a watchful eye on Kassandra, that he had hardly a moment to write Sophia a letter in reply.

But the end of their alliance was hardly something he could discuss in a letter, Stefan thought, shaking his head. Sophia deserved more than that. He would have to visit her at the von Starenberg estate later that day, after his meeting with Prince Eugene at his palace on Himmelpfortgasse within the city walls, and tell her himself. He would be gone the better part of the afternoon, and maybe into the early evening . . . a long time to be away from Kassandra. But there was no help for it.

Stefan walked over to a massive table with intricately carved legs, its dark, polished surface strewn with papers and rolled maps. He leaned on it for a long moment, his eyes barely focusing. His mind conjured forth a stirring image of flashing amethyst eyes fringed by lush, gold-tipped lashes, and smiling red lips. Kassandra . . . He clenched his jaw angrily, then with a sudden movement swept his arm across the table, sending maps tumbling to the floor and papers scattering high in the air, only to drift down and settle in disarray upon the woven carpet.

Damn, little good that's done! Stefan raged, shocked at his own anger. He sat down heavily in his leather chair, rubbing his forehead with his hand. What was she doing to him? It was as if he was beginning to doubt his instincts, and the heated memory that had driven him since that afternoon in the tavern. He was obsessed with a need to know the truth!

During the past two weeks, he had rarely let Kassandra out of his sight. He rode with her in the morning, entertained her in the library with tales of his travels and life as a soldier, joined her on the long walks she favored, accompanied her and Isabel into Vienna on several shopping trips—the pastime he least enjoyed!—and yet through it all she had given him no further sign that she was the woman who had so bewitched him. Not an expression, not a gesture, not a misspoken word—nothing!

Exasperated, Stefan rose from the chair and strode over to the window, planting his legs wide apart and crossing his arms as he looked out over the wide expanse of the snow-covered lawn. The first snow of the season had fallen last night, blanketing the landscape in a thin veil of white, the bare branches of the trees glistening like spun crystal under a transparent sheen of ice. No doubt it would melt soon. The bright morning sun was warm on his face through the windowpane, and already the snow on the curved drive was fast receding, clear rivulets of icy water streaking the packed dirt.

Best to set off for Vienna before the roads become a sea of mud, Stefan thought, sighing heavily. He glanced at the ornate clock on the shelf of a mahogany bookcase. His meeting with Prince Eugene was scheduled for half past eleven, barely two hours away. He had yet to dress in his dark blue uniform and, he scowled, noting the papers lying on the floor, reorganize the documents he needed for the meeting. He bent on one knee, quickly gathering up the rolled maps and papers.

Of one thing he was sure, he thought darkly, straightening to his feet and sorting through the documents. He would wait no longer for an admission from Kassandra. When he returned from Vienna he would confront her with the memory that was driving him mad, and if she denied it, perhaps her kiss would decide the matter once and for all.

Kassandra sat in the middle of her bed with her knees pulled up under her chin, her voluminous morning gown wrapped snugly about her, one stockinged foot tapping nervously on the satin bedspread. She could swear it had been almost an hour since Stefan had left the estate on his horse, Brand, an hour that had passed like an eternity as she forced herself to wait before making the slightest move. Although she knew he had gone into Vienna for a meeting with his commander, Prince Eugene, she wasn't about to take the chance that he might return unexpectedly.

It was the first time Stefan had left the estate by himself in two weeks, two confusing weeks that had been an ever-increasing torment for her. It had not taken her long to figure out that Isabel had assigned Stefan the task of being her guardian. Berdine, having heard it from Gisela, had confirmed her suspicions in a burst of giggling chatter.

From their first ride together the morning after the reception Stefan had dogged her every step, becoming a constant companion who, Kassandra loathed to admit, both infuriated her and excited her. His very presence was so powerfully masculine, so compelling, that her firm resolve to hate him was shaken every time they were together. She despised him for what he had done to her, yet she could not deny she was overwhelmingly attracted to him, beset by a scorching desire that was beyond her understanding. The aching memory of that afternoon haunted her every waking moment and filled her nights with unwanted dreams of his caress . . .

Kassandra shook her head and sprang from the bed. No, she would not think of him anymore! Especially not now, when she at last had her chance to rid herself of the garments hidden in the stable. She shrugged off her morning gown and tossed it on the bed, already dressed in her warm woolen riding habit. She ran to her closet and threw open the door, quickly pulling on her leather boots, then she whirled the new cape Isabel had bought her about her shoulders. Fastening it securely, she lifted the fur-lined hood over her head and hurried to the door.

At least Isabel is still sleeping, she thought gratefully, running lightly down the stairs. And Gisela was in Vienna at the market, so no one was here to spy upon her. She exhaled sharply as she stepped outside, the sharp, cold air taking her breath away. But the warm sun on her face lifted her spirits, and she walked briskly along the path leading to the stable.

"Hans?" she called when she reached the stable yard. She received no answer; a strange quiet hung over the place. Then she remembered Stefan had given the stableboys, several of the drivers, and other workers from the estate a free day to spend as they wished after laboring so long and hard in preparation for the coming winter.

No matter, she thought. She knew how to saddle a horse. She walked into the dark stable, silent but for the low rustling of horses in their stalls and an occasional whinny.

"Hello, girl," she said softly, stepping gingerly into a wide stall. The roan mare turned at the sound of her voice, nickering in greeting, and nudged Kassandra with her velvety nose.

"There you go," Kassandra murmured, reaching deep into the pocket of her skirt and pulling out a carrot stub. "I saved it just for you." As the mare munched contentedly, she hoisted the lightweight saddle onto her back, then fastened the girth below her belly. Lastly she drew the bridle over the mare's head, patting the white spot on her forehead, then led her from the stall.

Kassandra tethered the mare and ran over to the wall, exhaling with relief when she dug below the pile of straw and found the roll of clothing still there. Thankfully the stableboys had not found it. She tucked it under her arm and hurried back to the mare, then eased up on the saddle. Clucking softly, she ducked her head as they left the stable. At first the bright sunlight on the white snow blinded her, then they were off across the stable yard and along the road, the mare prancing friskily as they eased into a canter.

"Whoa, girl," Kassandra commanded, pulling up hard on the reins as the mare instinctively veered into the open field just off the road. "We're going this way today." She turned the mare in the opposite direction, heading her down an incline through a ditch drifted high with snow, then into the thick woods that she knew stretched for miles on this side of the road. It would be a far more secluded place to bury the clothing, and the cover of the trees would lessen the chance of being seen by anyone.

The forest was so dense that she had to slow to a walk, carefully winding around the trunks of towering trees and dodging fallen branches. She had never been this way before, and on any other day might have feared becoming lost. But it had snowed last night, and the mare's hoofprints made a welcome guide for the journey back.

Kassandra allowed herself to relax after several moments, the hushed quiet of the surrounding woods lulling her senses and easing the nervous tension that gripped her body. She allowed the mare to choose her own path while she looked around her at the glistening wonder of the winter scene.

"It's so beautiful . . ." she breathed, smiling as a pair of plump white-tailed rabbits hopped along the ground just in front of them, diving under the cover of a snow-laden thicket as the mare snorted and tossed her head in surprise. Two pair of velvet-brown eyes peeked out from beneath the low-lying branches, black noses and whiskers quivered, their furred bodies poised for flight.

The ground was crisscrossed with what seemed like hundreds of tracks. Squirrel, birds, rabbits, and deer; an intricate mosaic of forest life. Stefan had told her it was a favorite pastime for him to venture into the woods, not so much for hunting but for the solitude it offered—

Kassandra frowned, amazed at how quickly her thoughts flew back to Stefan. Her hands tightened on the reins once again. The man was such an infuriating contradiction! One day a rogue, with that taunting smile and hint of challenge in his eyes she remembered so vividly from the garden, and then the days thereafter a gentleman of gallantry, wit, and intelligence, with a droll sense of humor—the many qualities Isabel had so highly praised.

Kassandra sighed, perplexed. She knew she could never forgive him for what he had done to her, but she had to admit her guard was beginning to slip. He had done nothing within the past few weeks to indicate he had any desire to expose the secret they shared.

Perhaps he has decided there's nothing to gain from such a scandal, Kassandra reasoned. Or could it be that he feared for his own reputation? Surely he realized he would be punished severely, maybe even imprisoned, for his crime of assaulting the daughter of the English ambassador.

She grimaced, recalling a day when, walking with her father, they had come across the horrendous sight of several criminals being herded through the streets toward the prison, their arms pilloried, their backs viciously lashed and bleeding. He had told her the worst criminals were racked and broken on the wheel for their crimes, their mutilated bodies left outside the city walls as a gruesome reminder . . .

Kassandra shuddered. Hardly a fate Count Stefan von Furstenberg would wish upon himself! And even if he was still entertaining some plan of revealing their secret, after today she would have nothing to fear. There would no longer be any proof.

Kassandra pulled up sharply on the reins and

looked around her. There was a strange tension in the air—was it the wind?—and she was anxious to be done with her task. This place was as good as any, she decided quickly, sliding from the mare's back to the ground. Holding the roll of clothing in one hand, she walked to a sunlit clearing, her boots crunching in the snow.

What could she use to dig a hole? She cursed under her breath. How stupid of her to forget to bring a small shovel, or even a knife to hack through the cold earth. Obviously she would have to think of something else—perhaps . . . ?

Kassandra's eyes flew to a heavy stick lying a few feet away. It would have to do, she told herself, bending to pick it up. She returned to the center of the clearing and fell to her knees. Dropping the clothing beside her, she brushed the snow away from the spot with her gloved hands. She began to dig with the jagged end of the stick, slowly at first, then faster as the frozen topsoil gave way to moist black dirt.

Kassandra paused for the briefest moment to wipe away the hair that had escaped from the thick knot at her nape, then continued to dig furiously, her panting breaths forming clouds of vapor in the frigid air. At last there was a hole deep enough for the clothing. She dropped the roll gingerly into the hollow, wrinkling her nose in distaste, then pushed the dirt back in upon it, packing it smooth. Leaning on her hands at the edge of the covered hole, she fought to catch her breath, the icy air stinging her lungs.

At last it was done! she exulted, relief rushing through her. Sweat rolled down her back beneath the coat of her riding habit, but she didn't care. The tension and uncertainty that had gripped her for the past few weeks fell from her like a dead weight, and an overwhelming sense of freedom swelled within her heart.

Kassandra sat back on her heels, tossing her head back as she gazed up into the clear blue sky. As her laughter rang through the silent woods, a wild impulse seized her. She grabbed the stick and threw it with all her might into the trees.

"I'm glad I chose to stand over here, rather than in the way of your stick," a deep voice said behind her. "Your aim is deadly, my lady."

# Chapter 12

**K**assandra blanched, the laughter dying on her lips, the abrupt strangled sound an eerie echo in the forest. No, it can't be! she thought, her gloved fingers digging into the frozen earth as she knelt motionless, stricken with terror. He is in Vienna, with Prince Eugene. He must be, he must be . . . Surely, it is the wind, the rustle of dead leaves, a cruel trick of your imagination.

"It seems you have strayed from your usual riding path today, Kassandra," Stefan said lightly, stepping into the clearing. His casual tone belied the triumph surging within him; now she would confirm the truth and he would be free of this obsession to know. His eyes darkened to a vivid gray as he studied her lithe form, her back still to him, straight and stiff. He began to walk toward her.

He had been just outside the city wall when he realized he had forgotten a most important document that he was to present to his general. It was a map of the fortress city of Belgrade, Serbia, the site of the following year's campaign against the Turks, which had been secreted to him the night before by a well-paid Janissary spy. He had wheeled Brand around and ridden like the wind back to the estate, secured the map, then had set out again, only to find Kassandra ahead of him as she veered her mare from the road into the thick woods.

He had thought it strange, knowing how much she enjoyed riding across the open fields, and giving her a good lead, he had followed her to this clearing. She had been so engrossed in her mysterious task that she had not heard him approach, and he had stealthily watched her, a strong suspicion growing that she was on the verge of giving herself away.

She reminded him of a cornered doe, Stefan mused, seeing her tense at the sound of his approaching footsteps in the snow. Her head was tilted to one side as if she was aware of his every movement, her body taut and poised to flee.

"It's of small consequence, really, taking another path," he continued steadily. "The woods are beautiful at this time of year, especially with a dusting of snow. Still, I didn't expect to find you digging a hole in the ground, a strange pastime, you must admit, Kassandra, even for such a mysterious young woman as yourself."

Kassandra winced as stark realization, and a chilling despair, settled over her like a smothering cloud. It hadn't been the wind, or her imagination, she thought dully. Stefan must have been watching her for some time . . . must have seen everything . . .

Her limbs felt wooden, sapped of their lifeblood, as she rose to her feet and turned to face him, her gaze caught and held by his own. The familiar taunting challenge was there, but now something else struck her with numbing force. He looked so . . . resolute.

Stefan drew in his breath, stunned by Kassandra's poignant beauty. He had never seen her look so vulnerable, or so haunted. He longed to reach out and wipe away the smudge of dirt on her cheek, yet he held back.

No, he would not be swayed, he thought grimly.

The moment he had long awaited had come at last. He would play out the game to the end, and prove the victor, triumphant over this obsession that had so haunted his days and nights.

"Step aside, Kassandra," he breathed softly, so close to her now, he could see she was trembling uncontrollably, could smell the intoxicating scent of her floral perfume.

Kassandra opened her mouth to speak, but found she had no voice. She shook her head, her eyes never leaving his face.

Stefan had expected as much. "You must," he insisted, his voice low. He gently gripped her arm and drew her a few feet away from the carefully packed dirt where she had been standing. She offered no resistance, which puzzled him, but instead stood rigidly as he began to kick at the dirt with the heel of his leather boot. The packed soil soon gave way, revealing what appeared to be one end of a tightly wound roll of clothing, secured with twine.

Stefan squatted on his haunches and impatiently brushed away the remaining dirt, studying for a moment the contents of the shallow hole. His eyes widened in recognition and he glanced up at Kassandra, but she was no longer watching him, her gaze focused on some distant point in the woods, her features set and implacable as if finely chiseled in stone.

He pulled out the bundle and set it beside him. In one swift movement he drew a long hunting knife from a leather sheath at his belt and severed the knotted twine, replacing the knife as he rose to his feet. He shook out the clothing in a spray of moist dirt—a torn and wrinkled print gown, a pair of plain gray stockings that floated lightly to the ground, a petticoat, and a small velvet drawstring bag that fell near the toe of his boot with a chinking thud . . .

"So at last I have found you, my temptress," Stefan murmured, bending to pick up the small bag.

Flashing gold coins tumbled out the open end to the ground, in bright contrast to the black dirt mixed with snow. Yet it was not the money he was interested in, but his initials, finely embroidered in silver threads, upon the inside upper rim of the bag. His callused finger traced the smooth needlework— expertly sewn by Isabel, who had given the bag to him as a gift—the final proof he needed.

Stefan straightened just in time to see that Kassandra had turned toward him, the flash of her hand hurtling at his face. Before he could dodge the blow, she hit him with all the strength she could muster, a sharp, resounding smack. He nearly lost his balance, his cheek stinging painfully, but managed to keep his footing as she spun to flee.

Stefan lunged at her, grabbing her roughly, and twirled her to face him once again, his strong hands gripping her upper arms. He swallowed hard as he was struck by the full force of her gaze, like a tempest unleashed, her amethyst eyes, darkened to a stormy violet hue, glinting at him with sparks of fury.

"Bastard!" Kassandra shouted, nearly choking on the swell of emotions within her breast. Scalding tears blinded her, but she fought them back, determined not to give in to such a useless, feminine display. Sensing his momentary discomfiture, she wrenched free of his grasp, lashing out at him again with her arm. He deftly stepped aside and caught her wrist, twisting her arm behind her back and pulling her hard against his broad chest. He held her there, though she struggled and kicked, her attempts to escape him futile next to his powerful strength.

"You *are* the one," he breathed huskily into her fiery hair, now free of its pins and tumbling down her back and about her flushed face in riotous waves. Much the same as in the tavern, he recalled, drawing slightly away from her to study the exquisite lines of her high cheekbones, his finger instinctively tracing the curve of her jaw to her chin. When she tried to turn her face away from him, he entwined his hand in her lustrous hair and pulled her head back, bringing his mouth down upon her own.

Kassandra gasped, the memory of his kiss in the tavern, rough and demanding, and the shocking reality of his kiss at that moment, possessive yet almost tender, merging in her mind. This wasn't happening! she thought vainly, then thought no more as he deepened his kiss, forcing her lips apart, drawing panting breaths from her body.

Time stood still, then faded altogether. Kassandra did not know at what point she stopped fighting him, only to close her eyes and lean against his hard length, responding to his kiss with a burning ardor that matched his own. She felt dizzy, as if she were falling, a liquid warmth stirring deep within her and flooding her body with flaming desire.

Stefan tore his lips from hers and trailed a path of shivering kisses down her white throat, his mouth lingering at the pulse beating rapidly at the curved base of her neck. He inhaled the scent of her skin, her hair, a sense of conquest surging within him. He released her arm and brought both of his hands to her face, his thumbs caressing the satin smoothness of her cheeks as he reveled in her beauty.

Kassandra bent her head to the side at his touch, hypnotically immersed in the embrace of this man. But when she opened her eyes and met his searing gaze, she saw not only desire but sheer triumph. It chilled her to the bone, dousing her own desire as surely as if she had been drenched in an icy bath, and she remembered with a jolt why she so hated him.

Bile rose in her throat with the realization that this was merely a game with him, at her expense. It was clear he considered himself the victor, and her the spoils. But damn him, he had not won yet! In one swift movement she groped wildly for the sheath at his belt, then drew out the knife and pushed the flat end of the blade against his ribs.

"Let me go," she whispered vehemently, her eyes burning brightly. "Now!"

Stefan tensed and drew back suddenly, his arms dropping to his sides, his battle-honed instincts recognizing that Kassandra's tone bespoke no idle threat. He shook his head in amazement, but kept his attention on the knife as she stepped away from him, glancing occasionally over her shoulder to get her bearings in relation to the mare that was grazing contentedly on the dry grasses that edged the clearing.

Kassandra briefly turned her back to him when she reached the mare and grabbed the reins dangling to the ground, then whirled once again to find Stefan had not moved a muscle. She eyed him warily, the knife held expertly in one hand while she flipped the reins over the mare's head, stepped into the stirrup, and eased onto the saddle.

"Whoa, girl, steady," she murmured, pulling up on the reins with her free hand. Then without a word she lifted her arm and flung the flashing blade through the air. A grim smile lit her face when the knife cut into the earth only inches from Stefan's foot.

"As you can see, Count," she murmured tersely, lifting her chin with defiance, although inside she was quaking, "I am quite able to protect myself. I hope you take this as a warning, for if you come near me again, I will not be as charitable."

Kassandra nudged the mare with her heel; then, without a backward glance, they set off at a swift canter toward the estate, precariously dodging the trees lining the path they had left earlier in the snow.

Her heart was beating thunderously and she shivered, not so much from the cold as from the sheer boldness of her act. She had never threatened any living creature before, let alone a grown man, and a seasoned soldier at that. She only hoped she had swayed him from whatever game he was playing, or before heaven, she would make good on her threat.

Stefan's eyes flashed with open admiration as he watched Kassandra, seated proudly upon her mare, disappear into the dense trees. Then he bent down and grasped the handle of the knife, embedded to its polished hilt, and pulled it from the ground. He slid it into the sheath at his belt, then ran his fingers through his black hair, a wry smile curving his lips.

What a remarkable woman, Stefan mused. He had been in many fierce battles in his lifetime, but never had he been faced with such a beautiful, and possibly more deadly, opponent. It seemed she was full of surprises, and that her prowess extended to weaponry as well. He suddenly recalled waking up in the tavern to find his own sword lying on the bed, its razor-sharp blade pointed at his chest. Perhaps a thwarted attempt—fortunately for him!—by Kassandra to exact her retribution, he thought with a grimace.

Stefan uttered a low whistle for Brand, and barely a moment passed before the massive stallion appeared from the woods, snorting and tossing its regal head. He hoisted himself into the saddle, then wheeled the horse sharply and followed the path Kassandra had just taken.

At once he realized that instead of freeing him from his obsession for Kassandra, knowing the truth of who she was had further heightened his need for her, a need that seemed to rage within him like a burning fever. Never before had he seen such spirit in a woman. And now that his intuition was confirmed and he knew with certainty that Lady Kassandra Wyndham was the wench from the tavern, he would stop at nothing to make her his own.

Of course, he must marry her. Kassandra would become Countess von Furstenberg. If she had been a serving maid, tavern whore, or even married, it would have been different. But she was unmarried, a virgin until their fateful meeting, and an English peeress in her own right. No such woman would consent to anything less than marriage. No man of position and integrity would offer anything else. Marriage it would be!

Stefan smiled wryly, surprised at this turn of events. He was a man who cherished his freedom, a man who had known the pleasures of many women, and been most intrigued by the chase and the capture. But Kassandra was unique. In her he believed he had finally met his match.

And he had need of a wife. Isabel had driven home that point again and again. It was time he thought of the future, of his estate . . . an heir. He would offer Kassandra everything, his name, his wealth, and the chance to share his life. Perhaps that would make up for the one thing he could not offer her, his heart.

He was a soldier, first and foremost. There was no room in his life for useless and transient emotions. He knew well that any man ruled by his emotions rather than his intellect and gut instincts on the battlefield was not destined to live long. No, he could never give her love, but he would offer her an all-consuming desire reserved for no other woman.

Stefan drew up on the reins, a dark thought pressing in on him. Fool, what made him think she would accept his proposal of marriage? She was unconventional enough to think she didn't need his protection and stubborn enough to refuse his proposal outright. She clearly despised him. It was more likely she would throw his offer of marriage back in his face, with relish!

His hands tightened on the reins as an image flashed through his mind—Kassandra's eyes glinting angrily, her smiling red lips taunting him, her vehement denial—and his mouth set in a tight line.

No, he could not risk the public disgrace she would suffer if their liaison ever became known. And he could not deny his all-consuming need to possess her. He would not lose her, however ruthless he might seem, Stefan vowed. Tonight, after he returned from his meeting in Vienna, he would make his proposal . . . and he knew exactly what he had to say. She was too great a prize to leave anything to chance.

# Chapter 13

It was well past midnight when Stefan finally returned to the estate. A drowsy footman opened the door for him as he stepped inside the entrance hall, dark but for a few lighted candles still burning in the ornate chandelier. He stamped his feet and dusted the wet snow from his heavy cloak, then pulled it from his shoulders and dropped it over a high-backed chair against the wall as he walked into the library.

The room was also dark, the fire long since reduced to a pile of blackened ash, and there was a chill in the air. He sighed wearily, dropping the large leather bag that held his papers and maps, and rubbed his hands together to warm them. Guided by the dim light from the hall through the open door, he poured a snifter of brandy. He swallowed, the fragrant liquid burning his throat, then stood in silence, absently toying with the heavy glass.

Damn, it had been a long day, he thought, much longer than he had expected. Due to the length of his meeting with Prince Eugene, he still hadn't found time to visit Sophia.

He had been an hour late as it was, a breech the prince had fortunately forgiven, but then the discussions of war and strategy had gone on long into the night, with scarcely a pause for meat and refreshment. The map of Belgrade had been the focus of great interest and attention among the many officers present, affording a well-drawn diagram of the layout of the near impregnable fortress: valuable information that would hopefully insure another victory for Prince Eugene during the next summer's campaign.

Other discussions had centered upon the winter camp of the Imperial army, where the standing forces would be quartered until spring. Set in the Hungarian lowlands, the camp was a good day's ride from Vienna. He knew he would be called upon at some point during the winter to supervise his cavalry forces, for a month, maybe longer. But he hadn't told Isabel yet. There would be plenty of time for that, once the final date had been decided. She would no doubt be distressed to learn he was leaving again so soon.

Stefan set down his half-empty glass and rubbed his hands over his eyes. What would Kassandra think of his departure? Would she also be distressed . . . or elated?

"Milord?"

Gisela's soft inquiry intruded upon his thoughts. "Ah, Gisela, you are still up," he murmured warmly.

"Are you hungry, milord?" she asked. "The cook has kept a platter of beef and roasted potatoes warm for you. There was plenty left over this night, what with Countess Isabel's usually small appetite and Lady Kassandra shut away in her room all day—"

"What's that?" Stefan queried sharply. At the maid's surprised expression he softened his tone. "Lady Kassandra spent the day in her room?"

"Yes, milord," Gisela replied. "She came flying into the house earlier today, slamming the doors and such, and fled straight to her room. The door has been bolted, and no one has been allowed in, not even your sister, who pleaded in vain to find out what was the matter." She shrugged her narrow shoulders. "Perhaps her ride this morn did not agree with her."

Stefan frowned. If Gisela only knew how right she was! He suddenly moved past her and into the hall. "I won't be needing any dinner this night, Gisela, but my thanks. Rest well." He turned on his heel and took the steps two at a time, the wide-eyed maid staring after him in astonishment.

"Something's brewing this night," she mumbled, watching his tall form disappear down the corridor. Shaking her head, she held the candle in front of her and made her way to the kitchen.

Stefan strode down the hall, stopping abruptly at Kassandra's door. He had rehearsed his words over and over during his long ride back to the estate, all the while knowing no matter how he delivered them, they would be taken as ruthless and harsh. But he had no choice. He couldn't take the chance of losing her now . . . for both their sakes.

He paused, listening, and was not surprised to hear the floor creaking slightly from light footfalls pacing back and forth. He took a deep breath, then tried his hand on the doorknob while leaning his broad shoulder into the door. It held fast.

So it was still bolted, just as Gisela had said, he thought, his brow arching with displeasure. He stepped back, looking up and down the dimly lit corridor, then moved once again to the door. He no longer heard pacing within the room, only a heavy silence laced with palpable tension. Stefan knew she had guessed he was at her door.

"Unbolt the door, Kassandra," he whispered quietly, his soft tone belying his impatience. He waited a moment, but there was no sound. Damn. He would break the door down if need be! "I will not ask again, my lady," he murmured tightly. "Open

the door, or I will do so myself, in a manner you
will find most unpleasant.''

His threat was rewarded by the sound of footsteps
crossing the floor. Stefan smiled grimly. The bolt
grated and squeaked as it was suddenly drawn back,
then the footsteps fled and faded into the far recesses
of the room.

Stefan turned the doorknob and carefully pushed
open the door, not certain of his reception. He
stepped in gingerly and closed the door behind him
with a decisive click, scarcely daring to breathe. His
gaze swept the shadowed room, lit only by pale rays
of moonlight across the thick carpet, but there was
no sign of Kassandra.

He waited, tense and alert. It was only the sheer-
est whisper of a movement that caught his attention;
perhaps the rustle of a silken nightgown, he thought
heatedly, and he realized she was hiding behind the
oriental screen in the far corner of the room. Over-
coming a pang of guilt that he had so subdued her
brave spirit, he stood quietly by the door, his legs
spread, his arms crossed in front of him.

Kassandra crouched behind the screen, furiously
chewing her lower lip. Where was he? What was he
doing? Blackguard! He obviously wanted something
from her, but what? Wasn't it enough that he had
discovered her secret?

Several moments passed, each one an eternity for
her, and still Stefan made no movement toward her.
After another long silence, she had had enough. Her
knees were beginning to ache, kneeling on her
haunches as she was, a most uncomfortable position. This was her chamber, and here she was cow-
ering in it like a frightened lamb.

With a sigh of angry exasperation Kassandra rose
suddenly to her feet, wincing as pinpricks of sensation shot through her legs. She cursed under her
breath and leaned on the screen, but somehow mis-

judged the distance and lost her balance. The screen fell forward with a resounding crash, and she would have toppled with it if she hadn't grabbed the side of her tub, righting herself, just in time.

"Why don't you light a candle, my lady?" Stefan's voice, deep and husky, came to her from across the room. "It might make it easier for both of us to see . . . each other."

"Why would we want to do that?" Kassandra snapped. "I can assure you I have no wish to see you. Why don't you just leave!" She straightened shakily; then, as an afterthought, she moved to the fireplace not far from the tub and grabbed the poker propped against the wall. She might need it to protect herself, she thought fleetingly, holding it crosswise in front of her. After this morning in the woods, there was no telling what he might try to do.

"Very well. I'll light them," Stefan replied, unperturbed that Kassandra had armed herself once again. He could see in the dark, but for what he had to say to her, he thought it best if he could also read her expressions. He walked to the low table beside the bed, found the flint, steel, and tinderbox, and lit the three candles in the delicate porcelain candelabra, their flickering golden light settling over the room. Then he turned to face her.

Stefan inhaled sharply as his eyes moved over Kassandra, her beauty stunning to behold. She wore a cream lace nightgown that left little to his imagination, the curves of her lithe, long-limbed body barely concealed by the flowing folds of the gossamer fabric. Her long hair, brushed to a burnished glow, curled softly around her furious face and tumbled down the front of her gown, concealing the high, firm breasts he ached to caress. It was all he could do not to go to her and crush her in his arms, but he forced himself to think clearly, rationally. There would be time enough for that . . . later.

"That's better," he murmured, sitting down in one of the comfortable upholstered chairs at the foot of the bed. He stretched his long legs out in front of him and nodded toward the other one. "Sit down, Kassandra. We have an important matter to discuss."

She eyed him suspiciously, shaking her head. "No."

"Very well, then, stand if you wish—"

"We have nothing to discuss!" she stated hotly, cutting him off. She nervously fingered the poker. The blasted thing was so heavy. She set its point down upon the ceramic tiles in front of the fireplace on which she was standing, one hand still gripping the curved handle. "Now, I have already asked you to leave my chamber, Count von Furstenberg."

Stefan sighed. His attempts at civility were getting him nowhere. Best to get on with it, he decided quickly. He brought his legs up and leaned forward in the chair, his mild expression becoming deadly serious. "It's time to put an end to this charade, Kassandra," he said simply.

She paled, though she did not fully understand his meaning. "Charade?"

"I know you are the woman I found in the tavern, though why you were there, I have yet to discover. Our . . . encounter in the woods this morning only confirmed what I have believed all along, and what you have sought, for obvious reasons, to conceal from me since we met at the Hofburg." He paused, studying her face, but her lovely features were set and immobile. It was her eyes, wide and full of turmoil, that gave away her true feelings.

Do not be swayed, Stefan told himself. It is the only way you will have her. He continued relentlessly. "But I have not come to speak of our past, though it has much to do with why I am here, but of our future."

Our future . . . What could he possibly mean? Kassandra wondered dazedly. She licked her lips, a glimmer of fear coiling in the pit of her stomach. "What do you want from me?" she whispered, her throat constricted. So many tormented thoughts had assailed her while she had paced furiously back and forth across the room, playing out so many scenarios of what he might do now that he had discovered the telltale clothing and his cursed money bag. Yet as she faced him now, she could not fathom what he might demand from her.

Stefan rose from the chair and crossed to stand in front of her. Startled, she looked up at him, looming so large before her, his masculine frame so much broader and more powerful than she remembered. His eyes, so arresting, caught and held her own, penetrating to some hidden part of her, and it took all her effort not to tremble uncontrollably.

"I want you to become my wife."

# Chapter 14

**K**assandra stared stupidly up at him, uncomprehending, her grasp on the poker loosening. It dropped to the tiles with a clatter, but she did not even blink.

"I want you for my wife, Kassandra," Stefan repeated, noting the sudden pallor of her skin, her eyes blank and devoid of emotion. Her lack of response struck a painful chord within him, a feeling akin to rejection. But he shrugged it aside. By God, what had he expected? He knew her initial reaction was merely the calm before the storm. "But you must know I am not *asking* you to be my wife," he went on, his tone almost harsh. "I have decided that is what you *shall* be."

His last words sank into Kassandra like a knife cutting cruelly into her flesh. "Your . . . wife," she murmured, completely stunned. "You have decided?" Her eyes focused on his face once again, disbelief, fury, and incredulity boiling just below her facade of restraint. Never in her wildest imaginings would she have expected this preposterous demand! She could have exploded, screeched, and raged at him, but instead she felt a strange inner calm, an answer forcing itself to her lips with striking clarity.

"Impossible," she stated simply, brushing by him. "I despise you."

Stefan felt another jagged emotion at her words, a disquieting pain like nothing he had ever felt before. But again he defiantly stifled it, his face implacable as he grabbed her arm, pulling her roughly into his embrace.

Kassandra gasped in surprise, the coldness of his gaze striking fear into her heart. She tensed in his arms, scarcely breathing, his iron grip on her wrists a painful vise.

"But I haven't finished, my lady," Stefan said, his breath warm on her cheek. He almost smiled, recalling the sword on the bed and the episode with the knife that morning and thinking of the spirit she had shown. "I had anticipated your response, as you have already made known your feelings toward me on two occasions." He paused, pulling her so close she could feel the beating of his heart against her breast. "I offer you a choice."

"A ch-choice?" Kassandra stammered.

Stefan nodded, his chiseled lips a grim line. He had to have her—as much for her sake as his own. "I have already decided what I want. Now you must decide what you want. Either become my wife . . . or risk a scandal that could destroy not only your reputation, but your father's career as ambassador as well."

It was done, he had said it, Stefan thought dully, a stab of remorse shooting through him at the stricken look on her face. He had sworn he would do whatever was necessary to have her, yet the role of villain set uneasily upon him. Still, there was no turning back . . .

"It's a simple choice, Kassandra," he went on mercilessly. "You know there are those in the Austrian court who would delight in such a scandal, influential aristocrats with a distaste for the English

and their self-serving trade concerns with our enemies, the Turks. No doubt they would find the story
most amusing.''

Stefan bent his head and whispered against her
ear. ''I can hear them even now. An ambassador's
beautiful daughter seeks sensual diversion in wine
taverns . . . How gloriously decadent. You must
agree it would make for a perfect opportunity to
contribute to the downfall of an English ambassador.''

Kassandra stared at him, dumbstruck. This was
worse than she could ever have imagined. The man
was not merely a rogue, he was despicable, the devil
incarnate to force her to make such a choice! And
he seemed so sure of himself, as if he already sensed
what her answer would be. Rage mounted within
her at this infuriating realization, and a bitter retort,
a vehement refusal of his vile offer of marriage, rose
to her lips. She would pit her word against his own,
and see him rot in prison for what he had done to
her!

But she bit back her words, forcing herself to think
clearly. It was true. There were those in the Viennese court who would seize upon this story with
glee, if only to create such a stir that her father would
be recalled to England. Then all he had worked for
would be lost.

And she would be branded a whore, however un-
justly, the brunt of malicious gossip and innuendo,
just as her mother had been so many years ago. She
felt sickened by the cruel hand Fate had dealt her,
could almost feel the vicious lies and insults that
would consume her life if she chose to deny his offer.

And what of her father's relationship with Isabel?
The countess had made him happier than Kassandra
had ever seen him before, a lonely, driven man re-

juvenated by the power of her love. That, too, would be destroyed.

Would Stefan do that to his own sister? Kassandra wondered. A sister he clearly cherished? Hope flickered.

"But what of Isabel?" Kassandra blurted, her voice strained and shrill. "Have you thought of what such a scandal will do to her?"

Stefan exhaled sharply. He had suspected she might think of Isabel and her father, and he knew he had to answer carefully. If Kassandra sensed he would never do anything to harm his sister, then he would lose her. She would deny his proposal of marriage, and call his bluff. And if she did, what then? Would he go through with his threat? He doubted it. No, he had to play off her fears, which would only make him more loathsome in her eyes. But there was nothing else he could do; honor, integrity, and his overriding desire demanded that they wed.

"The choice is yours, Kassandra," he replied tersely. "You are responsible for the outcome of your decision, and whose lives will be affected by it."

Sudden tears stung Kassandra's eyes and she quickly looked down at her tightly held wrists, swallowing hard against the lump in her throat. She felt chilled to the very core of her being by his answer, so cold, so ruthlessly uncaring. What had she done to bring this upon herself? she cried wordlessly, struggling to understand. Why would he do this to her, knowing how she felt about him? She shuddered, the tears she had fought to quell coursing unchecked down her face. Sweet Lord, nothing was making sense anymore.

"Kassandra, your answer," Stefan demanded softly.

She started, his voice a death knell upon her heart. Yet there was one burning question she had to ask him before she would answer, one last attempt to dissuade him from shattering her life. She raised her head defiantly, her chin quivering, her vision blurred by her tears.

"What of love, Stefan?" she asked simply, her voice almost a whisper. "Would you not seek a bride who harbored some affection for you, rather than one who hates you, who abhors you for being no better than a beast who thinks only of his own selfish desires?"

Stefan flinched visibly at her words, which cut into him far deeper than he would ever admit. An angry tic worked along his jaw, his darkened eyes a maelstrom of unfathomable emotion. "Love has nothing to do with it, Kassandra," he said almost tonelessly. "I have no time for such a useless emotion. I am in need of a wife, in need of an heir, and I have chosen you for reasons that shall remain my own. Now make *your* choice."

There is no choice! Kassandra's inner voice screamed helplessly. Either way I will lose! Mustering all the strength in her body, she suddenly twisted free of his grasp and, before he could grab her, dashed across the floor in a flurry of cream lace and flying red-gold hair. But she stopped abruptly at the nearest chair, her back to him, one hand tightly gripping the upholstered rim.

You have already lost, Kassandra, she thought dazedly, her breasts heaving against her sheer gown. Though she would wish it a thousand times to be otherwise . . . Stefan had won. Perhaps she could endure the rest of her life branded as a whore, but she could never, never make her beloved father, and Isabel, suffer for her own folly.

Somehow she had to accept that, however unwittingly, she had brought herself to this moment, a fleeting moment that would remain forever etched in her memory, and to a marriage in which there would never be any chance for happiness . . . or love.

At least there was a way to prolong the inevitable, she consoled herself, lifting her hand and wiping the tears from her face, a tiny ember of hope still glowing within her. And perhaps give her the time she needed to think of a way out of this cursed agreement.

Kassandra turned, her eyes meeting Stefan's across the room. "I will marry you."

Stefan let out his breath, his heart pounding fiercely against his chest. He felt curiously hollow, the wild elation, the thrill of triumph conspicuously missing. "You have made a wise choice—" he began.

"When my father returns from Germany," Kassandra broke in with a faint smile at his look of dark displeasure. "Surely you realize we cannot marry, or publicly announce our betrothal, without his consent."

Stefan irritably ran his hand through his hair. Damn it all, that could be months. He had been so captivated by the idea of possessing her, of the marriage taking place without delay, that he had given little thought to the proprieties. He had no choice but to agree. To marry without Lord Harrington's consent would cause a scandal of its own.

"Of course," Stefan replied tightly, moving toward her, his eyes devouring every tantalizing inch of her.

Kassandra took a nervous step backward as he approached, clutching her nightgown and gathering it about her as if she could hide her near nakedness from his fervent gaze. Heaven help her, he wasn't going to force her to . . . to . . . ?

Impassioned thoughts, wanton memories of a shared afternoon, rose unbidden in her mind, and she shivered, her flesh tingling. She closed her eyes

in a futile attempt to dispel the throbbing images—
the rugged masculinity of his body, his kiss upon
her lips, the heat of his breath and hands upon her,
caressing her, evoking sensations she had never before imagined were possible—but she could not. For
a brief moment she was lost in the moment, reliving
it, her senses reeling in a wild tempest of delirious
remembrance of sight, sound, touch, taste.

The sound of the door to her chamber creaking
open forced her back to reality. Her eyes flew open
to find Stefan standing in the threshold, his face lost
in flickering shadow. "What—?" she choked, then
flushed with embarrassment, praying he had not
guessed her thoughts.

"In the morning I will have your belongings
moved to the room adjoining my own, the better to
know your comings and goings," he said evenly,
denying the raging fire that burned in his loins. He'd
surmised her thoughts a moment ago had matched
his own, and it had been all he could do to walk
away from her. But he was determined not to force
himself upon her again.

That she had agreed to the marriage was enough,
for now. In time, she would admit to the desire he
had seen smoldering in the depths of her eyes,
would admit to wanting him as much as he wanted
her. Then, and only then, would he come to her.

"If need be, Berdine will help you pack your belongings," Stefan continued. "I will not have my
future bride stealing out on any more solitary trips
into the city. Good night, Kassandra." He began to
close the door, but a sudden idea struck him.

"I strongly suggest you bolt your door at night, if
you wish to protect your virtue, my lady," he added,
noting that once again she was staring at him with
venom in her eyes, her fingers curled into tight fists.
"For if I ever find it unlocked, I will take it as an
invitation to enter."

"You may rest assured my door will remain barred against you," Kassandra murmured with vehemence, shaking visibly. "Now get out."

Stefan obliged her, closing the door firmly behind him. He paused, listening to the sound of her footsteps rushing to the door, then winced as the bolt grated into place.

He walked down the silent corridor to his chamber, sudden weariness overtaking him as he crossed to the tall window overlooking the snow-covered lawn, and stood there lost in thought.

He felt no glory in his victory, only a bitter taste in his mouth. He had won Kassandra, but at what price? Her biting words still rang in his ears. She despised him, just as he had feared.

What could he have done differently? Stefan agonized. If he had wooed her gently, would she have come to him on her own accord, the secret of their first meeting forgotten . . . forgiven? Perhaps, and then again, perhaps not.

Good God, what is coming over you, man? Stefan thought grimly, clenching his fists in utter frustration. He was a soldier, a rational man, not some fool who left his fate to chance or the whims of fickle emotion. He would not undo what he had done.

He turned abruptly from the window and sat down in the chair pulled close to the fireplace, watching as the orange flames in the dying fire curled and licked around the edges of the charred logs.

Kassandra. It seemed she had completely taken over his every conscious thought. And when at last he fell asleep, she would be in his dreams, a vision of fiery hair, porcelain skin, and bewitching violet eyes. He knew he would never forget how proud she had looked as she agreed to his proposal; how vulnerable and defiant—and more beautiful than any other woman.

Stefan sighed heavily, resting his head in his hand. Perhaps there was still a chance of winning some modicum of her favor before her father returned. Then she might look upon their marriage in a more promising light. It was worth a try.

Kassandra stood with her back against the door long after Stefan's footsteps faded down the hall. She felt as if she were being ripped apart by a storm of emotions . . . and all because of one man. She hated him—he was callous, cruel, selfish, a devil!—but no more than she hated herself.

For despite everything he had done, everything he had said to her, she could not quench the fury of desire that raged within her. A desire that had racked and tormented her since their first meeting, a desire so beyond her comprehension that its power left her shaken, her will no longer her own.

It was tearing out her very soul. Kassandra slumped to her knees, her realization sapping her last ounce of strength. She shook her head numbly, silent tears streaking her face. She had to defy him, or find herself forever in thrall to a man who could not love, who would use her only to beget children to carry on his name. Somehow, she vowed, her eyes closing with exhaustion, she would hurt him as much as he was hurting her now.

"And then, Count Stefan von Furstenberg," Kassandra swore bitterly, "you will rue the day you forced this choice upon me!"

# Chapter 15

**"S**tefan, is this really true?" Isabel asked breathlessly, her spoon suspended in midair, her vivid blue eyes dancing with excitement. "You and Kassandra are to be married?"

At his simple nod, the silver spoon fell from her hand and on to the table with a tinkling clatter. She bounded out of her chair with a squeal of delight and dashed around to the other side of the dining table. When she reached him she laughingly threw her slender arms about his neck, hugging him tightly, then plopped down in the chair beside him, her delicate features alight with a curious mix of happiness and bewilderment.

"But when was this decided, Stefan? It's so sudden, so unexpected! I had hoped you might consider it at some point . . . marrying Kassandra . . ." Isabel paused, blushing bright pink at the inadvertent confession of her secret hope, then threw up her hands, giggling sheepishly. "I mean, it was . . . I'd thought it an intriguing possibility . . . Oh, Stefan!" She looked down at her lap, flustered.

Stefan's deep laughter resounded through the high-ceilinged room. He was unused to seeing his poised and sophisticated younger sister at a complete loss. He lifted her chin, his gray eyes twinkling with merriment, a tender smile curving his lips. It was best to have her think she had some hand in the matter, he decided quickly.

"Your matchmaking has been no secret to me, Isabel," he said fondly. "Let me think. I believe you said something about my being a . . . now, what was it again? Oh yes. A warrior knight."

Isabel blushed anew at his teasing, but she smiled back at him. "You're impossible, Stefan," she blurted. "Now tell me, when did you propose—"

"Last night," he broke in, his smile tightening imperceptibly. "When I returned from Vienna."

"It must have been late. I waited up for you until ten o'clock, then decided to broach the matter this morning."

"What matter?"

"About Kassandra. She spent the entire day locked in her room," she said with concern, as Stefan turned his attention to the table, absently toying with the fork beside his plate, a plausible story taking shape in his mind. "Gisela saw her come in from her ride. She fled to her room without a word to anyone, slammed and bolted her door shut, and when I pleaded with her to come out, she would only say she wanted to be left alone!"

"I can easily explain, Isabel," Stefan said, turning back to her. "We had a slight disagreement before I left for Vienna yesterday morning, a situation that could not be remedied until I returned late last night. But all is well now, as you can surmise from my news."

"So that was it . . . a lover's quarrel," Isabel breathed with relief. She regarded him sharply. "You must have really upset her, Stefan. I have never heard her so distressed. What could you have possibly—"

"The matter was between Kassandra and myself," Stefan interjected, his expression strained.

"Forgive me, Stefan," Isabel apologized, chiding

herself for overstepping her bounds. They might be brother and sister, and very close, but they each had the right to privacy when it came to personal matters. She would no doubt have done the same if he had questioned her so tactlessly about Miles.

Isabel immediately sought to brighten the tone of the conversation and dispel the unsettling tension. "Have you considered a date for the wedding ceremony?" she asked lightly, curling her small hand within his.

Stefan sighed, his brow furrowing. The thought of possibly waiting until early spring to claim Kassandra as his own was almost more than he could bear. "That decision will have to wait until your Miles returns from Hanover and gives his consent to the marriage," he stated darkly.

Isabel did not miss the sudden coldness in his eyes, though she misread it. "But surely you don't think he will deny you, Stefan," she exclaimed. "He will be most amenable, I am sure of it."

She rose with a rustle of crisp silk and rested her arm reassuringly across his broad shoulders. "I will write to him this very moment, before I leave for Countess von Thurn's gala, and tell him the happy news. Then if you could post the letter in the city today"—she paused, thinking out loud—"let me see, it will probably take the post-carriage one or two weeks to reach Hanover, hmmm, maybe longer if the snows are deep . . ." She shrugged. "Well, he shall at least have it soon after the New Year."

Small comfort, Stefan thought wryly. Even if Lord Harrington received the letter within a few weeks, it did not necessarily mean its contents would hasten his return to Vienna. He would probably remain in Hanover as long as King George and his entourage were holding court there, in all likelihood until the worst of the snow had melted and the roads were once again safe to travel. It was well known that the

German-born king of England held little regard for the city of London, and no ability or inclination to speak the language. Surely he would linger in his home city to the last possible moment.

Stefan shook off his disgruntled thoughts, forcing a smile. "Go write your letter, Isabel, and bring it to me in the library when you are finished. I have an appointment this afternoon in the city, so I will post it then."

"An appointment?" Isabel asked, searching his face. An odd thought struck her, her red lips drawing into a pout. Surely he wasn't going to visit Sophia, not after what he had told her about Kassandra. "Stefan—"

"You know me too well, sister," Stefan interrupted her, reading her sullen expression. "Yes, I'm going to see Sophia—"

"But surely it is over between you," Isabel blurted angrily. "How can you do this—"

"Hear me out," Stefan admonished gently, taking her hand. "It is for that very reason that I must see her. Sophia and I have been friends—"

"Friends?" Isabel interjected with unusual sarcasm, her eyes flashing.

"Yes, friends, for a long time. And it's best she hear of Kassandra, and our plans to be married, from me. She deserves that much, Isabel."

Isabel sighed in frustration. Archduchess von Starenberg deserved nothing, as far as she was concerned. But she knew she had little sway over her brother's will. When he made up his mind to do something, it might as well be set in stone. "Very well, Stefan, do what you must. I am only glad you are at last breaking your . . . ties with that woman."

Her mood lifted at that gratifying thought. She bent and kissed him on the cheek, then hurried through the open archway. "It won't take long to write my letter, Stefan," she said over her shoulder.

"I shall only fill it with news of you and Kassandra. I have another letter already written for Miles, if you could post it as well." Then she was gone, her footsteps tapping across the parquet floor.

Stefan groaned, rubbing his forehead. His life had certainly changed since his return from the campaign, yet it was much the same. Just a few months ago he had been in the lowlands of Hungary, fighting alongside his men against the Turks, Tartars, and fierce Magyar tribesmen, and now here he was, doing battle with women instead.

He rose from the chair, threw his linen napkin on the table, and strode from the dining room. He only hoped his meeting with Sophia would be less fraught with difficulty.

Kassandra walked briskly up the steps leading to the front entrance of the mansion, exhilarated from her morning ride, her troubles temporarily forgotten. She cast a casual glance at the carriage fronted by four horses pawing anxiously at the frozen ground of the drive, then smiled broadly as she spied Zoltan atop the coachman's seat.

"Good morning to ye, miss," he shouted out heartily, lifting the woolen cap off his dark head with a flourish.

"And to you, Zoltan," she enthused, pausing on the last step. "Where are you bound this morning?"

"I'm takin' the countess to the von Thurn estate, not far from here," he replied, turning from her suddenly to scold one of the lead horses for leaning too heavily into its harness. "Whoa there, boy," he yelled out, pulling hard on the reins. "We'll be off in a flash, ye devil, so hold with ye."

Kassandra could not help laughing at Zoltan's colorful oaths. Her eyes were still on him as she moved toward the door, and she almost bumped into Isabel, who was just stepping outside. She gasped in surprise, drawing back.

"Kassandra!" Isabel exclaimed. "I was hoping to see you before I left for the gala. Stefan has told me your wonderful news. I'm so happy for both of you!"

Kassandra blushed hotly, the feelings she had managed to escape during her ride overpowering her once again. So already he was proclaiming his victory to the world, she thought angrily. She swallowed hard, stiffening as Isabel embraced her.

No, she must not give Isabel cause to think anything was amiss, Kassandra chided herself, willing her body to relax. She suddenly remembered something Stefan had said the night before about putting an end to the charade. She smiled at the irony. For her, the charade was only beginning.

"Th-thank you, Isabel," Kassandra murmured, bringing her arms up from her sides and returning the countess's embrace.

Isabel drew back, chattering excitedly. "There's so much we have to talk about, and so much to do. Perhaps we could even share a ceremony, Kassandra; wouldn't that be lovely? You and Stefan, your father and me." She smiled and pulled two sealed envelopes from her pocket. "And I have already written a letter to Miles, this one here; the other I wrote to him yesterday"—she flushed a becoming pink—"urging him to return as soon as possible. I know he has his diplomatic mission to consider, but perhaps it is nearing completion. We shall hope as much . . ."

Isabel stopped, a frown creasing her forehead. "I asked Stefan if he would post these letters for me when he goes into the city this afternoon, but he's not in the library. I thought perhaps he might be in the stable, saddling Brand, and I was about to take them to him."

"I just came from the stable," Kassandra said, her eyes fixed on the letters. "I didn't see him there."

"Oh, dear, and I really don't have time to look for him." Isabel sighed, then brightened. "Could you find him, Kassandra, and give him my letters?"

"Of-of course," she replied, her mouth suddenly dry. Her fingers trembled as Isabel handed her the two small packets.

"Good! Now I must go, or I will be late for Countess von Thurn's gala. We can talk more when I return." Isabel clasped Kassandra's arm, squeezing it warmly. "I'm so glad you're to be not only my stepdaughter, but my sister as well," she said sincerely. Then she turned away in a swirl of luxuriant gray fur and dusky blue velvet, and walked quickly to the carriage while Kassandra stepped through the front door, held open for her by the bewigged footman.

"And do tell Stefan not to worry about your father's consent," Kassandra heard her call as the carriage pulled away. "I'm sure Miles will be elated with your choice of a husband."

Kassandra flinched at Isabel's words, tightly clenching the letters. When she realized with a start what she was doing, she opened her palm and stared at them, the fine loops and curves of Isabel's handwriting burning like a brand into her mind. It was only the sound of Stefan's footsteps moving along the corridor at the top of the staircase that brought her back to reality, and she quickly came to a decision.

Kassandra held her breath as she tiptoed down the hall to the drawing room and closed the door quietly behind her. She dashed to the lacquered cabinet where Isabel usually wrote her letters and sat down on the delicate gilded chair. After pulling out several of the tiny drawers stacked one atop the other, she found what she was looking for, a thin silver letter opener with an ivory handle and the colored wax used for sealing envelopes.

Which one had Isabel said she wrote today? Kassandra tried to recall, her eyes darting back and forth between the two envelopes lying side by side in front of her. She shrugged, picking one. She slit open the fine cream paper, removed the one-page letter, and quickly perused it. Her expression tightened.

"A lucky guess," she whispered caustically under her breath, then tucked the paper into her bodice. This was one letter her father would never receive. Though she missed him terribly, she had no wish to hasten his return . . . and her cursed wedding. She would burn the letter later in her fireplace.

Kassandra replaced the letter with a blank sheet of paper she had hurriedly folded, then heated the stick of red wax over the candle burning brightly within a glass chimney on the top shelf of the cabinet, and dripped it over the back of the envelope. Lastly, she pressed Isabel's gold stamp into the warm wax, leaving the imprint of a rose.

With trembling fingers Kassandra cleared the polished surface of the cabinet and closed the drawers, then tentatively touched the wax on the letter. It had hardened. She swept up both letters and walked to the door, opening it slightly so she could peek into the hall. Feigning an air of nonchalance despite the wild beating of her heart, she stepped from the drawing room just as Stefan's voice rang out in the entranceway.

"Isabel?" Stefan queried, looking down the hallway leading to the drawing room. Expecting to see his sister, he was pleasantly surprised when Kassandra walked toward him, holding out the letters. He stared at her, appreciatively noting the form-fitting cut of her riding habit of rich russet wool, which heightened her vivid coloring.

"Isabel asked that I give you these," she mur-

mured, meeting his admiring gaze with icy reserve
as she handed him the letters. She might have to
live a lie to Isabel, and others, she thought defiantly,
but she would not hide her true feelings from him.
"She was in a great hurry, and could not find you
in the library, so she left them with me. Now if you
will excuse me," she finished pointedly, her gaze
indicating she wished to pass by him to the staircase. "I must go and pack my things."

Stefan stepped back, obliging her with a slight
bow and a rakish smile. Again he received only a
withering glance as she rounded the banister and
turned her back to him, walking stiffly up the stairs.
He watched her until she had disappeared down the
corridor, then he turned on his heel and strode to
the front door.

He might be determined to win her favor, Stefan
told himself, but she would fight him every inch of
the way. Strangely enough, the thought did not dis-
please him.

# Chapter 16

From her vantage point on the chaise longue, Archduchess Sophia von Starenberg surveyed with a jaundiced eye the cluster of elegantly dressed men and women. She was already bored to tears by their predictable chatter and idle gossip, and could hardly wait to leave, although she had arrived at her cousin Countess Maria von Thurn's gala only an hour ago.

She thumped her fan irritably on the brocaded cushion in response to a whispered conversation nearby, certain that if she heard one more miserable tale about a lover's infidelity, she would scream. How they ran on, she raged. The anecdote for that malady was simple. Find another lover.

Sophia sighed with annoyance and shifted on the plump cushions, carefully rearranging the glistening folds of her mauve damask gown. She had been longing for some harmless diversion, some trifling pastime, when Maria's invitation to this afternoon's gala had arrived at her country villa only yesterday. She had hoped it would be just the tonic to free her mind from plaguing thoughts of Stefan von Furstenberg. But she realized now such an escape was impossible. She could think of nothing, and no one, else.

Sophia chewed her lip. Damn him, where was he?

What could he possibly be doing that would keep him from her these past weeks? It was so unlike him to ignore her, especially after returning from such a long military campaign. She had envisioned them spending many luxurious hours in her bed, wanton hours filled with the sensual pleasures only she could give him. Instead they had shared just one fleeting moment of passion in the Hofburg gardens, hardly enough to satisfy her insatiable desire for such a magnificent man.

And why hadn't he answered her letters? She had never before deigned to write to any man. On the contrary, it was she who received the frantic, pleading missives from her lovers, fervent letters that did little more than amuse her. With Stefan it was different. For him, she would do anything.

Sophia leaned her head against the chaise and closed her eyes, rubbing her cheek thoughtfully with the mother-of-pearl fan. She summoned forth vivid memories of their other separations and impatiently awaited reunions, and she shivered deliciously, recalling the feel of him, the taste of him.

A wry smile curved her mouth, a slim eyebrow lifted archly. Who would have ever thought it? she mused. Sophia von Starenberg had finally fallen in love . . .

Certainly she had never expected it. She had been a young girl of sixteen when she had married her husband, a stooped, time-worn figure of three score years. But it had been an admirable match nonetheless, masterfully arranged by her debt-ridden parents. She had wanted it just as much as they, and had gladly traded the threadbare existence brought on by their incessant gambling for a life of wealth and luxury.

Her only regret was that she had wasted her virginity on such a man. Sophia grimaced with distaste, remembering. Fortunately the archduke's sexual demands had been mercifully few and had ceased altogether several years ago, but even now the memories of his fumbling, slack-lipped lovemaking were enough to fill her with disgust. Not long after the marriage she had taken a lover, the first of many, beginning eight years of casual alliances in which she honed her erotic skills to perfection.

Casual, until she met Stefan. From the moment she looked into his eyes, she knew she was lost. He was everything she craved in a lover, everything she admired in a man. After they had loved for the first time, when he lay sated and sleeping in her arms, she had sworn somehow she would become Countess von Furstenberg. She had only to rid herself of the one detestable thing standing in her way . . . her husband.

Sophia's eyes flew open, her grip tightening on her fan, her skin flushing with uncomfortable warmth. If only that man would die! She had gone herself to the poorest section of Vienna, where coin was precious and scruples unknown, her servant Adolph leading the way, to seek out an apothecary. They had finally stopped at a makeshift structure built against the city wall, and a small man with hawkish features had shuffled forth from the shadowed interior to greet them. She had not minced words. It was poison she wanted, but of a special nature.

"I believe what you are seeking is this," he rasped, holding up a dusty vial containing a grayish powder. He eyed her shrewdly. "But it is costly, my lady."

"Of that I have no doubt," Sophia replied tersely, without blinking. "Have no fear, man. I will pay you well for your powder . . . and your silence."

He nodded, a look of tacit understanding passing between them. "Dissolve a small portion into your . . . friend's tea or coffee once a day. It will bring

about a creeping death that has the appearance of
natural causes, like dying in one's sleep." He
laughed shortly, revealing a jagged row of blackened teeth. "We should all be as fortunate, eh?"

"How long will it take?" she demanded, ignoring
his remark and anxious to be gone from the place.
It rankled her nerves, what with rats skittering about
and the putrid stench of garbage.

"Two, maybe three weeks."

Liar! Sophia seethed. It had been two months
since her visit to the apothecary, and almost that
long since she had begun to poison her husband. It
was true his speech had become increasingly slurred,
his gait awkward and weaving, yet he clung to life
as tenaciously as he clung to his money. He even
managed to attend court functions, such as the reception at the Hofburg, though he fell asleep at the
most inopportune moments. And she had wanted
to be done with the unsavory business by the time
Stefan returned from Hungary.

Obviously she had been deceived by that dirty little man in the market, Sophia decided grimly. She
would have to seek out another apothecary, one
better-versed in his craft. And this time, she would
not fail.

Shrieks of feminine laughter broke rudely into her
thoughts, and her eyes narrowed at the group of
five women seated across the drawing room at a
finely wrought gaming table. They were merrily engrossed in a game of ombre, a three-handed card
game, while attentive gentlemen leaned over their
shoulders or stood behind their chairs, offering advice.

Another common diversion of these insufferable
galas. Sophia sighed with displeasure. Perhaps it
was time she left.

"A kreuzer for your thoughts, milady."

Sophia started in surprise, looking up into a pair

of ice-blue eyes that she could swear were laughing at her. She immediately recognized the strikingly handsome man, and just as easily she dismissed him, her brow arching as her gaze wandered over him. For if ever there was an aristocratic fop in the Viennese court, a true dandy who seemed to be in attendance at every social gathering, however inconsequential, it was Count Frederick Althann.

"Save your kreuzer, Count," she said breezily. "My thoughts belong to me alone." She smiled up at him, though her eyes were cold. "You're looking stylish today."

He was dressed in a full-skirted coat of dark blue brocade, a laced waistcoat, matching breeches, gartered silk stockings, and red-heeled shoes, with a lavish muslin cravat tied jauntily about his neck and a silver-hilted sword hanging at his left side. In one hand he held a pair of fringed gloves and a cane, his thumb caressing the polished gold crown. On his head he wore a powdered tiewig with a long, plaited queue down his back, tied at each end with a black bow, just a hint of his light blond hair peeking out at his forehead.

A pity he is only half a man, she mused wickedly, recalling the rampant rumors about the count's unnatural affinity for smooth-faced boys. Though it was hard to believe . . . he was really quite attractive: tall, fair, with an undeniable air of virility. And the excellent fit of his clothes revealed a lean, athletic body . . . yes, truly a pity.

"And you, Archduchess, take my breath away, as always," Frederick returned her compliment, bowing gallantly. He reached into his deep side pocket and pulled out an enameled snuffbox, flipped it open to reveal a tiny mirror on the inside of the lid, then deftly applied a pinch of the powdered tobacco to each nostril. Snorting delicately, he offered her the snuffbox with a flourish.

"No, thank you," Sophia murmured, wrinkling her nose with distaste. She turned away from him, her eyes widening as Isabel von Furstenberg swept into the drawing room.

Her cousin Maria hadn't told her Isabel would be attending her gala! Sophia thought, her mind racing. She watched motionless as the countess made her way through the crowd, exchanging light-hearted banter and greetings. Perhaps she might be able to tell her what had become of Stefan . . .

Sophia rose gracefully from the chaise. "If you will excuse me, Count Frederick," she murmured, brushing past him. She walked regally across the room, stopping just short of where Isabel stood talking with several young women.

"How wonderful to see you again, Countess," she broke in, keeping her voice light. She lay her hand on Isabel's arm.

Isabel froze at the sound of the familiar voice and the unexpected pressure on her arm, a shiver running through her. She turned, a fixed smile upon her lips. "Archduchess von Starenberg," she acknowledged coolly.

"I was wondering if perhaps we might talk, you and I," Sophia began somewhat lamely, noting a strange flash of triumph in Isabel's blue eyes. It momentarily unsettled her, though she could not imagine why. "About Stefan."

Isabel's heart seemed to stop within her breast as she turned back to the women at her side, who were listening with rapt attention, and quietly excused herself. They glided away, whispering behind their fluttering fans.

"I am not one to speak for my brother," Isabel said firmly, her eyes meeting Sophia's once again.

Sophia's temper flared at this remark, but she held herself tightly in check. She had always found Isabel particularly insufferable, and this moment was no exception. "I simply want to know why . . . that is, if Stefan . . ." She paused, then drew her red lips into a determined line. "What has become of Stefan?" she asked, her voice strained. "I've written him many times within the past weeks, yet I haven't received a single reply."

"Whatever do you mean?" Isabel asked sweetly. Heaven help her, it wasn't her place to reveal Stefan and Kassandra's engagement, but if this woman pushed her too far . . .

So that was it! Sophia fumed, her topaz eyes narrowing at the petite woman. "You have been intercepting my letters to Stefan, haven't you?" she queried, her voice a grating whisper. "You've never accepted my relationship with your brother, and now you wish to destroy it." She gripped Isabel's arm. "Well, it won't work, my dear Countess. There is nothing you can do that will tear us apart."

Isabel stepped back as if she had been struck, Sophia's unwarranted accusation ringing in her ears. "I know nothing of your letters," she retorted heatedly, visibly shaking, "but as to the other charge, yes, it is true. I have never liked you, or your *liaison*"—she spat out the word—"with my brother."

She wrenched her arm free of Sophia's grasp, fury overwhelming her, all thought of restraint banished from her mind. "As for tearing you and Stefan apart, it appears that unremarkable feat has already been accomplished. He has found another—" She bit off the words, her hand flying to her mouth.

Sophia blanched, her gaze widening in disbelief. "What do you mean . . . he has found another? Another what?"

Isabel decided quickly, throwing back her shoulders. She would face Stefan's wrath—for he would no doubt hear of this exchange from Sophia—regardless of what else she said.

"As I told you before, my dear Archduchess," she

mimicked with unaccustomed sarcasm, "I do not speak for my brother. But you may ask him yourself about the woman he will wed. He is planning to visit your estate this very day." With that Isabel whirled around, her slender back straight and proud, and walked across the room, where she joined a group of guests applauding a musician seated at a harpsichord.

*The woman he will wed . . . the woman he will wed.* Isabel's words echoed in Sophia's mind as she stood there, scarcely able to breathe. When she did at last inhale, low, husky laughter erupted from her throat.

"She lies, of course," Sophia whispered under her breath, her ears deaf to the strains of melodic music drifting through the drawing room. Isabel had never liked her, not that she cared in the least, and now she was spreading malicious lies in an obvious ploy to drive her and Stefan apart.

She would go back to her estate and wait for him, Sophia told herself, moving with statuesque grace to the door of the drawing room, a smile frozen on her lips as she nodded her good-byes. He would hold her in his arms and caress her, and tell her it was nothing but a lie . . .

# Chapter 17

**❝A**dolph, you must let me know the moment you see him," Sophia admonished from her dressing table, glancing at the misshapen little man, a dwarf since birth, standing on his tiptoes and peering out the window. He nodded in reply, intent on his appointed task. She turned back to the mirror, her attention riveted once again on the ministrations of the two serving maids hovering over her.

"Ouch! Take care with that, you stupid fool!" she snapped at the youngest maid, who was quickly unrolling the still warm clay curling tubes from Sophia's long, mahogany tresses. The girl jumped at the sudden reprimand, her shaking fingers inadvertently snagging another loose strand of her mistress's hair.

"That's enough!" Sophia exploded, wheeling in her chair, her beautiful face contorted in anger. "Will you pull every hair from my head, girl? Leave me at once! Marietta will finish your tasks. Go!"

"For-forgive me, milady," the hapless girl stammered, bobbing an awkward curtsy. With tears swimming in her eyes she cast a sideways glance at the other maid, then fled from the room.

"I thought you said she was well trained in dressing hair, Marietta," Sophia muttered tersely, settling back in front of the silver-framed mirror, her almond-shaped eyes scrutinizing her own reflection. Her slender fingers drummed impatiently on the dressing table as the matronly maid expertly lifted her hair and patted a light dusting of fine powder along her alabaster shoulders and long throat.

"Aye, well trained she is, mistress," Marietta replied calmly, accustomed by now to Sophia's outbursts. She had been in her employ since the archduchess had come to this house nine years ago as a bride, and could well remember the many times she had cried into her pillow at night, swearing she could never last another day with such a woman. But she had stayed, and by her stoic fortitude and patience had won Sophia's grudging respect. "But she is unused to working in such haste."

Sophia sighed with exasperation, but said no more, her lips drawn into a tight line. She watched in silence as Marietta deftly brushed out her thick hair and wound it atop her head in an elaborate coiffure, securing it with three gold combs set with seed pearls and square-cut emeralds. Then the maid applied her favorite perfume, a heady mixture of bergamot, musk, and amber imported from Spain, to her throat, behind her ears, pierced by glittering emerald earrings, and along the lush curve of her breasts.

"He comes, milady," Adolph said matter-of-factly in his high-pitched, nasal voice. He watched, unblinking, as Stefan rode up the drive on his black stallion and dismounted before the front entrance of the von Starenberg villa, then he dropped the hem of the brocade curtain he had been holding in his stubby fingers and waddled over to the dressing table. "Shall I meet him in the hall?"

Sophia rose so suddenly that he had to step back for fear the stiff whalebone hoopskirt beneath her voluminous gown would bowl him over. She looked distractedly at him. "Yes, yes, Adolph, greet him. I will be down in a few moments."

Adolph nodded, his piercing black eyes, overshadowed by his protruding forehead, studying her intently. He hadn't seen her so agitated before, though she was struggling to maintain a facade of nonchalance, nor so pathetically haunted. An almost imperceptible hint of fear hung about her like a cloying fragrance.

"What are you waiting for, Adolph?" she demanded irritably, shoving him forward with a rough push on his narrow shoulder. "Be off with you. Run!"

Adolph lost his balance and fell to the floor, grunting as the breath was knocked from his compact body. He struggled to sit up but could not; then, using a trick he had learned in the traveling menagerie where he had performed on a stage with puppets and monkeys, he brought his stunted arms against his chest and began to roll across the floor until he had gained enough momentum to right himself, bounding from his knees to his feet.

"And enough of your tricks," Sophia called out after him as he scampered through the door and ran down the hall as fast as his short legs could carry him.

Wheezing and puffing, Adolph took perverse pleasure in kicking Sophia's white Persian cat away from the top step of the staircase, where it was lolling sleepily. Its startled yowl echoed in the hall below. A lopsided grin split his reddened face as he hurried down the stairs, holding on to the railing so he would not fall, and once at the bottom, he took a moment to straighten his cropped coat. Then he strutted self-importantly up to Stefan, who turned from a portrait of Sophia he was studying.

"Milady bids you welcome, Count von Furstenberg," he stated formally, with a curt nod of his large head. He flourished his arm toward the salon. "I am Adolph. If you will follow me."

Stefan's gaze flickered over the little man, though he quickly masked his initial surprise. So it appeared Sophia had acquired a new servant while he was in Hungary, he thought, noting Adolph's flushed face and the sweat streaming from his brow. He was struck most by the coldness in his eyes, an impenetrable veil which, no doubt, hid the life of suffering he had endured due to his deformity.

"Lead on," Stefan murmured, following him into the white-paneled and gilt salon.

Stefan took a seat in a soft armchair, watching as Adolph poured him a brandy. The dwarf's short fingers fumbled with the crystal stopper in the decanter, and he almost dropped it.

Stefan frowned, turning to look out the window at the crisp, sunny day. He doubted he would ever grow accustomed to this latest passion of the aristocracy to possess these unfortunate beings, using them as servants and confidants, treating some as nothing more than pampered pets. Even the emperor and his wife kept a pair of dwarfs, cosseted and bejeweled favorites of the court, who often stood at Their Majesties' elbows during court functions.

"Thank you, Adolph, I will see to that." Sophia's husky voice interrupted Stefan's disapproving thoughts. He rose abruptly from his chair as she glided into the room with seductive grace and took the snifter of brandy from her servant's outstretched hands.

"Leave us now, Adolph," she said sweetly, though her eyes flashed as she looked down at him.

Adolph nodded and hurried from the room, reaching up on tiptoe to close first one, then the other of the double doors. Sophia waited, her heart hammering within her breast, until the staccato tapping of his boots died away before she spoke, breaking at last the thick silence that had descended over the room.

"I've missed you," she said simply, her ivory satin gown swishing against the carpeted floor as she moved toward Stefan, smiling provocatively. She held out the snifter to him, but he merely set it down on the table next to the chair.

Stefan's eyes swept appreciatively over her. Sophia was as stunning as ever, an incredibly desirable woman many a man would sell his soul to possess. It was no wonder he had been so drawn to her just over a year ago when they had first met, at a dinner gala at the Belvedere, Prince Eugene's summer palace. She had everything a man could want in a mistress, beauty, poise, and a sensual appetite that had amazed and delighted him time and again. But he no longer had need of a mistress . . .

Sophia thrilled at the open admiration in his gaze, her overwhelming relief making her limbs tremble. Isabel had lied! she exulted, so close to him now, she could feel the warmth emanating from his powerful body. With a sudden movement she wound her slim arms about his neck, nuzzling against him, at any moment expecting to feel the exciting pressure of his arms tightening as he returned her embrace.

"Oh, Stefan," she breathed, her pulse racing wildly. She tilted her head back, her half-closed eyes laden with desire, her parted lips aching for his kiss.

Stefan stared at her upturned face for the briefest moment, then brought his hands to the curve of her waist. With determined resolve he lifted her arms from his neck and drew them down to her sides.

It was the simplest of gestures. Yet in that fleeting moment, Sophia knew Isabel had spoken the truth.

"Sophia, I haven't much time," Stefan began, stepping away from her. "There is something we must discuss—"

"Who is she?" Sophia broke in, her back to him now, her voice strangely hollow.

Stefan started. How could she possibly have known? he wondered. Then he shrugged. He would never fathom the uncanny intuitions of women.

"You met her at the Hofburg . . . Lady Kassandra Wyndham," Stefan said evenly. "If you recall, she's the daughter of Isabel's betrothed, Lord Harrington."

Lady Kassandra Wyndham. The name struck like a dagger into Sophia's heart, and she fiercely bit her lower lip to keep from crying out. The bitter pain of this confirmation was almost more than she could bear. "She is your . . . new mistress, then?" she queried almost hopefully. She glanced at him, refusing to believe Isabel's words.

Stefan shook his head. "Sophia, there has never been any deception between us, and I will not have it now. I have decided to marry Lady Kassandra as soon as her father returns from Hanover and gives his consent. I think it is best, meanwhile, for our relationship to cease."

Sophia looked away, tremendous fury flaring within her, quelling all other emotions. No! *She* was to become Countess von Furstenberg, she raged, not some English bitch who was little more than a schoolgirl! Somehow she found her voice, forcing it to remain calm. "Her father is in Germany? Ah yes, I had almost forgotten. When do you expect his return, Stefan?"

"By spring," Stefan replied tersely. "Though it is my hope it will be earlier."

Sophia's eyes glittered ferally, a slow smile curving her lips. Then all was not lost, she mused. Spring was yet a long time away. She whirled to face him.

"I am so happy for you, Stefan!" she exclaimed, bustling forward and kissing him lightly on the cheek. "Truly I am. And of course, it stands to reason our relationship must cease . . . for now. It would hardly be suitable for us to continue our present arrangement, considering you lack the good ambassador's consent. As an Englishman, he is hardly versed in our Viennese customs.'' She chuckled knowingly. ''You would not have him thinking you were a rogue.''

Stefan studied her beautiful face with wry amusement. He was pleased she was taking his news so well, though for a moment he had begun to have his doubts.

He relaxed. It seemed he had not underestimated her good sense after all. As to her insinuation they might continue their affair at some later point, perhaps after his marriage—well, for now he would let it go. It was enough that she had accepted his news with such obvious grace. Eventually he would have to make it very clear that his burning desire for Kassandra left no room in his life for any other woman.

''Let us share a drink to your marriage, Stefan,'' Sophia suggested suddenly, interrupting his thoughts. She poured herself a good measure of sherry while Stefan picked up the brandy snifter, then held the crystal goblet in front of her. ''To your future bride . . . Countess von Furstenberg.''

''Yes,'' he agreed. ''To Kassandra.'' He tossed down the fiery contents in one draft.

Sophia's hand shook as she raised the goblet to her lips, the sweet wine nearly making her gag. Yes, to Lady Kassandra Wyndham, she thought malevolently, smiling at Stefan. The bride who would never live to see her wedding day.

''Now I must go,'' Stefan said, setting down his glass. ''There are matters I must attend to at the estate.''

''Of—of course,'' Sophia replied, momentarily taken aback by his abrupt manner. ''I will walk with you to the door—''

"No, but thank you, Sophia. I can see my way out," he murmured. He strode to the double doors of the salon, anxious to be on his way. There was no sense in prolonging this meeting.

"Stefan," Sophia called out, her knuckles white as she gripped the goblet.

"Yes?"

Sophia swallowed hard, a tremulous smile fixed upon her face. "Please give my fondest greetings to your future bride," she murmured.

Stefan nodded, then with a flashing smile he was gone, his footsteps echoing across the hall, followed by the awful finality of the front door closing behind him. Sophia waited, motionless, until the thundering of hooves upon the drive had faded away, then she threw her goblet against the tall enameled stove in the corner, sending shards and splinters of glass flying everywhere.

"Adolph!" she screamed, rushing into the hall. "Adolph!"

It was only a moment before he appeared from the kitchen, hastily swallowing a mouthful of cold mutton and wiping his greasy fingers on his breeches. "I am here, milady," he muttered, eyeing her cautiously. He marveled that such a beautiful face could contort so viciously, revealing the true nature of the woman he had no choice but to serve.

Sophia looked down at him, her hands clenched into fists, her breasts heaving against the stiff fabric of her bodice. It was really a simple matter, she thought shrewdly, a scheme forming in her mind as she appraised him. Once this Kassandra was dealt with, then Stefan would come back to her and all would be as before. And she possessed the very accomplice to carry out her bidding . . .

"I have a task for you, Adolph, an important task," she commanded imperiously. "One in which you will be able to use all the . . . *skills*"—her eyes narrowed—"and attributes that your previous owner claimed you possessed."

She knelt, her gaze level with his own. "If you succeed in this task," she murmured sweetly, "I will be sure to reward you well. If you fail . . ." She shook her head, sighing regretfully. "Well, you can imagine, eh, Adolph?"

He licked his lips, nodding, a flicker of fear lighting the depths of his black eyes.

"Good. Now come with me to my chamber, and we will discuss this task . . . further." She rose to her feet and glided across the polished floor to the staircase, then turned and held out her hand. "Come along, Adolph."

# Chapter 18

Kassandra closed the thin volume of English verse she had been reading for most of the morning and leaned against the leather chair. It had been unexpectedly generous of Stefan to allow her the use of his extensive library, she mused, and she had done so with great pleasure on many occasions during the past weeks—but only when she was certain he would not be there. It was unnerving to be alone in the same room with him.

She had tried once, at his insistent invitation, to read a book there while he was poring over various maps and manuscripts at the massive table he used for a desk. But she had been unable to concentrate on the page before her, his every movement, every rustle of paper, a jarring torment.

It seemed each time she looked up he would be studying her intently, almost curiously, as if he sought to know what she was thinking. His gaze alone was enough to send her mind reeling, tinged with the desire that was always reflected there, and something else she could not fathom. Flustered, she had hurriedly sought her page again, but finally gave up and fled the room, fearful that he might see her own hated desire smoldering in her eyes.

No, it was far more to her liking to be here by herself, among the hundreds of leather-bound vol-

umes gracing tall shelves that reached to the ceiling.
Her gaze drifted around the large room, silent but
for the ticking of the ornate gilded clock on the mantelpiece, and she noted the trappings—oak paneling,
heavy, imposing furniture, a collection of swords
and pistols upon the walls—that gave it a decidedly
masculine ambience. The only liberty she allowed
herself whenever she entered the library was to draw
back the velvet drapes so the bright winter sunlight
could stream into the room.

Kassandra sighed as she set the book on a table
beside the chair, then rose to her feet and crossed to
the window. She gazed out, the sunlight warm on
her face, marveling at the blinding snow covering
the ground. She had never seen a winter quite like
this one, so unlike those she had known in Sussex.
It snowed very little there, if at all. Here, although
it was only January, the sparkling drifts already
reached well above the lower panes of the windows.

Kassandra's fair brow furrowed in thought. Surprisingly enough, the deep snows had not kept them
confined to the estate, as she might have expected.
The past few weeks had been a blur of activity, much
of it due to the Christmas season and the coming of
the New Year. She suspected some of it was due to
the unsettling conversation she and Stefan had
shared a few days after she had moved her belongings into the sumptuous bedchamber adjoining his
own.

She had done her very best to avoid him altogether, or at the very least spend as much time in
Isabel's company as possible so he would not catch
her alone. But on this particular night Isabel had retired early, so she'd sought the solace of the drawing room.

Sitting down at the harpsichord, she had skimmed
her fingers lightly over the keys, her lilting soprano
quietly accompanying her favorite melodies. She was

so lost in her music, she did not hear the door open and close quietly, nor did she realize Stefan was silently watching her until his voice sounded from across the room.

"Do you play only sad melodies?" he queried gently, stepping from the shadowed background into the flickering light cast by the candelabra atop the harpsichord.

Kassandra's hands froze on the smooth keys, and she flushed with sudden warmth. It never ceased to amaze her how even the sound of his voice could send her senses reeling. But she quickly regained her composure. "I play what is in my heart," she retorted hotly. "If it is not to your liking, you have only to leave."

Stefan chuckled softly, seemingly unperturbed at her tone. "Ah, but it is very much to my liking, Kassandra. You sing beautifully," he murmured, pulling up a chair. He seated himself, then leaned forward, a pleasant smile on his handsome face. "Please go on."

Kassandra had no wish to remain in this room with him. His accommodating mood hardly suited the picture of him—cruel, callous, a blackguard of the worse kind—she nurtured as a constant reminder of what he had done to her.

She stood up from her chair and swept hurriedly across the room, leaving a good distance between them. She was almost to the door when his next question caused her to stop abruptly in her flight. Her heart lurched within her breast.

"How did you come to be in that tavern, Kassandra?" he asked gently.

At first she was too stunned to answer, but the bitterness of her recollection soon forced her to speak. "What does it matter, especially to you?"

"I wish to know," he replied softly.

Kassandra sighed heavily, pondering his request.

Her eyes stared unseeing at the intricate pattern woven into the carpet. Then she shrugged. There was no reason not to tell him, she decided. She no longer had anything to hide.

"I wanted to lose myself in the city," she began, her voice a monotone. "To experience Vienna without the burden of my identity as the daughter of an ambassador. So I dressed as a maid and set out on my own through the streets, chancing upon a cattle parade. One of the oxen broke loose, and there was a great deal of commotion"—she paused, taking a deep breath, the vivid memory looming before her— "and I was fortunate enough to stumble into the tavern, probably saving my life."

Kassandra looked directly at Stefan, her gaze locking with his. "Yet it seems in truth I was not so fortunate. Your city was not what I imagined it to be, nor its inhabitants. I lost my life at that moment, or at least control of my own fate, almost as surely as if I had been trampled to death," she whispered fiercely, startled to see his expression of pain. But it quickly passed, and only a slight tension in his square-cut jaw betrayed any emotion. "May I go now?" she queried tersely.

His only answer was a short nod, then he looked away. She swept angrily from the room, and was making her way up the stairs, guided by a footman holding a silver candlestick, when she heard him call out her name. She turned to find him standing at the bottom, one foot resting on the step above it, his arm braced against the balustrade . . . as if he had stopped himself from following her.

"Beginning tomorrow, I will show you a different Vienna," he said seriously. "One of beauty . . . and laughter." His eyes gleamed with an intense emotion she had never before seen there. "You cannot blame the city for what fate has ordained, Kassandra."

A stinging retort flew to her lips, but she bit it back. She could see by his determined stance that he would not be swayed. And she was too tired to battle with him further tonight, even if it was only a war of words. "As you wish," she replied, turning her back on him.

And so it had been, Kassandra mused, absently fingering the delicate gold chain around her neck, just as Stefan had said. During the past weeks he had given her a glimpse of the imperial city she might never have experienced without him, a peek into the splendid wonder that was Vienna.

A few times Isabel accompanied them, but after a while she claimed she was not well suited for the role of chaperone. With a playful glance at her brother, she laughingly insisted they were better off without her. Kassandra had protested, albeit lightly, always fearful that she might give Isabel the impression that something was amiss. It was to no avail. Like it or not, she had to contend with Stefan as her sole companion.

Yet aside from the interminable carriage rides, which passed in uncomfortable silence on her part and studied amusement on Stefan's, at least she had some consolation. Everywhere he had taken her there had always been other people, so in her mind they were never truly alone.

They attended all manner of musical events, from impromptu concerts of flute, violin, and zither held in luxurious cafés, to the grandest performances of the Hofmusikkapelle, or Court Orchestra, at the Hofburg. She watched in astonishment as Charles VI himself, from sheer love of music, conducted the orchestra from the harpsichord, his virtuosity a wonder to behold. Stefan whispered in her ear that the emperor spent several hours each day working at his singing and playing various instruments, as a refuge from the burdens of power and responsibilities of court life.

They went to an opera where the wonderful singing was nearly surpassed by the amazing light effects—a wild storm complete with thunder and jagged streaks of lightning, then the twinkling of stars as the veiled clouds rolled away. Remarkable whirring machines had moved the scenery to and fro, some causing the actors to disappear beneath the floor as if by witchery.

Stefan even took her to a puppet show, though she found it very strange . . . a ballet performed by dwarfs and lifelike marionettes. At times it was hard to discern what was real, and what was illusion. The ballet was coupled with the latest optical effects: lanterns that projected phantoms upon pale backdrops, eerie winds stirring the curtain. And all the while, moaning voices carried forth from the sides and back of the stage, sending shivers down her spine.

They had twice dined in sumptuous restaurants, Stefan insisting she sample specialties from many nations—Slav, Italian, German, and Czech—and varieties of wine, both red and white. Each time, she declined more than a few sips of the fragrant vintages, fearful lest she lose control of her wits. She was determined to remain wary of him, despite his obvious efforts to win some measure of her favor.

For that was exactly what he was doing, Kassandra reflected, settling herself on the wide windowsill. She was no fool. For some reason Stefan was showing her a different side of himself, more like the man Isabel had so fondly described to her before she had met him. In the fascinating whirl of the past weeks it was all Kassandra could do to remind herself of his true character, lurking just beneath his devastating charm.

Kassandra's eyes darkened, her head racked with turmoil. She would be a liar to say she was not af-

fected by him. Each passing day was becoming an
increasing torment for her, and she had still to think
of a way out of her predicament. She tugged with
exasperation at the jeweled locket dangling from her
necklace, then looked down at it, wincing. Set with
precious rubies and diamonds, it caught the sunlight, glittering brightly in the palm of her hand.

Kassandra cursed under her breath. Stefan had
given her the necklace on Christmas Day with a
touching sincerity that had left her breathless and
perplexed. She had wanted to refuse it, but he had
a deliberate habit of presenting her with gifts in front
of Isabel, so she had no choice but to accept. He had
drawn it about her neck, his fingers brushing lightly
against her nape as he fastened the clasp, causing
her to tremble. The locket fell just above the hollow
between her breasts, its smooth weight against the
beating of her heart a much-needed reminder of his
selfish treachery.

Kassandra rose abruptly from the sill and began
to pace the library, chewing her lower lip. What of
the music box he had given her, with the tiny nightingale perched on a branch of ivory, which trilled
when the silver lid was opened?

And most unexpected of all, the beautiful Arabian
mare he had presented to her on the first morning
of the New Year, its gleaming coat the same pure
white as the snow that blanketed the ground. If he
sought to touch her heart, he had come closest in
that moment. She had made no secret of her love
for horses.

Damn him! she raged. Did Stefan really think she
would be so easily swayed by these gifts, that all
which had passed between them would be forgiven,
even forgotten? A troubling thought struck her. Perhaps he hoped it was a way to cajole her into leaving
her chamber door, the one leading to his own chamber, unbolted at night . . .

Kassandra stopped suddenly and drew her arms tightly against her chest. Every evening since she had moved into the room adjoining his, she had lain awake in her bed, listening wide-eyed to his pacing footsteps like a lithe, stalking animal's. Then he would try her door, and every fiber in her body went taut with shivering tension as he slowly turned the knob, only to find it bolted securely against him.

Sometimes his furious pacing would begin anew, while other times it would cease and there would be only silence, perhaps a sign that he slept at last. Then there had been the nights when she heard him leave his chamber, slamming the door behind him. Moments later she would watch from her window as he rode out into the darkness on his stallion, not to return until the next morning—

A sharp rap on the door startled Kassandra from her reverie. Stefan stepped into the library, a smile spreading across his rugged features. "I was hoping I would find you here," he murmured, his gaze raking over her. She was ravishing in her lilac morning gown, its simple lines heightening her singular beauty. He liked the way the silken fabric skimmed closely against her lithe body, buoyed only by a single petticoat rather than those infernal hoopskirts. Unfortunately the gown was not suitable dress for the theater. Regrettably, something more formal was required.

His black brow rose quizzically. "I see you are not dressed for our excursion into the city, Kassandra. Have you forgotten about the comedy this afternoon?"

"Co-comedy?" she asked blankly, blushing under his frank perusal, her flesh tingling. Then with a start she remembered. Her eyes flew to the clock on the mantelpiece. It was half past one already. Stefan had requested she be ready to leave by two o'clock.

"Oh dear," she began, flustered. "I was reading . . . and the time has flown—"

"It's no matter," he interrupted, chuckling lightly. "There is still time for you to change." He took a step toward her. "If I could dictate women's fashion, I would have you go just as you are."

Anger shot through her at the blatant desire in his eyes, yet it was tinged with a strange, unsettling excitement. The man could make her feel as though she were standing before him as God had created her, though she was fully clothed. Obviously he was becoming quite sure of himself, and far too sure of her . . . something she would remedy at once.

"I have decided I am not in the mood for a comedy," she said in a rush. "Perhaps Isabel might accompany you in my stead." Her gaze moved to the door, but she knew from experience not to brush past him. Instead she held her ground, her chin lifted defiantly.

Stefan's expression tightened. "The invitation was extended to you, Kassandra, not Isabel," he murmured. "I am afraid you have little choice. Either be at the door within the half hour, or I shall personally see that you are suitably dressed and carried forthwith to the carriage." He paused, his voice low and husky. "And if you have any doubts as to my knowledge of women's clothing, rest assured I am well versed in lacing . . . and unlacing," he emphasized darkly, "those garments you call corsets. Am I understood?"

Kassandra drew herself up, glaring at him. He wouldn't dare! Then, as if reading her mind, Stefan nodded, his steady gaze glinting a challenge. She swallowed hard. Yes, he would, she thought grimly. However vexing, it was clear that he had bested her once again. "If you will excuse me, my lord," she acquiesced, her eyes flashing, "I will go and change."

Stefan stepped aside as she walked by him, her back stiff and proud. "Within the half hour, Kassandra," he said softly.

She threw him a withering look, then fled up the stairs.

# Chapter 19

Stefan studied Kassandra's face in the dim light of the theater, fascinated by her range of expression. Wonder, shock, astonishment, delight . . . Her face was like an open book, almost as easily read as a child's, yet endlessly intriguing.

He smiled wryly. He doubted she suspected she was far more entertaining than the action on the stage. She was paying him little heed, her eyes drawn with rapt attention to the wild antics of the actors dressed in flowing Greek costumes. Occasionally she laughed, a bright, carefree sound that delighted him—a sound he heard far too rarely—or she would shake her head, blushing becomingly at an indecent word or a crude gesture.

Suddenly Kassandra gasped aloud. Startled, he glanced toward the stage, his brow lifting at the sight of two young male actors dropping their breeches in full view of the audience. He laughed shortly. He had seen this celebrated comedy once before, but this time the author was taking unusual liberties with his interpretation. Yet despite the bawdy rendition, the audience seemed well pleased with the entertainment. Uproarious laughter echoed under the painted and gilt ceiling, and the common people seated on the ground floor were elbowing and jostling each other roughly, to further enhance the joke.

Stefan leaned back in his chair, his gaze drifting around the crowded theater and back to Kassandra. He was glad he had paid a gold ducat for their front box. It offered the best seats in the house, situated as it was on the second tier above and to the right of the stage. He hoped Kassandra was pleased as well. Though in this last instant, he thought ruefully, their box was perhaps closer than she might have wished.

He exhaled slowly, his forehead furrowed. He had never before been so baffled by a woman. Here he was, wondering if she was pleased, and she hadn't even wanted to attend the comedy in the first place. It was only because he had once again forced his will upon her that she had relented. His actions had probably set him back even further in her opinion, making for naught his efforts of the previous weeks to win her favor.

Stefan shifted uncomfortably in his chair, stretching his long legs in front of him. He cursed under his breath. Damn it all, what was coming over him? Since when had he been at a total loss as to how to win a woman's favor?

He glanced at Kassandra, innocently unaware of his dilemma. Or was she? he wondered, thinking back over the past weeks. During their outings together she had seemed to enjoy herself, though she had remained coolly distant toward him. His gifts—even the costly Arabian mare that he had hand-picked for her from a renowned merchant—had brought a temporary light to her eyes, a fleeting smile, but then she had closed herself off from him again.

Stefan's gaze lingered over the sculpted perfection of her profile, coming to rest on the delicate curve of her lips, seductively parted in a smile. His blood coursed hot within his veins at the memory of their soft warmth against his own. She was such a bewitching contradiction. For despite her outward reserve, his gut instincts told him she was wavering.

He could swear on several occasions he had caught a glimpse of desire in the depths of those stirring amethyst eyes, a hint of the tempestuous passion she held so determinedly in check, as if it were a wild spirit within her, desperate to be free; the very same passion that inspired him to pursue her so mercilessly.

Perhaps it would just take more time to convince her that their marriage would not be the nightmare she envisioned, Stefan considered, though the grim prospect of waiting a moment longer did not set well with him. It had been difficult enough during the past month. He had spent many hours with her, during the day and into the early evening, torturous hours in which he played the part of the perfect gentleman, though he longed to crush her in his arms.

It was the nights that were pure hell. He'd been a fool to insist she move into the chamber adjoining his own. The thought of her so close to him—her fiery hair in disarray on the pillow, her body lushly curved, inviting, known only to him—was proving too much of a temptation. He grimaced, recalling nights he'd spent in near pain, his body inflamed from wanting her. On many an occasion, he had thought of breaking down the bolted door that separated them, but his sense of honor had always stopped him.

Stefan stared blindly at the stage, gripping the arms of his chair as a stab of remorse cut through him. Never again would he force himself upon her. He had seen enough of the aftermath of war and the misery inflicted upon conquered peoples—death, starvation, and brutal rape—to set his stomach churning at the thought. He shook his head fiercely, dispelling the stark images from his mind.

No, he had always sought willing women for his

bed. And so it would be with Kassandra. He would wait until he was certain she wanted him as much as he wanted her. To insure his intent, he would continue to spend nights at his hunting lodge several miles from the mansion. He was not about to jeopardize whatever progress he had made with her by his impatience to possess her completely.

A burst of thunderous applause erupted from the audience, halting his thoughts, and he looked over to find Kassandra studying him quizzically.

"Did you enjoy the performance, my lord?" she repeated, louder this time to be heard over the hoots of approval and stamping feet. Though she doubted he'd seen much of it at all, she thought irritably. She'd been hard pressed during much of the comedy to ignore his constant staring and keep her mind on what was transpiring onstage.

Stefan smiled, noting her flushed cheeks and slightly sarcastic tone. So she had felt his gaze after all . . . Never underestimate this woman, he admonished himself, rising to his feet. "Yes, I did," he replied, holding out a hand to her. "The scenery was inspired."

Kassandra ignored his remark, and his proffered assistance. She rose gracefully from her chair and glanced over her shoulder, her gaze sweeping the quickly emptying theater, searching for someone. Then she spied him, the dark-haired dwarf who had also been watching her for most of the performance from his seat just below their box. He was pushing his way down the crowded aisle, his booted heels grinding rudely on the toes of unfortunate patrons in his haste to leave the theater.

Strange, Kassandra mused. She had no idea why the little man had scrutinized her so. She had never seen him before, though his fine suit of clothes indicated he was probably the servant to a wealthy

aristocrat. She quickly dismissed him from her mind
at the pressure of Stefan's hand upon her elbow.

"There is a wonderful inn near the Danube, the
Golden Rose, where I thought we might enjoy a light
supper," he murmured, holding back the red velvet
curtain that separated the box from the corridor.
"It's a bit rustic, but a favorite of mine."

Kassandra nodded in quick agreement. Though
she did not want to prolong this outing, she had to
admit she was hungry. She had eaten only a thin
slice of toasted bread and orange-scented tea since
early that morning. Her stomach growled painfully
as she stepped from the box, and she blushed in
embarrassment. A hint of amusement glinted in Stefan's eyes, but he gave no other indication that he
had heard.

Together they walked down the narrow corridor,
lit by small oil lamps set in ornate gilt sconces, then
down the plush carpeted stairs that led to the main
hall of the theater. Stefan wasted no time in retriev-
ing her fur-trimmed cape from a liveried footman
and wrapped it about her shoulders, his fingers
brushing her throat as he insisted upon fastening
the embroidered frogging himself. Kassandra shivered at his touch and turned her face away from him.
She did not trust herself to look into his eyes. He
threw on his own heavy cloak and took her arm,
guiding her through the milling crowd to the front
entrance.

It was only half past five o'clock, but the sun had
long ago disappeared behind the gray, snow-laden
clouds. Streetlamps glowed hazily along the street,
their golden light dimmed by an icy drizzle, and the
air was crisp and cold. Kassandra lifted her hood
over her head, then plunged her hands into her deep
side pockets to warm them. In her haste earlier that
day she had forgotten her long woolen gloves.

"Wait here, Kassandra," Stefan bade her gently,

with a light squeeze on her arm. "I'll be back in a moment." He strode down the walkway, searching the shadowed street for Zoltan and the carriage.

Several moments passed, and still Stefan did not return. Kassandra stamped her numbed feet, the satin shoes beneath her gown no protection from the chilling wind. Her teeth were chattering, and she doubted she could withstand the cold much longer. She decided to wait for him across the street from the theater, beneath an overhanging second-story balcony, where she would at least have some shelter from the freezing drafts.

Stepping into the snow-packed street, Kassandra did not hear the thundering hooves until they were almost upon her.

"Look out, miss!" a woman screamed behind her. "Oh God, the carriage!"

Kassandra turned her head, her eyes widening in horror as a black carriage, led by four galloping horses—like snorting dragons, she thought fleetingly—careened directly at her. There was no time to flee. She closed her eyes, bracing herself for the awful impact.

Suddenly she was yanked violently backwards and hit something broad and hard. The breath was knocked from her body and her eyes flew open in surprise, just in time to see a face peering out at her from the dark interior of the carriage as it raced by her, the deadly metal-rimmed wheels barely a foot away.

Kassandra gasped for air, her dazed mind unable to register that visage. Then she realized. It was the dwarf from the theater! But her thoughts were interrupted as she was roughly spun around, and enveloped in a fierce embrace, that left her feet dangling above the ground.

"Kassandra, my love," Stefan murmured raggedly against her silken hair, his heart clamoring within his chest. Dear God, if he had arrived a moment later! He shuddered, drawing her closer, her jasmine scent enveloping his senses. In the next instant a great surge of anger welled up inside him, and he wanted to shake her for her incredible folly. He set her down so abruptly that her head snapped back, his hands gripping her upper arms like a vise, his eyes searching her ashen face with grim intensity.

"Good God, woman, what were you thinking?" he demanded, his voice dangerously low. "You could have been killed." With a brusque nod he indicated where he had left her standing. "I told you to wait over there."

Kassandra stared up at him, dumbstruck. Stefan had saved her! Yet his harsh tone stirred her own anger, and she railed at him, her eyes flashing. "What do you mean, what was I thinking? What were *you* thinking, to leave me standing on the corner, freezing to death? None of this would have happened if you had asked Zoltan to wait for us near the front of the theater!"

Stunned by her shrewish tone, Stefan loosened his grip on her arms, though he did not release her. Obviously she was overwrought by what had happened . . . perhaps even in shock, he thought grimly, noting the pallor of her skin and her glittering, overbright eyes. He sighed heavily. It was best to leave at once for the estate.

"Zoltan!" he called out, waving his arm. The carriage, set on smooth wooden traineaus that enabled it to be drawn through the deep snow like a sleigh, pulled up alongside them. Zoltan jumped to the ground with a grunt, his dark eyes clouded with concern, and held the door open as Stefan lifted Kassandra and stepped up into the carriage.

"Drive swiftly, man," Stefan muttered as the door closed firmly behind them. Zoltan nodded, then climbed into his seat and cracked his whip above the heads of the dappled horses. The carriage jerked into motion, then slid effortlessly along the winding street, guided by lighted lanterns swinging from curved hooks on both sides of the front panels.

Atop his lap, Kassandra struggled against Stefan's firm hold on her, but finally slumped against his chest in futility. A ragged sigh escaped her as she glanced up at him, his expression barely discernible in the dark interior.

"I can assure you, my lord," she said through gritted teeth, "that I am quite able to sit upon the seat *without* your assistance." To emphasize her words she wriggled some more, but to no avail. He merely tightened his arms.

"Be still, Kassandra," he admonished softly, yet in a tone that brooked no argument. He said no more, but held her against him all the way back to the estate as if he would never let her go.

# Chapter 20

A dolph walked slowly into the darkened hall of the von Starenberg villa, its high ceiling and paneled walls draped in black crepe. His every step took great effort as he made his way to the salon where the archduchess awaited him, or, more aptly, he thought with a grimace, awaited the news she longed to hear . . . that Lady Kassandra Wyndham was dead . . . as dead as her own recently departed husband.

Outside the double doors, he inhaled a great breath. The archduchess would not be pleased, he thought miserably, then defiantly clenched his small hands.

"What's the matter with you, Adolph?" he chided himself in an indignant whisper. The devil knew, he had faced worse before. Let the witch do with him what she would. He squared his narrow shoulders with false bravado and rapped boldly on the door.

"Enter," a dusky voice sounded from within, bringing on a fit of trembling. He swallowed hard as he opened one of the doors and stepped into the salon, then froze at the incongruous sight of his beautiful mistress, dressed from head to toe in black mourning. Her topaz eyes gleamed in the candlelight, reminding him fleetingly of a cat just before it pounced on its unwitting prey.

"What news have you, Adolph?" Sophia asked breathlessly, rising from her chair and walking toward him. "Have your little spy games paid off? Were you able to find your quarry?"

Adolph nodded slowly. "It was a perfect opportunity, milady, the one I had been awaiting for many weeks." He looked down, gaining courage, then raised his head and steadily met her gaze, though he was quaking in his boots. "But it was not to be."

"Not to be?" Sophia queried sharply, her expression hardening. "Spare me your riddles, Adolph. Tell me simply—does she still live?"

"Y-yes, milady," he stammered, taking a small step backward, then rushed on in hasty explanation. "It was the count himself who saved her from the wheels of the carriage. Death was so close, milady, only a hair's breadth away—"

"Then you will have to try again, Adolph," Sophia cut him off, gripping the starched fabric of her skirt and turning away. "And still again, if need be, until the task is completed."

Adolph gaped at her stiff back, stunned by her simple response. It was so unlike the blind rage—and the beating—he had expected. "V-very well, milday," he managed.

"Now leave me."

Adolph turned on his heel so suddenly that he nearly bumped into the door. With his heart thumping in his chest, he hurried from the salon and fled across the hall and up the stairs as if the hounds of Satan were snapping at his heels.

"I'm fine, Isabel, truly I am," Kassandra insisted, throwing back the woolen blankets the countess had draped on top of the goosedown coverlet on her bed. "It was only a scare, nothing more. I don't have a fever, or chills, and I certainly don't need these extra blankets. But I am tired—"

"Of course you are tired, Kassandra; forgive me," Isabel interjected, her delicate features etched with anxious concern. She wrung her small hands together, at a loss. "Are you sure there isn't something I may bring you—hot tea, perhaps, or a sip of brandy to help you sleep?"

Kassandra shook her head and settled back upon the soft pillows. "You are so kind, Isabel, to worry after me so, but I think all I need now is a good rest." She smiled and held out her hand, and Isabel rushed forward, squeezing it affectionately. "With Prince Eugene's dinner gala tomorrow, you should also get some rest."

Isabel nodded. Indeed she was tired, and after this unexpected turn to the evening, she could hardly wait to seek the solace of her bed. Her nerves were fairly frazzled. "Very well, then," she agreed. "But I shall have Berdine sit outside your door for a while in case you need anything." She bent and lightly kissed Kassandra's forehead. "I am only grateful Stefan was there with you, Kassandra. I cannot bear to think of what might have—" She stopped abruptly, shuddering. "Well, it's enough that you are safe. Sleep well."

Kassandra watched as Isabel cupped her hand and blew out the candles beside the bed, then turned, and with a last glance over her shoulder, quietly left the darkened room.

Kassandra sighed heavily and closed her eyes, longing for sleep. Instead her thoughts flew unbidden to the vivid image of the black carriage bearing down upon her. She tensed, in her mind's eyes reliving the terrifying moment, then just as suddenly her body relaxed as she recalled the soothing strength of Stefan's arms.

It was as if he had come out of nowhere to save her from certain death, she mused, remembering the stricken look on his face, his breath warm and comforting against her hair. And he had said something to her . . . What was it? She tried in vain to recall his words, but they escaped her, lost forever in the panic of that moment.

Another face, malevolent and cold, loomed suddenly in her memory, and she shivered despite the warmth of the coverlet drawn up under her chin. Had it been the dwarf peering out at her from the carriage? she wondered. It had all happened so fast, she really wasn't sure anymore. Perhaps she had only imagined it . . .

No, she didn't want to think of that odd little dwarf, or the dreadful incident, anymore. She rolled onto her side, plumping the pillows beneath her head, then froze at the sound of muffled voices just outside her door. She could not make out the words, but she recognized Berdine's girlish chatter, and the richer, deeper voice . . . Stefan's.

Kassandra sat upright in her bed, her hand flying to her throat. Sweet Lord, she had forgotten to bolt the door to her chamber! She frantically threw back the thick coverlet and swung her legs over the side of the mattress, then ran barefooted to the door and slid the bolt firmly into place. Relief swept through her at the sound of his footsteps moving down the hall, then they faded altogether.

Kassandra walked slowly back to bed, her forehead crinkled in thought. She had not seen Stefan since they had arrived back at the estate. He had carried her up the stairs and into her chamber, laying her gently on the bed. For a fleeting moment it had seemed he wanted to tell her something, then Isabel had rushed into the room, clearly overwrought and demanding to know what had happened. After a terse explanation on his part, Stefan had abruptly left them.

Wasn't it just like him to wait until Isabel had gone to her chamber, then try Kassandra's door! He was obviously thinking only of his own selfish desires, even after she had almost been killed. She brushed off a niggling thought that he might have simply come to inquire after her, perhaps to see that she was well. No, that was unlikely. Such concern did not match his true character!

Kassandra plopped down on the edge of her bed, then restlessly rose once again and moved to the window, the folds of her linen nightgown swirling about her slim legs. She leaned against the sill and gazed out over the snow-covered lawn, glowing an eerie white in the light of the full moon. Then she tilted her head back, marveling at the myriad stars glittering in the dark blue heavens. It never ceased to amaze her how there could be so much turmoil in the world, and in her own life, yet the night sky was always so peaceful . . .

An odd shiver disrupted her quiet reflection. Why did she feel someone was watching her? She looked down, her eyes widening at the sight of a cloaked figure seated atop a black horse just below her window. Though she could not see the rider's upturned face in the dark, she instinctively knew who it was.

Her breath caught in her throat as Stefan sharply veered the stallion about in a spray of glittering snow and set off at a breakneck gallop down the drive. In a moment he was gone, disappearing into the darkness as he had done so many other nights while she watched from her window, wondering where he was going . . .

Probably on his way to see that mistress of his. Kassandra sniffed with feigned indifference. Or perhaps some other tart he'd found in a tavern somewhere. A stab of jealousy pierced her, surprising in its fierceness. But she quickly stifled it and turned furiously from the window.

She didn't care one whit where Stefan was off to! she raged, throwing herself on her bed. But jealousy flared in her heart once again as she imagined him in another woman's arms, a statuesque beauty with almond eyes . . . and she knew she lied. Heaven help her, she did care, more than she would ever admit. And this startling realization only made the harsh reality of her predicament even harder to bear.

Kassandra futilely pounded her fist into the bed, outraged tears filling her eyes. Bastard! To think he would use her only to beget children, yet all the while continue his whoring with his mistresses, too.

She cried until she was spent, her wracking sobs fueled by confusion, anger, and hopelessness, then she rolled onto her back and wiped the tears from her face with the back of her hand. She felt dazed, numb, yet one thought echoed in her mind. Somehow she had to find a way to defy him. Somehow . . .

Suddenly an idea of such simplicity, such clarity took her breath away. It was perfect! She turned on her side and leaned on one elbow, propping her head in her hand, her expression rebelliously determined.

"I will find a lover," Kassandra murmured. If she was condemned to a loveless marriage, it would only be fair. It was an accepted practice in Vienna for married women to have their paramours, obliging gentlemen who supplied the affection and devotion missing in many an arranged—or forced—marriage. She, for one, had no intention of going through her life without ever knowing what it was to love and be loved in return.

Feeling a sudden chill through the thin fabric of her nightgown, Kassandra crawled under the coverlet and settled into the snug warmth of her bed, a plan taking shape in her mind. Yes, that was exactly what she would do. Though she wasn't yet married, there was no harm in casting her eye about for a lover. Then when the wretched day of her wedding finally arrived—if she could find no way to escape it—and she became Countess von Furstenberg, she would have someone to give her what Stefan could not . . .

Growing drowsy, Kassandra closed her heavy eyelids. What would he be like? she wondered languidly, attempting to conjure a vision of this future lover. But as sleep overcame her all she could think of was a man with piercing gray eyes with a hint of blue, hair as black as midnight, and a smile that even now dared her to enact her plan.

# Chapter 21

"So this is the famous Winter Palace," Kassandra breathed excitedly, her gaze sweeping the length of the building as Stefan lifted her from the carriage, his strong hands encircling her slender waist beneath her cape. He set her down gently upon the walk, a black brow lifted in puzzlement at her winsome smile, surprisingly directed at him.

"And you say Prince Eugene lives here all alone, Stefan, in this massive place?" she asked, enchanted by the way the high white walls gleamed golden in the light of the streetlamps. She accepted his proffered arm.

Stefan nodded, the light pressure of her hand in the crook of his arm and the sound of his name upon her lips unexpected favors. She called him by his name so rarely, usually making do with either his title, a simple 'my lord,' or, he considered wryly, a wide range of colorful expletives that would set a nun's ears to burning.

Come to think of it, he mused, walking alongside her to the main entranceway, she was unusually animated this evening. He had seen her laughing and conversing gaily in Isabel's presence, but never alone with him . . . at least not since those first few weeks at the estate when they had spent a great deal of time together and she had played out her pretty cha-

179

rade with remarkable verisimilitude. But Isabel
would not be with them tonight. She had taken ill
at the last moment with a headache, so it was just
he and Kassandra in attendance at the gala.

He was amazed that Kassandra had agreed to accompany him after the shock she had suffered the
night before at the theater. Then again, he thought
ruefully, she had been well enough to bolt the door
when he had neared her chamber to inquire after
her comfort.

A few moments later, when he had saddled Brand
and was preparing to ride from the estate, he had
spied her at her window, gazing dreamily at the
moon. He had been mesmerized by the ethereal picture she made, the fiery luster of her hair in stunning contrast to her creamy skin and flowing white
nightgown.

He gazed down at her as she walked past the long
line of gleaming carriages, as much a vision now as
she had been the night before. Her eyes shone with
excitement and her cheeks blushed with a healthy
glow. Yes, all in all, she had made a remarkable re-
covery.

Which was more than he could say for himself, he
thought, feeling strangely subdued. He had spent
the night at his hunting lodge, not for fear he might
be tempted to break down her door, but because he
needed to be alone. Kassandra's close brush with
death had shaken him deeply, unleashing a barrage
of feelings within him. He had slept little, instead
pacing the wood-planked floor and raging at the four
walls over what he had done to her, and agonizing
about what he could do to make amends . . . to show
her how much he loved her—

His expression grew mildly self-mocking. Yes, he,
Stefan von Furstenberg, a man who had sworn he
would never be ruled by his emotions, had finally

fallen in love, and it had taken a near disaster for him to realize it.

Ah, but this dinner gala was neither the time nor the place to bare his soul to her. When the time was right, he would know it.

His lips drew into a faint smile. This shift in her manner seemed to be evidence that perhaps her heart had softened toward him. Yet it was so sudden, he couldn't help wondering how it had come about.

Could it simply be gratitude for saving her life? Or had his efforts of these past weeks at last won her favor and acceptance? Whatever it was, it was enough to give him some hope that all was not lost between them.

Kassandra paused in front of the center doorway, the largest of the three flanking the street. She tilted her head back to admire the monumental building, created by the joint efforts of Vienna's greatest architects, Hildebrandt and Fischer von Erlach. There were seventeen tall windows on the first story, above each window an elaborate ornament, while the three windows above the doorways had graceful balconies. The building was crowned with a richly sculptured frieze, a balustrade, and eighteen statues, each posed differently.

"Impressive, isn't it?"

Kassandra felt Stefan tense at the unfamiliar though pleasant male voice. How strange, she thought, glancing over her shoulder to return a most engaging smile. The extremely stylish aristocrat standing just to her left seemed hardly the person to elicit such a reaction from Stefan. He looked harmless enough, in his powdered bobwig and elaborate plum-colored coat bedecked with frothy cream lace.

"Yes, it is," Kassandra replied, suppressing an urge to giggle. She had never before seen such a preening dandy. She extended her hand as he stepped beside her, then glanced up pointedly at Stefan.

He caught her look, and frowned with displeasure. "Lady Kassandra Wyndham . . . Count Frederick Althann," he said gruffly. He watched disdainfully as the younger man pulled his tricornered hat from his head with a decidedly feminine flourish, then bent over Kassandra's gloved hand and lightly kissed her fingers.

"I am most honored," Frederick murmured pleasantly. He straightened, his gaze moving to Stefan. "I have not had the pleasure of congratulating you, Count von Furstenberg, on the glorious success of the last campaign. As ever, your legendary valor is to be commended."

Stefan merely nodded in acknowledgment. "If you will excuse us, Count Althann," he said tersely, cueing Kassandra with a light squeeze on her elbow. She looked up at him, perplexed by his rudeness, then sighed and walked with him up the curved steps and through the entranceway, determined to query him about his behavior later. She sensed that the young count followed not far behind, and when Stefan wasn't looking, she threw him an apologetic smile.

A flurry of liveried servants rushed to and fro in the marble hall just beyond the entranceway, taking capes, canes, and hats from the arriving guests. As Stefan shrugged off his dark woolen cloak, Kassandra could not help but notice how strikingly handsome he looked this evening.

He was dressed with intensely masculine flair, from the fine cut of his brocade coat, a deep burgundy that heightened his bronzed coloring, and the laced waistcoat beneath it that stretched across the powerful breadth of his chest and shoulders, to the dark breeches that hugged his muscled thighs, and the well-fitting black boots that came to just below his knees. He wore no wig—he had been vocal on several occasions regarding how much he despised them—and though it went against fashion, his thick hair was tied together at his nape with a black ribbon.

It suited him, Kassandra mused, lowering her eyes as she smoothed a satin flounce on her gown. For if there was one thing she had learned about Stefan von Furstenberg, it was that he was his own man, and did exactly as he pleased.

She looked up, not surprised to find him also appraising her. Liquid warmth raced through her limbs as his heated gaze moved slowly over her, from the elegant coif of her hair, which had been swept up and fastened at her crown with two silver combs, then allowed to tumble down her back in a riot of curls interwoven with silver ribbon, to her satin shoes, which peeked from beneath the hem of her skirt. Her gown was a rich sapphire-blue concoction bedecked with matching satin ribbons and delicately embroidered flowers in silver threads, and a daringly low neckline that showed off to perfection her flawless breasts and shoulders.

Kassandra used her fluttering fan to hide her smile. She had once sworn never to wear such a gown again, but on this occasion she was pleased by his obvious approval. She had dressed for the dinner gala with special care, and she was determined to enjoy herself, even to the extent of letting down her guard toward Stefan. She did not want their verbal sparring to spoil this evening.

For, though as a rule she disliked these social gatherings and was not accustomed to playing the coquette, tonight was different. Tonight was the perfect opportunity to begin her search for a lover. And if Stefan found her alluring, perhaps other gentlemen might as well . . .

Kassandra again took Stefan's arm as they were ushered up the white spiraling staircase, which was supported at the landings by writhing stone giants, and into the ballroom. A portly footman announced their names in reserved tones to the thirty or so guests present.

Kassandra's gaze swept with pleasure about the well-appointed room, lit by gleaming chandeliers holding hundreds of candles. Although this room was built on a much smaller scale than the ballroom at the Hofburg, it far surpassed it in richness of decoration and furnishing, like a finely wrought jewel box filled with gems.

She marveled at the profusion of gilding and elaborate carving about the tall windows and the doors leading to the balconies. The windows were polished to a sparkling shine and framed by curtains of the finest Genoa damask, the hems fringed in gold lace. Paintings by well-known masters graced the paneled walls, while manicured orange and lemon trees were set about in large gilt pots. In the center of the ballroom, a curved table in the shape of a horseshoe was dressed with the whitest of linen tablecloths, polished silver candelabra, and china plates edged with gold.

"As you can see," Stefan murmured, following her gaze, "the emperor well rewards those who serve him. For a man who has saved our country from the Turks, there can never be enough praise or compensation."

Kassandra nodded, following him through the throng of guests to where Prince Eugene was engrossed in sober discourse with a thin, sallow-faced man, who, like most everyone in the room, seemed to tower over him. The general turned at their approach, his dark eyes flickering over her and quickly lighting with recognition.

"Lady Kassandra Wyndham," he murmured graciously, his lips barely grazing her fingers. "It is a distinct pleasure to see you again." He glanced at Stefan, his expression genuinely warm. "I should commend you, Count, for escorting such rare beauty to my hall. Rousseau here"—he nodded toward the middle-aged man at his side—"would do well to set his pen to paper and write a glorious ode in her honor." He quickly commenced introductions to the celebrated French poet, who was under his patronage during a brief stay in Vienna.

"I am charmed, mademoiselle," Rousseau murmured, bending over her hand. He straightened, studying her intently, as a painter might appraise a model. "My kind patron is most apt in his assessment of your beauty. You are lovely indeed. I would be delighted to compose a poem for you."

His peaked features grew animated as he warmed to his favorite subject. "In truth, I have begun one already, dedicated to the beauteous ladies of the Viennese court. Each verse is represented by a different flower. When completed, it will be a bouquet of prose to enrapture the senses. Hmmm . . . which shall you be?"

"I love roses," Kassandra offered, flattered. "Cream roses, tipped with scarlet."

"So it shall be," the poet agreed with a thin smile.

"You will have to meet Count Stefan's sister, Rousseau," Prince Eugene said with indulgent humor. "No doubt you will wish to include her in your composition as well." He glanced around the room. "But where is Countess Isabel?"

"Unfortunately she has taken ill," Stefan began, his gaze moving from Kassandra's pleased expression to his general.

"Nothing serious, I trust."

"No, my lord, but she sends her fond greetings, and her regrets. She had been looking forward to this evening for some time."

"As have I," Kassandra broke in, smiling prettily. "Isabel has told me that you possess a remarkable library, sir. Perhaps I might have the opportunity to view your collection at some point in the evening?"

"So, an intellectual as well," Prince Eugene remarked, his sparse brow lifting with interest. The faintest of smiles touched his serious face. "An unusual trait in a woman, but one to be admired and encouraged." He held out his arm to her. "I fear that once the banquet begins, there will be little chance for a tour, my lady. But if you would care to view the library at this moment, I would be more than happy to show you its treasures."

"Oh, yes, that would be delightful," Kassandra agreed, taking his arm. She glanced at Stefan. "Do you mind—"

"Not at all," he interjected evenly, quelling his sharp jealousy. The emotion startled him, for it was not one he had ever felt before, and so strongly. Yet he knew he had nothing to fear from his commanding general. Prince Eugene's life was devoted to his passion for military conquest and strategy, his longstanding affair with Countess Eleanor Batthyany the only sensual diversion he allowed himself. Kassandra's request had merely appealed to his love of books and his great pride in his library.

"Will you accompany us, Rousseau?" Prince Eugene queried. "I would swear you know more about my library than I."

Stefan watched silently as Kassandra and Prince Eugene strolled arm in arm from the ballroom, followed by the poet. He could not help chuckling. Obviously his general was far more aware of propriety than he had allowed.

"Oh, what a pity." A woman's sultry voice broke into his thoughts, a bejeweled hand pressing intimately upon his arm. "And I was so hoping to congratulate her on your marriage plans, Stefan."

He turned, his eyes narrowing imperceptibly. "Sophia," he murmured with a short nod. "You look well." His gaze flickered over her, the black satin gown she was wearing incongruously extravagant for a woman in mourning. "Kassandra will return shortly, and you may greet her then," he continued tersely. "Though I must ask you to refrain from discussing our marriage openly. Consent has not yet been given."

"Oh, yes, Stefan, forgive me," Sophia murmured, removing her hand from his arm. "I had forgotten." She gazed up at him from beneath thick, curling lashes. "There has been so much on my mind of late."

Stefan shifted uncomfortably, chiding himself for his callous lack of manners. "I was saddened to hear the news of your husband's death," he offered in a gentler tone. "Though many a man would envy such a peaceful end. Archduke von Starenberg was a respected minister of the court. I am sure the emperor will miss his thoughtful wisdom, as well as his company."

Sophia sighed deeply, averting her gaze. "Yes," she agreed. "It was so kind of Prince Eugene to invite me to this splendid gala," she exclaimed, abruptly changing the subject. "I can hardly wait for the dancing later. I have not been out of the house since—" She glanced back at him, wrinkling her nose in distaste, then caught herself. She turned away, feigning a light sneeze. "Excuse me, Stefan," she said, pulling a black lace handkerchief from her pocket and delicately dabbing her nose.

Stefan eyed her quizzically, laughter welling up inside him. He had almost been fooled by her display of grief, but this last gesture confirmed his suspicions. He knew Sophia far too well. She had never expressed any concern for her husband while he was alive. Why should it be different after his death? He lifted her chin, her topaz eyes meeting his steadily.

"Sophia, you cannot fool me," he said, smiling. "You are incredibly wealthy and free at last from a marriage you despised. Now, tell me. What will you do with this newfound freedom?"

Sophia did not speak for the briefest instant, her gaze softening, then her red lips drew into a smile. "Oh . . . there are many things to occupy me for a time," she breathed huskily. "But when they are completed, perhaps I shall seek a husband . . . someone who is more worthy of me."

"Then as you drank a toast to me, I shall drink to you," Stefan offered gallantly. He signaled to a servant bearing a silver tray laden with crystal glasses filled with red wine. With a flourish he took two glasses from the tray and held one out to her, then lifted his own. "To this most worthy of husbands . . . may he bring you happiness."

Sophia raised the glass to her lips and drank deeply, her eyes never leaving his face.

# Chapter 22

⟨⟨◯◯⟩⟩

**"Y**our knowledge of literature is extraordinary," Prince Eugene complimented Kassandra as they walked along the hall leading back to the ballroom, the thin poet following them like a discreet shadow. "My library is open to you whenever you should take a fancy to visit it," he offered graciously.

Kassandra smiled her thanks. She studied with interest the paintings, lustrous clusters of rock crystal displayed on marble pedestals, and alabaster statues he pointed out to her along the way, his comments punctuated by knowledgeable remarks from Rousseau. She had very much enjoyed her tour, even though it had passed so quickly, and truly hoped she would have occasion to visit the palace again.

Prince Eugene had shown her not only his magnificent library, which was filled from floor to ceiling with thousands of books bound in Moroccan and Turkish leather dyed red, blue, and yellow, but also three drawing rooms hung with portraits, both life-size and miniature, and the finest tapestries from Brussels. He had even allowed her a glimpse of the Blue Room, with its splendid furnishings upholstered in complementary shades of blue and turquoise, and the Golden Cabinet, its walls hung with shimmering gold brocade.

"And now, Lady Kassandra, I must take my leave," Prince Eugene murmured, with a courteous bow, at the entrance to the ballroom. "The banquet is soon to begin, and I must see that all is in readiness. Perhaps we may have a chance to converse again later in the evening."

He lifted her hand to his lips and lightly kissed her fingers. "You have been most charming, my lady," he added, his dark eyes twinkling kindly. "Count Stefan is a man to be envied. I must congratulate him on his excellent fortune."

Kassandra gazed after him as he moved away, followed by Rousseau after he, too, had expressed his pleasure in her company. The two distinguished men were immediately surrounded by other guests.

Congratulate Stefan? she wondered, mulling over his words. Surely he hadn't already told Prince Eugene of their marriage plans . . .

*His* marriage plans, she amended irritably, her gaze sweeping the ballroom. Blackguard! He had no right to discuss even the possibility of a wedding until they had received consent from her fath—

All thoughts fled her mind, her gaze widening in shock as it came to rest on Stefan. He was seated upon a wide divan, engrossed in conversation with a curvaceous dark-haired woman whose back was turned to her. She watched, motionless, her feet rooted to the floor, as he threw back his head and laughed at some private joke, then suddenly spied her across the room. After a quick word to the woman, he abruptly rose and strode toward her.

It was only when the woman rose as well, in a swirl of shimmering black satin, and began to follow him, that Kassandra recognized her. "Sophia," she whispered, her heart lurching within her breast, just as Stefan reached her side.

"Did you enjoy your tour?" he asked with some concern, noting the heightened color on her cheeks and the animosity simmering in her eyes. Strange, he thought fleetingly. Her expression was hardly what he would have expected, considering she had been so gay only a half hour past, when she had left with Prince Eugene.

"Perhaps not quite as much as you have enjoyed my absence," she replied cryptically, barely restraining her angry words. Damn him! It wasn't enough that he sought the company of his mistress virtually every night. Now he was flaunting their sordid relationship in her face so she would have no doubt as to her own role in his life.

What the devil could she have meant by that? Stefan wondered, puzzled. But Sophia's graceful approach prevented him from answering, much to his rising irritation.

"What a pleasure to see you again, Lady Kassandra," Sophia purred smoothly. Her careful expression was one of polite concern, but her almond eyes glinted harshly. "Stefan has told me of your narrow escape from serious harm at the theater yesterday afternoon." She leaned forward and lightly touched Kassandra's arm. "You must be watchful of Viennese carriage drivers, my dear," she murmured, shaking her head. "They are the most daring in the world, and the most skillful, but often foolhardy in their haste to reach a destination."

Kassandra shivered at her touch and stepped back. "I shall take your advice to heart, Archduchess von Starenberg," she said with a fixed smile, though her throat constricted painfully. "Now if you will both excuse me, I believe I shall find my place at the table. Prince Eugene has informed me the banquet is soon to begin."

With a stiff nod, she brushed by them and walked swiftly to the table, searching the gold engraved placards set beside each plate for her name. She was so intent in her task that she bumped headlong into

Count Frederick Althann as they both converged
upon the same chair.

"My apologies, my lady," he exclaimed, catching
her around the waist. Fighting to regain his own
balance, he brought her hard up against his chest,
one hand firmly grasping the back of the nearest
chair as his other arm held her tightly.

"Oh!" Kassandra gasped, blushing with acute
embarrassment. Yet she could not help thinking he
was amazingly strong, all vestiges of the effeminate
posturing he had displayed earlier now vanished.
Then, just as suddenly, he drew away from her,
fluttering his hands about his person, adjusting his
linen cravat, smoothing his waistcoat, and checking
the alignment of his wig, which had been knocked
slightly askew.

Kassandra stared up at him, both bemused and
intrigued. How odd, she thought, quickly regaining
her composure. She could almost swear this gentleman was pretending to be something he was not.

"I believe this seat is yours, my lady, not mine as
I had thought," Frederick offered, one red-heeled
shoe placed before the other as he bowed elegantly.
He pulled the cushioned chair away from the table,
waiting until she was seated before pulling out his
own and sitting down beside her. He pursed his lips
indignantly. "The servants have placed the placards
so close together, it's hardly clear which seat be-
longs to whom—"

"Please, it was a simple mistake," Kassandra interrupted, studying his features. "Don't trouble
yourself any further."

"You are most forgiving, my lady," Frederick
murmured, averting his eyes and fussing with the
napkin on his plate. Careful, man, he berated himself. This is the closest you have come to giving
yourself away . . .

He let out a breath. It was just his luck that he

was seated next to the most beautiful woman in the room, making his foppish role all the more difficult to play. He had seen the flash of intuition in Lady Kassandra's gaze when she looked at him a moment before. No doubt it would take all of his resources not to further arouse her suspicions, as well as keep his mind on his mission . . . to see and hear everything, and forget nothing.

Just think of the Sultan's gold, Frederick, he admonished himself sarcastically, with a faint smile. It always gets you through.

Kassandra started at the jarring sound of a chair scraping along the floor and turned her head, noting that Stefan was sitting across the wide table that separated them. Her face fired heatedly at his dark scowl, directed more at the gentleman on her left than at her, but it gave her an idea.

Two can play at your little game, Stefan von Furstenberg, she thought defiantly, pointedly ignoring him and turning back to Count Althann. She quickly appraised him. He was handsome enough, with his ice-blue eyes and angular features, as blond as Stefan was dark. Though she wasn't attracted to him, she could not deny that she sensed an air of mystery about him, as revealed to her during their mishap.

Not a lover . . . but an intriguing dinner partner, to be sure, she mused, leaning toward him and returning his smile.

Stefan stood at one end of the ballroom, watching in grim silence as two lines of couples met at the center of the polished floor where the table had been, now cleared away for the dancing that would last well into the evening. The lilting strains of a minuet floated through the air and the first dance began, the men bowing and advancing, the women retreating in a rustle of petticoats, silk, and satin. Then the women advanced, dipping and swaying, and joined hands with the men, each graceful turn punctuated by whispered compliments, furtive glances, and seductive smiles.

Stefan took a long swallow of brandy, his eyes darkened with fury. He briefly noted Sophia in the group of dancers, then dismissed her from his mind, his gaze moving instinctively to Kassandra. He followed her every movement, her lighthearted laughter ringing in his ears, as she stepped blithely from one gentleman to the next, finally arriving again at her original partner, Count Frederick Althann.

Stefan's hand tightened on the glass, his jaw set in anger. Damn it all! If Count Althann wasn't such a useless fop, he would have called him out at dinner and been done with it. But somehow he had restrained himself. He knew he could hardly test his sword against a man who was better known for his impeccable taste in clothes—and his rumored predilection for young boys, he thought with disgust—than his prowess with weapons.

Stefan's lips drew into a sardonic smile. He could not believe he was so jealous of such a man, if one could even call him that. But he was, painfully so. Or perhaps it was any man who looked at Kassandra with the slightest interest; he had certainly seen many occasions this night. It seemed she had charmed every gentleman at the gala, including his commanding general.

As she has never sought to charm you, he thought fiercely.

He quickly set down his glass for fear he might crush it in his hand. Try as he might, he could not suppress the feelings Kassandra roused in him, feelings of wild, extraordinary proportions. That she would bestow her vivacious charms, smiles, such precious laughter, on other men infuriated him beyond reason. Except for the brief period when they had first arrived at the gala, she had never granted him what she was so freely giving this night!

Women! He would never understand them. He had actually begun to think he had won her favor, then only the devil knew what had happened to cause her sudden change of heart. Now he was no longer sure of anything.

Except that she is playing you for a fool, he mused grimly. And he would know the reason . . .

Stefan strode toward the dancers, but a hand tugging on his arm stopped him. His eyes flashed angrily at this sudden hindrance, only to find Prince Eugene's personal chamberlain at his elbow.

"My lord, Prince Eugene must speak with you," Clemens whispered urgently, out of breath. "If you would follow me, he is waiting in his library."

Stefan nodded, and with a last glance over his shoulder at Kassandra, he left the ballroom. His expression was guarded as he entered the impressive library, for he surmised it could only be an important military matter that would draw his commander away from his guests. He noted the sodden and exhausted messenger standing at attention beside Prince Eugene's desk, confirming his suspicion.

"Forgive me for calling you away from the dancing, Count Stefan," Prince Eugene began, looking up from a letter spread before him. He indicated the messenger with a slight nod. "This man has just arrived from the winter camp. It seems Commander von Paar has been injured in a riding accident and must return to Vienna for immediate care. I want you to replace him as commander in chief."

Stefan's gaze widened imperceptibly, his mind working fast. He had already prepared to leave for the camp within the week to join his cavalry forces, and had even told Isabel as much. But he hadn't expected this! And he had yet to say anything to

Kassandra. Now there would be little time, if any, to discuss the matter.

"I accept with honor, General," he stated.

Prince Eugene studied him intently. "It is a heavy responsibility, Count Stefan, and usually reserved for an officer with more years under his belt. But you have proven your ability to command time and again with the cavalry. When I join you at the camp in early spring, I shall expect to find the men well trained and keen for battle."

"And so they will be. I shall leave this very night," Stefan said, already looking forward to the challenge.

"Tomorrow morning will be soon enough," Prince Eugene replied, rising to his feet. "The roads are far too treacherous by night." He turned to the messenger, a lad of scarcely seventeen years. "I commend you for your bravery, young man, riding well past sunset as you did to reach me with your message. So you say the wolves are fierce this winter?"

"Yes, General. They brought down my extra horse, and would have taken me down as well if I had not carried another pistol at the ready."

Prince Eugene patted him on the shoulder. He glanced at Stefan. "I'd say he would make a fine candidate for the cavalry, wouldn't you, Commander?"

"I shall consider him one of my own men from this day," Stefan agreed seriously, "for he certainly deserves it."

"Th-thank you, my lords," the lad stammered, a proud grin splitting his face as he looked from Prince Eugene to Stefan.

"Now, Clemens, see that he is fed and given a warm bed to sleep in," Prince Eugene told his chamberlain. "He will have a long ride back to the camp on the morrow, in the company of my esteemed commander in chief."

"Yes, my lord," Clemens replied with a bow. "Come with me, lad." He hastened from the library with the messenger at his heels.

Prince Eugene sat back down at his desk, perusing the papers before him. "It appears I must forgo my guests for a short while," he said matter-of-factly. "I must write some letters to the other officers at the camp, notifying them of my decision. They will follow your commands explicitly. I'll give them to you in the morning, before you set out. If you leave Vienna by eight o'clock, you should be at the camp by late afternoon."

He glanced up at Stefan, his serious expression softening. "Go and enjoy what is left of the evening, Count Stefan. No doubt Lady Kassandra is anxious for your return to the ballroom. I would not leave such a charming beauty waiting much longer."

Stefan winced, his thoughts flying back to Kassandra. What he would give if that were true. "Very well, my lord." He bowed, then turned and walked from the library. His footsteps echoed down the long hall as he made his way to the ballroom, a strange eagerness seizing him. It felt as if he had been away from her side for hours rather than a few moments. Now they had so little time left . . .

Familiar feminine laughter greeted him at the entrance to the ballroom, setting his pulse racing. But he stopped cold in his tracks at the sight of Kassandra surrounded by four young gentlemen, the ever-present Count Althann hovering close to her like a preening butterfly. She was smiling prettily at some remark, then out of the corner of her eye she spied him. She laced her arm through the nearest gentleman's, her lilting voice loud enough for him to hear.

"Of course I will dance with you, Count Bonneval, and the rest of you gentlemen, if you will only await your turns."

Damn it all, he had heard and seen enough! Ste-

fan raged, unreasoning jealousy seizing his heart
once again. He would not share the woman who
was to become his wife! He strode after them and
gripped Kassandra's arm just before she and her
companion joined the swirl of dancers.

"I believe you have reserved this dance for me,
Lady Kassandra," he muttered tersely, throwing a
dangerous look at the hapless gentleman at her side.

"In-indeed, Count von Furstenberg, I had no
idea," the stunned aristocrat acquiesced, stepping
back as if he had been stung. He bobbed his head
to Kassandra, then hurried away.

"How dare you," Kassandra gritted, though a
quiver of fear shot through her at the dark, storm-
tossed expression in his narrowed eyes. She bit her
lower lip to keep from crying out, his tight hold a
painful vise on her arm. "You're hurting me."

Stefan did not answer, merely steered her toward
the arched entrance to the ballroom. He would have
to offer his regrets to Prince Eugene in the morning,
but at least he now had another excuse besides Kassandra's wanton display for leaving the gala early.

"Where are we going? What about the gala?"
Kassandra whispered. Her cheeks fired with embarrassment at the inquisitive looks being cast their way
by guests—Count Althann, Count Bonneval, a sullen Sophia—and servants alike, and she said no
more, her eyes downcast.

Stefan ignored her, paying little heed that she had
to practically run to keep up with his long strides as
they hurried through the hallway and down the
winding staircase to the marble entrance hall. "Our
capes, man," he grated to the startled footman, who
quickly obliged them. "Go to the kitchen and tell
my driver we are leaving at once." The footman
nodded and fled down the corridor, holding on to
his wig.

They were ushered out the great doorway, a servant holding a lantern high as they made their way in the new-fallen snow to the carriage. By the time they were settled, with piles of warm furs wrapped around their legs and draped over their laps, the driver had hoisted himself into his seat and the carriage slid into the street, borne upon sleek wooden traineaus.

# Chapter 23

~~~~~~~ ∞ ~~~~~~~

**K**assandra's face burned with humiliation and fury, so much so that she kept her head turned away from Stefan during the entire journey. Her tear-glazed eyes stared blindly out the window at the darkened streets, then into the inky blackness of the forest along the road leading to the estate. She did not trust herself to speak. There was too much emotion, too much pain, welling up inside her, threatening a storm over which she would have no control.

The tension was palpable in the carriage, like a living presence between them. Stefan made little movement and no sound but for his steady breathing. Yet she could feel him watching her in the darkness, provoking shivers within her.

In the pressure of his muscled thigh against her own beneath the furs, the warmth of his body searing through her clothing, she could sense his tightly reined restraint. She chewed her lower lip, wishing desperately for the solace of her chamber and the safety of her doors bolted firmly against him.

At last the carriage came to a jarring halt. The flurry of neighing horses, footmen opening the door and lifting her to the ground, then assisting her up the steps to the front entrance, was a welcome diversion from the unnerving silence. She was grateful the hour was so late. She had no wish to face Isabel, or the prying Gisela. But no sooner had she shed her cape in the dimly lit foyer then Stefan took her arm once again and escorted her up the grand staircase and down the corridor to their adjoining chambers.

"Good night, Kassandra," he murmured tersely when they reached her door, his expression masked by the shadows filling the hall. "It has been a most pleasant evening."

Kassandra's throat constricted at his coldness. "M-my lord," she finally managed. She fumbled with the doorknob, then the door opened and she stepped inside with a sweeping sense of relief. She fairly slammed it in her haste to be free of his unsettling gaze, her fingers flying to the bolt and sliding it into place. She slumped against the door, scarcely breathing as she listened for the sound of Stefan's footsteps moving down the hall. But there were none.

Stefan's eyes narrowed furiously, the door slamming in his face a booming echo in his mind. Only her silence during the journey back to the estate had held his rage in check. Now, with this last act of defiance, he felt his temper finally snap.

"Open the door, Kassandra," he demanded, his voice low and menacing.

Stunned, Kassandra backed away from the door, slowly shaking her head with disbelief.

"I will not ask again, my lady," Stefan murmured vehemently, leaning his broad shoulder against the doorjamb. "The choice is simple. Open this door, or I will break it down." He laughed harshly. "Believe me, Kassandra, no bolt will keep me from you."

Kassandra's hand clutched at her throat, her mind racing wildly at his last words. But she had no more time to think as he tested the doorknob, still held fast against him.

"Very well—"

"No, wait!" she exclaimed, flying to the door. Her fingers shook uncontrollably as she withdrew the bolt, stark realization flooding through her that perhaps she had gone too far at the gala. Then the door swung open and she darted away, Stefan's powerful form filling the room where she had stood only a moment before. He closed the door firmly behind him, and bolted it.

Kassandra backed away as he moved slowly toward her, his striking features, set, implacable, illuminated in the pale moonlight streaming through her windows. It was then she recognized the scorching desire reflected in his gaze . . . the same look she remembered so vividly from the tavern, only heightened by flashing anger. Her worst fears were confirmed. Her limbs suddenly felt weak and she could not still her trembling. Her gaze skipped about the room for any means of escape, but there was none.

"Oh!" she gasped, backing into the divan placed near her bed. She scrambled around it, taking some fleeting comfort that there was an obstacle between them.

Stefan stopped his relentless advance, one hand resting on the back of the divan. His eyes raked over her. "Tell me, Kassandra," he breathed softly, belying the torment twisting within him. "What game have you been playing tonight . . . and with so many?"

Ire coursed through her, jolting the fear from her heart and giving her courage. Bastard! He spoke of games . . . to her! She drew herself up before him, her gaze meeting his with defiance. "Game, my lord?" she retorted, throwing all caution to the wind. "I play no game. I am merely exercising my prerogative to choose a lover. That is the custom in Vienna, is it not?''

Stefan's expression hardened, his jaw clenching perceptibly. But before he could reply, she rushed on breathlessly.

"From what I have seen, it's only fair. God knows to whose bed you ride out almost every night. Obviously you have your whores . . . your mistresses . . . that . . . that Sophia!'' she spat angrily. "I see no reason why I might not have a lover as well!''

Stefan exhaled sharply, momentarily confused. Sophia? What the devil could she mean by . . . ? Then suddenly it all made perfect sense to him. An amused smile tugged at his mouth, the anger ebbing from his body, overwhelmed by an emotion far more intense. He threw back his head and laughed deeply, loudly.

Kassandra stared at him in shock, hardly expecting this reaction. But she misread his mirth, thinking he was mocking her. "Don't let me keep you, my lord,'' she grated, her chin lifted truculently. "I have no doubt your mistress awaits you.'' Her eyes flickered toward the door. "Now get out of my room.''

Stefan's smile faded and he took a step toward her, glancing down at the divan blocking his way. Then he raised his head, his eyes glittering in the moonlight. "You are correct on one count, Kassandra,'' he murmured lightly. "I agree wholeheartedly that you should have a lover.''

"Y-you agree?'' Kassandra queried, astonished. She gaped at him, caught completely off guard by his unexpected acquiescence. And in that same moment, he shoved the divan roughly out of the way and caught her within his arms. He drew her against his chest, and though she struggled wildly, he held her fast.

"Yes,'' he whispered in her ear, his breath hot against her neck, "but I must tell you, Kassandra, your other accusations are way off the mark.'' He brought his hand up and tilted her chin so she would look at him. ''I have no mistress . . . not since we met that night in the garden. You are the only woman I desire, the only woman I long to possess.''

He paused, drawing a shuddering breath, his un-flinching gaze searing into the violet depths of her eyes. ''As to your other charge, you must be refer-ring to the nights I have spent alone at my hunting lodge, my only refuge against the torment of having you so close to me . . . wanting you, more than I have ever wanted any woman, while I have waited for that moment when you admit to the desire that is raging within you, a desire that is matched only by my own.''

''No . . .'' Kassandra whispered fiercely, tossing her head. ''No, it's not true. I hate you . . . despise you!'' She felt as if she were being ripped apart, long-repressed emotions welling up inside her, vivid memories of shared passion, shivering sensations . . . aching desire.

''It's true,'' Stefan insisted, drawing her closer, his powerful arms like bands of iron. ''For you have just revealed something to me this night, Kassandra, something I have not seen before,'' he murmured, stroking her hair, then running his finger lightly along her cheek. ''Your jealousy.''

Stunned, she renewed her struggles, kicking, lashing out with her arms, anything to be free of him. ''Blackguard! You're mad!'' she exclaimed, striking his chest with her doubled fists. But he eas-ily caught her hands and drew them behind her back, making her lithe body arch against his.

''And when there is jealousy, Kassandra . . . there is desire,'' he said softly, his eyes holding her own with an intensity that took her breath away. ''I know that because I, too, have felt unreasoning jealousy possess me tonight. I believe you want me now as much as I want you."

She shook her head, the fierce pounding of her heart a deafening roar in her ears. It seemed the room was crashing down around her, along with her will, her resolve to resist him. Nothing made sense anymore but the truth in his words, and the stirring power of his arms.

"Then deny it and I swear I will leave you," Stefan said abruptly, releasing her.

She fell back against the foot of the bed, groping for the corner post so she might regain her balance. Her breath tore at her throat, her breasts heaving against her taut bodice as she brought herself around to face him.

Sweet Lord, deny him! her inner voice screamed. Deny him! She met his eyes, and in that fleeting moment he knew . . . as she knew. She opened her mouth to speak, to cry out, but no words came.

Kassandra's hands slid limply down the corner post and she slumped to her knees, her gown fanning out around her. She bowed her head in defeat and sighed raggedly. She could no more deny him than she could deny she lived and breathed.

When Stefan bent over her and lifted her gently to her feet, she did not protest. The muscled strength of his arms around her once again thrilled her, and she returned his embrace, knowing she was lost . . . yet no longer caring. She lifted her head, her eyes meeting his, a mirror to his fervent desire. Then his lips touched her own, tentatively, sweetly, deepening into a kiss that seemed to draw her soul from her body.

"Kassandra, my only love," Stefan murmured huskily against her mouth, as she entwined her slim arms about his neck. They twirled slowly about in the center of the room, lost in their embrace, their solitary dance serenaded by moonlight and the rustle of satin.

Then his hands were sliding over her while his mouth continued its tender assault down her throat. He expertly unpinned the outer robe of her gown from her bodice and pulled it gently from her shoulders and arms, letting it drift to the floor in a cloud of sapphire blue and glinting silver threads. Then he deftly untied the drawstring of her satin overskirt, and next her hoopskirt. The heavy garments fell from the graceful curve of her hips and sank to the floor. All that was left were her stays, with the beribboned bodice pinned to its front, her stockings and satin shoes, and her linen drawers.

Stefan lifted Kassandra from the midst of her crumpled gown as easily as if she weighed nothing at all, holding her against his chest as he moved to the door adjoining their rooms. He unbolted the lock, pulled open the door, and crossed the threshold into his own chamber. Laying her gently on the great bed, he moved away for the briefest moment, quickly kicking off his boots and stripping away his clothing.

Kassandra watched through eyes half-closed with passion as Stefan's magnificent body was revealed to her, a ruggedly powerful silhouette in the flood of moonlight from the tall windows. Then he was sitting beside her, and she rose up to meet him, her arms once again weaving about his neck as his strong hands caressed her. She shivered deliciously as his fingers crept beneath the stiff fabric of her stays to the curve of her waist, exploring a silken path to the small of her back, where he reached up and around and quickly untied the laces, flinging them with her bodice to the floor.

"Lie back, my love," Stefan murmured thickly, kneeling over her as she sank languidly against the down pillows. He kissed the tempting hollow be-

tween her breasts, their taunting beauty at last bared
to his torrid gaze. He eased off her shoes and unrolled her stockings from her long legs, his feather-
light touch sending shivers of anticipation through
her body. She caught a glimpse of a roguish smile,
a flash of white in the shadows, as he tossed her
hose playfully over his shoulder, then bent his dark
head to grasp the delicate laces of her drawers with
his teeth, untying the tiny bows one by one.

Kassandra arched against the tingling warmth of
his breath playing across her skin, impatient to be
free of this last vestige of clothing. Stefan seemed to
sense her thoughts. In one swift movement he
slipped the drawers from her body and cast them to
the end of the bed, then stretched his hard-muscled
length atop her and captured her mouth with his
own.

It was a savage kiss, possessive, all-encompassing,
as Stefan sought to slake his driving need, too long
denied. He rolled onto his back, pulling Kassandra
with him, his fingers freeing the silver combs and
ribbons from her hair and entwining in the fire-gold
mass cascading about them like a gossamer veil.

A low moan escaped Kassandra's throat as her re-
pressed desire for this man exploded within her, and
she returned his kiss deliriously. Her moan suddenly became a gasp of pleasure as his warm mouth
moved down her throat, across her smooth shoulder, seeking her breasts.

He nibbled at the pouting nipples, flicking them
with his moist tongue, suckling lingeringly, exulting
in the sweetness of her skin, and marveling that
there could ever have been a woman fashioned as
beautifully as she.

Kassandra knelt above him, her thighs hugging
his tapered hips, the swell of her womanhood
pressed against the hardness of his desire. A flutter
in her belly surged outward through her limbs, a

tightening, a hunger building up inside her that she knew only he could fulfill. She trembled, her hands resting on the sculpted span of his chest, her fingers enmeshed in the dark mat of curls. She reveled in the sinewy strength of his battle-hardened muscles, rippling beneath her palms with his slightest movement.

Then he was lifting her from him and she felt strangely bereft, moaning the loss of the overwhelming sensations, only to find herself suddenly impaled upon his thrusting manhood. He filled her completely, and an impassioned cry tore from her throat as he began to move within her, slowly at first, then faster, his large hands gripping her to him, urging her on with sweet words and whispers, her name a caress upon his lips.

Kassandra arched against him, again and again, panting breathlessly, her skin bathed in a fine wash of perspiration as he sought to lose himself within the soft warmth of her body. She felt him tremble beneath her, heard him groan with passionate urgency, then she knew nothing more as jagged streaks of light burst before her closed eyelids, her mind, body, her very soul lost in the shuddering rapture that enveloped her. She cried out, dragging her nails across his chest, and felt his own throbbing release deep within her, as he pulled her to him, crushing her lips with his own.

They clung together for a long time, drawing breath after ragged breath, a tangle of limbs and flaming hair. Then Stefan gently rolled to his side, bringing her with him, and stroked the sleek line of her hips while she rested peacefully with her head nestled on his shoulder. He gazed down at her face, swathed in moonlight, his heart aching with love for this one woman.

He knew he was hardly sated. He would rouse her soon, even now his overwhelming desire for her was rekindling in his loins. He had no doubt that this storm of passion finally unleashed between them—wild, shared, freely given—would rage well into the night, even until the first rays from the rising sun streaked the morning sky.

# Chapter 24

**K**assandra's eyes flickered half-open and she brought her arms above her head, stretching languorously. She yawned, covering her mouth with the back of her hand, then smiled contentedly and closed her eyes again. She rolled to her side, fitting her hands under her chin, and snuggled into the downy warmth of the bedding. Sighing softly, she felt sleep stealing over her once more, seducing her, lulling her . . .

"A good morning to you, milady," Berdine said cheerfully, bustling into the room with a silver tray laden with a steaming teapot, toasted bread slathered with butter and honey, and two boiled eggs set in a china bowl that rattled against the delicate teacup and saucer. Humming a lilting tune, she set the tray on a small table near the bed and moved to the window, drawing aside the lacy curtains.

Kassandra's eyes flew wide open, her brow knit in confusion. Where was she? she wondered hazily, her thoughts muddled with fragments of dreams and whispered memories. She was in Stefan's room, wasn't she? A sudden wave of panic gripped her. Dear God, Berdine had found her in his bed!

Kassandra sat up abruptly, her unfocused gaze darting about the bright room, decorated in feminine shades of rose, cream, and pale lavender. With a start she realized she was in her own chamber. She sank back onto the bed, relieved yet still bewildered.

"Or perhaps I should say 'good afternoon' to you," Berdine said, giggling.

"W-what time is it?" Kassandra murmured, almost afraid to ask.

"Why, three o'clock, milady. Prince Eugene's gala must truly have been grand to keep you up till all hours. You've slept through two meals this day." She set the pot down upon the tray. "It was Countess Isabel who decided I should wake you."

Berdine plopped the silver tea ball into the cup, glancing over her shoulder while she allowed the tea to steep. "I would have come to your room to help you undress, milady, however late, if you had only called me," she apologized, her gaze shifting back to Kassandra. "But it appears to me you had no trouble at all, even with your stays."

Kassandra sat up at this statement, her eyes widening at the sight of her gown—overskirt, hoopskirt, stockings, everything!—neatly draped over the divan, which was set exactly where it should be, at the foot of her bed. Even her satin shoes were placed toe to toe near her closet. She shivered despite the warmth of her linen nightgown.

Nightgown! Kassandra's glance fell to the fine lace garment, her cheeks flushing heatedly. She had no recollection of donning a nightgown . . . Her gaze flew to the door adjoining her chamber with Stefan's. It was bolted securely, as if it had never been opened.

"Now lean back, milady, and I'll hand you your tea," Berdine murmured, plumping up the large down pillows.

Kassandra did as she was told, her mind racing. Surely she hadn't imagined last night, she thought dazedly. A blush crept across her skin as a secret smile touched her lips. No, never in her wildest dreams could she have envisioned such a night . . . or such a lover.

"I hope the tea is to your liking, milady," Berdine said, handing the teacup to her carefully. She slid the table a little closer to the bed. "And the cook made a nice breakfast for you." She paused, smiling. "Well, brunch, that is. Now then, will there be anything else?"

"No. This is wonderful, Berdine, thank you," Kassandra replied. She blew gently on the surface of her tea, then took a sip. It was one of her favorites, sweet cinnamon.

"Very well, milady. I will return in a short while and prepare your bath. The water should be just about heated in the kitchen." Berdine bobbed a short curtsy, then hurried from the room and closed the door behind her.

Kassandra took another sip of tea, her gaze sweeping the room. There could only be one explanation. Stefan must have carried her into her chamber while she slept, slipped a nightgown over her head, and tucked her into bed, then arranged her clothing to look as if she had done so herself. He knew as well as she the impropriety of being found sharing a bed together, despite their plans for marriage.

Their plans for marriage . . . Funny, she mused. For the first time, the thought of marrying Stefan did not rankle. She set the teacup on the tray and rested her head against the pillow, closing her eyes. She tentatively touched her lips, still tender from the fiery passion of his kiss, her skin tingling with vibrant memories of his embrace.

A warm sense of fulfillment welled up inside her. It enveloped her completely, and she sighed, recalling the male scent of him, the taste of his mouth, the rough texture of his skin, the giddy excitement whenever his eyes, startling in their gray depths, caught and held her own. And most of all, his words of love and desire, thrilling her still as they echoed in her mind. He had called her his only love . . .

Kassandra's eyes drifted open and she gazed at the bolted door with a glimmer of hope. Perhaps it might be possible for them to find some happiness together after all, she considered, despite what had gone before. She could no longer deny to herself, or him, that she yearned for him with a passion beyond her understanding.

Perhaps what they had shared the night before signified a new beginning. She could not help wondering if there might be something more between them than desire, something not yet touched upon . . .

A soft rap at the door dispelled her thoughts. Could it be Stefan? She smoothed the coverlet and ran trembling fingers through her tangled hair, feeling as foolish as a blushing girl half her age.

"Come in," she called breathlessly.

Berdine opened the door. "I've summoned your bath, milady."

Kassandra could barely mask her disappointment. "Thank you, Berdine," she murmured, sinking back against the pillows. Ah, well, she would go and find him when she was finished with her bath and dressed. She waited until the maidservants had filled the porcelain tub, set near the decorative heating stove in one corner of the room, before she threw back the coverlet and swung her feet to the floor.

Berdine arranged the painted screen around the tub to afford Kassandra some privacy as she stripped off her nightgown, pinned up her hair, and stepped into the steaming water. She bathed hurriedly, much to the surprise of the young maid, who was used to her lingering over her bath. Then she was out of the tub and buffing herself dry with a thick towel as she walked to the closet, leaving a trail of wet footprints upon the carpet.

Kassandra dressed with unusual care in an emerald silk morning gown. Sitting impatiently at her dressing table, she bade Berdine not to bother overmuch with her long hair. A few simple brushstrokes soon had it gleaming with brilliant highlights, and two gold combs, her only decoration, swept the heavy mass away from her forehead. She donned a pair of soft slippers and skipped lightly toward the door.

"But milady, what about your meal?" Berdine asked, glancing at the untouched tray.

"I'm not really hungry," she called over her shoulder as she left the room. "But if you would like, Berdine, you're welcome to it."

Kassandra paused in the corridor, looking both ways before reaching a decision. Instead of walking toward the staircase, she turned in the other direction, stopping when she came to Stefan's door.

She tested the doorknob, unable to resist the urge to see if he was in his chamber. The door opened easily and she peeked inside, but the room was empty. She began to close the door, but her curiosity got the better of her and she ventured inside. She had never seen his chamber before last night, and she was not surprised she could remember little about it.

The brightly lit room was extremely large, with a massive fireplace at one end. It was sparsely furnished, almost spartan, the great bed near the tall windows the dominant feature in the room. Her skin heated like wildfire as she drew closer, running her hand along the brocade bedspread. She could almost sense Stefan's presence there, vivid images of the night before flashing through her mind. She closed her eyes, remembering. A long time passed before she left the room, her breath caught in her throat, fearful that one of the servants might find her there.

Kassandra hurried past her door and continued down the hallway, her steps light and buoyant. She felt happier than she had in months. She almost ran down the stairs, checking first his library, which was dark and empty, then the dining room. But there was no sign of Stefan, or anyone else for that matter. Next she tried the kitchen, but its only occupants were the cook and several maidservants, busily preparing the evening meal. Last she tried the drawing room, nearly colliding with Isabel as she pushed open the door.

"Kassandra!" Isabel gasped, stepping back in surprise, the letters she had been holding now scattered on the floor. But she merely laughed, a pretty smile lighting her features. "I was beginning to wonder if you were going to spend the entire day abed." She bent down and began to pick up her letters, and Kassandra knelt by her side to help.

"Forgive me, Isabel," she began, rising and handing over several crisp packets. "The gala went much later than I had imagined—"

"So Stefan told me," Isabel interjected. "But come and sit down, and tell me everything." She settled in a soft armchair near the harpsichord while Kassandra pulled out the high-backed chair in front of the writing cabinet. "I had hoped to hear more from him, but he was in such a hurry to be on his way this morning."

Kassandra glanced up sharply as she took her seat. "On his way?"

"Yes. He left for the winter camp of the Imperial army, a day's ride from here. But of course, you know all about it, Kassandra. So tell me, was the gala absolutely splendid? If only I hadn't been plagued by that awful headache. I would have loved to have been there."

"What winter camp?" Kassandra asked softly, suddenly finding it difficult to breathe.

Isabel leaned forward in her chair. "Stefan did not tell you?"

Kassandra shook her head, twisting the silken fabric of her skirt.

"Why, just yesterday morning he said he'd be leaving in about a week. He knows how much I dislike to see him go, so he always waits until the last moment to tell me anything. Then last night, Prince Eugene told him he had to leave much earlier than expected. But I cannot believe he didn't mention all this to you."

Isabel shrugged her delicate shoulders, sighing deeply. "Men and their unfathomable passion for war," she murmured. "They seem to think of little else." She quickly explained the camp's purpose, then rushed on. "All Stefan really told me was they are beginning preparations for the summer campaign against the Turks. But where the Imperial army will strike, and when, is a most closely guarded secret."

"How long will he be gone?" Kassandra queried, her gaze focused blindly on some point in front of her, a hard lump in her throat.

"Until early spring, I believe," Isabel replied. She patted Kassandra's hand, noting with dismay that it was ice-cold. "I'm truly sorry, Kassandra, that Stefan didn't tell you. As I said, he had originally planned to leave at the end of the week, but then the most unexpected thing happened last night at the gala. He was named commander in chief of the camp—well, at least temporarily, until Prince Eugene takes full command in the spring. I'm so proud of him. It's quite an honor. Perhaps his mind was so full of his duties and responsibilities—"

"Of course, that must be it." Kassandra fixed a smile upon her face as she squeezed Isabel's hand.

"I'm sure he will write a letter, and explain everything."

"Oh, I know he will," Isabel agreed, relieved that she was taking the news so well. Though for the life of her, she could not imagine why Stefan had neglected to apprise Kassandra of his plans. It was so thoughtless of him.

Isabel paced the floor excitedly. "But we shall have a marvelous time together, you and I, and the days will pass so quickly, he will be back before we know it. And there is so much to do before your wedding . . . I mean, there's certainly no harm in beginning some preparations, Kassandra, your gown, your trousseau." She paused, sighing. "I haven't received a single reply yet from Miles to any of my letters, and heaven only knows if he has even received them due to this nasty winter and all the snow. But I believe the last of our worries should be receiving his consent to your marriage."

Isabel glanced down at the letters clutched in her hand. "Speaking of which, I must have Zoltan take these into Vienna and post them for me at once." She hurried to the door. "I'll be back in a moment, Kassandra," she called over her shoulder. "Say a prayer that one of these letters reaches your father." Then she was gone.

Kassandra sat motionless in her chair, silence descending over the room like a suffocating vapor. So Stefan had known he was leaving . . . and hadn't bothered to tell her. Cold fury welled up inside her. Not even last night, when they lay in each other's arms after . . . after . . .

"Damn you to hell, Stefan von Furstenberg!" Kassandra raged under her breath, rising to her feet so suddenly that the chair fell to the carpeted floor with a resounding thud. She stormed to the window, her arms clasped tightly to her chest as she stared out across the snow-covered lawn.

It was all so painfully clear, she thought bitterly, swallowing hard against the tears stinging her eyes. Obviously she was good enough to bear the brunt of his endearing lies . . . and his lust, but hardly worth including in other facets of his life!

Kassandra felt almost a physical pain as the promising notions she had entertained so briefly vanished from her mind like whispering phantoms. It was just as Stefan had said. He had need of a wife, an heir. It was only her body he was interested in, not her. She meant nothing to him. Nothing.

Another wrenching thought struck her. The bastard! Maybe last night was merely a cruel ploy to hasten along his desire for an heir!

Kassandra wiped the tears rolling down her face with the back of her hand. What a fool she was! For a few fleeting hours she had actually believed Stefan cared for her. She could have sworn she saw some affection in his eyes, felt it in his caress, heard it in his whispered words of passion. But it was all an illusion, a heartless play on her emotions, a calculated ploy to get what he wanted from her.

Well, damn him, she would not be so easily deceived again, no matter what he might say or do! When he returned from this camp of his, she would give him a welcome he would not soon forget.

# Chapter 25

**"A**lert me at once when Prince Eugene arrives at the camp," Stefan ordered of his aide, who was standing at rigid attention in front of the plain wooden table strewn with papers and maps.

"Yes, Commander," the young officer replied with an eager bow of his head. He wheeled smartly and strode from the room, his spit-polished boots black and gleaming.

Stefan sat back in his chair, barely suppressing a grin. For the life of him he could not imagine how his new aide, the middle son of an archduke, kept his boots so clean. The camp was a sea of mud, brought on by the spring thaw and torrential rains that had plagued them for several weeks now.

Stefan toyed absently with his ink pen, wondering if he had ever been as green as that newly recruited soldier. Probably, he mused with a short laugh. No doubt he, too, had been overly enthusiastic, anxious to please, reveling in the pomp and grandeur of military life, the parades, the pageantry.

His expression darkened. That had ended soon enough with his first battle, his true initiation into the startling realities of his profession. He could recall all too well his brash exhilaration and hotheaded bravado, soon tempered by scenes of brutal war. Each successive battle had transformed him gradually into the seasoned soldier he had become—what his young aide would have to become if he was to survive.

A knock on the door broke into his grim thoughts. "Enter," Stefan called out, leaning forward in his chair.

A mud-splattered courier stepped into the room, wiping his damp, dirtied face with his cap. "I have brought the mail from Vienna, Commander von Furstenberg," he said.

"Good. Set it here," Stefan replied, clearing a place amidst the stack of papers. The courier quickly obliged him, dropping the leather bag atop the table and unfastening the metal buckles. He threw open the flap and dumped a pile of letters and several rolled documents in front of Stefan, then brought the emptied bag up under his arm. "That's all I have, sir," he murmured.

"You'll find a warm meal in the cooking tent, a short walk from here. Have one of the men show you the way," Stefan said, dismissing him with a nod.

"My thanks, Commander." The courier quickly left the room, his stomach growling hungrily, visions of salt pork, boiled potatoes, and good, strong beer urging him on.

Stefan set aside the rolled documents, deciding he would look at them later. He sorted through the letters, searching for any familiar handwriting. He was nearly to the bottom of the pile when he spied a letter from Isabel, and though he was pleased to receive it, he could not help feeling keen disappointment that there was nothing from Kassandra.

He grimaced. He was hardly surprised. She hadn't answered any of his letters these past two months, his only word of her having come through Isabel's frequent missives. Isabel had regaled him with myriad details of how they spent their days, their shopping trips into the city, visiting this milliner or that dressmaker, searching out the perfect point lace, or the most exquisite fabric. There had been occasional galas, usually only Isabel in attendance, and quiet evenings spent in his library, she at her needlework, Kassandra curled up in a chair, reading. In last week's letter had come unexpected word that Miles Wyndham would be returning to Vienna in early April.

All of this hardly whetted Stefan's appetite for the news he was craving, news only Kassandra could afford him. How was she spending her time when Isabel was away from the estate? Was she riding the Arabian mare he had given her, walking in the woods? Was she thinking of him with loving thoughts, as he hoped, or angry thoughts, as her lack of correspondence seemed to suggest?

"Enough with torturing yourself," Stefan muttered under his breath, glancing down at the letter in his hand. He broke the wax seal with his thumb and slit open the crisp packet with a thin-bladed silver opener, then drew the folded letter from the envelope. It was dated only three days ago. A faint smile touched his lips as he read Isabel's affectionate salutation, but it faded abruptly, his brow furrowed into a frown, his hand clenching the ivory paper.

"What the devil," he exclaimed, reading the body of the letter with heated intensity.

She and Kassandra could have been killed . . . Their carriage had suddenly lost a wheel and overturned in a ditch along the road leading to the estate . . . Zoltan was thrown to the ground and severely injured . . . The two horses, horribly maimed, were shot dead where they lay . . .

Stefan read on in disbelief. Isabel's handwriting, usually so graceful, was a blotted scrawl, as if she had written not long after the terrifying incident she was so vividly describing. But her last paragraph calmed him somewhat, filled with assurances that she and Kassandra were fine, though bruised and badly shaken, and closing with a fervent wish that he return home soon.

Stefan set the letter down and leaned his head in his hands. Gut-wrenching emotions assailed him—worry, helplessness, frustration—and overwhelming relief that they were unharmed. He sighed heavily. He had wished so many times he could be there, now, after this letter, more than ever. But he could not return to Vienna until Prince Eugene relieved him of his duties at the winter camp, duties that were becoming increasingly difficult to concentrate on. It had been so long since he had seen Kassandra and held her in his arms, her jasmine-scented hair and her silken skin enveloping his senses . . .

Suddenly he brought his fist down hard upon the table, the sound reverberating through the sparsely furnished room. Damn it, man, you cannot allow your personal desires to overrule your sense of duty, he berated himself fiercely. Yet even as he tried to force her from his mind, she was there, like a vision before him.

"Kassandra . . ." he murmured under his breath, closing his eyes so he could see her more clearly. She had bewitched his thoughts as surely as she had captured his heart.

Everything about her haunted his memory—her rich voice, her singular beauty, her wit and intelligence, her indomitable spirit. He could not forget how she had looked the morning he left for the camp . . . with the dawn light spilling across her pillow, her flaming tresses flecked with gold, and a soft smile curving her lips as she lay sleeping peacefully. How he had longed to wake her and tell her he was leaving and why, but most important of all, how much he loved her. Yet something had stopped him.

Stefan opened his eyes and stared blindly at the

letter, his feelings at that moment rushing back to him. Even on the battlefield he had never felt so vulnerable. He had so much to tell her, so much to explain, and there had been so little time. How could he make sense of what lay deepest in his heart, in the few precious moments before he had to set out for Vienna, then the winter camp?

And he had been afraid. Afraid that after declaring his love, she would still denounce him. Even after the night they had shared, after she had at last admitted her desire for him, perhaps nothing, not even his love, could erase what had happened between them at the tavern or how relentlessly he had pursued her, forcing her into a marriage she did not want.

Finally he had left her room, unable to bear the thought that she might refuse his love. He wanted to remember her as she was, sated from the heat of passion, his name, cried out during their sweetest release, upon her lips.

Perhaps his fears had been justified all along, Stefan thought dully, rubbing his forehead. Perhaps what had stopped him was the very reason she refused to answer his letters, even that first one, in which he had poured out his soul . . .

Stefan's jaw tightened in determination. No, he would not believe it until he spoke with her face-to-face! Whatever her reasons for not answering his letters, he was not prepared to give up so easily. Especially now, when after being away from her for two interminable months, he had reached a decision that might finally sway her heart in his favor.

"Commander, Prince Eugene and his retinue have been sighted just beyond the camp. He will be here shortly," the aide blurted as he burst in the door, his loud voice jarring rudely into Stefan's thoughts.

"Don't you know enough to knock, man?" Stefan demanded, then softened his tone at the young officer's crestfallen look. He rose from his chair. "Is all in readiness?"

The aide brightened visibly, snapping to attention. "Yes, Commander. The trumpets are sounding and the pennants are raised. All other commanders have been alerted, and their soldiers are joining ranks at this very moment."

"Very good," Stefan said, striding from the room and through the narrow foyer, then down the front steps of his quarters, with the aide not far behind him. He stepped into the bright afternoon sunlight, his keen eyes surveying the scene before him.

Uniformed men were rushing into formation from all directions of the camp, streaming from tents, long-timbered barracks, even from the muddy parade fields where they had been practicing drills. It took only a few moments for everyone to scramble into line, each man in his place, row upon dark blue row, regiments of cavalry atop their mounts and infantry alike at stiff attention.

Brightly colored pennants flapped in the cool March breeze. Horses neighed and snorted impatiently. An expectant hush hung in the air, for Prince Eugene was coming to take command of his Imperial army, in preparation for the summer's campaign against the Turks.

Stefan mounted Brand and took the reins from his nervous aide, who was doing his best to hide his fear of the mighty war-horse. A fine candidate for the infantry, he thought dryly, as he was soon flanked by generals from the various contingents of the army. They set out along the puddled road between the long, broad lines in formation to meet their commander in chief, just now passing through the guarded entrance to the camp.

"Sound the cannonade!" Stefan roared above the stillness, his voice echoed by thundering blasts from eighty cannon. The heavy artillery pieces were quickly reloaded, then fired three more times, the steady beating of drums filling in the intervals between each grand salute.

Prince Eugene drew closer, riding well in front of his plumed retinue on a prancing white stallion. Resplendent in a navy uniform edged with gold braid, he radiated supreme confidence despite his slight figure. His dark eyes swept from side to side, proudly but solemnly surveying his forces. He reined in his mount as Stefan rode up alongside him, acknowledging his approach with a bow of his head.

"You have done exceedingly well, Count Stefan," he said seriously, meeting his gaze. "The men look fit and ready to fight."

"My thanks, General," Stefan replied. "But it is the men who are to be commended. They have been training long and hard since the worst of the winter subsided. They know well the strength of their enemy."

Prince Eugene nodded gravely, always one to identify with the common soldier. He had worked his way up through the ranks and considered himself one of them. He was even known to sleep upon the ground wrapped in a soldier's cloak, and not for lack of better lodging.

"And so they shall be commended," he agreed, raising his voice to be heard. "See that each man is given double his monthly pay, on behalf of our gracious emperor! And spare no meat this night, nor brandy. We shall feast in honor of our enemy, who await their defeat!"

A great roar went up from the men nearby, and for those who hadn't yet heard, shouts echoing his words passed along the formation like wildfire. Soon the entire camp resounded with cheers and hurrahs, drawing the faintest of smiles to Prince Eugene's thin lips. He turned once again to Stefan.

"You know as well as I that there is much to be

done, more training, more preparation, before we set out for Belgrade in May. Ride with me now to the council hall, then summon every commanding officer. The men may feast, but we have much to discuss tonight.''

Stefan nodded, reining Brand in alongside Prince Eugene's white stallion. Soon they were joined by other commanders, forming a long procession as they rode toward the council hall in the center of the camp.

Yet even amidst the clamor and excitement, Stefan's thoughts flew unbidden to Kassandra, never far from his mind, and always within his heart. As he rode beside his general, he resolved then and there that he would request a few weeks leave as soon as their initial meetings were completed. He had to talk to her at once, before her father returned from Hanover, and tell her of his love . . . and his decision.

For it was his plan to release her from her promise to marry him. He would rather risk losing her, and perhaps gain her love, than force her to go through with their marriage, and earn only her hate.

# Chapter 26

~~~~~~~~~~~~~~~~~~~~

**"A** ride, Kassandra? But it looks as if it might storm this morning," Isabel murmured doubtfully, her hand falling from the lace curtain at one of the tall windows flanking the front entranceway. "And I can't imagine you would even consider climbing atop a horse. I'm so stiff and sore, I can barely walk without cringing." Truly, Isabel thought, it was taking her much longer to mend from that carriage accident last week than she had imagined.

Kassandra pulled on her riding gloves, then glanced up at Isabel. "I'm feeling much better today, Isabel, really," she insisted. "And it's the first morning it hasn't been raining for weeks now. I'll only be gone for a short while." She smiled away the footman and opened the door for herself. "Now go and sit down. The physician said you must rest as much as possible."

Isabel sighed. "Very well, but if it begins to storm, you will come back at once?"

Kassandra nodded, a reassuring smile upon her lips. "Rest, Isabel," she admonished gently. "Father will be most displeased to find you still limping about—"

"All right, I'm convinced," Isabel interjected with a laugh. As she watched Kassandra walk down the

227

front steps, a sudden thought struck her. "I know it's only the first day of April, so it might still be too early, but if you see any wildflowers, you must bring me some," she called out.

Kassandra waved and set out along the muddy path leading to the stable, swinging her arms. It felt so good to be outdoors! She took in great breaths of the moist air, tinged with the fresh scent of green grass and damp, musty earth. The water-soaked ground squished under her boots, and birds trilled gaily in the budding trees, sounds that delighted her. They meant the coming of spring, her favorite time of year.

Yet this year was different, she reminded herself. Spring also meant her father's imminent arrival, hastening the wretched marriage that loomed before her like an inescapable trap.

No! She would not think about it, at least not this morning. She walked determinedly toward the stable, smiling once again as Hans, the stableboy who saw to her mare, rushed out to greet her. He was nearly a full head taller, and she marveled anew at how much he had grown over the long winter.

"Good morning to ye, milady," he exclaimed, doffing his cap. He ran his hand self-consciously through his unruly light brown hair, a warm blush burning his freckled cheeks. "Shall I saddle yer fine mare?"

"Yes, Hans, if it will be no trouble for you," she murmured, noting with faint amusement how he stared at her with guileless admiration.

"No trouble at all, milady," he replied eagerly, dashing into the stable. "I'll bring her out to ye."

Kassandra leaned against a splintered fence post, humming a tune while she absently smoothed the light woolen skirt of her riding habit. It seemed only a few moments passed before Hans was leading the spirited mare into the stable yard.

"She's a beauty, that she is," Hans said soothingly, running his hand along the mare's glistening
white flank. The animal nickered, tossing its head
and flipping its long, silky tail. One front hoof dug
impatiently into the damp earth. "But a spitfire, to
be sure. She bit poor Penn in the seat of his breeches
t'other day, whilst he was shoveling feed into her
trough."

Kassandra gasped. "Is he all right?" she asked,
barely suppressing a giggle behind her gloved hand
as she envisioned the awkward scene.

"Oh, aye, milady, he's fine," Hans said, "except
for sittin' down." He laughed and held the mare
steady while Kassandra hoisted herself into the sidesaddle. He then handed her the reins. "Best to hold
her in for a ways, milady, before ye give her full
rein," he cautioned. "She may be a bit skittish this
morning. Remember, she's not been rid since last
month, only set free to run in the paddock every
day."

"I'll heed your advice, Hans," Kassandra said,
drawing up the reins. Her tone grew serious.
"How's Zoltan faring?"

"He's better, milady, though his leg will take a
good while to mend, or so the physician says. It was
a bad fall."

"Yes, it was," Kassandra agreed, shuddering at
the memory of that day. "Well, give him my fond
greetings," she murmured. "And tell him if there is
anything he needs, he must send word to the countess or myself at once."

"Aye, milady." Hans bobbed his head as Kassandra nudged the mare with her boot, and they set
out at a trot across the stable yard. "Enjoy yer ride,"
he called, waving his cap.

Kassandra steered the mare out onto the road
leading from the estate, but it was nothing more than
a rutted mire. She decided to ride out across the

unplowed fields instead, where the short grasses had hopefully absorbed the worst of the recent rainfall. She bit her lower lip against the pain jolting through her bruised right leg as the mare jumped across a shallow ravine. She eased the mare into a walk while she massaged her thigh.

She flinched as she touched a sore spot. Obviously she was not quite as recovered as she had thought. The purplish green bruises had finally faded to a faint brown, but the dull pain still lingered. And if she hurt even this much, she could well imagine how Isabel must feel.

The countess had borne the brunt of the accident. She had been sitting on the far side of the carriage when it lost a wheel and toppled down the embankment, and she was thrown against the right door. Kassandra had escaped worse injury by being shoved roughly into the padded wall next to her seat, bumping her head and bruising the right side of her body. The physician had marveled that they had escaped with their lives, surmising that Isabel would have suffered far more but for the protection of the stiff whalebone hoopskirt, which had cushioned her fall. One good thing he could say for the preposterous contraptions!

It was all Stefan's fault, Kassandra thought irritably. If he hadn't insisted on forcing her into this marriage, they would never have gone to the city that day to look for fabric . . . for a wedding gown.

She frowned. It had been hard enough to block Stefan from her mind without Isabel talking of wedding preparations all the time, which she had done constantly since his departure for the winter camp. Now Kassandra had this nagging pain to remind her of him.

And the stack of unopened letters lying in the bottom of her drawer, Kassandra amended darkly. Letters she had not allowed herself to read for fear of being swayed by his lies. She had done her best to harden her heart against him, and had succeeded for the most part. Until night fell, when she would lie awake in her bed, the heavy silence emanating from his adjoining chamber almost more than she could bear. It was then she could not deny to herself how much she truly missed him, with a poignant ache deep within her that she could not quell.

It had become almost a nightly ritual. She would leave her bed and walk to her armoire, open the drawer, and pull out the pile of letters, held together by a delicate red ribbon. She would stand there in the darkness and stare at them for the longest time, wondering what he could possibly have to say to her that would warrant so much correspondence.

Then, with a ragged sigh, she would set them resolutely back in the drawer, seeking once again the solace of her bed. Sleep would elude her until the early hours of the morning, tormenting thoughts of Stefan, and their last night together, burning like a firebrand into her mind. Sheer exhaustion was her only release, pulling her at last into dreamless slumber.

Suddenly the mare stopped in her tracks, her sharp, nervous whinny breaking into Kassandra's disturbing reverie.

"What is it, girl?" she murmured, gazing along the thick line of trees bordering the open field. She saw nothing, only the branches swaying in the wind, which had picked up slightly. She turned in the saddle and looked over her shoulder, but again there was nothing, the empty field stretching out behind them, a carpet of velvet green against the clouded sky, the road they had left a tiny black ribbon wending back to the estate.

Kassandra faced forward again and patted the mare's silken neck. "There now, you see, it's nothing," she said reassuringly. But she started when a

covey of blackbirds, flapping and cawing, were
flushed from a nearby tree. They hovered above
them ominously, circling, then flew off across the
sky.

Perhaps it was a deer, she thought, willing her
body to relax. Or a fox, stalking along the ground
for its next meal, or some other harmless forest creature. She clucked her tongue, and they set out once
more across the field.

Kassandra nudged the mare's flank, urging her
into a gallop. The pain of her bruises was forgotten
as they flew across the fields, her waist-length hair
streaming out behind her, her cheeks flushed with
exhilaration. An occasional shaft of sunlight broke
through the heavy gray clouds, lending a hazy
golden sheen to the scenery. The sheer beauty of it
enlivened her spirits, and she laughed. And when
they had come to the end of the fields she plunged
the mare into the forest, a netherworld of shadow
and light. The hushed stillness was broken only by
the crackling of underbrush beneath the mare's
flashing hooves, and her own panting breaths.

They rode on and on, sometimes slowing to a trot
as they wound through dense trees, other times at
a breakneck canter through wide clearings that
opened to the sky. She had no time to think, only
to react. Her hands held the reins with assurance as
she ducked low-lying branches or hugged the mare's
powerful neck as they soared over fallen logs
stretched across their path.

She did not hear the thundering of hooves close
behind her, nor the cocking of a pistol. She only
heard the loud report, echoing from the trees and
shattering her single-minded concentration, a
strange whizzing by her ear, and the terrified snorting of her mare. Then she was flung from the saddle
as the animal reared up on its back legs and frantically pawed the air.

Kassandra hit the ground with a sickening thud, the breath knocked from her lungs. She stared up into the darkening sky, her vision blurred, a grotesque face floating above her for a fleeting moment. Then all was black, and she sank into unconsciousness.

"Your aim is failing, Adolph—"

"Shut up!" he snapped, glancing up at the stout, bearded man standing at his side. "I paid you to ride the horse, not to offer me worthless criticisms." His black eyes narrowed shrewdly on Kassandra's prostrate form. Perfect, he thought coldly. It appeared the fall had done its damage. Her forehead was bleeding where she had bumped it on that log, her skin was ashen . . .

"Let's get out of here," he ordered tersely. "We'll let the wolves finish her off. Once they get a whiff of that fresh blood . . ." He shrugged, grinning broadly. "It will look like the accident it was meant to be." He brushed by his companion and strode with his stilted walk toward the dappled horse tethered nearby.

"Ah, so you never meant to shoot her, then."

Adolph wheeled about, his eyes glittering dangerously. "You ask too many questions, my friend."

The bearded man shifted uncomfortably, his swarthy face flushing bright red. Without a word he moved to the horse and mounted, then reached down to Adolph and lifted him easily to the saddle.

"Ride," Adolph grated, settling himself. He leaned against his companion's chest as they set off through the woods, the wind howling around them.

Kassandra blinked against the cold rain pelting her face and licked some of the moisture from her lips, then swallowed weakly, a poor attempt at cooling her parched throat. The awful pounding in her head was excruciating. It radiated from just above her left temple, and she tentatively touched the spot. As she drew her hand away, her gaze widened in horror at the blood staining her gloved fingers.

"Sweet Lord!" she whispered faintly, struggling to sit up. Dizziness assailed her and she sank back down upon the ground. She lay there for a moment, shielding her face from the rain, but after a few deep breaths she tried again, ever so slowly. This time she was successful. The throbbing pain in her head increased tenfold and she thought she might scream, then it suddenly subsided to a dull ache.

Kassandra looked about her dazedly, at a total loss as to her surroundings. Then she remembered. Her gaze skipped about, searching for any sign of her mare, and she twisted to look behind her, but she was alone.

A booming clap of thunder caused her to cry out, and she stared up into the sky, boiling with darkened clouds and crisscrossed by streaks of jagged lightning. The rain was falling heavier now, stinging sheets that felt like biting pinpricks through her drenched clothing. She rose shakily to her feet, almost losing her balance, but managed to stagger over to a gnarled tree trunk. She clung to it, rivulets of water streaming down her face and blinding her, her hair plastered to her head and down her back. She fought to collect her bearings, her consuming thought to strike out at once for the estate.

But which way should she go? she wondered with a burst of panic. There were no landmarks, and there was little daylight left. Shadowed trees loomed around her, each looking much the same as the next, and if there had been any tracks, they had been washed away by the rain and oozing mud.

You'll get nowhere just standing here, Kassandra, she chided herself. Summoning her courage, she pushed away from the tree and set off in one direction, holding up her soggy skirt as she sloshed through puddles of standing water, then stopped, her instincts telling her she was going the wrong way. She turned and tried another direction, walking for well over a half hour before she sensed it, too, was leading her farther away from her destination.

It was growing dark, almost nightfall, and with a sinking feeling Kassandra realized she must have been unconscious for several hours. She leaned against a tree, her labored breaths tearing at her throat, a sense of hopelessness unlike anything she had ever felt before welling up inside her. She was lost in the woods.

The storm was increasing in fury with every passing moment; the wind buffeted her with lashing rain. She knew her strength was failing, her body chilled to the marrow. She had to find the way back, or she would surely die from exposure.

Or the wolves would find her . . . That horrible thought gave her the impetus she needed. Summoning the last ounce of her will, she stumbled onward, almost bumping headlong into a sturdy logged wall.

Relief engulfed her; scalding tears streaked her face. She followed the rough-hewn contours of the wall, placing one hand over the next, until she found the door. She pushed on it with the last of her strength, nearly falling as it gave way easily. Her eyes quickly adjusted to the large, dim room. Wood was stacked near a stone fireplace, and a wide bed covered with piles of furs stood in one corner. She could hardly believe her good fortune.

She was too exhausted to build a fire. She shut the door firmly behind her, the interior of the rustic building as silent as a tomb compared to the shrieking storm. She peeled the sodden clothing from her body as quickly as she could, leaving only her chemise. Then she pulled off her ankle-high boots and stumbled to the bed. With a moan she climbed under the warm furs, her teeth still chattering as she fell asleep.

# Chapter 27

❦

Stefan arrived at the estate just as the thunderstorm exploded in all its fury. It had been a long ride from the winter camp, much of it accompanied by wind and rain, and he was soaked to the skin despite his heavy cloak. As he drew closer to the stable, he could think of nothing better than the warmth of a fire and good brandy to drive the chill from his body . . . and Kassandra's welcome company.

A wry smile tugged at the corners of his mouth. God only knew how she would greet him, he thought, wiping his hand over his wet face. But anything had to be better than the raging wrath of this storm.

He reined Brand in at the stable doors and dismounted, his boots sinking into the thick mud. Perhaps he should have written to Isabel and let her know he was coming, he considered, pushing open the wide door. Well, it was too late now. Besides, he had wanted it to be a surprise. He chuckled under his breath, envisioning the scene. Kassandra's reaction would be immediate and unrehearsed, a true gauge of her current frame of mind toward him. And from that he would decide how best to proceed with his plan.

He led Brand into the stable. The well-lighted interior was unusual for this time of the evening and it threw him off guard. What was even more unusual was the intense level of activity—stableboys intent upon brushing down drenched horses whose heaving flanks were streaked with mud and foam, menservants shrugging out of sodden wraps, their brows raised and anxious, while others were leading fresh horses from their stalls and quickly saddling them, shouting orders to the bustling stableboys. No one took any notice of him at all.

"What's going on here?" he roared, startling everyone into gaping silence. Nervous whinnies and rustlings from the horses sounded loudly in the ensuing lull.

"My lord!" Karl Loos blurted in the next instant, rushing forward. The overseer's face was drawn and worried. "It is Lady Kassandra, my lord. She's missing. We've been out searching for her these past hours—"

"What do you mean, missing?" Stefan demanded, his heart lurching.

"Her ladyship went for a ride this morning, milord," Hans broke in breathlessly, scuttling up beside the overseer. "Well before the storm broke. I saddled her horse myself, the Arabian." He nodded to the white mare standing in her stall with a blanket thrown over her back. "A few hours later, the horse trotted back into the stable yard, saddle and all, but no milady. I went out to the road, thinkin' she might have decided to walk the last bit, as she does sometimes, but she wasn't there, not anywhere to be seen. I thought it strange, and went to find Karl as fast as I could run."

"Where have you searched?" Stefan asked, his eyes moving back to the overseer.

"The fields, the woods for several miles surrounding the house, even your hunting lodge, my lord," Karl answered, "but there's no sign of her. We

had a track to follow for a while, then the rains began . . .'' He shook his head, at a loss.

Stefan took immediate command, his mind working fast. ''Hans, see to Brand, have another horse
saddled for me at once, and bring it to the house.''

''Aye, milord!'' the boy answered, dashing off.

''Karl, make sure every able man is sent out, drivers, footmen, all of them, but in pairs. Have them
cover the same ground again, then fan out and go
even farther. She's out there somewhere, maybe injured.'' He paused, his voice almost breaking. God
help him, he could not think of it. Swallowing hard,
he rushed on. ''I'll join you in a few moments, after
I see Isabel.''

His blazing eyes swept the stable, falling on every
man present. ''Get on with it, all of you,'' he ordered. ''We must find her.'' At his words the furious activity began anew, with heightened urgency.
Stefan turned on his heel and strode from the stable,
breaking into a hard run down the path leading to
the mansion. He burst through the front door before
the startled footman could rise to his feet.

''Where is Countess Isabel?'' he cried out, streams
of water running off his cloak and forming puddles
on the floor.

''In her ch-chamber, my lord,'' the man stammered, taken by surprise. ''She has taken to her
bed—''

''Count Stefan!'' Gisela exclaimed, cutting off the
footman's words as she rounded the corner from the
dining room. She set the silver tray she held upon
a nearby table and rushed to meet him. ''I cannot
believe it's you!'' She wrung her hands nervously.
''Have you heard about Lady Kassandra?''

''Yes,'' Stefan answered, shrugging out of his
sodden cloak. His low aside to the footman sent him
scurrying up the stairs and down the corridor to his

lord's chamber for a dry cloak. Stefan turned back
to Gisela. ''Has Isabel taken ill?''

''No, my lord. But the strain, coupled with the
recent accident . . .'' She shook her head miserably.
''I have never seen her so distraught.''

''Go to her at once, and tell her I have gone in
search of Kassandra. Hopefully the news will comfort her.'' His gaze moved from her face to the footman rushing down the stairs with a cloak draped
over his arm, then back to Gisela again. ''Tell Isabel
not to worry. I will find her.''

Gisela could only nod, her throat constricted painfully at Stefan's determined expression. She knew
him too well. He was putting up a brave front, but
his eyes told her a different story. They were
wracked by torment . . . and fear.

Stefan quickly donned the proffered cloak, then
he was out the front door, down the steps, and
mounting the powerful roan stallion just brought to
him from the stable. The keening wind tore at him
with incredible force, and thunder split the sky as
he rode along the drive, meeting up with Karl and
seven other riders at the crest of the hill. Each held
a covered oil lantern.

''The storm is growing worse,'' he shouted, rain
lashing at his face. ''Search for as long as you can,
but do not endanger your own lives.''

Karl's reply was lost on the wind, but Stefan did
not wait for him to repeat it. With sure hands he
tugged upon the reins and dug his booted heels into
the stallion's sides. The animal surged forward,
leaving the others well behind as it galloped along
the road and jumped over the flooded ravine into
the fields.

The lightning that surged across the boiling sky
was Stefan's guide, illuminating the great expanse
of field and forest. He rode like a man possessed.
Cold terror gripped him for the first time in his life,

driving him on. He knew the estate and Kassandra's favorite trails like the back of his hand. He was determined to search along each one, no matter how long it took him.

Stefan's lips moved in a fervent prayer, then straightened into a grim line. He knew if he lost Kassandra, he would never forgive himself for how wretchedly he had treated her.

But as the agonizing minutes dragged into an hour of fruitless search, it seemed as if his impassioned plea would go unanswered. The storm was like a wild thing determined to thwart him. Small branches hurtled through the air, striking his chest. Rain whipped his face. And as they rode into the thick of the forest, trees were felled from the terrible force of the wind, one nearly crashing down upon them.

Stefan had no doubt he was by himself now, convinced the others had been driven back by the ferocity of the storm. But perhaps it was right that he suffer alone. He rode on relentlessly, until at last it was raining so hard, he could see barely a few feet in front of him. With a sinking heart, he had to face reality. He would have to seek the cover of his hunting lodge until the worst of the storm had passed, then strike out again. It would be a waste of precious time, but there was nothing to be done about it.

Veering the stallion sharply around, he rode directly west until he at last came to the lodge. He dismounted and led the exhausted animal into the shelter of the small stable some distance from the logged building. After rubbing him down and filling the trough with hay, he set out again in the stinging rain. His footsteps were heavy as he slogged to the front door. He pushed it open and stepped inside, closing it regretfully behind him.

Stefan leaned on the door for a long time, his eyes adjusting to the darkness. Fatigue assaulted him, mixed with incredible despair. But he would not allow himself to give in to it. He walked resolutely over to the stone fireplace, where he removed his cloak, shook it out, and hung it over the back of a chair. Wiping his hands over his face, he sat down on his haunches and began stacking wood on the iron grates. Before long he had a fire blazing in the fireplace, its warmth slowly creeping into the far corners of the large room. But it could do little to dispel the chill that penetrated his heart.

Stefan stared blindly into the orange flames, the pain welling inside him so bitter, it felt as if a knife was twisting cruelly. He listened to the howl of the wind just outside the door, the deafening thunder, the rain pelting against the windows, and vehemently cursed the storm that was holding him hostage within the shelter of his lodge. How could he fight against such an enemy?

Kassandra was out there, maybe hurt . . . maybe worse. And here he was, virtually helpless, at the mercy of a storm that seemed to be roaring with laughter at his plight.

A low sigh suddenly drifted across the room, raising the short hairs on the back of Stefan's neck. Instantly alert, he whirled and crouched low on the floor, drawing the long knife he always carried from the belt at his waist. His gaze darted about the shadowed room, falling upon the wide bed in the far corner. The furs he had stacked there several months ago were piled oddly on the mattress, as if someone was huddled beneath them . . .

So a poacher had also sought refuge from the storm, he thought darkly, creeping on his hands and knees toward the bed. This was not the first time he had found one of the thieving bastards in his lodge. Holding his breath, he drew back the furs, one by one, with the tip of his knife, until he was down to the last. He raised the flashing blade, poised and ready in case he was attacked, and flung the fur aside.

Stefan's eyes widened in disbelief, his knife dropping to the mattress at the sight of Kassandra huddled there. She was shivering uncontrollably in her sleep, her lips tinged with blue. His mind raced. Karl had said they searched the lodge . . . She must have stumbled upon it after they had already gone.

"Kassandra," he murmured softly, wild with relief. But it quickly turned to alarm when he ran his finger tenderly down her cheekbone. Her skin was clammy and feverish.

Stefan rose to his feet and with a mighty heave pulled the bed near the center of the room, where the warmth from the fire could reach it. Kassandra moaned at the sudden jarring, but did not stir. He stripped the damp chemise from her body, wincing at the dark bruises on her pale skin, and tossed it on the floor. Covering her gently with the furs, he quickly shed his own clothes and climbed into the bed beside her. He knew the warmth of his body was the surest way to drive the wracking chill from her own.

Cradling her in his arms, Stefan gazed down at the woman he loved more than his own life. He touched his lips to the bruised welt at her temple and lightly kissed her mouth, willing his strength into her. Then he lay his head down upon the bed, offering a silent prayer of thanks that his plea had been answered.

# Chapter 28

✦⊙⊙✦

Kassandra snuggled closer against the broad warmth at her back, lost in the most extraordinary dream. It was sensory more than visual, a swirling collage of fragmented impressions: soft whispers, sweet words, evocative scents, thrilling sensations. She stretched luxuriously, her legs entangling with muscled strength. She felt so safe, so secure, her body enveloped in a comforting presence.

She sighed and shivered, a hint of pressure sliding along the curve of a breast, circling, circling, just grazing a hardened nipple, then it was gone. Powerful bands drew her back possessively, holding her closer. A warm breath blew against her earlobe . . . oh, it tickled!

Kassandra's eyes drifted open, her hand swiping languidly at her ear. She drew a deep breath, her dreamy gaze caught and held by shafts of golden sunlight streaming through the small window near her head. She watched, mesmerized, still half-asleep, as twirling flecks of dust danced in midair. Smiling, she leaned forward, her arm outstretched, to catch a sparkling handful.

She gasped, her eyes widening in shock as strong, bronzed arms pulled her back and tightened around her. She froze, not daring to breathe, suddenly fully

awake. Her heart pounded with fright. Memories of
the storm tumbled through her mind, converging
with her dream of only moments before and the
sheer terror now gripping her. The hand at her
breast . . . Dear God, protect her, it was real!

Her gaze fell on a crumpled pile of clothing on the
floor near the bed. Dark overcoat, breeches, black
boots, with her white linen chemise peeking out
from beneath in striking contrast. Desperately she
began to struggle, her body taut and straining for
escape.

"Easy, Kassandra, it's me," Stefan murmured
soothingly, holding her fast within his arms.

Kassandra's heart leaped as she instantly recognized the deep, rough-edged voice. Stefan! Her
limbs felt weak and useless as wild relief engulfed
her, along with a giddy rush like butterflies in her
stomach, and a strange, excited happiness. Dazed
questions filled her mind. How? When?

Then a startling realization struck her and she
forced herself to think clearly. Even if it was Stefan,
she was still in peril. She had not forgotten how he
had deceived her the last time they were together.
And at this moment she could not be more vulnerable, lying within his arms, unclothed, the heat of
his skin burning into her own. She fought to stay
calm despite her trembling.

"How . . . how did you find me?" she finally
managed, hazarding a peek at him over her shoulder. She felt a jolt, a tingling, as she was struck by
the rugged hollows and planes of his face, the inky
blackness of his hair, the penetrating depths of his
gaze, all like an unspoken embrace. Her memories
of him had hardly done him justice.

Stefan rose up on his elbow and gently rolled her
onto her back, his breath catching in his throat as he
drank in the sight of her. Her color had returned,
her skin flushed with rose, her lips lush and red.

Gratitude filled him, a prayer of thanks in his heart. For a moment he simply could not answer. His fingers gently stroked her silken hair, fanning out like a fiery halo about her head. He swallowed against the hard lump in his throat, finally trusting himself to speak.

"It appears you stumbled into my hunting lodge, my lady," he began softly.

"Your hunting lodge?" Kassandra breathed in surprise. Her gaze flew about the decidedly masculine room, noting its rustic yet comfortable furnishings. So this was where he claimed to have gone those many nights. It was amazing enough she had found any place in the storm, but the coincidence of finding his private refuge was truly unsettling.

"Yes. Your disappearance created quite a stir last night, Kassandra. I arrived late, hoping to surprise you, only to discover you were missing and my entire household in an uproar. You gave us . . . me, quite a scare."

Kassandra's pulse quickened at his last words, but she turned away to hide his dizzying effect on her. She marveled at how even his simplest phrase, his slightest glance, could fluster her so completely. It was all she could do to remember his deceit.

"I set out looking for you, but the storm became so intense, I was forced to seek shelter here, planning to stay only until it subsided." He chuckled. "I heard a noise, and thought there was a poacher in my bed. It was you," he finished quietly. He traced lightly along the swollen bump on the side of her forehead. "Does it hurt?"

She winced, drawing in her breath. "Yes," she murmured.

"What happened?"

She turned back to him, shrugging. Her brow furrowed in confusion. "I don't know, really. I was riding, then I heard a shot, from a pistol, I think. It all happened so fast. I was thrown to the ground, and that's all I remember, until I awoke and it was almost dark.''

The faint memory of a face peering down at her entered her mind, but she quickly dismissed it. For all she knew, it could have been her mare nudging her. "I tried to find my way back," she continued, "but the storm was so fierce, I got lost. Then somehow I found this place.''

"There must have been poachers on my land after all," Stefan muttered darkly. If he ever found one, he swore vehemently, he would surely kill the man. To think what an errant shot might have taken away from him . . . his love, his life.

This last statement hurt Kassandra to the quick, but she masked it with irritation. Here she could have been killed, and he thought only of poachers! She began to sit up, but he pushed her gently back down on the bed, which infuriated her further, especially since the soft fur had fallen away from her breasts, leaving them exposed to his view.

Stefan's gaze went instinctively to the tempting mounds, his blood shooting hot through his veins. He longed to savor the sweetness of a rose-tipped peak, to explore the fascinating length of her body pressed so intimately against his own, its graceful curves, its womanly secrets. Yet he knew that now was not the time. He tore his eyes away and caught her gaze. The flashing amethyst depths had darkened to a stormy violet hue.

Stefan exhaled sharply. It was a look he knew only too well, and he could hardly blame her. Except for his attempts to win her favor and their last evening together, he had given her little cause to regard him otherwise. But hopefully after she heard what he had to tell her, that would change.

Kassandra clutched the fur and drew it up over her body. "I would like to get dressed, my lord," she said tersely. "So if you will kindly release me—"

Stefan silenced her with a gentle finger to her lips. "I have something to say to you, Kassandra," he murmured.

She jerked her head away. Whatever it was, she had no wish to hear it. "Surely it can wait until later," she objected. "No doubt your servants are searching for us even at this moment. It would be most unseemly if we were found here together"— she blushed hotly—"like . . . like this."

Stefan could not help but chuckle at her discomfort, then he grew serious. Out with it, man, he told himself. You have kept silent long enough, too long. He drew her chin back to face him, ignoring the defiant glint in her eyes. "Listen to me, Kassandra," he said softly. "I love you."

Kassandra blinked, but she said nothing. She could not. Her heart was in her throat.

"I love you, Kassandra," he repeated earnestly, "and I have been a fool not to tell you before now."

Kassandra flinched as if she had been struck. Love. It was as if by hearing the word spoken aloud, the bewildering torrent of emotion, the terrible longing, and the aching desire that had wracked her since their night of passion had finally been given a name. Love . . . How she loved him! And seeing him again, feeling the stirring strength of his arms around her, she could no longer deny it.

Yet with this shattering realization, she knew she had to resist him. Especially now. For he had the power to hurt her far more than ever before if she fell prey to his charms again. His words were false. He did not love her. He had told her before that to him, love was a useless emotion. He was only saying he loved her because he wanted her body, nothing more! She had to protect herself, or be lost to his lies forever.

"No!" Kassandra exclaimed fiercely, shoving at him with all her might. Taken totally by surprise, Stefan lost his hold on her and fell back against the log wall. In that moment she sprang swiftly from the bed, snatching up her chemise from the floor. She ran to the other side of the room and dressed hurriedly, slipping the thin lace straps over her shoulders. Then she moved to the door, eyeing him warily as she fumbled with the latch.

"Will you run out in only your chemise, then?" Stefan queried, throwing back the fur and rising from the bed.

Kassandra's knees quaked at the sight of him. He was so devastatingly handsome, the rippling power of his body more beautiful than any form she had ever seen. During her wide-eyed hesitation, he strode across the floor and pulled her in his arms again before she could even think to flee.

"Why don't you believe me?" he asked raggedly, molding her supple form to his own, his hands tightening desperately on her narrow waist. God help him, he was baring his soul to a woman for the first time in his life, and she refused to believe him! His tormented gaze caught and held her own. "I swear to you, Kassandra, I love you more than life itself!"

She shook her head, bringing her hands up and clasping them over her ears. She was in agony, her soul being ripped apart. If only she could believe him! She could forgive him anything, everything, if only his words were true. But he lied, he lied!

"No, please," she cried, trying to twist free of his grasp. But he captured her face in his hands and brought his mouth down upon her own, as if by the power of his kiss, their panting breaths merging as one, he could convince her of his words. He plundered her lips, forcing them apart, his tongue delving into her, his arms pulling her closer, closer . . .

Tears stung Kassandra's eyes as she returned his kiss, deeply, deliriously, for she was powerless against it. She gave herself completely, forgetting her rage, her anguish, the lies, the deceit, the past, the future . . . everything fading into insignificance but for the breathless splendor of the moment.

But when he wrenched his mouth from her own at last, something snapped deep within her. She knew there was only one thing she could do. She would have to lie as well, to hurt him as cruelly as he was torturing her . . . by appealing to the one emotion she knew he possessed, the emotion she had seen in his heated gaze at Prince Eugene's gala. His jealous pride.

"Your kiss tells me what you will not," Stefan breathed huskily, his thumbs caressing her silken cheeks. "Say it, my love. Let me hear it from your lips that you believe me," he demanded softly.

"It does not matter if I believe you or not," she replied steadily, defiance flaring in her eyes. "Your love is wasted on me, Stefan." How strange, she thought fleetingly. Her voice sounded so distant, as if it were coming from someone else.

"What do you mean?" he asked, stunned, his brow knit in confusion.

"I love another, my lord. Save your eloquent words for your mistress, or someone who might better appreciate them."

A strained silence fell over the room, broken only by the sound of their jagged breathing. Stefan stared at her, his expression unfathomable, his body strangely relaxed, nothing belying the depth of his furious agony but his eyes. They were darkened to the color of slate, burning into her own as if he could read her very soul. Then suddenly his hands slipped to her upper arms, gripping her brutally.

"Have you given yourself to another man, Kassandra?" he grated, his voice dangerously low.

Kassandra hesitated, fear surging through her. But she threw back her head and lifted her chin. "Yes!" she tossed at him. She was stunned by the poignant flash of pain in his face, matched only by the haunted look in his eyes, and she almost regretted her words. Was it possible she might have been wrong?

The door swung open so suddenly, she jumped in his arms, all thoughts forgotten as it struck the timbered wall with a resounding crash. Karl stepped over the threshold, stopping with one leg still out the door. He gaped, red-faced, at Stefan and Kassandra, then backed out again, loudly clearing his throat and looking at the ground.

"Forgive me, Count Stefan," the overseer blurted uncomfortably. "Though I must say I am relieved we have found you and the lady . . . alive and well."

Not in the least embarrassed by his nakedness, Stefan released Kassandra and moved to the door. "We'll be out in a few moments, Karl," he said tersely. "Is there an extra horse for the lady?"

"Yes, my lord."

"Good."

Stefan shut the door firmly and turned to Kassandra. "Get dressed," he muttered. He strode to the bed, grabbed his clothes, and quickly put them on, his face set and grim.

Kassandra did not hesitate. She gathered her clothes from the floor and retreated to a far corner, where she dressed hurriedly with her back to him. Her fingers fumbled uselessly with the mother-of-pearl buttons on her riding jacket, which was still damp from the night before. But she didn't care. All she wanted was to be free of the oppressive tension in the lodge, and free of him.

When they were both ready, Stefan opened the door once again and bowed to Kassandra. "After you, my lady."

She kept her eyes down, her face flushing miserably as she stepped into the bright morning sun. She could imagine what Karl must think. She only hoped he was discreet enough to keep what he had seen to himself.

Stefan followed directly behind her, hoisting her up into the saddle of the white Arabian. Then he mounted the roan stallion and they were off, a strangely silent party wending its way back to the estate.

# Chapter 29

Sophia threw open the white latticed doors and strolled onto her private balcony. She leaned against the smooth balustrade, caressing the polished marble as her almond eyes swept the grandeur of her formal gardens. It seemed that, during the few short days since the horrendous thunderstorm, spring had finally come to Vienna.

She languidly inhaled the morning air, tinged with the scent of flowers that had appeared in the gardens as if overnight. The bright sunshine was deliciously warm upon her skin. A light breeze played through her mahogany tresses, which Marietta had just brushed to a burnished glow, the glorious mass trailing down the bodice of her cream satin morning gown to cover the swell of her breasts.

Sophia wound her fingers in a silken tendril, her eyes narrowing with interest at one of the gardeners, an Italian youth of eighteen, as he knelt over a flower bed. Her gaze traveled across the sculpted breadth of his shoulders and back, the muscles rippling in his arms as he dug methodically, then down the curve of spine to his firm buttocks, their masculine beauty heightened by his tight breeches.

Desire quivered inside her, dusky laughter bubbling in her throat. Angelo. Her angel. For want of the man she craved above all others, he had been only one of the diversions who had amused her over the dreary past winter.

Sophia's smile quickly faded, her hands gripping the balustrade like talons. Diversions that had gone on far longer than she had planned . . .

"Milady," Marietta murmured, standing by one of the latticed doors. "Adolph is here."

Sophia tensed, though she spoke calmly. "Bring him to me." She listened to the rustle of Marietta's starched skirt as the maid moved swiftly across the room, opening and closing the chamber door with a click.

"The little beast," Sophia muttered vehemently, the familiar thud of his bootheels upon the carpeted floor grating against her nerves. She should choose her assassins as carefully as she chose her gardeners.

"You sent for me, milady?" Adolph asked, stopping on the threshold. He grinned expectantly. Perhaps she was going to present him with the emerald ring she had promised, for the successful completion of his task. The bauble was worth a fortune, and could very well mean his freedom if he found the right buyer for it.

Sophia waved Marietta away, waiting to speak until she had left the room. Her topaz eyes glinted with deep-seated rage as she studied her servant. At the click of the door she drew herself up, towering over him. "It seems you have failed me once again, Adolph," she stated darkly.

Adolph shook his head vigorously, his heart sinking to his boots. The low timbre of her voice, dripping with hidden intent, was like a death knell to him. "No, mistress, that's not possible!" he blurted. "She could not have survived her fall . . . I saw it, milady. It would have killed the strongest man!"

"She lives, Adolph; it is as simple as that," Sophia muttered with disgust. "I saw Countess Isabel at a gala last evening, looking none the worse for your bungled carriage accident. I overheard her talking to several of her simpering friends about Kassandra's . . ." she viciously spat out the hated name ". . . unfortunate fall and Stefan's daring rescue. It was so gushingly recounted, I thought I might retch!"

Adolph took a step back, cold fear gripping him. "I c-could have sw-sworn . . ." he stammered, the words dying on his lips as she cruelly clasped his shoulder.

"You are obviously not capable of performing the task you have been given, my little friend."

Adolph fell to his knees, his compact body shaking uncontrollably. "Please . . . please, mistress, allow me one more chance," he pleaded, sweat breaking out upon his protruding brow.

"Why, Adolph?" Sophia sneered. "So you can fail me again? This is all becoming quite an embarrassment to me. And one more failed attempt will surely look suspicious, if it doesn't already. I don't think I can risk another—"

"I promise, milady, I will not fail you!" Adolph broke in, his high-pitched voice wavering. He swallowed hard, as her fingers bit painfully into his shoulder. "I swear on my life!"

Sophia abruptly released him, and he toppled over onto the floor. "Aptly put, Adolph. On your miserable life . . ." She wheeled around, her skirt hitting him across the face, and strode to one end of the balcony, her back to him. "Now get out of my sight," she ordered. "You have until this evening to come up with a plan . . . a very good plan."

"Yes, milady!" Adolph nodded furiously, rising quickly to his knees. He grasped the balcony doorknob and pulled himself to his feet, bowing as he backed away. "Until this evening—"

"Go!"

Adolph did not hesitate. He sped to the door, nearly tripping on his own boots in his haste to leave her chamber.

Sophia sighed with satisfaction as the door slammed behind him. She leaned slightly over the balustrade and plucked a flowering bud from a tall tree growing near the wall, her gaze moving once again to the gardener toiling below. Holding the bud in the palm of her hand, she admired its fragile beauty and inhaled its delicate fragrance.

"Angelo!" she called out. She gestured to him with a wave of her hand. He smiled knowingly up at her, and she smiled in return, her eyes dancing with lusty anticipation. Then she turned and sauntered from the balcony, crushing the bud between her fingers and dropping it to the floor.

Adolph took another draft of warm beer, then licked the foam from his lips. His black eyes roamed the dingy interior of the tavern, dimmed with smoke from countless cooking fires and cheap tobacco, resting here and there on familiar faces: the tavern keep, a giant of a man, nearly seven feet tall and strong as a bear, whom he had known from his days with the traveling menagerie; the whores who worked the riverfront inn next door, with their heavily rouged cheeks and hardened glances. Yet these women always smiled when he would visit his favorite haunt, never cringed when he offered to pay for their affection. He felt more comfortable in this ramshackle tavern than anywhere else on earth. Less a dwarf, condemned by an accident of nature to a life of ridicule and hardship, and more of a man. It was to this place he had come to think.

Adolph barely suppressed a shudder, recalling Sophia's cold threats. He did not doubt she meant every word. Never in his life had he known such a woman, or dreamed such a woman could exist, until he was sold into her service late last summer. He had known ruthless cruelty, but usually at the hands of men. The archduchess was a witch, a murderess, the devil incarnate swathed in female flesh of the finest alabaster and the most voluptuous curves, her face a study of extraordinary beauty that gave no hint to the evil lurking in her heart.

If the bitch *had* a heart, he amended wryly. He took another draft of beer, the pungent liquid buoying his flagging spirits, and emptied his mug. He set it down on the rough-hewn table with a thud, the heavy pewter clinking against the other two mugs in front of him, and waved for another. He rested his head in his hands while he waited, his thoughts tumbling over and over in his mind.

He had to think of a new plan, and fast, he mused grimly, or he, not Lady Kassandra Wyndham, would become Sophia's next victim. But what? It was by mere chance that his three previous attempts had failed. This time he had to come up with an idea that was foolproof, one that would convince Sophia he could carry it through to completion. Perhaps poison might do the trick. He knew of many kinds, arsenic, hemlock, nightshade, and many ways to conceal their use, so one's death might resemble an accident—

A chair grating across the planked floor jarred him out of his thoughts and he looked up as two cloaked men sat down at the table next to his own, the one nearest the corner. They were dressed as Bohemian peasants, in rough woolen garments and low-slung caps that covered their heads, not an uncommon sight, especially this close to the Danube. There were many Slavic races who had merged into the fabric of Vienna, plying their trades along the river.

Yet there was something about these two men that struck him as odd. His instincts told him that these two peasants were not what they seemed.

Adolph blinked in surprise when a sallow serving wench placed another mug of frothy beer in front of him—he had forgotten his request for more in his curious observation of the strangers. He paid her, shrewdly watching the newcomers as they, too, ordered beers, then resumed their soft-spoken conversation. He listened carefully, his ears attuned to even the quietest sounds, a talent he had learned to insure his own survival. He was not disappointed at the furtive discussion that drifted over to him. He kept his head down and slowly sipped his beer.

"You must deliver this message to Sultan Achmet," one of the men muttered, furtively sliding a folded letter across the table. "I have made all the arrangements for you. The boat will leave tomorrow night, taking you to Belgrade. There you must alert Mustapha Pasha to the Imperialist threat, but stay no longer than it takes you to recite the message. You must press on, traveling as swiftly as you can."

"So you believe it is to be Belgrade, then?" the other asked in faintly clipped tones.

Adolph started. He had heard that accent before, long ago, as a youth, when his traveling troupe had performed in Constantinople. The man was Turkish.

"Yes. It seems Prince Eugene is eager to surpass his victories of last year by attempting to capture the great fortress. He has maps, diagrams, everything he needs to lay siege to the city."

"But the garrison in Belgrade can hardly defend the fortress alone. They are well armed, well trained, to be sure, and the fortress is heavily fortified. It could withstand a long siege, but if the lines are broken . . ." The Turk paused, shaking his head. "It would be twenty men to one in favor of the Imperialists."

"True. Prince Eugene can be stopped only if the grand vizier, Halil Pasha, assembles his field army and prepares to march from Constantinople in defense of the city. That is the contents of your message, Hasan. That is why it is urgent you deliver it to the Sultan as quickly as possible. I should know in a few days when the Imperial forces plan to leave Vienna. I shall carry this news first to Belgrade, and give Mustapha some advance warning, then travel on and hopefully meet up with Halil's army on its way north. So, you see, I will be following close on your heels."

"You have done well, Count Althann."

Adolph's eyes widened. Count Althann . . . He knew that name. Sophia had insisted he learn all the names of the aristocratic families in Vienna, and some of their history. But which Althann?

The two men fell silent as the serving maid brought their beers, waiting until she had moved well away before continuing their hushed discussion. The Turk laughed at some whispered remark, then Adolph heard the unmistakable chink of money, muffled by a cloth bag. He surmised shrewdly that gold was changing hands, the opiate of any spy.

"We had agreed on twice this amount, if I recall, my friend," Althann muttered, his blue eyes searing into his companion's dark gaze.

"Ah, how stupid of me," the Turk replied, his voice echoed by another thud upon the table. "You have a good memory, Frederick."

"That is why I am so well paid, Hasan."

Adolph shook his head in disbelief. So Count Frederick Althann, one of the most favored young aristocrats at the Viennese court, and a godson of the emperor, was a spy for Achmet III, Sultan of the Ottoman Empire! Yet it made sense. He was the fourth son in his family, heir to little but the title of count. What quicker way to earn his fortune than as a spy?

Adolph's face split into a sarcastic grin, though he hid it well with his sleeve, pretending to wipe his nose.

"Let us leave this place," Hasan murmured, his cunning eyes sweeping the darkened room, lit only by shallow oil lamps and the cooking fire roaring beneath a greasy hearth. He could barely mask his disgust. "Surely you know of another more comfortable establishment, where one might sample the delicacy of a refined Viennese courtesan?"

Frederick nodded. "I know of such a house," he murmured with a wry smile. "But I must warn you, Hasan. The women there could steal a man's soul. They are well versed in all manner of carnal . . . amusement."

"All the better! Let us be on our way, my friend," Hasan replied eagerly. "I have only one night to taste the pleasures of this city."

Adolph watched as the two men rose from their chairs. They passed by him so closely that the Turk's cloak swept against his table. Grateful that he had changed from his rich clothes into more drab attire, he feigned idiocy by staring with glazed eyes straight ahead and drooling into his beer.

"In my country they kill poor wretches like him at birth," Hasan muttered scornfully. "That creature is repulsive."

Adolph winced, Frederick's terse comment lost to him as they moved away. He glanced over his shoulder when he heard the door swing shut, then shoved the beer away and leaned back in his chair, an idea forming in his mind.

A slow smile cut across his face. It was perfect, he thought slyly. The perfect solution to his dilemma. Here was a man who would no doubt do anything—anything—to preserve his deadly secret and his life. All that was needed was one little word to Sophia, and this traitor, this spy against his own people, would take the distasteful responsibility of Lady Kassandra Wyndham from his hands forever.

Adolph threw a few coins on the table for the serving maid, then stood on the low stool on which his feet were resting and jumped to the floor. He could not wait to tell his mistress of his ingenious plan. It was the stuff of which her wicked dreams were made.

# Chapter 30

Count Frederick Althann stepped elegantly from the gleaming carriage, ignoring the bewigged footman holding the door for him. His shrewd gaze swept along the grand façade of the von Starenberg mansion. It gleamed blinding white in the bright afternoon sun, like a great iced cake, with exuberant ornamentation flanking the tall windows and front entranceway. He lifted his tricornered hat from his head with a practiced flourish and settled it under his arm, then turned to the driver.

"Wait here, man. I won't be long."

"As you wish, my lord." The carriage driver nodded, tightening his grip on the reins. The two barrel-chested bays stamped their hooves upon the drive at this restraint, their black manes and tails twitching impatiently.

Frederick walked up the marble steps and through the open doorway, his own impatience barely concealed beneath his polished veneer of nonchalance. His final meeting with Hasan was scheduled for later that afternoon, at the same riverfront tavern where they had met the night before. He had little time for unexpected social calls, though this one he could hardly have refused. Rank and position always dictated special consideration.

Frederick handed his hat, gold-topped cane, and

gloves to another footman, allowing himself just a moment to straighten his silk cravat. He had absolutely no idea why Archduchess Sophia had summoned him, and with such insistent urgency.

Their acquaintance stretched back several years, but it had always been on a purely superficial level. They moved within the same aristocratic circle, attended many of the same court functions and galas, but that was the extent of their interaction. He had long ago sensed in her a temperament much like his own, a dangerous combination he had done his best to avoid. Theirs had been merely a relationship of flowered flattery, simple jests, and the most frivolous exchanges.

"Archduchess von Starenberg awaits you in the salon, my lord," the footman intoned.

"Lead on, then," he murmured, following the stiff-backed servant across the hall to a set of double doors. They were quietly opened, revealing a room of startling white and gilt, awash with sunshine streaming from tall, arching windows. Yet there were candles burning in a glittering chandelier, the light reflecting off furnishings upholstered in the most opulent gold brocade. And ensconced on a wide divan, the archduchess herself, a stunning vision in scarlet satin embroidered with gold thread.

Easy . . . Frederick cautioned himself, his pulse racing at the sight of her seductive beauty. Do not forget your role. He extended a silk-stockinged leg in front of him and swept her a low bow.

"Count Althann . . . Frederick, if I may," Sophia purred, a beguiling smile curving her lips. What an amusing game this would be, she thought fleetingly, as he straightened once again. She had not missed the hot flash of admiration in his ice-blue eyes, hardly the reaction a woman would receive from a man with a preference for boys . . . "Please, come in.'' She gracefully waved her hand toward an armchair set near the divan. "Sit down."

Frederick obliged her, affecting his most grandiose walk as he crossed the floor to the chair. He sat down with fastidious poise, sweeping his coattails from beneath him and crossing his legs carefully at the knee, the better to show off his fine silk garters imported from Italy, and red-heeled shoes. He leaned casually on one elbow, his gaze not meeting hers until he had flicked an imaginary speck of dust from his breeches.

"Are you comfortable?" Sophia asked, when it seemed he was finally settled.

"Oh, quite, my lady," Frederick replied, pulling a white lace handkerchief from his pocket. It was the fop's counterpart to a lady's fan, used for emphasis in speech, or to coyly hide an expression in its scented folds. He pursed his lips, sniffing delicately. "You sent for me with some urgency, Archduchess von Starenberg," he began. "Might I inquire—"

"Please, call me Sophia," she interjected, marveling at the pretty show he was affording her. If Adolph had not apprised her of this man's true character and vocation—a spy for the Turks, no less—she would never have guessed it in a thousand years. His foppish performance was flawless.

Frederick was slightly taken aback by her intimate request, but he shrugged it off. Anything to indulge the lady, he thought dryly. "Very well. Sophia," he murmured, with a deferential nod. "Your invitation was most unexpected, and though I am charmed by your sudden interest, perhaps you could tell me why I have been so honored."

"Of course, Frederick," Sophia replied, leaning forward on the divan. "There is a certain matter I wish to discuss with you—"

A sharp rap on the door interrupted her, and she rose in a cool rustle of silk. "Ah, I believe Adolph has brought us some refreshment," she murmured. Perfect, my little man, she mused. You are right on cue.

Frederick glanced over his shoulder, blanching as a dwarf, swathed in a Turkish costume complete with turban and boots with curled-up tips, stepped into the room bearing a silver tray laden with crystal goblets and a tall decanter filled with deep red wine. An unsettling feeling gripped him. He could swear he had seen that dwarf somewhere before. But where?

Sophia noted his expression with a satisfied smile. All was proceeding exactly as she had planned. Adolph stopped in front of her and held the tray while she poured wine into the two goblets, then she set the decanter on a nearby table and offered one of the goblets to Frederick. He rose from his chair and accepted it, waiting as she lifted up her own.

"Leave us, Adolph," she commanded softly. "But stand just beyond the door, in case I have need of you."

Frederick's gaze followed the dwarf as he quietly left the room. Then he looked back at Sophia.

"Surely you realize, my lady, that all things Turkish are banned in Vienna." He sniffed, holding his handkerchief to his nose in feigned distaste. A reaction any outraged citizen would have made if presented with such a scene, he thought shrewdly.

Sophia waved off his comment. "Only a trifling indulgence on my part, Frederick, within the confines of my home," she explained with a throaty laugh. "I am sure there are many in this city who harbor a fascination for . . . the Orient."

Frederick's hand tightened imperceptibly on the stem of his goblet, but he smiled and nodded. "It shall be our secret, then," he offered gallantly.

"Our secret," Sophia agreed, raising her goblet.

She threw back her head, her topaz eyes alight with a strange fire. "Let us drink a toast, Frederick."

"Very well."

"To secrets . . . may they be well kept . . . and to our new alliance."

The rim of the goblet stopped abruptly against Frederick's mouth, some of the wine sloshing out and staining his cream silk cravat. "Alliance?" he queried, perplexed, lowering the goblet to his side. "What alliance?"

Sophia set her glass down next to the decanter. Her wine, too, was untouched. Her smile had faded, replaced by an expression of deadly seriousness. "Funny," she murmured, almost under her breath. "If you were truly a fop, as you pretend to be, you would have been more concerned with your precious cravat than with what I have just said."

Frederick set down his goblet and took a step toward her. "What are you talking about?"

"Cease your game, Frederick. It has grown tiresome," she replied. "I know everything about you. Everything." Her eyes narrowed with cunning. "Perhaps in the future, when you frequent decrepit taverns for your clandestine . . . *meetings*, you might do well to look about you first. You never know who might be listening."

As if by an arranged signal, Adolph stepped into the room, grinning from ear to ear. He leveled a cocked pistol at Frederick's chest, knowing well that desperate actions were committed by desperate men. "My lord," he muttered with a slight bow of his turbaned head. "Your costume today fits you far better than that of a Bohemian peasant."

Frederick felt a sickening knot in his stomach, his thoughts racing. The tavern . . . That's where he had seen this ugly little dwarf, drooling into his beer! Stunned, he looked from Adolph back to Sophia, her sinister smile sending a cold shiver through his body. He longed for nothing more at that moment than to grab her by her slender throat and throttle the self-satisfied expression from her face. But with the pistol trained at his heart, it appeared these two accomplices had thought of everything.

Except for the emperor's guard, he mused darkly. If he was discovered, then where were the authorities? Surely Sophia was aware of the rich reward paid for the capture of spies.

Sophia's dusky laughter broke into his thoughts as if she had read his mind. "You're far too precious a commodity to waste upon the bloody rack, Frederick. And as you can see"—she waved her arm around the opulent room,—"I have no use for the emperor's reward." She took a step toward him, her eyes flashing menacingly. "What I do have need of is an assassin," she stated bluntly.

Frederick understood immediately, though he said nothing. Obviously there was a bargain to be struck here, an evil one.

Sophia paced slowly in front of him, the heavy scent of her perfume drifting over him like an ominous cloud. "You're no fool, Frederick," she began, studying his face. "I'm sure you are aware that your life is forfeit if it becomes known you are a spy for the Turks. But perhaps, to avoid such an unpleasant fate, you might consider taking on a certain task, of a distasteful nature in itself but one in which you would earn my undying gratitude . . . and my silence." She stopped in front of him. "Shall I go on?" she queried.

"Please," Frederick muttered.

"Good. It's quite simple, really. If you accomplish my task, then I will keep your secret. Now, what do you say?"

There was no choice but one, Frederick mused grimly. Life . . . or death.

"What is your task, my lady?" he asked quietly,

an unspoken agreement passing between them. As she clapped her hands together with sheer pleasure, he could only guess as to the depths of her depravity.

"There is a young woman who must die," she said simply. "Her name is Lady Kassandra Wyndham."

Frederick's eyes widened in shock, but again he held his tongue.

Sophia had not missed his response. "Yes, you know her. That simpering English girl," she muttered bitterly, her almond eyes reflecting the intensity of her hatred. "She must die at once . . . for reasons that shall remain my own."

At his terse nod, Sophia moved closer to him. "I do not wish to know of your method, Frederick . . . Just see that it is done. And one other thing," she murmured, smiling faintly. "It must appear to be an unfortunate accident, or our agreement is waived. Do I make myself quite clear?"

Frederick could barely suppress a shudder. He did not doubt she meant exactly what she said. "Yes," he said.

"Splendid," she purred, trailing a cold finger down the side of his face. "Oh yes, Frederick, I'd almost forgotten. If you perhaps entertain any thoughts of revenge, I would suggest you consider such a move very carefully. I've written a letter, which is in safekeeping, outlining everything we have discussed this day, including your chosen profession as a spy. A letter that would certainly fall into the proper hands if, shall we say, anything should happen to me . . ."

Bitch! Now he truly had no alternatives, Frederick thought. He was not only a spy, but a soon-to-be murderer. He might as well have sold his soul to the devil, for it seemed that Satan and Sophia were one and the same.

Sophia moved away from him so suddenly, he was taken by surprise. She sat down on the divan and leaned back against its soft upholstery. "You may leave us, Adolph," she commanded. "I think we have nothing to fear from our handsome spy." She waited until he had left the room, than she spoke again, her voice almost a whisper.

"Adolph told me something else about you, Frederick," she murmured, stretching her arms languidly above her head. "I don't think I believe those rumors about you anymore . . . that you prefer boys to women."

Frederick appraised her heatedly, desire flaring within him at the open invitation gleaming in those unfathomable topaz depths. So he was to be her whore as well. Well, there were worse fates, he considered with dark amusement. He walked slowly to the divan and knelt down beside her.

"Show me that you are a man, Frederick," she breathed huskily, her arms snaking around his neck. Her laughter echoed as he expertly forced her scarlet bodice down beneath her breasts, the voluptuous globes, high and firm, leaping into his hands. She laughed no more, but shrieked in wild delight as he bent his head over a taut nipple, and bit it.

# Chapter 31

Isabel sighed heavily as she closed the door to Stefan's chamber, her attempt to discover the reason for the lovers' quarrel between him and Kassandra thwarted once again. She simply could not get an explanation out of either of them! A strained pall had hung over the mansion for over a week now, ever since they had been found safe and unharmed—much to her tearful relief!—at the hunting lodge the morning after that dreadful thunderstorm.

She walked slowly down the corridor, shaking her head in bewilderment. She had never seen such strife between two people who were intending to be married. Stefan and Kassandra had virtually avoided each other at every turn.

When she would breakfast with Kassandra, and Stefan would walk into the room, he would wheel around and stalk out again. Or when she was discussing an estate matter with Stefan in the library and Kassandra would enter, she would slam her book shut and practically flee at the sight of him.

And then there was the evening that, in hopes of encouraging a reconciliation, she had planned a special dinner for them, complete with many of the cook's most elaborate dishes—pheasant, roast mutton stuffed with oysters, brandied custard sprinkled with sugared almonds for dessert, and more. But she had ended up eating alone, Kassandra pleading a headache and Stefan concocting some nonsense about important letters he had to write. The past few days had been a dizzying whirl of such perplexing events, with, unfortunately, no end in sight.

It was not the homecoming she had envisioned for Miles, she thought unhappily. She had wanted everything to be perfect. But there seemed to be no rhyme or reason when it came to matters of the heart, especially between those two. They couldn't be more stubborn and strong-minded. And though she fervently wished it otherwise, there didn't seem to be anything she could do about it. Obviously this quarrel would have to take its natural course, without any help from her.

At least she was feeling more like herself, she mused, pausing at a large oval mirror to study her reflection. Her lively blue eyes stared back at her, fringed by black, curling lashes, and she forced a smile, her right cheek dimpling becomingly. It would not do for Miles to find her so glum when he finally arrived at the estate.

Isabel turned from the mirror, her smile fading. Whenever that might be, she thought, her dark mood drifting over her once again. She had been expecting him for well over a week. They had been separated for so long, and these last few days had been achingly slow, their tedium compounded by Stefan and Kassandra's silly quarrel.

Perhaps Miles can set things to rights once he gets here, Isabel consoled herself, continuing down the corridor. She could only hope his diplomatic skills extended to Kassandra as well. She held out her hand for the banister as she reached the staircase, but stopped it midair at the sound of a familiar voice wafting up to her from the hall below, deep, resonant, tinged with good humor. Her heart skipped a beat, her skin flushing with warmth. Could it be . . . ?

"Miles, is that you?" she cried out, barely able to contain her excitement. She leaned over the banister, her face lighting with happiness at the tall gentleman standing just inside the front doorway, a beaming Gisela at his side. He turned and looked up at her, grinning broadly, his light blue eyes crinkling at the corners.

"Miles!" Isabel fairly flew down the stairs, her arms outstretched, laughing and crying at the same time as he rushed to meet her at the bottom of the staircase. Lost in his embrace, Isabel felt as if time stood still for her, the private agony of many months of waiting washed away in a single moment.

"Oh, Miles . . ." she sobbed, standing on tiptoe, her delicate frame pressed against his well-toned body. She hugged him as if she would never let him go, and truly, she swore to herself, she never would again.

"Isabel, my love," Miles Wyndham murmured soothingly, tasting the salt of her tears as he kissed first her cheek, then her mouth. They drew life's breath from each other, embracing, tenderly caressing, their kisses punctuated by joyous laughter, oblivious to the comings and goings of their silent audience.

Gisela, her eyes shining with approval, watched her mistress with her handsome beloved for a fleeting moment. Then she rushed to the kitchen to bid the cook prepare a hearty midday meal for his lordship, who most certainly must be starved after his long journey.

Stefan, his expression haunted, watched them from the banister on the second floor. He had heard Isabel's outburst from his chamber and had decided to go and greet his future brother-in-law, dropping the documents he had been merely staring at anyway. But upon seeing them, so blissfully lost in their embrace, he had changed his mind. He swallowed against the bitter taste in his mouth, knowing he would never possess such a love as theirs, knowing Kassandra was lost to him.

He had no one to blame but himself. He alone was responsible for what had happened at his hunting lodge. Now he could only curse the day he had forced Kassandra to agree to their marriage, curse his arrogant pride, his impatience, his selfishness.

He had offered her everything but love . . . Kassandra, who was meant for a great love. And when he had finally offered her his heart, it was too late. She had done what any woman in her situation might have done . . . found someone to give her what he said had no meaning for him. He had lost her love to another man.

A far worthier man, he thought grimly. Disconsolate, he quietly turned on his heel and disappeared down the corridor.

Kassandra was just returning from her morning ride, her cheeks flushed and rosy as she breezed through the front door, only to blanch at the unexpected sight of her father. She stood rooted to the floor, torn between unbridled happiness at his safe return, and heart-wrenching distress.

So, the day she had dreaded for so long had finally come, she thought miserably. She had no doubt Stefan would ask for consent to their marriage at the earliest opportunity. And she would have no choice but to accept her father's inevitable reply, even when she and Stefan were so far apart. She had given her word . . . It might as well have been written in blood.

Overwhelmed, Kassandra turned as if to flee, hoping to collect her thoughts in the solace of her favorite garden before greeting her father. But she froze on the threshold at the sound of her name echoing about the hall.

"Kassandra!" her father repeated, holding Isabel's hand as they both hurried to greet her.

"Papa," she murmured, a tremulous smile upon her lips. She moved toward him, tears welling in her eyes. She forced them back, a familiar litany droning in her mind. She must give him no cause to think there was anything amiss . . . She must give him no cause . . . She had only to read the radiant joy on his face, and Isabel's, to know there was too much at stake to do otherwise.

"Papa, what a wonderful surprise!" she exclaimed as his strong arms embraced her. She buried her face against his broad shoulder. He smelled of fragrant pipe tobacco and woodsy cologne, scents she had known since childhood. "I've missed you so."

Miles drew away from her, his admiring gaze sweeping over her from head to foot. "You've grown even lovelier since I left, Kassandra," he said with pride. He would not say aloud how much she resembled her mother, with her flaming hair and violet eyes, for fear of hurting Isabel. God knows, he would never do that, however unintentionally.

He glanced over at his beautiful betrothed, reaching for her hand and squeezing it. The past could never be forgotten, nor should it be, he thought fleetingly. But he had been granted a glorious second love to fill the void that had long tormented his heart. "She has thrived under your care, Isabel," he voiced tenderly.

"Yes, Isabel has been like a mother to me during your absence, Papa . . . and a dear friend," Kassandra quickly agreed.

"Well, if she has thrived, I certainly can't take all the credit," Isabel objected with a bright laugh. "Stefan is most to be thanked for that."

Kassandra nearly choked in surprise, but she held her tongue as Isabel chattered on.

"We've had more than our share of adventures, and miracles, while you've been away, Miles. I've told you about most of them in my letters, but some of the things that have happened recently—" Isabel paused in midsentence, her pretty features darkening with feigned exasperation. "Did you receive any of my letters, Miles? If you did, your replies were most infrequent, scarcely four in just as many months. I had begun to think you had forgotten me."

"Never, my love," Miles replied, shaking his head. He brought her hand to his lips and kissed it gently. "I wrote you often. But I learned during my journey that many post carriages en route to Vienna were lost this past winter, along with their passengers and cargo. What with the thieves that constantly plagued the route between this city and Hanover, it was a wonder the post ever reached its destination." He uttered a short laugh. "Though I must say some of my letters would hardly have proved any entertainment at all. King George's home court was a somber place to spend the winter."

"But what of my letters, Miles?" Isabel persisted. "I wrote to you every week."

"I received a few, but I think most of them suffered the same fate as my own," he replied. He put his arm about her waist. "It is no matter, my love. We are together now, with all the time in the world to catch up on events." He bent down and lightly kissed the tip of her nose, then straightened and studied her quizzically. "Though I did receive the most curious letter, Isabel, addressed to me with your handwriting. But the paper inside was blank."

Kassandra started, her cheeks firing hotly.

"Blank? How odd," Isabel murmured, perplexed.

Then she gasped, her eyes widening like china saucers. "Well then, Miles, have you heard the wonderful news about Stefan and—"

"Oh, Papa, it is so good to see you again!" Kassandra blurted, interrupting. She threw her arms around his neck and hugged him fiercely. "But I'm sure you and Isabel must have so much to discuss, and"—she glanced down at the dirty hem of her riding skirt for emphasis—"I really should change. One could practically choke from this dust!"

With an apologetic smile, she hurried to the staircase. "We can talk later, Papa," she called over her shoulder. She wanted to gather her skirt and run up the steps, but she forced herself to walk, her heart thundering.

Sweet Lord, she simply could not face it, she raged silently. At least not right now. Perhaps later that afternoon, perhaps . . . Oh, damn it all!

Kassandra moved swiftly down the corridor to her chamber, swiping at the loose strands of hair that had fallen from the thick knot at her nape. Her door was slightly ajar, but she thought nothing of it, her head down as she walked into the sunlit room. She closed it firmly behind her and turned around, gasping in surprise as Stefan rose from the divan.

"Wh-what are you doing here?" she sputtered, backing against the door.

"I've been waiting for you, Kassandra," he began, his expression grim. "Your father has returned—"

His voice sent a shiver through her. It was the first time he had spoken to her since . . . She shook her head, willing her thoughts back to the present. "Yes, yes, I know," she said, her blood pounding. "I just saw him."

Was this how it was to be, then? she wondered wildly. Her father had just arrived, and here was

Stefan, ready to capture his long-awaited prize, like
. . . like some relentless bird of prey.

Stefan sighed raggedly, reading the desperation in
her eyes. It could hardly match his own. He was being split apart, a final furious debate warring within
his mind, his heart, his very soul. He had been possessed by it the entire week, unable to face her, unable to face himself. Even now, when it was time to
make a decision, it raged like an unquenchable fire
within him.

He knew he could still hold her to their agreement. At least then he would not lose her completely . . .

Or he could let her go . . . She would be free to
enjoy her newfound happiness, and most of all, free
of the cruel havoc he had wreaked upon her life.

Stefan's hands clenched into helpless fists. He
knew well within his deepest heart that he had decided. To take Kassandra for his wife knowing she
loved another man was more than he could bear. It
was not enough to possess her body. He wanted her
love—the one thing that would never be his.

Enough, he thought with resignation. She's lost
to you. Get on with it.

Stefan took a step toward her, his tortured gaze
meeting her own. ''I release you from your agreement to marry me, Kassandra,'' he said abruptly.
How easily said, he mused, for a statement that
would haunt him for a lifetime.

Kassandra merely gaped at him, so stunned she
barely registered his words.

''It was my plan to tell you this at the hunting
lodge, but it was not meant to be.'' He paused,
swallowing against the raw emotion constricting
his throat, then continued, his voice a dull monotone. ''You have nothing to fear from me, Kassandra.
There will be no scandal. What happened in the tav-

ern is between you and me alone . . . our secret. On
that, you have my word. Now I must go."

Stefan moved toward the door, not surprised
when Kassandra quickly stepped out of his way. It
seemed fitting that she would run from him, even
now. He opened the door. "I wish you happiness
with your lover, Kassandra, whoever he may be,"
he murmured softly. "He is more fortunate than he
will ever know." Then he was gone, the door closing firmly behind him, his footsteps echoing down
the corridor before fading altogether.

Kassandra could not move. Stefan's words seemed
to hang in the air—*I release you, Kassandra, release you,
release you,*—as they tumbled over and over in her
mind. She was free of her cursed agreement . . .
free.

Yet how strange, she mused. She felt nothing. No
joy, no wild elation, no relief, no sense of triumph,
only a swirling emptiness. Never in a thousand years
would she have expected this . . .

Her legs were wooden as she at last walked to the
divan and sank down upon it, her head resting in
her hand. She stared blindly at the rose-patterned
brocade, a single thought pressing in upon her, insistent, demanding.

What had Stefan said? *It was my plan to tell you at
the hunting lodge* . . . Yes, those had been his words.
*But it was not meant to be* . . . Why? Why wasn't it
meant to be? Why hadn't he told her?

She drew in her breath sharply. Because before
he'd had a chance, she'd spurned him, saying she
loved another . . .

Kassandra raised her head, the haunting memory
of his expression at that moment a striking image in
her mind. Why would Stefan have planned to release her from her agreement to marry him if his
words of love were not true? After all that had

passed between them, perhaps it was the only way he could prove he truly loved her . . .

"Oh, Kassandra, what have you done?" she whispered under her breath, rising from the divan. She had sworn she would forgive him anything, everything, if only he spoke the truth. And he had, dear God, he had! Stefan loved her!

As she loved him . . .

A fierce ache welled up in her heart and she cried out his name as she fled to the door and flung it wide. There was only one thing she could do. She had to find him. She only hoped it wasn't too late.

Holding up the skirt of her riding habit, Kassandra raced down the silent corridor and dashed down the stairs, almost running into Isabel, who was rounding the corner from the dining room.

"Kassandra, I was just on my way up to fetch you. Your father is in the drawing room changing out of his traveling clothes, but as soon as he's ready, we're to have dinner. We thought you might join us. The cook has prepared the most wonderful meal—"

"Isabel, please, have you seen Stefan?" she blurted breathlessly, her eyes darting to the closed door of the library.

"Why, he just left, Kassandra, only moments ago."

"Just left?"

"Yes. I asked him to stay for dinner, but he mumbled something about going for a ride and wanting to be left alone for a while." She shook her head. "He seemed upset. And if I know Stefan, I have no doubt he has set out for his hunting lodge. It's where he always goes when he wishes to be alone."

Kassandra gave Isabel a quick kiss on the cheek, flashed her a smile, then, without saying a word, hurried to the door and opened it before the footman had a chance.

"What shall I tell your father?" Isabel called out, her brow knit in confusion. When she received no answer, she shrugged her delicate shoulders, at a momentary loss. Then a slow smile spread across her features, and she laughed.

"What is so amusing?" Miles queried, walking up behind her and wrapping his arms about her petite waist. He bent down and nuzzled her neck, the sweet rose scent of her perfume enveloping his senses.

Isabel sighed and leaned her head back against his chest. "If I am any judge at all in matters of the heart, I believe Kassandra and Stefan are soon to end their quarrel," she murmured, almost to herself.

"What quarrel?"

Isabel turned in his arms, her eyes filling with admiration as they swept over him. He looked so handsome in his light wool waistcoat and breeches, the air of a dignified statesman clinging to him like a fine fragrance. He was no longer wearing a wig; instead his dark brown hair, graying at the temples, was neatly combed from his strong forehead. She took his hand and walked with him into the dining room. "Oh, it is nothing, my lord. Come, our dinner is waiting."

# Chapter 32

◠◠◠◠◠

The sun had climbed well up in the midday sky by the time Kassandra neared the hunting lodge. She slowed her mare to a trot, shading her eyes from its bright glare as she searched for any sign of Stefan or Brand. A low nicker drifted to them from the small stable, and she felt a rush of nervous excitement. That meant Stefan was here, just as Isabel had said he might be.

She dismounted in front of the stable door, opened to allow the spring breezes to waft in and out, and led the mare inside the darkened building. It was empty but for Brand, who snorted and tossed his proud head in greeting. She settled her mare into a nearby stall, then stepped out again into the sunlight, but not in time to see another horse and rider melt into a copse of trees a short distance away.

She walked to the lodge, a giddy tightness in her chest, her breath frozen in her throat. But when she pushed open the door and stepped inside, her gaze sweeping the sunlit interior, Stefan was not there. She couldn't even tell if anyone had been in the lodge since the week before—

A dry stick snapped outside, startling her. "Stefan?" she called out, rushing from the lodge. She was greeted only by the chirping of birds, perched high in the swaying branches of the trees that encir-

cled the logged building, and the gentle rustling of
new leaves, shimmering and waving in the sun.

Where could he be? Then she remembered something Isabel had told her once about a favorite place
of Stefan's, along an arm of the Danube River that
served as the northeastern boundary of their land.
She had said he used to spend many hours there as
a boy, fishing or dreaming. She had even caught
him fencing at imaginary enemies, a wooden sword
in his hand, one day when she had ridden out to
meet him.

Kassandra smiled faintly, conjuring up the scene,
then her thoughts returned quickly to the reason she
had followed him here. But where was this river?
She had never seen it herself, for she never rode this
far north. She had no idea if it ran anywhere near
the hunting lodge . . .

It must be close by, she reasoned. Otherwise
Brand would not be in the stable. She walked determinedly around the lodge, searching for any sign of
a path. She was rewarded when she spied a well-
worn trail leading through the dense woods at the
rear of the lodge.

She began to follow it, almost running, a sense of
urgency spurring her on. The trail wound through
the forest for a short way, skirted a wide clearing,
and finally sloped back into the trees and down a
gradual hill. She could hear the sound of rushing
water growing louder and louder, yet she was hardly
prepared for the majesty of the river when she came
upon it, a winding torrent of light and vibrant color.
She leaned against a tree while she caught her
breath, her eyes wide as she drank in the stunning
view.

Sunlight sparkled upon the water, interwoven
streaks of gold broken only by the white-flecked current, a splashing fish, or a gusting breeze. Reflected
in its depths was a sky of azure blue. Lush green

grass covered the rolling banks, like a velvet carpet falling into the water, and towering trees lined ragged shores—

Kassandra's heart pitched as her wide-eyed gaze suddenly fell upon Stefan. He was sitting with his back to her almost at the edge of a grassy knoll overlooking the river, a short distance from where she stood.

Quelling a rush of apprehension, she pushed away from the tree. She moved slowly behind him, her footfalls masked by the soft grass. She could tell he was lost in thought, his arms around a raised knee, his other leg stretched out in front of him. It was only when she laid her hand gently upon his shoulder that he started in surprise and jumped to his feet, whirling to face her.

"Kassandra! What the devil?" he shouted. He eyed her warily. "What are you doing here?"

She hesitated a moment. She had so much to say to him, to explain to him . . . she didn't know how to begin. She took a tentative step toward him, her eyes locking with his own.

"I've come to meet the man who has won my love," she murmured evenly, ignoring the fierce beating of her heart.

Stefan winced, his face darkening. So this must have been where she would meet her lover, he thought angrily. How ironic that she had discovered this particular spot on the river, his favorite sanctuary, for her liaisons. How fitting. But, damn it all, why did she have to torture him? Did she hate him so much she would now flaunt her lover before him?

He turned to study the shoreline. There was no sign of anyone yet. He looked back at her, consumed with barely controlled rage. No! He would not have it. Elsewhere perhaps, but not on his land, and not here.

"If the man is fool enough to trespass on my

land," Stefan grated, "he will surely face the sting of my sword."

Kassandra couldn't breathe, the force of his pain almost too much to bear. She saw it reflected in his eyes, the gray depths that could stir her with only a casual glance; she read it in the taut stance of his powerful body and in his expression, his ruggedly handsome features set, implacable, strangely pale despite his bronzed skin. How she had hurt him. How they had hurt each other. She had to choose her words carefully, carefully . . .

"If that is so," she said softly, "then you will be plunging your blade into your own heart."

Stefan stood motionless, his blood roaring in his ears. When he spoke at last, his voice was a dangerous whisper. "So you mock me even now, Kassandra."

"No!" she exclaimed, rushing up to him and placing her fingers upon his lips. "Never." He flinched at her touch, seizing her wrist in a cruel grip.

Kassandra winced against the pain but held her ground, her chin trembling as she shook her head. "There has never been another man, Stefan," she murmured. "Only you."

He quaked at her words, shaken to the very depths of his soul. Ever so gradually, as the agonizing torment ebbed from his body, his grip loosened. His eyes burned into her own as he brought her hand to his mouth, his lips searing into her flesh as he kissed her open palm. "Kassandra . . ." he moaned raggedly, his arm encircling her waist, drawing her close. "Kassandra . . ."

She lifted her hand to his bent head, her fingers stroking his thick black hair. "I love you, Stefan."

His mouth captured her own before she could draw a breath. He kissed her with all the passion he possessed, yet with infinite tenderness, saying without words what was etched indelibly upon his heart.

Nothing else mattered, no explanations, no apologies . . . only the kiss they shared. The past was forgotten, lost in the face of impassioned forgiveness, and there was only the future, shining before them.

With an exultant cry, Stefan picked her up in his arms, her feet dangling off the ground. They twirled around and around, a wild shower of kisses raining upon cheeks, eyelids, tips of noses, smiling lips. Incredible joy, the sweetest rapture . . . they were drunk with it, giddy, then it seemed the ground moved from beneath them, and they were falling through space—

Kassandra shrieked in shock as they hit the cold water with a mighty splash, her cry cut off when she sank beneath the sunlit surface. Then she was catapulted upward by Stefan's strong arms, sputtering and gasping for air as she emerged from the shoulder-high depths. Stunned, she gaped at him through spiky lashes, her chest heaving, her teeth chattering, her riding habit a sodden weight upon her chilled body. He was as drenched as she, rivulets running down his face, his clothes molded to the rugged breadth of his shoulders and chest. And he was grinning from ear to ear.

"It appears, my lady, that I . . . misjudged . . . the shoreline!" he gasped, holding her close against him to prevent the strong underlying currents from forcing them apart. He kissed her with a loud smack, a low chuckle rumbling in his throat. Then he threw back his head and laughed uproariously, the deep, rich peals echoing all around them.

Kassandra thrilled at the sound, joining in, her bright laughter merging with his own. It felt so good to laugh, to love! She entwined her arms around his neck as he lifted her easily in his arms and waded to shore against the tugging current, climbing onto the sloping bank, where he sank to his knees and set her gently upon the soft grass.

He fell beside her and rolled onto his back, wiping his hands across his face and through his hair. They lay there for a few moments, staring up into the wide blue sky, their panting breaths punctuated by short bursts of laughter.

Kassandra threw her arms above her head, luxuriating in the golden warmth of the sun through her soaked clothing. But the mid-April breeze was cool. She shivered, her teeth still chattering.

"I . . . I w-wonder what Isabel and . . . m-my . . . father . . . will think when th-they see us," she stammered, glancing at Stefan with a quivering smile.

"They'll be none the wiser," Stefan answered enigmatically, sitting up. He bent over her and planted a warm, lingering kiss on her chilled lips, then drew away and rose to his feet. He held out his hand to her. "Come with me, Kassandra."

With a puzzled look she took his hand. He pulled her up beside him, and they walked back to the grassy knoll where he had been sitting. He picked up his light woolen cloak and wrapped it securely around her shoulders. Then they set out hand in hand along the trail to the hunting lodge. The walk seemed much shorter going back, despite numerous pauses for breathless kisses, and soon they were standing just outside the lodge.

Kassandra gasped in surprise as he swept her in his arms and carried her through the door, standing ajar, just as she had left it. He kicked it shut and set her down in the middle of the floor, then moved to the fireplace. In a matter of minutes, tiny orange flames were licking at the dry kindling and logs piled high upon the grates.

Stefan rose to his feet and shrugged off his drenched outercoat, his fingers working at the but-

tons on his sodden waistcoat. "Take off your clothes,
Kassandra, and we'll dry them in front of the fireplace," he murmured with his back to her.

With a deep laugh he removed his boots and
poured the water from them into a bucket, before
setting them aside, then draped his dripping garments over a chair near the fire. That left only his
breeches. He turned, unfastening the row of vertical
buttons, but stopped at the stricken look on Kassandra's face. She was still standing in the middle of
the room, a small puddle forming around her feet.

Kassandra's skin fired hotly at his startled expression, and she lowered her eyes, embarrassed. She
felt like such a fool! But when he began to undress,
she could not quell the hint of fear that this was all
a dream. Scarcely a week had passed, and now suddenly everything was so different between them.
Things were happening so fast! She needed some
time before . . . before . . .

She blushed bright pink, so lost in her confused
thoughts, she didn't hear him walk up to her. She
started as he gently lifted her chin, his eyes searching her own.

"Kassandra, we have all the time in the world,"
Stefan murmured soothingly, as if he had read her
mind. "There is no need to rush things. When you
are ready, we'll both know it. It's enough for now
that we love." He bent and tenderly kissed her
flushed cheek. "If you'd like, I shall turn my back
and close my eyes as you undress," he offered with
a playful smile, "and I'll leave these on." He glanced
down at his breeches. "Agreed?"

Kassandra nodded, blinking back the tears swimming in her eyes as Stefan walked to the fireplace
and leaned his muscled arms on the mantel. She
cast off his cloak and undressed quickly, peeling off
layer after layer of soaked clothing, her riding coat,
wide skirt, petticoat, chemise, boots, stockings. She

hung everything on the other high-backed chair, propping her boots beside Stefan's.

"Why don't you wrap yourself in a fur, my love," Stefan suggested, sensing she was near him. It was all he could do to keep his eyes closed, knowing what a fetching sight she must be. But he was determined not to betray her trust, despite the burning ache in his loins. "There are plenty on the bed."

Kassandra's gaze darted from his face, his striking profile highlighted in the glow of the flames, his eyelids tightly shut, to the bed. She ran across the floor and seized a soft fur, whirling it around her shoulders and clutching it to her body. She turned from the bed, and was about to tell him he could open his eyes, but the words died on her lips.

Her heart pounded wildly as her gaze traveled along the powerful length of his body, from the broad span of his shoulders, the muscles firm and knotted, his black hair falling to just below his nape, to the sculpted definition of his back, tapering to a slim waist, banded with muscle. His breeches, wet and molded to his lower body like a second skin, did little to hide the taut outline of his buttocks and the strength of his thighs . . .

Kassandra shivered, a rush of liquid desire tingling from her scalp to her toes. These were the thoughts of a woman, and here she was acting like a frightened child. This was not a dream. Stefan was real, of flesh and blood . . . He was her love, the air she breathed. She didn't need more time to tell her that. She needed his arms about her, the warm pressure of his lips upon her own, his touch . . .

"Stefan?" she murmured, her voice barely above a whisper. She tensed as he turned, her breathing shallow, her lips parted. His bronzed body was outlined in an aura of flame, magnificent, virile, and she could not tear her eyes away. Her hands loosened their hold on the fur and it drifted along her skin to the floor, the whisper-soft sensation exciting her beyond measure. She moaned faintly, crying out in yearning for this one man. She stretched out her arms, wanting him, wanting him . . .

For a moment Stefan could only gaze at her, mesmerized by the startling vision she made. Her porcelain beauty was awash in gold from the warm sunlight streaming through the windows, her damp hair clinging to the lithe curves of her body and down her back, streaking across her high, pouting breasts. She swayed slightly, and something winked and sparkled between the tempting hollow, the jeweled locket he had given her.

Diamonds, rubies—they paled beside her loveliness, he thought fleetingly. She was the rarest jewel, with facets of fire-gold and cream, brilliant amethyst and palest rose, goddess, woman . . . perfection. And she was his.

He walked slowly toward her, his eyes capturing her own, holding them in thrall. He reached out for her, their hands entwining, and drew her against him, his breath catching in his throat as her hardened nipples grazed his chest. But he held himself back, gazing down into her face, searching. Only a few moments ago she had shied away from him, confused, uncertain. He had to be sure she wanted him as much as he wanted her . . .

Sensing his inner turmoil, Kassandra lowered her head and trailed a line of kisses across his chest to just left of his breastbone, where she pressed her lips fervently to the beating of his heart. ''Love me, Stefan,'' she murmured, her breath hot against his skin. ''Love me . . .''

He groaned, her words unleashing within him an explosion of raging desire. In one fluid motion he lifted her in his arms and laid her upon the bed, the pale cream of her body in striking contrast to the glistening furs beneath her.

Kassandra rolled languidly onto her side, watching with intense fascination as Stefan stripped off his breeches. Emboldened by her love, she traced her finger along the dark swath of hair trailing down his taut belly, past sleek, narrow hips, to end in a mass of black curls between sinewed thighs. His erect manhood seemed to leap against her hand and she gasped in surprise, falling back onto the furs.

Stefan chuckled lustily, gathering her into his arms as he lay down beside her. "I warn you, my lady," he whispered in her ear. "To touch a man so can only bring about the most dire consequences." He gently bit her earlobe, as if to emphasize his words, then it was he who gasped when Kassandra's hand tentatively touched his pulsating hardness once again.

Her fingers wrapped around him, unsure at first, but growing more bold as she slowly caressed him, reveling in the silken feel of his skin, the satin smoothness, the crispness of the curls nestled there. He moaned against her ear, his breaths panting, ragged, and she marveled that she could pleasure him so. She began to stroke him faster, innately sensing that she could please him still further, only to start when he suddenly drew her hand away.

"Enough, my love," he whispered hoarsely, pushing her back down upon the furs. He knelt above her, his muscled thighs straddling her hips, his throbbing shaft pressed against the silken mound between her legs. His flint-gray eyes, inflamed with passion, seared into her own. "Now it is my turn."

He bent over her, supporting his powerful weight with his hands, and tenderly kissed her forehead, her eyelids, his lips brushing against her gold-tipped lashes. His kiss became possessive when he sought her lips, demanding, drawing the breath from her body as his tongue savored the recesses of her mouth, tasting its sweetness, lingering there. When Kassandra's arms instinctively wound about his neck, returning his impassioned kiss, he forced them down above her head, gripping her wrists gently with one hand while his other hand stroked her breast.

Kassandra sharply inhaled as his nails lightly raked across her hardened nipple, until she thought she might scream from the delicious sensations pouring through her body. Each time she arched her back, her hips moved beneath him, stoking a fire deep within her belly as the tip of his hardness pressed urgently against the aching bud of her desire.

Suddenly Stefan released her wrists and shifted his weight, pushing her long legs apart and kneeling between them. His hands were everywhere, caressing, teasing, his mouth, hot, insistent, capturing first one rose-tipped crest, then the other, while his fingers explored the silken cleft of her womanhood, entwining in russet curls. He knew she was ready, but he wanted to push her still further to the brink of ecstasy. He bent down and cupped her buttocks, his tongue delving into her where his fingers had been only a moment before.

There was a wildness to his movements, an urgent intensity, matched only by Kassandra's driving need. She writhed against him, trembling, calling his name, pleading for him to stop, pleading for him to linger, pleading for what she knew was to come.

Then Stefan was above her, knowing she could wait no longer, knowing he could wait no longer to possess her. As he plunged into her, she cried out her pleasure, tears of rapture stinging her eyes, her jagged breaths melding with his own. She felt storm-tossed, buffeted, adrift in a raging sea of delirious sensation, then she was hovering above it for a blinding instant, hovering . . . until she dove back down into the boiling sea, wave after wave of furious ecstasy crashing in upon her, crashing in upon Stefan, drowning them in all-encompassing delight.

# Chapter 33

❦

It was Stefan who first opened his eyes, blinking against the dappled sunlight playing across the wide bed. He rose up on his elbow and glanced out the window. The sun was settling into the trees, its bright rays winking through the leafy branches.

It must be three, or perhaps four o'clock, he thought, somewhat dazed. He was not used to sleeping in the middle of the afternoon. The flames had died in the fireplace; nothing was left of the logs but glowing embers that hissed faintly, the only other sound in the lodge the steady rhythm of Kassandra's breathing.

Smiling, he gazed down at her, nestled against his chest. She was so touchingly beautiful . . . He wrapped his arm about her protectively, a sense of overwhelming fulfillment settling over him. He had never known such happiness, such peace. He could hardly wait to share his joy, their joy, with Isabel and Lord Harrington.

Stefan bent his head and touched his lips to her cheek, stroking the silken softness of her hair. "Kassandra, it's time to wake," he whispered.

She merely sighed, snuggling closer, lost to sleep.

He suppressed a laugh and tried again, this time gently shaking her shoulder. "Awake, my love."

Kassandra's eyelids slowly flickered open, a contented smile lighting her features. "Hmmm . . ." she murmured, stretching languorously, the crisp curls on his chest tickling her nose. She inhaled, breathing in his warm, male scent.

Stefan groaned, the pressure of her lithe body against him rekindling his desire. He would never get enough of her! This afternoon was proof of that. They had loved until breathless exhaustion had overtaken them, and even now he could think of nothing better than spending another delightful hour in bed. But he forced his mind to the stir that was probably brewing at the mansion over their long absence. He didn't think Karl could stand the shock of finding them like this again. It was time they made their way back.

"Kassandra, the afternoon has fled," he began. "Your father is no doubt wondering—"

"Father!" Kassandra exclaimed, her eyes widening. She sat up beside him, oblivious of her nakedness. "Oh, Stefan, we should return at once. I hope they haven't sent anyone out looking for us."

"My thoughts exactly," he replied, tracing his finger down her arm, his eyes feasting upon the tempting silhouette of her breasts.

Kassandra shivered at his touch, playfully pushing his hand away. "Stefan . . ."

"I know, I know," he said reluctantly. Suddenly he forced her back down upon the mattress and rolled on top of her, supporting his weight on his elbows. He grinned rakishly, entwining his fingers in her fire-gold hair. "But when we are married, my lady, you will not so easily escape my bed."

"I shall hold you to your threat, my lord," Kassandra answered with a lusty gleam in her eye that both astounded and delighted him. Chuckling, Stefan bent his head and kissed her soundly, then rolled away from her to the edge of the bed and swung his long legs to the floor. He stood up, offering her his hand.

"Let us not delay our wedding any further, my lady," he said. "There is the small matter of your father's consent I must address as soon as we get back."

Kassandra blushed hotly, taking his hand. He drew her from the bed and into his arms, embracing her fiercely. "Do you think I have a chance?" he queried lightly, though his expression was serious.

Kassandra pulled away, her gaze meeting his. "My father wishes only for my happiness," she murmured. "He will see that I have found it with you, Stefan."

As if to seal her words, she stood on tiptoe and touched her lips to his in the sweetest kiss he had ever known. It was timeless, lingering, until at last she drew away, smiling up at him. "Then I have nothing to fear," he whispered almost to himself.

Kassandra shook her head with certainty. "Nothing, my lord."

Stefan released her, his broad smile returning to his face as he swept up his breeches from the floor. He put them on, eyeing her roguishly. She was watching him, her gaze one of bold admiration. "Perhaps you might dress, Kassandra, unless you would prefer to ride as you are," he teased. He appraised her heatedly. "Although I, for one, would not mind in the least."

Kassandra blushed anew and scurried over to the chair where she had hung her clothes, her fingers trembling as she snatched up her chemise. She drew it on, aware that he was watching her, and reveling in that knowledge. She dressed hurriedly, though, and was almost ready when he spoke again.

"I'll saddle the horses while you finish," he said, walking up behind her. He nuzzled her neck, his breath a stirring warmth against her nape, and draped his blue cloak about her shoulders. "Wrap yourself in this, my love. I'll not have you catching a chill on the ride home." Then he was gone from her, striding across the planked floor, the door opening and closing behind him.

Minutes later, Kassandra fumbled with the last buttons on her riding coat, her back to the door as she bent and drew on her boots. She heard it creak open, and she straightened, clutching the cloak about her body. "That was quick, Stef—"

A thick cloth pressed roughly against her nose and mouth cut off her words. Her eyes widened in fright, her fingers clawing at the gloved hand that held it, a cloyingly sweet odor swamping her senses. Her vision dimmed and she felt as if she was choking. Then there was only blackness as she slumped unconscious to the floor.

That was the easy part, Frederick thought grimly, pocketing the cloth. He wasted no time as he knelt and lifted her in his arms, hoisting her over his shoulder. He knew he had only minutes before Stefan would return with the horses.

He strode quickly to the door, peering out toward the stable, located some distance away, but thankfully there was no sign of him. With his heart thundering in his chest, Frederick took off at a run to the back of the lodge, where he plunged along the trail leading to the river. He had left his horse tethered there, just in case the opportunity he had been awaiting all afternoon should present itself.

Frederick's mind raced, his chest heaving from exertion as he half ran, half walked along the path. It had been too perfect, he marveled, especially after he had missed two excellent chances earlier that day. When Kassandra had gone for her morning ride, he had not counted on her masterful ability with horses, and he had been hard-pressed to overtake her, let alone keep up with her.

When she had arrived at the lodge, he should have grabbed her before she found Stefan. But their rendezvous at the river had given him the idea for her accidental demise, if he could only abduct her. He had kept himself hidden just outside the lodge for the past few hours, waiting, listening, hoping desperately for the slightest chance he might catch Kassandra alone, even for a few moments. His silent prayer had been answered when Stefan left the lodge for the stable. He had seized the opportunity, and he had proved the victor!

At least so far, Frederick amended darkly. He was no fool. Time was of the essence in this deadly game. He knew that as soon as Stefan discovered she was missing, he would search everywhere, probably even to the river. Which was exactly what Frederick wanted . . .

He shifted Kassandra's weight on his shoulder, grateful that she was so light. He could hear the roar of the rushing water just beyond the wooded hill, and he increased his pace, almost sliding down the trail. Nervous relief filled him as he reached the river, and he made his way quickly to the grassy knoll where Stefan and Kassandra had shared their fleeting moment of happiness, a touching scene that had been most entertaining.

Frederick dropped to his knees and laid Kassandra upon the ground. He studied her for a moment, her beautiful features, her lush breasts outlined beneath the riding coat.

Yes, it would truly be a pity to squander such loveliness, he thought, cold cunning reflected in his gaze. It seemed fate had intervened in his original intent to cast her into the river, where, unconscious, she would quickly drown. While hiding outside the lodge, he had thought of a much better plan to rid Archduchess Sophia of Lady Kassandra Wyndham . . . forever. He could not suppress a laugh. He would not only save his own neck, but reap a profit in gold as well!

From what he knew of her now, she was not only well versed in lovemaking, but charming and witty as well. He remembered their pleasant conversation at Prince Eugene's gala a few months ago, her graceful skill at dancing and flirting, and her winsome smiles. He had almost given away his true nature that night, thinking perhaps she might be enamored of him . . .

A sharp twinge of remorse stabbed at Frederick, but he quickly stifled it. He had no time for regret, nor pity, not when his own life was at stake. At least he was allowing her to live.

Though she might wish she had died, he mused darkly, once she learned she was bound for a harem as a morsel to tempt a jaded Turkish palate. He had in mind exactly which harem, and which man would become her master. As far as Sophia was concerned, Kassandra would be as good as dead. No woman who entered a harem was ever seen or heard from again.

Get on with it, man, Frederick chided himself, ripping the blue woolen cloak from her shoulders. You've still got to make it look like her disappearance was a tragic accident.

He stood up and strode to the water's edge, his keen eyes judging the distance and angle of approach to several trees farther down the shoreline, now knocked over and half-submerged because of the fierce storm of the past week. He cast the cloak into the river, watching as it drifted on the swiftly flowing current. He felt a rush of triumph when it snagged on a branch. Perfect! Then he dug his bootheels into the muddy bank, so it appeared as if someone had slipped into the water at that point.

Frederick grimly turned his back on the river and hurried to Kassandra, hoisting her once again over his shoulder. He walked upstream a short way to where he had tethered his horse, laid her crosswise over the saddle, mounted, and set off at a fast canter through the woods. He veered north, intending to avoid the von Furstenberg estate altogether. He would cut back toward Vienna when he was well past it.

Raw excitement gripped him and he spurred the spirited stallion on with a sharp nudge of his boot. Tomorrow he would at last be able to leave the city and head south along the Danube to Belgrade, Serbia. It was only Sophia's unexpected task that had prevented him from leaving several days sooner. He had finally discovered the date the Imperial army would depart for the summer campaign. Halil Pasha would be most pleased by this information . . . as well as by the seductive gift he would present to him.

Now there was nothing left to do but hire a boat and send a message to Archduchess Sophia von Starenberg that Lady Kassandra Wyndham was dead.

Stefan led the two horses toward the lodge, amazed at his light step. How different from when he had arrived there earlier in the day.

"Kassandra!" he called, surprised that she wasn't waiting for him at the door. He had been in the stable for a quarter hour, plenty of time for her to finish dressing. He shrugged, raising his voice again. "Kassandra!"

When he received no answer, he tethered Brand and the Arabian mare to a tree stump and strode into the sun-washed interior. It was empty.

Stefan turned on his heel and walked back outside, surveying the clearing surrounding the lodge. Perhaps she was teasing him, hiding behind a tree, as a game . . .

He laughed shortly, his voice tinged with feigned exasperation. "Kassandra, come out. We don't have time for games this afternoon. I want to reach the mansion before dark."

There was no reply, not even a giggle. All was hushed, still, except for the wind rustling through the trees and the haunting call of a mourning dove.

A mourning dove. A shiver ran down his spine, but he quelled it angrily. He had never been one for superstitious nonsense, and he wasn't going to begin now!

It was simple, he reasoned. He had taken longer than she had thought he would, so she had decided to entertain herself with a stroll. The woods were magical at this time of the year, with the sun filtering through the new leaves, dappling the ground in light and shadow, and the scurrying of forest creatures and their young. The forest had intrigued him as a boy, and drew him even now, stirring his senses. Kassandra and he were alike in that regard.

Perhaps she had strolled back toward the river, he considered. It was worth a look.

He mounted Brand and urged him into a trot, skirting the lodge and setting out along the trail. Every few moments he called out her name, but only his voice came back to him, echoing in the silent woods. He searched for the blue cloak he'd lent her; its color would surely stand out amidst the forest hues. But there was no sign of her anywhere.

Stefan's spirits lifted as he neared the river. Something inexplicable told him she was there, waiting for him, perhaps to share a last kiss in memory of the day. She was a romantic at heart—another trait he loved about her.

He pulled up on the reins at the foot of the hill and dismounted, walking the rest of the way to the river. But when he reached his favorite spot, he was disappointed once again. She was nowhere to be seen.

"Kassandra!" he shouted above the rushing torrent, looking first upstream, then the other way. "Kassan—"

His voice froze in his throat, fear cutting through him. Was that his cloak, caught within the branches . . . ? He moved closer to the shoreline to get a better view, his feet slipping in the mud at the water's edge, and he had to catch himself from sliding in. He looked down, his heart lurching sickeningly in his chest. Someone had fallen here, not long ago . . .

Kassandra!

Stefan began to run along the rolling bank, faster and faster, desperation spurring him on. He did not stop until he reached the fallen tree, half of its splintered length stretching out across the water, its branches reaching for the sky like bony fingers. Floating on the surface of the white-flecked currents was his blue cloak, snagged by one of the outermost branches.

Kassandra . . .

"No . . ." he whispered vehemently, as if he could will away the thought burning into his mind. "No!" He wrenched off his boots and dove into the water, frantically searching the muddy river bottom and along the length of the submerged tree . . . nothing. He came up for great, gasping breaths only to dive beneath the sunlit surface again and again, swimming with powerful strokes to the place where he had slipped, diving, searching, diving . . . nothing . . . nothing!

The horrible minutes dragged on, the agonized cries that tore at his throat melding with the ragged breaths for air that rasped in his lungs. At last, spent and exhausted, he dragged himself from the water and fell to his hands and knees, his chest heaving, water running from his clothes and pooling on the ground.

"Brand!" he shouted hoarsely, fighting to catch his breath. "Brand!"

A shrill whinny carried to him on the breeze, then the thunder of hooves sounded upon the grassy bank as the black steed galloped toward him.

"Steady, boy, steady," Stefan gasped, staggering to his feet and leaning on Brand's glistening flank. His hands, scratched and bleeding, seized the reins, and with a groan he hoisted himself into the saddle. He nudged the stallion into a fast trot, veering along the rolling bank.

He would search the entire length of this river, he swore vehemently, and on to where it joined the Danube, if need be. He would find her . . . he would find her! Alive or—

No, he would not think of it! Desperate tears stung his eyes. He tried to choke them back . . . He had never cried before in his life. But they welled up once again, streaking the hardened planes of his face, dimming his vision as his tortured gaze followed the line of the shore . . . the life that had held so much promise suddenly become a living hell.

# Chapter 34

Kassandra tossed her head from side to side, lost in the depths of an all-consuming nightmare. There were no shapes, only faceless, creeping shadows. They advanced, looming over her, then receded, disappearing into a smothering gray mass, a dense cloud, settling over her, covering her. She couldn't breathe . . . she couldn't breathe!

Kassandra gasped, her body jerking spasmodically. She dragged open the oppressive weight of her eyelids, only to close them once again. Her lungs drew in great gasps of air, tinged with the fetid odor of rotting fish, damp wood, and mildew. The smell unsettled her empty stomach and she gagged, rolling heavily onto her side, afraid she might choke.

She was ill . . . something was wrong with her, she thought dazedly, trying to lift her head. It fell back to the thin mattress with a thud, the throbbing at her temples heightening into piercing pain. She cried out, her hands cradling her forehead, her moans echoing about the cramped cabin, dark but for the thin slivers of light squeezing through the small slatted window.

A key grated in a lock and the door creaked open, lamplight flooding in from a narrow hallway. Kassandra blinked against the brightness. Two figures were framed in the light, their whispering voices carrying to her from a few feet away.

What were they saying? she wondered crazily, not recognizing their clipped language. Who were they? Where was she? The door slammed shut on her unanswered questions, the key twisted, and footsteps scurried down a hall, fading into silence.

Kassandra rose up on her elbows and lifted her head, tucking her hands beneath her chin. She stared straight in front of her at the window, forcing herself to take slow, even breaths. Gradually the stabbing pain in her head subsided, becoming a dull ache. Her blurred vision began to focus, and the queasy feeling in her stomach settled into a gnawing emptiness. Yet she still felt as if she was rocking up and down, a dizzying motion that occasionally pitched the bed forward, bumping the headboard into the planked wall.

Strange, she mused, the muddled fog clearing from her mind, her thoughts growing sharper. She had felt this motion before, last summer, on the boat that had taken her and her father down the Danube from Ratisbon to Vienna . . .

She started, her eyes widening in horror. Sweet Lord, she was on a boat! She twisted around, her gaze flying about the shadowed cabin. It was very small and plainly furnished with a chair and an armoire upon which was stacked a pile of books. The bed she lay upon was very narrow, the mattress hard and lumpy. The ceiling was low; an unlit oil lamp swung overhead, back and forth, back and forth, further testament that she was aboard a vessel of some kind. But how?

"What is happening?" Kassandra whispered plaintively under her breath. She struggled to sit up, almost falling back upon the mattress as dizziness assailed her. She grabbed on to the headboard until the vertigo passed, her forehead furrowed in desperate thought, remembering.

She had been waiting for Stefan in the hunting lodge . . . she bent over to pull on her boots . . . she heard the door open . . . the cloth, pressed over her mouth . . . now she was here, on a boat.

Maybe it was all a terrible dream, Kassandra thought numbly, peering out the thin slats of the window. Tears stung her eyes at the wide expanse of glistening water between her and the rolling shoreline, green and thickly wooded.

It wasn't a dream! Panic-stricken, she sprang suddenly from the bed, her legs buckling beneath her. She fell heavily to the floor, expelling her breath in a loud gasp. Stunned, she lay inert, wincing as feeling flowed back into her limbs, pricking her like sharp pins and needles. She began to crawl toward the door, where she grabbed on to the latch and pulled herself to her knees.

"Help! Please, someone help me!" she cried, tears streaming down her flushed face. She rattled the latch up and down, but to no avail. The door was locked. With great effort she rose to her feet, the room spinning. She clung to the door, pounding on it weakly. "Please, let me out! Let me out!"

Loud footsteps sounded, a key was fitted into the lock, then the door was pushed open so abruptly that Kassandra fell back against the armoire. Pain shot through her shoulder, but she ignored it, swiping the tears from her face as she rushed forward, straight into the arms of a tall man standing just inside the threshold.

"Light the lamp, man," Frederick gritted to the scrawny sailor behind him.

Kassandra tensed at the familiar voice, though she did not understand his words, spoken in a language wholly foreign to her. She stared up at him, but in the dark she couldn't see his face. It was only when someone brushed by her and lit the oil lamp that her eyes widened in startled surprise as she recognized the man who held her as Count Frederick Althann.

Wild with relief, she collapsed against his chest. Whatever had brought about this nightmare was now, thankfully, at an end. What a coincidence that Count Frederick should rescue her from this confusion. She embraced him gratefully, her mind racing with questions. Then she shrugged, stifling giddy laughter. What did her questions matter? She was safe!

Frederick held her against him, stroking her silken hair, well able to imagine her thoughts. He hardened his heart. A pity. But not to be helped. He suddenly extricated himself from her embrace, nodding to the sailor. The man grabbed Kassandra's arms at the elbow and dragged her back, shoving her onto the bed.

"Wh-what?" she blurted, her eyes moving from Frederick to the sailor, who was lustfully appraising her, a crooked grin on his face. "Count Frederick . . . ?"

"You must forgive his rudeness, Lady Kassandra," he murmured, bowing slightly. "He knows no better." He nodded to the sailor, who quickly left the cabin, then walked over to the chair, pulled it closer to the bed, and sat down. "How are you feeling, my lady? You have been asleep for well over a day."

Kassandra gaped at him in total astonishment. What was going on? Here she was in a cramped cabin, on a strange boat, bound for God knew where, and Count Frederick was asking after her health!

An unsettling thought struck her. This serious-faced man sitting across from her was hardly the fop she remembered from Prince Eugene's gala. There was nothing effeminate about him, not in the simple cut of his clothes, not in his posture, not in his steady, intense gaze. She blushed, noting his eyes were fixed on the rapid rise and fall of her chest. He was not the same man at all!

"I-I am dizzy, my lord," she stammered. "I . . ." She paused, biting her lower lip. How did he know she had been asleep for a day? Unless . . . unless he had something to do with why she was here.

Kassandra stifled the twinge of fear in her heart, rising to her feet. "What game are you playing, Count Frederick?" she asked, indignation fueling her courage. "Where is Stefan? I demand to know what this is all about."

Frederick, amused by her pretty show of temper, allowed his thin lips to curve into a smile. But it faded as he leaned forward in his chair, his ice-blue eyes piercing her own. "You demand, my lady? You are in no position to demand anything. And as for Count von Furstenberg, he is quite far away. Now, sit down."

What did he mean, Stefan was far away? Kassandra shuddered, gripped by an icy chill. She sank down upon the bed, her hands falling numbly to her lap.

"I am now responsible for your fate, Kassandra." He laughed dryly. "I hope you don't mind my calling you by your given name. We shall be in close quarters for the next few weeks, and I think it best to dispense with . . . all formalities." His gaze raked over her. "You may call me Frederick."

He settled into his chair, deciding to toy with her a little. "You really should thank me, Kassandra. I have spared your life. That is why you are here"—he paused, his hand sweeping about the cabin—"and not at the bottom of some river."

Kassandra's eyes narrowed at him, her chin trembling. Spared her life? What had she ever done to him that he would wish to harm her? "Was it you at the hunting lodge?" she asked in disbelief.

"Yes," he answered. "The dizziness you complained of will soon pass, an unpleasant complication of the mild drug I used on the cloth." He raised a blond eyebrow. "It seems you've made some enemies in high places, Kassandra," he continued cryptically. "Or should I say, one enemy, although one seems to be quite enough in your case. This . . . enemy would see you dead."

Kassandra's thoughts raced. "Wh-what enemy?" she queried shakily. "Who would w-wish my dea—?" She stopped, blanching, unable to say the word. She swallowed hard. "And why would you—"

"You mustn't trouble yourself with questions for which there are no answers, Kassandra," Frederick interrupted soothingly, placing his hand atop hers. "There are some things that must remain a secret." His fingers caressed hers. "But you needn't worry. You have nothing further to fear from this enemy."

Kassandra slowly drew in her breath. Suddenly it was all becoming horribly clear. If what Count Frederick was telling her was true, and he had spared her life, then it was for some other dark purpose entirely of his own making. He had already alluded to a journey lasting several weeks, had said he was now the master of her fate. Yet what fate, she could not begin to imagine.

Kassandra pulled her hand away. "On the contrary, Frederick, I believe I have much to fear," she objected, grim understanding reflected in her steady gaze. How strange, she thought fleetingly. She could not believe the calm that had settled over her, despite her obvious peril. "Where are you taking me?" she queried.

Frederick's eyes widened, startled by her sudden grasp of her situation. He sat back, clearing his throat. "Suffice it to say we are journeying south, Kassandra, far from Vienna." He rose abruptly. "That is enough talk for now. You need rest, to recover from the shock you have suffered." Indeed she does, he considered, noting the dark smudges beneath her eyes. He could not have her looking pale and wan.

"I must apologize for the accommodations. This Croatian fishing vessel was the only transport available on such short notice." He smiled faintly. "I believe you will find everything you need in the armoire, even some books to while away the hours. I recall you saying how much you enjoyed reading. If there is anything further you wish, you have only to ask—"

"I wish to return to Vienna," Kassandra interjected softly.

Frederick stiffened but ignored her comment and walked to the door. Almost as an afterthought, he turned, his eyes flashing dangerously. "I must warn you, Kassandra. If you are entertaining any fantasies of escape, you would do well to reconsider. The crew have been well paid for their services, one of which is to guard you well, and will resist all bribes for fear of losing their reward . . . and possibly their heads, if I am deceived before we reach our destination."

He began to close the door behind him, pausing to glance once again at her. "And if you anticipate any daring rescue on the part of your . . . lover," he stated coldly, "rest assured, my lady, there will be none. He believes you have drowned, and is no doubt, at this moment, mourning your death." At her stricken expression, he looked away. "Your midday meal will be brought to you shortly. I hope you like fish stew." He shut the door with a resounding thud, the key grating in the lock.

Kassandra stared blankly in front of her, her hands

clasped tightly in her lap. She felt as if she were suffocating in the confines of the small cabin, her sense of restrained calm crumbling in the face of desperate anguish.

"Stefan . . ." she whispered. No! No! She was not drowned, not dead! She was here! She had to get out. She had to get out!

Kassandra jumped from the bed and hurled herself at the window, her clenched fists beating at the slats. They held fast. She slipped her fingertips through one of the tiny openings. Maybe she could pry one loose . . . and if one, then another! She could create a space wide enough to slip through and swim to shore. She yanked and pulled, but again she was defeated. The openings were too narrow. Damn it all, she simply could not get a firm hold.

She sank helplessly onto the bed, tears of frustration swimming in her eyes. Soon they tumbled down her face, a tormented flood as wrenching sobs wracked her body. Yet through it all she kept silent, her hand clasped against her mouth, until finally she threw herself on the bed and buried her cries in the woolen coverlet, one defiant thought burning in her mind. She would not give that . . . that bastard the satisfaction of hearing her grief!

When her tears were spent at last, she rolled onto her back and stared at the planked ceiling, a plan forming in her mind. She would not give in to despair. She was alive, and that was all that mattered. Somehow she would escape and find her way back to Vienna, and Stefan.

Kassandra's doubled fists pounded into the bed. And she would make her captivity so difficult for Count Frederick, he would rue the day he had brought her aboard this wretched boat.

# Chapter 35

"**B**ut I tell you, Stefan is not seeing anyone,"
Isabel insisted, her hands pressing into her
black crepe skirt. Oh, if only she had been closer to
the door, she thought irritably. She would never
have allowed the footman to grant this woman entrance.

"Isabel . . ." Sophia purred, her eyes narrowing.
"It has been over a week since"—she paused, shaking her head sadly—"well, since the unfortunate accident. Surely he would allow a visit from a friend,
an old friend, who wishes only to offer him comfort
and condolences at this trying time."

Isabel shook her head firmly, raising her voice.
"No, Archduchess von Starenberg, that simply
won't be possible. Stefan has left express wishes that
he does not want to be disturb—"

"But I insist on seeing him!" Sophia exclaimed,
cutting her off. "I lost my own husband, dearest
Stanislav, only a few months ago, and I can well
imagine what Stefan must be feeling. Who better
than I to offer him consolation, when I have recently
experienced such grief, such anguish, myself." With
a determined smile fixed upon her beautiful face,
she swept past Isabel, her voluminous mauve taffeta
gown rustling vigorously. "Where is he, in the library?"

Isabel rushed after her, grabbing her arm, undaunted by Sophia's height. "I demand that you leave at once, Archduchess. You are sorely testing the limits of my hospitality, which when it comes to you, are narrow indeed!"

. "What is going on out here?" Stefan shouted, opening the door to the library. His eyes widened at the sight of Sophia, his expression hardening.

"I-I'm sorry, Stefan," Isabel murmured. "I told her you did not wish to be disturbed."

"Oh, Stefan, I only wanted to let you know how truly sorry I am," Sophia began, composing her features into an appropriate expression of sympathy. She took a step forward. He didn't appear to be suffering overmuch, she thought with quick appraisal. He was dressed well, in his dark blue uniform, shaven . . . all in all, a good sign. "If we could talk, for only a moment."

Stefan abruptly threw open the door and strode back into the room. "It's all right, Isabel," he said over his shoulder.

"You see," Sophia murmured in an aside to Isabel. "We're old friends." She threw a smug smile, then flounced into the library, closing the door firmly behind her.

The room was dark, the curtains drawn, and only a few candles lit here and there. Sophia shuddered. What a dreary place, she mused. Well, when she was Countess von Furstenberg, she would redecorate the room more to her liking. Her gaze settled on Stefan, who was intent upon throwing documents and rolled maps into a leather satchel. He was clearly ignoring her, and she didn't appreciate being ignored.

"You're packing?" she inquired, trying to keep her tone light.

"Yes. I'm leaving shortly for the Imperial camp.

You have excellent timing, Sophia. A few moments longer and you would have missed me entirely.''

Sophia smiled, not sure whether his words were a compliment or not. But she remained unruffled. She took a few light steps forward. ''What a pity, Stefan. I was hoping I might persuade you to leave this gloomy house for a while and share supper with me tonight.'' She mistook his raised brow for interest. ''Perhaps you might reconsider your journey, and linger another day or two—''

Stefan's lips drew into a tight line. Was the woman mad? he mused incredulously. Surely she didn't think he might be interested in . . . His mouth curved into a sardonic half smile. With Sophia, nothing surprised him.

''I will have to decline your invitation,'' he stated bluntly, resuming his packing. ''Prince Eugene is expecting my arrival by nightfall.''

''Prince Eugene, Prince Eugene,'' Sophia muttered. She had heard enough of that pompous little man and his plans for glory and conquest! It seemed the talk in Vienna was of nothing else but the summer campaign, which would part them again for six months or better. Why did she have to fall in love with a soldier?

Ah, but what a soldier. Sophia sighed softly, her gaze moving over him, her pink tongue flicking over her lips. Although he was fully clothed, she could imagine the sinewed muscles beneath the taut fit of his uniform, the sculpted planes of his body, the black hair matting evenly across his chest, trailing down the tight muscles of his belly, past his navel, that tempting hollow she longed to kiss and suckle, trailing to the dark triangle at the juncture of his powerful thighs . . .

She drew in her breath, her face flushing. How she wanted him, how she loved him. Now there was no one between them, no husband, no meddling

English bitch . . . nothing but this odious summer campaign. Sophia slapped her fan irritably against her palm, her ire rising once again. Perhaps she should rid Austria of Prince Eugene as well.

Stefan buckled the flap on the satchel, and the clicking sound startled Sophia from her venomous reverie. She reached a quick decision. She was not about to give up so easily, not after she had expended so much effort to free them of any entanglements. She sauntered over to him and laid her hand on his arm, caressing his sleeve.

"You are a commander yourself, Stefan," she purred persuasively. "One of the highest-ranking officers in the Imperial army. Surely you have the power to determine your own schedule. What will another evening matter?" She leaned against him, plying him with all of her seductive power. "I promise you, I could help you forget."

Stefan flinched at her words, his eyes flashing angrily. "As you have so quickly forgotten your own husband, Sophia?" he tossed at her, his tone dripping with sarcasm. "I think not. I do not wish to insult you, but nothing you could say—or do—will help me forget Kassandra. Nothing." He moved away, his breathing hard, his hands doubled into tight fists. "If this is your idea of offering sympathy, Sophia, it's a wasted effort. Now, if you'll excuse me, I still have much to do before I leave."

Sophia stiffened, the blood rushing from her face. If he had struck her, she could not have been more stunned. He'd never spoken to her like this before, never! She whirled, seeking to hurt him as well. But she bit her tongue. She knew he didn't really mean it. He was merely speaking out of his momentary grief. Stefan was a virile, passionate man. It wouldn't be long before he sought out the company of a woman. And when he did, she would be there, waiting. She decided to try another tack.

"I've heard they have not as yet found a body—"

"Not a body," Stefan cut her off vehemently, "Kassandra."

"Oh, so you still hope to find her alive, then?" Sophia scoffed lightly, not surprised when he did not answer.

Thankfully that would never happen, she mused. She had no doubt that Frederick had carried out his end of their agreement; he would be a complete fool to have done otherwise. His gloating letter had assured her that Kassandra had drowned, that he had accomplished his task easily, and well.

It was no matter to her that there was no body. Kassandra could rot at the bottom of the river for all she cared. But it seemed Stefan needed some sort of final proof before he could be free of her. Well, it was only a matter of time before her bloated corpse would float to the surface, squelching the last remnant of his misplaced hope.

"You will have to face the truth eventually, Stefan. Kassandra is dead," she stated matter-of-factly. "Perhaps your heart will start to mend when they finally lay her in the ground. I assume they will continue the search while you are at camp?"

"Enough!" Stefan demanded. He strode to the door and wrenched it open. "I think it's best you leave, Sophia. Now."

She sighed heavily. Obviously this would take more time than she had ever imagined. But he was worth it. She would just have to be patient. It was enough, for now, that she had finally gotten rid of that English tart.

She waltzed slowly to the door, stopping in front of him. "You may not believe it now, Stefan, but one day you will be over this . . . dreadful incident. I want you to know that I'll be here, on that day, waiting for you." She leaned forward and suddenly brushed her lips against his cheek, then swept from the library. She grimaced as the door slammed behind her, but she shrugged it off.

Remember, my girl, she consoled herself, the worst is over. It will only take a bit more time to become Countess von Furstenberg. She smiled tightly at Isabel, who was standing near the staircase, a distinguished gentleman at her side. He was dressed from head to toe in black mourning. She started. Lord Harrington . . .

"My dear ambassador," she murmured, holding out her hand to him as she hurried across the floor. "I was just offering my condolences to Stefan at his loss. I should offer them to you as well. What a terrible misfortune."

Isabel barely managed the amenities, her blue eyes flashing fire. "Archduchess Sophia von Starenberg . . . my betrothed, Lord Harrington."

"You have my deepest sympathies, Lord Harrington," Sophia rushed on as Miles bent his head and brushed his lips atop her hand. "Your only daughter. How tragic. And in the prime of her youth and beauty."

Miles straightened, swallowing against the choking lump in his throat. He was not adept at judging human character, but he could swear he saw triumph in those striking topaz eyes. Yet before he could reply she had turned to Isabel.

"My dear Countess, I hope you and Lord Harrington are able to find some happiness in the midst of such sorrow." She did not wait for an answer, but whirled and flounced toward the opened door.

Wasn't that the final coup, she gloated, stepping up into her carriage with the assistance of her liveried footman. She settled on the plush seat, an amused smile lighting her face.

A kiss on the hand from the father of the girl she had consigned to death. How rare!

# Chapter 36

～◦◯◯◦～

Kneeling in front of her small window, Kassandra sighed heavily, watching through the thin slats as another magnificent sunset torched the western sky. The sun was a glowing orange ball, then a crescent, sinking beyond the distant plains, finally fading into the shimmering horizon, awash in startling hues of crimson, violet, and gold fire. She had never seen such beauty, nor felt such piercing desolation. She had counted ten sunsets so far, marking the passing of ten interminable days, each one taking her farther and farther from the man she loved.

Where was Stefan? What was he thinking at that moment? Of her, perhaps, as she thought only of him? The same questions had tormented her every hour, every minute, since she had awoken in this dingy cabin. She had no relief from her questions, nor did she want any. Strangely, they gave her hope amidst the despair that settled over her, a despair she continued to fight against, even as one day melted into the next, the numbing sameness of her routine broken only by her wretched meals and her afternoon walks upon the deck.

Kassandra leaned away from the window, settling on her haunches. She smiled, recalling the feeling of the wind in her hair that afternoon, her face lifted to the warm sun. She had closed her eyes, for a moment nursing the illusion that she was free, free of Frederick, free of the boat and its leering crew, free of what lay ahead for her, free of everything. But her reverie had been shattered at the sound of Frederick's hated voice, telling her it was time to return to her cabin.

Kassandra shifted her legs and settled into the corner, drawing her knees up under her chin and arranging her plain cotton gown about her slippered feet. She rested her forehead on her arms, Frederick's words coming back to haunt her like unbidden ghosts.

They were never far from her mind. She had gone over and over them, analyzing, debating, wondering, hoping to gain some spark of insight into her predicament. Frederick had said little else to her since that first day, only inquiring after her health, so she had no new information to go on. It seemed he purposefully avoided her, except for escorting her to and from the deck, which was fine with her. She wanted as little to do with him as possible.

She knew now they were traveling south along the Danube, passing through Hungary. Simple geography had told her that. As to their destination, she still had no clue. She had also decided the strange series of accidents that had plagued her in Vienna must somehow have been related. She could not forget the image of the dwarf's face, staring out at her from the carriage, and the blurred visage looking down at her after she fell from her mare. Were they one and same? Yet when she tried to imagine who might be at the center of this plot, she always drew a blank, the same questions tormenting her. Who could hate her so that they would wish her dead? Who?

She had wracked her mind anxiously, sorting through every memory for any slight she might have committed, any inadvertent insult. But there were none. Her lips drew into a faint smile. The only person she had insulted time and again was Stefan. And to reward her, he had given her his love!

"Stefan . . ." she murmured, closing her eyes tightly, conjuring a vision of him in her mind. She shivered, remembering his touch, his kiss, the stirring sensation of his piercing eyes upon her, his rugged features, his body so gloriously male . . . Sweet Lord, she could not bear the thought that she might never see him again.

"If only I could escape," she murmured, lifting her head. But her door was constantly locked, the window totally impenetrable. Frederick had taken the precaution of boarding it up still further on the outside, in case she might manage to break through the slats. And whenever she was escorted from the cabin to the deck, she not only had him by her side, but two sailors as well, one posted in front of her and one following behind. She had no more chance of escape than a nightingale in a cage.

Kassandra grimaced. Her only other recourse, her plan to make her captivity as difficult as possible for him, had gone awry on the second day. She had refused her meals, railing and cursing at whoever entered her room to deliver them, on one occasion even dumping the disgusting contents of her bowl on the sailor's head.

Her belligerent behavior had brought Frederick's wrath down upon her more quickly than she had imagined. He had threatened to suspend her meals entirely for several days, which hardly caused her to blink, but then warned her he would tie her hands and feet to her bed for the duration of the journey, to lie in her own filth if need be, if she did not curb her actions at once. His threat had been so coldly uttered, she did not doubt for a moment he would act on his word. She had immediately relented rather than face such degrading humiliation.

A key suddenly grated in the lock, startling her. She slid to the edge of the mattress and leaned against the window, as far away from the door as she could possibly be within the confines of her cabin. She held her breath as the scrawny sailor she had nicknamed Jack stepped through the door, bearing her supper tray. He nodded to her, throwing her his usual crooked grin that reminded her more of a grimace, then turned his back to her while he set the tray on top of the armoire.

Kassandra's gaze darted to the open doorway, the key still in the lock and no other guards in sight. Seizing the unexpected opportunity, she sprang from the bed and rushed to the door, slamming it shut behind her and turning the key. She barely heard the sailor's startled cries of alarm as she raced down the empty hallway, blood pounding in her ears, and up the wooden stairs leading to the deck.

Darkness had fallen. The deck was lit by oil lanterns set here and there. Several sailors were standing nearby, engrossed in low conversation, their backs to her, and she held her breath as she crept stealthily to the side of the boat. She knew it would be only a matter of moments before Jack's disappearance would arouse suspicion, if his howls for help hadn't already.

She ducked her head, dodging rigging, and jumped over coiled ropes and piles of netting as she made her way quickly to the stern. All the while her lips moved in fervent prayer, hoping against hope she had not been seen. She was almost to the stern when she heard her name called out, Frederick's commanding voice carrying over the water.

Kassandra's heart skipped, but she paid him no heed, hoisting herself up on the railing and swinging her legs over the side. She hesitated for an in-

stant, staring down into the black river. She knew it
would be a long swim, but she had to chance it. The
alternative was too frightening to contemplate.

"Before you jump, Kassandra, you might consider what you'll find upon reaching the shore. We
are passing the homeland of the Tartars, have been
all day."

Kassandra froze at Frederick's words. Tartars! She
had heard stories of these wild tribesmen from Stefan. They fought alongside the Turks and were
known for their ferocity and cruel bloodlust, rumored even to feast on raw horsemeat. She gripped
the railing, indecision wracking her.

Frederick inched closer. "If you manage to reach
the shore, Kassandra, without drowning from the
undertow for which this river is legendary, let me
tell you what will happen to you," he murmured
quietly, not taking his eyes from her. "You may
manage to evade them for a day, maybe longer, but
eventually they will find you. They ride like cen-
taurs, hardly a match for a young woman struggling
through unknown terrain on foot."

His voice grew to just above a whisper. "And
when they find you, Kassandra, despite your rare
beauty, every man of that particular band will rape
you, to sample the wares for which he will bid. If
you survive such handling by ten or fifteen strong
men, they will cast lots to possess you. You will become a slave, Kassandra, to be brutalized at whim,
worked or ridden to death before you see the year's
end." He stopped just a few feet from her, sensing
her fright and uncertainty, a palpable presence between them. "Jump . . . if you dare."

Kassandra's blood froze in her veins at his taunt,
and she quickly made up her mind. Bastard. She
would take the risk! Nothing could be worse than
the fate he most likely planned for her! She closed
her eyes and pushed off from the railing, screaming

painfully as Frederick caught her by the hair and one shoulder, hoisting her back up and over the side of the boat.

She struggled and kicked, tears blurring her eyes as she flailed at him, striking him furiously with her fists, but to no avail. He lifted her easily and threw her over his shoulder, ignoring her cries and curses as he carried her back along the deck and down the wooden ladder to the cabins below. He grunted in pain, one of her fists finding its mark along his ribs, but kept going, striding into her cabin and tossing her onto her bed. Then he kicked the door shut and whirled to face her, his fair features twisted in rage.

Fear swelled within her and she edged away from him until she could go no farther, her back up against the wall. He merely grabbed the hem of her skirt and dragged her toward him, catching her about her narrow waist. He brought her up against him so hard that the breath was wrenched from her body, and she gaped at him in stunned surprise.

"You have tried me sorely this night, Kassandra," he said, his ice-blue eyes searing into her widened gaze. "I tell you, I will not have it." Suddenly his mouth crushed down on hers, his tongue forcing entry between her bruised lips. She tried to pull away, but he held her fast, his hands cruelly gripping her face.

Kassandra began choking, cries of protest caught in her throat. She writhed against him, his tongue filling her mouth, her body awash in fear and loathing. With all of her strength she brought up her hands and violently pulled his blond hair, then she raked her nails down his face.

Frederick sucked in his breath at the stinging sensation, tearing his lips away. He swiped his hand across his cheek, his eyes widening at the vivid blood staining his fingers. "Bitch!" he yelled, striking her across the jaw. She fell onto the bed with a

moan, her head reeling from the shock of his blow.
But she forced back the blackness that was threatening to overwhelm her and leaned up on her elbows, her breasts heaving against her bodice, her
violet eyes ablaze.

"If you come near me again, Count Frederick, I
swear I will kill myself," she whispered vehemently. "Then you will have nothing to show for
your pains."

Frederick pretended he had not heard her threat.
"For this, you will remain in this cabin until we
reach Belgrade," he spat angrily. He turned
abruptly, wiping his hand on his breeches, leaving
bloody fingerprints, and stormed from the cabin. He
ground the key into the lock with a vengeance.

Kassandra dropped back onto the bed, staring
blindly at the planked ceiling and the lamp, swinging back and forth, back and forth. She could have
cried, but she had already spent her tears. There
was nothing inside her but a desolate emptiness, and
one word searing into her mind.

Belgrade. So at last she had learned her destination. And she knew her fate was sealed. Belgrade
was in the hands of the Turks. God only knew what
Frederick was planning to do with her there.

# Chapter 37

*Belgrade, Serbia*

**F**rederick's eyes narrowed as a gilt and painted carriage, covered with scarlet cloth fitted over a frame and harnessed to a matched set of silver-gray oxen, came to a halt along the teeming riverfront wharf, not far from where the fishing boat had docked only an hour before. The carriage was flanked by a motley group of twenty Janissary soldiers on foot, ten on each side, a tiny fraction of the large garrison assigned to protect the city. Yet they looked more like outlaws in their mismatched uniforms, the white cotton turbans on their heads the only item that distinguished them as members of the Sultan's elite corps of infantry soldiers.

And, indeed, they were outlaws. Renegades, protecting a distant military outpost far from the control of Sultan Achmet. Hasan had told him how they had murdered the last pasha of Belgrade, cutting him into small pieces with their scimitars for no reason other than that he restrained them from plundering the surrounding countryside.

Now Mustapha Pasha was general here, commanded by his own Janissaries. He had not dared to punish them for his predecessor's murder, for fear of his own life. On the contrary, he had applauded their action, showering them with gold and blessing their fierce raids into Hungary, where they raped and pillaged, burning everything in their destructive wake.

It was to this man, a ruthless coward, that Frederick was entrusting Kassandra's care and protection while he traveled on to meet the grand vizier.

Frederick shrugged. He had no choice but to leave her here in Belgrade. There was simply too much at stake to do otherwise. He could not have her slowing him down on his journey toward Constantinople, a journey that would be treacherous enough for him and his Janissary escort.

Frederick's lips thinned into a tight line. He only hoped Mustapha nursed a healthy fear of his powerful cousin, Halil, as well, and would think twice before touching Kassandra while she was in his safekeeping. He would have to make it very clear she was destined as a gift to the man who was second in command only to the Sultan himself . . . a man who could end his life, cousin or no, with the flick of his hand or a simple nod if Mustapha sampled what did not belong to him.

Frederick watched silently as the driver of the carriage and the accompanying servant jumped from their high seats to the ground. The driver flung open a corner of the rich cloth to reveal the silken interior, while the servant rushed along the length of the boat. When he spied Frederick standing near the prow he stopped abruptly, raising his voice as he bowed numerous times.

"His Grace, Mustapha Pasha, welcomes you to Belgrade, Count Althann." He bowed again, sweeping his arm toward the carriage. "Please, His Grace awaits you anxiously at the fortress."

Frederick's expression remained impassive as he bowed his head ever so slightly in acknowledgment of the well-dressed slave. He turned to the two sailors standing just behind him, and spoke to them in Serbo-Croatian, their native language.

"Fetch the woman. But first see that her hands are tied and she is blindfolded."

They nodded, ducking their heads as they clattered down the wooden steps into the hold. A few moments later they returned, a subdued Kassandra stumbling between them.

Frederick could not suppress a wry smile, noting they had also gagged her. He had not heard her this quiet since they left Vienna. But his smile quickly faded as he studied her more closely. This was the first time he had seen her since the night she had tried to escape.

Her cheeks were very pale, her hair unwashed and stringy, her cotton gown hopelessly wrinkled. He had held good to his threat, and she had spent the last week below deck, confined to her cabin. Obviously the lack of sunshine and fresh air had dampened her spirits, though it had done little to mar her beauty. She was as lovely as ever.

He had taken her impassioned oath to heart as well. It had shaken him deeply. Never before had a woman vowed to take her life if he so much as touched her. And that was one thing he did not want to have on his conscience. It was bad enough he couldn't sleep at night, thinking about the fate that soon would be hers. Yet it was not enough to sway him. He was as much of a coward as Mustapha, fearful of his own wretched life above all else . . .

Damn Sophia to hell! he raged, his fists clenching as he willed the disturbing thoughts from his mind. One day he would repay her for what he had been forced to do to this innocent girl!

"Take her to the carriage," he said gruffly, following the two sailors as they hurried down the plank and onto the wharf, carrying Kassandra between them.

Like a lamb to the slaughter, Frederick could not help thinking, climbing into the silken interior of the carriage and settling himself on the plush cushions piled upon the lacquered floor. He watched grimly as Kassandra was propped up beside him, then the scarlet curtain was closed.

But this lamb would know her fate, he decided suddenly, and who had so drastically altered the course of her life. At least he could give her that. Perhaps her hate for him, for Sophia, would give her courage to face what was to come.

The carriage jerked into motion, the sound of the Janissaries' boots striking up a measured cadence as they began the long ascent up the rocky hill to the massive fortress overlooking the city.

"Welcome, Count Althann," Mustapha Pasha exclaimed, clapping his pudgy hands, his gold rings, encrusted with precious jewels, glittering from every finger. "Your reputation of excellent service to Our Most Supreme Sovereign, the Sultan Achmet, precedes you."

His wide smile suddenly faded and he clucked his tongue in agitation. "Hasan Aziz was here only six days past, with such news, such news. The Imperialist dogs! He is well on his way to Constantinople by now, to alert the Sultan . . ." He paused, waving away the unsettling news as if he were swatting a pestering fly. "Ah, but we can talk of this later. You are most welcome."

He stepped closer, his slippered feet making no sound on the polished marble floor that shone like glass. "But who is this?" he asked softly, studying with veiled curiosity the gagged and blindfolded woman kneeling beside Frederick.

"She is a gift for His Grace, Halil Pasha, upon his arrival in Belgrade," Frederick replied pointedly, stressing the grand vizier's name. "I have brought

her to you for safekeeping, until she may be presented to him. Her name is Kassandra.''

''Ah . . .'' Mustapha breathed, his hands forming
a triangle as he rested his index fingers on his broad
lips. Frederick watched as he walked around both
of them very slowly, his gown of purple silk stretching taut over his vast stomach and falling into swirling folds around his short legs, the ermine hem of
his white pelisse brushing along the floor.

Kassandra started at the sound of her name. Once
again she did not understand the language being
spoken, but she knew it was Turkish. As she now
knew Frederick was a spy for the Turks.

And that it was Archduchess Sophia von Starenberg who had brought such wretched injustice upon
her . . .

She winced, shifting uncomfortably, her knees
aching from the cold, hard floor. Yet she was grateful for the pain. It was the only thing that made her
feel half-alive, the numbing shock of everything
Frederick had told her during the carriage ride to the
fortress becoming stark reality in her mind.

It had spilled from him like a flood, like a wild
confession—Sophia discovering he was a spy
through her dwarf, Adolph, who was probably the
same little man she had seen at the theater, in the
carriage, and after her fall; Sophia's demand that
Kassandra be killed if Frederick wanted to preserve
his secret; the drowning hoax; on and on. And now
she knew her life had been spared for a fate perhaps
crueler than death. She was to remain in Belgrade
under constant guard until she was presented to the
grand vizier as a slave for his harem!

Frederick had told her about everything, his cow-
ardice, his greed, as if he believed she would never
be able to use such knowledge against him. As if
she were to disappear from the face of the earth. The

only thing he hadn't told her was why Sophia had done this to her . . . why?

Kassandra felt an anguished scream rise up in her throat, stifled only by the filthy gag in her mouth. Deep in her heart, she knew the reason. It was as old as time itself. Jealousy. Sophia loved Stefan . . . and would stop at nothing to have him.

Had she succeeded? Kassandra wondered wildly, tears stinging her eyes beneath the blindfold. Would Stefan forget her so easily, to find solace in the arms of the woman who had plotted her death? Sophia had been his mistress; he must have some feelings for her. Oh God, please tell her he hadn't forgotten her!

Kassandra drew in her breath, her roiling thoughts shoved rudely into the recesses of her mind as a moist hand, smelling of sweet perfume, glided across her cheek. A silken garment whispered about her arm and shoulder. Mustapha Pasha! Would this nightmare never end?

"Is her tongue like a serpent's, sharp and tinged with venom, that you have her mouth bound so?" Mustapha asked, standing in front of Frederick once again. "Are her eyes, like Medusa's, able to turn a man to stone? I think not." He sniffed delicately, lifting his hand to his nose. "She is unclean, but from what I can see, that is her only true fault. Yes?"

Frederick studied him shrewdly. He nodded. "Yes, Sire, her only fault."

Mustapha clapped his hands together, and two female slaves appeared as if from nowhere. They prostrated themselves on the floor before him.

"See that this woman is bathed, her body completely shaved as is our custom, and dress her in something more befitting of her beauty," he commanded. The two women sprang from the floor and gently seized Kassandra's arms, pulling her to her feet. She stood there shakily, voicing a muffled objection, trying futilely to wrench her arms free.

"She may . . . protest such treatment," Frederick murmured.

Mustapha chuckled with amusement, his eyes alighting on the flaring red scratches on Frederick's cheeks. "So I see," he commented dryly. He turned to the slaves. "A little opium in a goblet of chilled water or in a bite of baklava," he suggested. They nodded solemnly, their faces expressionless.

He turned back to Frederick as they hurried her away. "She will give us no trouble." Then he bowed with his hand to his heart. "I am honored, Count Althann, to harbor such a prize for my esteemed cousin, Halil." He straightened, a look of understanding passing between them. Then he gestured to a low table set by a marble fountain, plump brocaded pillows placed around it on the floor. "Come, let us eat. We have much of importance to discuss."

Frederick followed him to the table, glancing one last time over his shoulder. But Kassandra was gone, the great carved doors leading from the pillored reception hall slamming shut behind her and the two slave women. The fierce guards with flashing scimitars held crosswise against their chests returned to their places on either side of the doors, staring coldly back at him. He turned away, a hard lump in his throat.

He had sealed her fate. By voicing his intent to Mustapha, it could not be undone. It was sacred, inviolable. Kassandra now belonged to Halil Pasha, her protector . . . her master.

Frederick sat down at the table across from Mustapha, his appetite no match for the forty elaborate dishes served on plates of gold by silent slaves. The meal dragged on for several hours, punctuated by their talk of war, strategy, when the Imperial army could be expected at the fortified ramparts of Belgrade—most likely within a month's time, mid-June—and how there was no doubt but that Halil's field army would prove victorious, his advantage lying in strength of numbers. The message Hasan was delivering to the Sultan had included information on the probable size of Prince Eugene's forces; the grand vizier would bring an army twice, three times that size to ensure his enemy's defeat.

At last, after sherbet had been served in delicate china bowls, followed by ink-black coffee, fragrant with cinnamon, pipes had been smoked, and silence was hovering over them, the pasha reclining heavily upon his pillows, Frederick rose to take his leave without fear of offending his host. The final amenities were observed, then he was escorted from the reception hall, his thoughts already on the long journey ahead.

Mustapha watched through half-closed lids, waiting, his arms stretched languidly across his protruding belly, until Frederick disappeared through another set of massive doors. As soon as they closed behind him, he clapped his hands sharply together. Four slaves rushed forward, lifting him with barely concealed effort to his feet. He waved them away, straightening his gown and pelisse as he hurried across the floor to the great doors leading to his harem, which were opened wide.

He made his way swiftly along shadowed corridors, and down winding stairs, his short legs propelling his unwieldy bulk forward with great speed. His panting breaths were accompanied by a guttural wheezing from deep in his throat, but he did not stop until he reached the room he was seeking. He entered quietly, hiding behind a latticed partition, his fingers hooking in the crisscrossing wood strips, his sweating face illuminated by diamond patterns of light.

So, he had timed it perfectly, Mustapha commended himself, licking his lips as he peered through the partition. He sucked in his breath, a surge of desire rippling through his trembling body. Allah could not have fashioned a more beautiful sight!

Kassandra stood on a small, raised platform, her limp body supported by a black eunuch, her head lolling against his shoulder, his large hands gripping her curved waist. Her white skin, flushed with rose, stood out in startling contrast, buffed to a glossy sheen and devoid of any offensive hair. The two female slaves were dressing her quickly, slipping her long legs into transparent jade-green trousers of silk damask, lifting her arms and pulling a delicate white chemise over her head, then bringing them down to her sides and draping a close-fitting gold tunic over her shoulders. Last came a pair of white slippers of soft leather.

Mustapha watched, spellbound, as they laid Kassandra upon tasseled pillows, large and small, where she would rest in drug-induced slumber until her chamber was prepared. His dark eyes sought the shallow rise and fall of her full breasts, the hardened nipples pressing through her silken garments. It was all he could do not to dash from behind the partition and cover her prostrate body with his own, to rip off her trousers and delve into the perfect white softness . . .

Mustapha cursed under his ragged breath, licking the sweat from his upper lip. He knew he could no sooner possess her than to deny his faith. The woman belonged to Halil.

Ah, but there was no one to prevent him from watching her, he mused with a lascivious grin. This fortress abounded in secret passageways, hidden closets, holes bored into the walls at his command, where he could spy on his harem women at their baths, in the sanctity of their chambers, and seek his own private pleasure.

"Kassandra," he whispered, rolling her name upon his tongue like honey. Yes, she would be a most welcome diversion from the trying weeks to come.

# Chapter 38

Stefan shielded his eyes from the late afternoon sun, his narrowed gaze sweeping the wide perimeter of the Imperial camp. Prince Eugene had picked their strategic position carefully, the camp stretching out across the barren plain lying just south of Belgrade, along the Sava River, which intersected with the Danube. Both rivers had been closed off to all water traffic since the siege had begun more than seven weeks ago, cutting off any possibility that food, ammunition, or fresh water would reach either the city or the fortress overlooking it. Yet still the siege dragged on, fully a month longer than Prince Eugene and his commanders had anticipated.

They had already surmised Mustapha Pasha and his Janissary garrison knew well in advance of their plan to attack Belgrade. No doubt the work of a well informed spy, Stefan considered grimly. Traitor! May he rot in hell!

The Turks had obviously prepared for a lengthy siege. It seemed their supply of ammunition was inexhaustible. A steady barrage of fire from the cannons surrounding the fortress had prevented the Imperial army from drawing any closer, virtually holding them hostage on the banks of the Sava. Time was slipping away, lives were being lost, and still they could get no closer to the fortress, their every attempt to storm the city thwarted by the deadly fire.

Already the first week of August had come and gone, and here they sat under the vicious sun baking in heat that had dropped many a man. Now, to compound their desperate situation, Halil Pasha had arrived a few days ago from Constantinople, come to rescue the garrison from the Imperialists. He had brought with him a field army twice the size of their own, setting up his colorful tents on a high plateau to the east of the city. His artillery had soon joined in the barrage, and Prince Eugene had been forced to move the camp back several hundred feet to escape the worst of this new threat.

"Damn!" Stefan cursed, raging at his feelings of impotence. Before Halil Pasha had marched upon Belgrade, he and his cavalry had managed to make some successful forays near the city under cover of darkness, overtaking a few outlying regiments of Janissaries camped on the other side of the Sava. But these efforts had brought them no closer to their goal of capturing the fortress, a prospect that seemed more remote with each passing day. Something had to be done, and soon, or the Imperial army would find itself retreating toward Vienna in defeat.

Stefan wheeled around suddenly to face the small group of officers standing just to his left. "See that the men are prepared to ride out again this evening across the Sava," he barked, taking them wholly by surprise. "I'll not sit by while these Turks gloat around their fires wondering what became of their fierce enemy."

"Yes, Commander!" they answered as if with one voice, exchanging shaken looks as Stefan stormed into his tent. Each man hurried off in a different direction to do his bidding, wondering what had happened to the stoic commander they knew from previous campaigns.

Stefan strode over to his cot and sat down heavily, running his hand through his sweat-soaked hair. The shadowed coolness of the tent soothed his temper somewhat and he began to think more rationally. He knew he couldn't send his men out without express orders from Prince Eugene, orders he had been denied since the arrival of Halil Pasha's forces. If there was to be an attack, it must be a concerted one, infantry and cavalry combined to break the Ottoman lines.

What was happening to him? Stefan wondered. Yet even as he asked himself, he knew the answer. He had not been the same since Kassandra's disappearance. He had become relentless, like a man possessed, driving his men as hard as he drove himself.

"No, she is not dead! She cannot be dead!" Stefan whispered passionately, rising from the cot to pace about the tent. They had found no body, no clothing, nothing of Kassandra's.

The last letter he had received from Isabel, written only three weeks ago, had stated as much. It had been delivered by swift courier along with the rest of the post for Prince Eugene. Trembling, Stefan had held it in his hand, until at last he had ripped it open, reading desperately, his heart in his throat. After another exhaustive search, nothing had been found. And until that day—God help him if it ever came!—he would not believe that Kassandra was dead.

Stefan sat down on the wooden chair set near the cot, his arms resting on his elbows, his head in his hands. He had never felt so desolate, so haunted, in all his life, hardly the trait a soldier would wish for in his commander. Perhaps he should relinquish his leadership, rather than endanger the lives of his men from lack of good judgment—

"Commander von Furstenberg!"

Stefan started, looking up at the young lieutenant standing at the entrance to his tent.

"Yes?"

"Prince Eugene has called a council of war, Commander. You are requested to come to his tent at sundown. The general also requests you command your men to begin preparations for battle." Then he was gone, the flap falling back into place.

A council of war. Prepare for battle. Those were the words he had been waiting to hear for weeks . . .

Studied excitement gripped Stefan, clearing his mind of any self-doubt. Years of battle-honed instinct took over, racing through his blood, his emotions receding into the background. He knew they would assail him again in a quiet moment—when he slept, when he dreamed of her—but for now, there was much to be done.

Stefan strode from his tent, into the receding light of the afternoon. He had not forgotten her. The vivid pain was still there, only suppressed for a time in the face of what he was trained to do.

Halil Pasha waved his hand irritably, silencing the loud bickering among his assembled generals. His piercing black eyes settled on one after the other, the expression on his narrow, olive-skinned face brooking no argument.

"The Imperialists are cowards," he murmured in a low, commanding voice. "They would sooner retreat than attack. It is clear they have felt the strength of our superior numbers, striking cold fear into their hearts. We shall see them tear down their camp within the week, and set out for the safety of Vienna."

"But that Savoyard, Prince Eugene, is unpredictable, Your Grace," one of the generals protested weakly in the face of such firm resolve. He looked nervously at his peers, then back at Halil. "We cannot forget Peterwardein, or Temesvar, last summer—"

"Enough!" Halil rose from his cross-legged position upon the carpeted floor to stand in their midst. "There shall be no more discussion, no argument. It has been decided. We shall continue the heavy bombardment, deterring any movement on their part toward the fortress. We have nothing to fear from these infidels. It has been read thus in the astrological omens, and so it shall be done. Belgrade is ours, and shall remain so."

He turned his back on them and strode to where a slave was kneeling, head bent, eyes downcast, holding up a silver bowl of cool water. Dipping his hands, he washed them, a signal to his generals that their war council was at an end. One by one they rose, bowing at the waist, then left the ornate tent, their flowing caftans rustling.

Halil dried his hands on a soft linen towel offered to him by another slave, then tossed it upon the floor. It was quickly retrieved, and the two slaves crept silently away.

"Send in the spy," Halil commanded to his ever-present Chief Eunuch, a black man towering well over six feet tall and of immense girth, who had been in charge of his harem for many years. Even in war, a powerful man traveled with his wives, his concubines. The sensory pleasures of life could not be denied because of conflict.

"Yes, Sire," the Chief Eunuch murmured in his strange half-tenor voice, his slippered feet belying his bulk as he padded across the thick silk carpets to the guarded entrance to the tent. Curved scimitars were drawn aside, allowing him to pass.

Halil settled himself on a raised sofa, arranging the brocaded pillows comfortably behind his back. He waited, a soft breeze swirling from waving goose feather fans. A quizzical smile lit his full lips as he remembered Count Frederick's words of a few days ago: *"It is only my wish to remind you, Sire, of a special gift I have brought for you from Vienna."*

"Ah, the Englishwoman," Halil answered softly, trying to conjure an image of her in his mind.

Count Frederick had first mentioned her when he had arrived in Constantinople. How had he described her? Oh, yes. He had said she was very beautiful, like a white goddess, with skin of finest cream, hair the color of fire, and eyes of purest amethyst, like crystalline violet pools.

Virgin? he had inquired. No, Sire, not a virgin. But Halil had only shrugged. It was no matter to him. Virgins could be difficult, prone to shedding tears. They brought him little pleasure. It was a woman skilled at lovemaking who stirred his blood.

"I have not forgotten her, Count Frederick," he had continued, his interest piqued. But their conversation had been interrupted by one of his generals, and he had not thought of her again. Until now.

Perhaps it was time he summoned this "goddess" from the fortress, he mused. He certainly felt the need of some diversion to break the monotony of this campaign. It was more of a stalemate, until the Imperialists turned and fled, he thought confidently, rubbing his pointed beard, black as jet. Yes, a sensuous diversion, an Englishwoman, no less! His first . . .

"Count Frederick Althann, Your Grace," the Chief Eunuch announced, gliding back to stand near the tented wall. He wrapped his thick arms about his barrel chest, a look of watchful attention on his broad face, all-seeing, all-hearing, ready to serve his master with his very life if need be.

Halil looked up, shrewdly studying the tall blond man as he entered. He hated spies. They were vermin, maggots, feeding upon deceit and avarice, the glint of gold reflected in their eyes. But they were a necessary evil, and this one had virtually insured him a victory over the hated Austrians, with his timely information. Now Count Frederick had a gift for him as well. Truly he was a man who knew how to please his benefactors.

"Your Grace," Frederick said, bowing low, his hand to his chest.

"I wish to see this gift you have spoken so much about," Halil began, before Frederick had even straightened.

Frederick inhaled softly. "As it pleases you, Your Grace." So the grand vizier had finally voiced a summons, he thought fleetingly. He had begun to wonder if Kassandra might end up with that disgusting pig, Mustapha, after all. At least with this man her worth would be truly recognized and she would be treated accordingly, some small consolation for the treachery he had inflicted upon her.

"Take several soldiers with you and travel with great caution," Halil ordered. "I will not have you, or your gift, falling into the hands of the infidels." He dismissed him with a curt nod. "Now go."

Frederick winced as he turned and strode from the tent. She would not fall into Stefan's hands, he amended darkly. There was no chance of that. The Imperialists had been completely held down at their camp for the past week, the heavy bombardment discouraging any troop movement, even routine patrols along the Sava. Besides, to reach the secret entrance at the base of the fortress he and Kassandra would be skirting the Danube, far from any Austrian river blockade. He had done it many times already, carrying messages from Halil to Mustapha.

If he had not been entirely confident that this campaign would fall to the Ottomans' favor, he would never have left Kassandra in Belgrade, he thought, hoisting himself atop a magnificent Persian war-horse and kicking it into a gallop, four mounted guards thundering close behind him. He would have gone on with her to Constantinople, hindrance or not, and deposited her in a harem there. He was no fool!

# Chapter 39

⟡ ⟊⟊ ⟡

Kassandra braced herself against the rough stone wall, her feet balancing on a three-legged brass stool as she peered out the high, narrow window in her chamber. Her eyes piercing the gathering dusk, gazing longingly at the Imperial camp, whose tents spread like a carpet to the south of the Sava. Soon it would be dark and she would be able to see only the glow of scattered fires and the blinding bursts of artillery blasts as the heavy cannon of the fortress began their nightly vigil of holding the besiegers at bay.

She had stood just so at her window every day, every night, since the Imperial army had arrived to lay siege to the fortress. She'd instantly recognized the fluttering banners of the emperor, her heart soaring with hope, knowing Stefan was out there, in one of those long rows of tents.

Yet as the days had turned into weeks, then almost two months, her hope had grown dim. Prince Eugene's army had to be faring badly. They had already retreated once, well over a week ago.

That had been the worst day of her life. She had watched in disbelief as the tents were struck down, thinking they were leaving—oh God!—thinking she was being left behind! She had screamed out to them, calling out her name, calling out to Stefan, but

342

her desperate shouts had been lost to the deafening cannon fire.

But not lost to the white eunuch in charge of the harem. He had rushed in and subdued her easily, despite her thrashing and struggling, and shoved a red opium pill into her mouth. She tried to spit it out, but he held her jaw clamped shut and covered her nose with his massive hand until she swallowed, gagging as it slid down her throat. Soon the pill had taken effect, her head falling back limply upon the thick carpet, her limbs awash in languid, drunken sensation, the room spinning like a dizzying whirlpool of color, cannon fire, and the eunuch's pasty white face hovering above her, until she saw no more.

When she had awoken at last, bright morning sunlight streaming in a narrow shaft across her face, it had taken her a moment to remember why she was lying upon the carpeted floor. She had struggled slowly to her feet, the blood rushing in her ears, cold dread seizing her as she stumbled toward the window. Tottering on the stool, she had looked out, expecting to see only a wide, barren plain. But the Imperial camp was still there, pulled back a good ways from the river, but there! She had never felt such incredible joy, not since that day at the river when she told Stefan she loved him . . .

Kassandra leaned her forehead on the stone ledge, shuddering as she willed the poignant splendor of that memory from her mind. There was no use in torturing herself. She and Stefan couldn't be farther apart if a wild ocean separated them. He was out there, thinking she was dead. And she was a prisoner in this dismal fortress, locked within the harem of that fat abomination of a man, Mustapha Pasha.

Bile welled up in her throat at the thought of him, and she had to hold her breath for fear she might gag. It seemed he had gone out of his way to make her life here a nightmare, as if he derived some perverse pleasure from her obvious loathing of him.

He had forced her to share interminable meals with him in his bedchamber, a large, ornately decorated room that reeked of debauched excess, though thankfully he had never touched her. He had drugged her whenever she displayed the least hint of rebellion, and had kept her locked away in this chamber without the solace of any other human company besides the vile eunuch who checked on her constantly. On many occasions she had felt Mustapha was somehow watching her, when she was dressing, when she bathed in the morning, as if the very walls had eyes. She had tried to shrug it off, but the niggling feeling had stubbornly persisted.

The hours she had spent in the main baths, she had been alone except for the same two mute female slaves, though the myriad perfumes of other women lingered in the hot, steaming chambers. She was forced several times a week to endure their meticulous and humiliating ministrations. Her skin chafed and burned from their unnatural plucking and shaving, their pummeling and massage a torture she could not endure without feeling the urge to scream. But she had learned early to quell her outbursts, if only to stave off the inevitable opium they forced down her throat if she resisted. If she was ever to escape, she needed to have her wits about her.

A despairing laugh broke from Kassandra's throat. If she was ever to escape . . . An impossible thought! She could no sooner escape her captivity than she could squeeze through this window and fly away, straight into Stefan's arms.

No, her only escape would be a summons from this Halil Pasha, and mercifully it had not yet come. But she knew he'd already arrived with his army from Constantinople, as Frederick had said he would. She couldn't see the Ottoman camp from her window, but the Janissary guard on the ramparts below had more than tripled, and heavy cannon were sounding from the east, firing round after round upon the Imperial camp.

"Guard yourself well, my love," Kassandra whispered fervently, peering out into the darkness at the tiny flickers of light to the south. "Guard yourself well."

A key grated in the lock and she started, jumping down from the stool. She whirled to face the white eunuch as he entered her room, silent as a slithering snake, fattened and bloated from its kill.

He loomed in the doorway, his portly frame swathed in lime-green silk tied with a wide sash around his middle, and stared at her. The veiled expression in his unfathomable pale eyes, devoid of any emotion, unsettled her, and she swallowed hard, wondering what he could possibly want. Then he made a slight gesture with his hand and forefinger, indicating for her to follow him.

Kassandra clutched her silver damask tunic tightly about her body, feeling a sudden chill despite the humid warmth of her chamber. She reluctantly followed him into the hallway, lit by torches fitted in polished sconces, past the baths, through a labyrinth of like hallways, up a flight of winding stairs. It felt as if she were being led through a maze, and when she and the eunuch stopped in front of a set of massive double doors, richly carved and painted with erotic scenes of copulation, it finally dawned on her that she was leaving the harem. Blushing hotly at the pictures, she looked away.

The white eunuch picked up an ornamental gold-knobbed cane propped against the wall and struck one of the double doors several times. As they swung open into a vast marble hall, he set down the

cane and walked on, once again indicating for Kassandra to follow.

Kassandra took a few tentative steps. She saw a
tall man dressed in rich Turkish garb, a white turban
upon his head, standing with his back to her next to
a sullen Mustapha Pasha and two fierce-looking Janissary guards, who were studying her appraisingly.

What was going on? she wondered wildly, freezing in her tracks. She gasped, her eyes locking with
Frederick's ice-blue gaze as he turned to face her,
and in that moment she knew she was lost. The
summons from Halil Pasha had finally come.

Kassandra turned to flee but stopped abruptly, realizing with a hysterical giggle there was only Mustapha's harem behind her. She was trying to escape
one harem by hiding in another! Before she had a
chance to attempt another direction, the white eunuch grabbed her arm and wrenched her around,
nearly dragging her across the polished floor toward
the group of men. The great doors slammed shut
behind them with a resounding thud, the wickedly
curved scimitars held by the eunuch guards slicing
through the air with a terrifying whoosh as they resumed their places.

Frederick could not tear his eyes from Kassandra
as she was brought in front of him and forced to her
knees, her head down. She was so breathtakingly
beautiful! She was thinner, perhaps, than he remembered, the hollows beneath her cheekbones further defining her startling beauty. Her skin glowed
with a pale translucence, no doubt the result of long
hours spent in the warm steam of the Turkish baths.

He could not suppress his pity for her when the
eunuch whipped several silken scarves from a deep
pocket of his pelisse and wrapped one over her
mouth, gagging her before she could cry out, another over her eyes, blindfolding her. There was

nothing he could do. Not now. He was merely the messenger, the gift bearer.

At least she was free of this repugnant man, Frederick thought, turning back to Mustapha as the eunuch finished tying Kassandra's wrists together with another scarf and whisked a silken cloak around her, covering her in a shimmering shroud.

Frederick bowed, smiling thinly. "My thanks, Sire, for your gracious care of this slave," he murmured formally. "His Grace, Halil Pasha, will be most pleased with his new acquisition."

Mustapha merely nodded, not at all pleased. He had hoped his cousin had conveniently forgotten about her. Ah well, Allah had decreed that it be so. She was but a slave, nothing more. And she had given him many hours of secret pleasure, albeit without her knowledge.

"Give my cousin this message," he answered, brushing off what Frederick had just said. He handed him a rolled slip of parchment paper, sealed and tied with black cord. "I wish an answer tonight."

Frederick took the parchment, and secured it in the folds of his sash. "I will return as quickly as I can," he replied, nodding at the Janissary guards. One of them bent down and hoisted Kassandra over his shoulder, then the small party walked from the hall, Mustapha staring after them.

Kassandra fought to stay calm, knowing it was useless to struggle. Her only power lay in keeping her wits about her. But it was difficult to breathe with the gag tied so thoroughly over her mouth. She forced herself to take slow, deep breaths through her nose, her senses acutely attuned to everything that was happening.

Her head bounced lightly against a broad back . . . They were climbing down seemingly hundreds of stairs. She smelled a dankness in the air, a stuffiness that almost caused her to sneeze, then a wooden door creaked open. An eerie silence settled over her captors, and the man who held her ducked and straightened, the door thudding closed.

She smelled fresh air, felt a breeze cooling her skin through the silken cloak as they stepped into the open, where the sounds of the night were all around them . . . chirping crickets, a hooting owl, and the roar of the cannon coming from the fortress ramparts. Pebbles skittered beneath heavy boots, sliding down a slope and plunking into water. A rocking motion dizzied her senses, then she heard the scraping of oars and water lapping at the sides of a boat as it glided across a river.

On the other side there were restless horses, nervous whinnies, new voices, more soldiers. She was grabbed by another man, held for a moment, then lifted high into a saddle and settled against a stocky chest, a muscled arm wrapping around her waist. Her head snapped back as they set off at a hard run, and she closed her eyes to the swamping dizziness of riding blind, the earth moving beneath them, the thundering of hooves in her ears.

They were climbing, climbing, away from the river, horses straining, pulling, voices growing animated, less tense, as they reached familiar ground. She could see glowing light through her blindfold, inhaled the scents of cooking food and wood fires. Low male laughter resounded, the buzz of hundreds, thousands, of voices, soldiers everywhere, the clash of weapons in mock battle drills, and still the roar of the cannon, farther away now, as if from a distant precipice, pummeling the earth below.

They slowed gradually to a trot, then came to an abrupt halt, the horse quivering beneath her. The pressure of her captor's arm disappeared and she was sliding from the saddle, gasping, caught by another's arms, lifted against another chest. Her heart

beat fiercely in her breast, cold fear welling up as
strong legs carried her forward into a hushed place,
the outdoor sounds fading altogether. Faint strains
of music, zither and lute, drifted to her from some
distance ahead, growing louder, louder, melodic,
undulating, her nostrils flaring at the heavy scent of
incense and perfume.

Kassandra sharply drew in her breath as whoever
held her suddenly knelt and lay her with a slight
bump upon a carpeted floor. Hands clutched at the
silken cloak, then with a strong tug it was pulled
from beneath her and she was sent rolling across the
floor, over and over, her head spinning. She came
to a stop on her back, her tousled hair streaking
across her face and heaving breasts.

"Lady Kassandra Wyndham," she heard Frederick announce, his voice echoing in her mind . . . her
name upon his lips a sentence of death.

# Chapter 40

Halil Pasha appraised the trembling, long-limbed woman lying at his feet, his black eyes lighting with keen interest. He glanced up at Frederick. "Quite a presentation, Count Althann," he murmured with a low chuckle.

Rubbing his pointed beard, he looked back down at her and stepped over her supine body to study her from a different angle. The sable trim of his black pelisse swept lightly across her chest, and he noted with a smile her raised nipples, hardened and taut, straining against her silver tunic.

She was easily aroused, he mused, intense lust filling him at the thought, centering upon the hot fire flaring in his loins. The sign of a truly passionate woman.

Halil glanced up again, clearing his throat, his narrowed gaze falling upon his Chief Eunuch. Unspoken communication passed between master and slave, a command. The Chief Eunuch walked over to a large chest, ornately wrought in silver and gold, and raised the lid. He pulled out a silk bag, heavy with chinking gold coins, and held it in one huge hand as he moved silently to Frederick. He held out the bag, his broad face expressionless, his bald head glistening in the golden light of myriad candles.

Frederick hesitated, looking from the silk bag to

Kassandra's prostrate form. But at Halil's questioning look he seized it from the eunuch's hand, knowing from the bag's weight that it was more gold than he had ever imagined. With this generous reward, and the payments he'd received during the last few months, his wealth and comfort were assured, for life.

"I am pleased with your gift, Count Althann," Halil stated simply, walking around Kassandra to stand at her slippered feet. "If anything, your praise of this woman's . . . Kassandra's . . ." he amended, "beauty was too modest. But now you must leave."

Indeed, Halil thought impatiently. He could hardly wait to divest this Englishwoman of her silken garments, like the petals of a flower, and reveal the fragrant hidden bud.

Frederick started, but quickly recovered. Of course you must leave, fool! he berated himself. Your work is done here. He bowed low at the waist, clutching the silk bag to his chest. Then he remembered the message Mustapha had given him, hidden in his sash. He straightened, pulling out the rolled parchment and handing it to the Chief Eunuch, who inspected it and handed it to Halil.

"A message from His Grace, Mustapha," Frederick said, watching as Halil deftly slit the cord with the jeweled dagger at his waist, broke the seal, and unrolled the slip of parchment, reading quickly. The grand vizier's expression became one of extreme annoyance. Frederick surmised there was no love lost between these two men, bound by blood but little else.

Halil turned abruptly to the Chief Eunuch. "Inscribe a letter. Tell my cousin exactly what was discussed earlier today at the war council. It seems he wonders why I have not ordered an attack upon the Imperialists. Sniveling fool! He grows weak with worry in his fortress, fearing they shall make an un-

expected move. Can he not see they are quivering
in their tents, the cowards, soon to retreat? They
have no chance in heaven against the strength of my
army!''

Frederick said nothing. He had not been called
upon to answer. He stood silently, waiting as the
Chief Eunuch sat down at a nearby writing desk and
put pen to parchment, recording his master's words
and blowing upon the rich black ink as it slowly
dried. At last the letter was completed. The eunuch
folded it into a square, affixed the grand vizier's seal,
then handed it deferentially to Halil.

''Take this to my cousin, along with this verbal
message,'' Halil said, his black eyes full of anger as
he gave the letter to Frederick. ''If he wishes to re-
tain his position in Belgrade, he would do well to
acquire some backbone. It seems he is growing soft,
perhaps spending too much time in the company of
his women.''

Frederick nodded and slid the letter within his
sash. ''It shall be done, Sire.'' He stole a last glance
at Kassandra, then turned on his heel, his flowing
caftan swirling about his long legs as he strode from
the inner chamber of the tent, through a vast adjoining antechamber, a shadowed corridor, then once
again into the night.

Halil's forehead creased in speculation, watching
the heavy folds at the entrance to the tent cascade
back into place behind Frederick's tall figure. He had
not missed the flicker of guilt in his unsettling blue
eyes as he looked for the last time upon the Englishwoman. It was a surprising emotion in such a man.
And a liability in a spy.

Perhaps Count Althann's days of service to the
Sultan should be drawing to an end, before such an
emotion could lead to a fatal misstep. But he dismissed the thought, deciding to wait until morning

to take any action. Now there was only pleasure on his mind.

He waved away his Chief Eunuch, who disappeared like a creeping phantom into an adjoining chamber, and turned back to Kassandra, kneeling beside her. She started, panting, as he cut the knotted scarf binding her wrists. He could sense the fear emanating from her like a dense fragrance. It excited him beyond measure.

Kassandra winced at the touch of cold steel against her cheek and the sound of a sharp blade easily swiping through the gag just below her ear. She ran her tongue across her dry lips, not knowing what her simple gesture was doing to the man kneeling over her. Next the blade slit her blindfold in two, the severed scarf falling away from her eyes. She blinked from the sudden flood of light, squinting up into the piercing black gaze of Halil Pasha. Her whole body tensed as he swept the long strands of hair from her face, his fingers lightly brushing her skin.

Halil sucked in his breath, marveling at the wondrous beauty of his new slave. She was perfection, a goddess, just as Count Althann had said.

He had never seen such an incredible color as the luminous amethyst pools staring up at him, set off by thick, dark lashes beneath winged brows. He leaned over her, trailing a smooth-tipped finger from the center of her forehead, down the straight line of her nose, brushing the sensuous curve of her lips and resting on her trembling chin. Perfection. And he could wait no longer to possess her. His need was great; it cried out for satisfaction. He had held himself back from his other concubines all afternoon in anticipation of this moment.

A pity he did not speak her language, he thought, rising to his feet in one lithe movement to tower above her. No matter. What he wanted to do at that moment required no words. It was a language of gesture, expression, touch, perfectly understood by man and woman, master and slave. He held out his hand to her, a commanding motion, his eyes reflecting his immediate intent.

Kassandra did not move. She did not even blink. She simply stared up at him, looming like a great black falcon above her, her body awash in loathing, fear, and terrifying awe. Everything about him was black, his close-cropped hair, his glistening beard, his eyes, tinged with cruelty and burning lust. Black pelisse, black trousers, black slippers . . . black, absence of color, symbol of death.

His face was pale against the blackness, narrow with long features, a high forehead, a hooked nose, and generous lips that curved into a cunning half smile. His white hand reached out to her, but she would not take it. She shuddered with disgust and turned away, repulsed, sickened . . . fearfully defiant.

Halil's smile fled his lips, incredulity and rage welling up inside him. No slave had ever insulted him so before! Nor had any slave ever excited him so . . . His blood coursed hotly through his veins. He would take up her challenge. If she would not accept his hand and allow herself to be led to the low dais, turning her back on the silken comfort of his bed, then he would take her on the floor. She would learn not to defy her sovereign master, her lord—this . . . this slave!

With a ragged sigh Halil fell on top of her, his lean frame, toughened, scarred from battle, a warrior's body, pressing her into the floor. She screamed, a high, piercing sound, but he only laughed wildly in reply, his Chief Eunuch and numerous guards, standing at attention just beyond the inner chamber, staying their hands upon their scimitars, his laughter assuring them there was no cause for alarm.

Kassandra struggled and kicked, tossing her head, but her strength was no match for his own. She heard a ripping sound, and inhaled sharply as her tunic and chemise fell from her breasts, baring them to his black gaze. He held her shoulders to the floor, kneeling astride her now, his fingers splayed and biting cruelly into her flesh, while he bent his head and captured a rose-crested nub with his mouth, suckling hungrily, his hideous groans ringing in her ears.

Kassandra twisted desperately beneath him, crying out again when he grabbed her wrists and wrenched them high above her head, his other hand fumbling with her silken trousers, pulling them down around her hips. His leg delved between her legs, forcing them apart.

"No!" she screamed, her breaths tearing in great gasps from her throat. She summoned every ounce of her flagging strength in a final effort to thwart him. "No!" She jerked sharply to one side, her arms breaking free of his grasp, her hands flying to the wide sash at his waist, groping, searching for the one thing that would save her, not from death, which would swiftly follow her final act, but from this brutal rape.

She laughed in frenzied relief, her fingers suddenly circling around the hilt of his dagger. Too late, Halil sensed her intent, and his mortal danger. Before he could stop her, she brought it up high above him, then down, down, the flashing blade slicing into his arm just as he managed to roll away from her, saving his own life by the barest instant. He jumped to his feet, screaming in pain and outrage, shouting curses, his hand pressed to his upper arm, blood trickling between his fingers and running down his sleeve.

The Chief Eunuch was the first to rush into the inner chamber, his saber drawn, followed by eunuch guards and Janissaries pouring in from the front entrance and adjoining antechambers, scimitars poised. They converged upon Kassandra, who lay on her back with her eyes tightly closed, her breasts heaving, her body wracked by shuddering spasms, too exhausted to cover her nakedness and beyond caring.

She said a swift prayer, expecting at any moment to feel the sting of many blades cutting into her flesh. And, indeed, if she had looked up at that moment, she would have seen a glittering canopy of scimitars raised high above her, suspended, as the guards looked to Halil for the slight nod that would end her life. All was hushed, deathly still, with no sound but for jagged breathing and the faint ring of steel upon steel as scimitars wavered, brushing blade to blade.

Halil exhaled slowly, glancing from his arm, the bleeding partially staunched, to the woman lying defenseless upon the floor. He quickly made up his mind. He shook his head, in that small gesture sparing her life. The scimitars were withdrawn, and the Janissaries and guards moved back to their places. Only the Chief Eunuch remained, with another eunuch of lesser rank by his side.

"Cover her," Halil finally managed to say through gritted teeth, struggling to catch his breath. He watched as the Chief Eunuch lifted Kassandra roughly to her feet and threw his brocade pelisse around her while the other eunuch supported her limp body. She opened her eyes briefly, her gaze widening as if she was stunned to find she still lived and breathed, then she closed them again, her chin dropping to her chest.

Yes, you will live to regret what you have done, slave, Halil thought fiercely, as if reading her mind. You will wish time and again that you had died this day.

"Take her . . . to the harem," he said, gasping.

"Isolate her from the other women . . . but do not deal too harshly . . . with my tigress. Perhaps a few days without food or water . . . will tame her wild manners."

"Yes, Sire," the Chief Eunuch murmured, though his expression, usually set and composed, was doubtful. He nodded to the other eunuch, and together they dragged Kassandra from the inner chamber.

Halil winced, pulling away his hand to examine the oozing wound. His private physician entered the chamber, rushing forward, but he waved him away.

"It is only a scratch," he said, sinking down upon a divan. His voice fell to a whisper. "Only a scratch."

Hardly worth the loss of such dazzling beauty . . . and a passionate spirit to match, he mused. Cold cruelty glittered in his black eyes. A spirit that he would break, bit by bit, until she begged for his caress with open arms.

His full lips drew into a smile, the thought giving him great pleasure. He leaned back upon the divan, allowing the hovering physician to approach him at last.

etching out and blan[...], the handwrit[...]
[dif]ficult to pick a path through the [...] and [...]
[...]g boulders. It was even more difficult [...]
[...] they now had no moon to [...]

# Chapter 41

$\sim\!\!\sim\!\!\infty\!\!\infty\!\!\sim$

**F**rederick leaned well back in his saddle as the Persian war-horse galloped down the steep hill leading from the Ottoman camp, Kassandra's piercing scream echoing in his mind.

He had heard it carrying from deep within the grand vizier's tent just as he mounted and rode away. The four Janissary guards riding with him had laughed coarsely, praising the prowess of their commander. He tried to blot it out, to think of anything but what was happening to her right now, but he could not.

Damn it, man, you did what you had to do. It was either this, or your own skin. At least she lives. But his reasoning did little to assuage his guilt, nor did the weight of the gold, hidden in the folds of his trousers, which pressed against his hip. He felt he was choking on guilt, drowning in it, even as he tried to force his mind back to his mission . . . delivering Halil's letter to Mustapha.

Frederick eased up on the reins when he reached the bottom of the slope, veering the stallion toward the rocky shore of the Danube. The Janissaries pulled up behind him, flanking his rear.

It was pitch-dark, the moon barely visible in the sky, a pale beacon hidden behind a thick bank of clouds. A swirling fog was settling over the river, reaching out and blanketing the shoreline, making it difficult to pick a path through the rocks and hulking boulders. It was even more difficult to sight the small boat they had upturned and secured beneath armloads of underbrush, the boat they would need to cross the river to the fortress.

Frederick knew it was close by, but with each passing moment he could see less and less. The fog had become so dense, it obscured anything more than a few feet away. He did not see the silent shadows crouching behind a mass of boulders until it was too late, could not even have guessed that a regiment of Imperial soldiers had been sent out along the Danube as advance scouts for the battle to come.

He and his Janissary guard passed unwittingly right through the midst of them, realizing their danger only when they were attacked with a swiftness that sent them sprawling from their saddles. Three of the Janissaries died at once, quietly, neatly, their throats slit, their lifeblood staining the sandy soil. The remaining guard was wounded, but not mortally, subdued by four silent soldiers.

Frederick fell hard upon the ground, a soldier immediately astride his chest while two others pinned him down. The white turban was knocked from his head, the cold point of a dagger pressed beneath his chin, piercing the skin. He looked up into the clouded sky, awaiting death. Instead he heard a sharp intake of breath and a deep chuckle.

"Look at what we have here, Commander," his captor muttered incredulously, peering at him in the dark. "Either this Turk had a blond, light-eyed mother, or I would swear he is no Turk at all!"

Another man drew close and bent over him, squinting closely at his face. He straightened, quickly voicing low-spoken commands. "Get this man to his feet at once. You three will accompany me back to the camp, while the others hold their position here until we return.''

A numbness washed over Frederick, a swift death denied him with these words. He could not believe how quickly fate had turned against him. His deadly game had been well played for almost three years, and now suddenly he had lost, without even a fight, just as he had attained the wealth that would free him from his role as a spy. That gold was useless to him now. It could not spare him from what lay ahead, a death far worse than anything he could imagine.

Frederick was pulled roughly to his feet, his hands bound with leather cord, a gag stuffed into his mouth. He waited as a boat was brought from behind the rocks and slid across the gravel into the river. A sharp push propelled him forward, and he stepped shakily into the rocking vessel, strong hands pushing him onto a planked seat.

''Perhaps you might explain to Prince Eugene why you wear the clothes of the enemy, lad,'' the officer murmured tersely, settling behind him, a blade at his back.

After the men heaved the unconscious Janissary guard into the bottom of the boat, they pushed off from the shore and drifted silently downstream. For fear any sound might bring the Turks down upon them, no oars touched the water until they reached the point where the Sava flowed into the Danube. Then they rowed like hell against the conflicting currents, making straight for the Imperial camp.

Stefan stepped from Prince Eugene's tent, the council of war having drawn to a close. It was already well past ten o'clock. The camp was hushed, still, but for the intermittent bursts of artillery fire near the Sava, the Turk's remedy for holding them at bay, even during the night. Except for the continuous guard posted around the camp, most of the soldiers were catching a few precious hours rest, which was also his plan. Three o'clock in the morning, when the camp would rouse to make final preparations for battle, would come swiftly enough.

He drew in a great breath of the damp night air, murmuring a prayer of thanks for the heavy fog that blanketed the camp and the surrounding countryside. He could barely see the lighted windows of the fortress high above Belgrade. Hopefully the fog would hold to serve as their ally and shield in the dark hours before morning.

Stefan turned and strode toward his own tent, his mind working over the events of past hours, the council of war, the lengthy discussions, planning a course of attack, on and on. Yet one event stood at the forefront of his thoughts. He shook his head, still astounded. He could hardly believe that Count Frederick Althann, the court fop, was a spy for Sultan Achmet.

It had been the most incredible scene. They had all been gathered about a large oaken table, Prince Eugene and every commander save one plotting the battle that would commence well before dawn.

Prince Eugene had already discussed with them his decision to launch a surprise attack against the Ottoman lines. The long siege and the constant bombardment had taken a heavy toll on his forces, in both manpower and morale, until the Imperial army was on the verge of collapse. Believing his hand to be forced, he had to choose between retreat, hardly an option for the brilliant general, or striking out in a daring retaliation, despite the heavy odds against them. He had opted for retaliation, with the full support of his commanders.

At the height of their discussions, they had been suddenly interrupted by a commotion outside the tent. The commander of the regiment that had been sent to scout the Ottoman camp had burst in, followed by a retinue of soldiers, two bedraggled prisoners in their midst. One of them was a Turk, slumped between his guards, his shoulder bloodied and his right arm hanging uselessly by his side, and the other was Count Frederick, dressed as a Turkish officer.

A stunned silence had fallen while the commander grimly recounted how he had captured the prisoners, then he handed Prince Eugene a letter that had been found on Count Frederick. An aide familiar with the Turkish language was summoned, the general's expression darkening as the young lieutenant read it aloud.

Never had Stefan heard more overbearing confidence than was expressed in that letter. It elicited a terse response from Prince Eugene.

"This letter shall be Halil Pasha's undoing," he murmured, his dark gaze falling on every man in the tent. "His misplaced confidence proves once and for all that we must make a stand. It will be the last thing he expects. Cowards? The grand vizier will soon know the meaning of the word when his soldiers are routed and scattered in retreat, his tents razed to the ground!"

If ever there had been evidence to condemn a man as a spy, and a traitor, it was that letter. Yet through the reading, Count Frederick remained aloof, silent, with a studied dignity, as if that was the only weapon remaining to him. It was clear to everyone that he was hardly the preening fop he had played at court, an ingenious role he had devised to cover a far more dangerous pursuit.

At last, after refusing to answer any questions, he had been dragged away for torture along with the Turkish soldier captured with him. His death—as for all spies, impalement on a sharpened stake driven into the earth—would come later, after they had gotten any useful information from him that might help them in the battle the next morning.

Stefan sighed heavily. That had been several hours ago. No doubt by now Frederick hardly resembled the same man. Torture was a cruel, but necessary evil in wartime. The information he had given to the Turks had already cost hundreds of Austrian lives, a price he would pay with his own.

Stefan slowed his pace as he drew closer to his tent, recalling the piercing look Frederick had shot at him before he was hauled away. A strange chill had coursed through him, but why, he had no clue.

"Commander von Furstenberg!"

Stefan wheeled at the agitated cry, but he saw no one through the damp mists. He turned back, continuing toward his tent.

"Commander . . . von Furstenberg! I must . . . speak with you!" the voice called again, and this time when Stefan turned, he saw a dark form running toward him, taking shape in the mists. He recognized the captain of the prison tent, where not only the prisoners but also unruly and undisciplined soldiers were being held.

"What is it, man?" Stefan asked as the burly captain drew up alongside him, panting as he fought to catch his breath.

"I just came . . . from Prince Eugene's . . . tent." He gasped, bending down and resting his hands on his thighs, his chest heaving. "His aide . . . said you had left . . . only a moment . . . ago."

Stefan nodded. "So you have found me. But what's the urgency here—"

"The prisoner, sir . . . Count Althann," the captain interrupted, straightening. "He is asking for you, Commander. He says . . . he will speak to no one . . . but you."

Stefan's expression hardened. What could the

traitor possibly have to say to him? Then he shrugged. He only hoped it was useful information.

He nodded. "Lead on, man." They set off through the fog, the shorter man fighting to keep up with Stefan's longer strides. When they reached the prison tent, the guards quickly lowered their muskets and stepped aside, allowing them entrance.

It took a moment for Stefan's eyes to adjust to the dark interior, lit only by scattered oil lamps. Unkempt soldiers were shackled to their cots, a row along each wall, deserters, thieves, ruffians, the lowest dregs of any army. The air was stuffy, smelling of human waste and sweat. The war prisoners were kept off by themselves in an adjoining tent. The morale in this place was low enough already without having to listen to a man's agonizing screams during torture.

Stefan passed quickly through the main tent, looking neither left nor right, then through a wide fenced area and into a smaller tent. He stopped short, his eyes widening as his gaze shifted from the Turkish guard, lashed and hanging limply from a wooden post, to an outstretched form bound hand and foot, and lying on a blood-soaked cot. He moved closer, his lips tightened into a grim line. It was not a pretty sight.

Frederick's naked body was streaked with blood and dank sweat, his face black and blue, his eyes swollen shut. His fingers and toes had been mutilated, and scorch marks crisscrossed his chest where a hot brand had seared into his flesh. His left leg had been broken, and twisted cruelly beneath him, shattered white bone breaking through his thigh.

Stefan fought back a wave of unexpected nausea. He had seen far worse on the battlefield time and time again, but there was something about this man that struck him to the core. His body had been reduced to ruin, yet he lay there with a quivering defiance Stefan had seen in few others, friend or foe.

"He has refused to say anything for two hours," the captain blurted, standing at his side. He had regained his breath, an incredulous look upon his swarthy face. "He grinds his teeth, screams, moans, cries out for God, but other than that, says nothing . . . even through this." He shook his head, perplexed. "Just when I begin to think he will take any information he possesses to his grave, all of a sudden he asks for you, Commander."

Stefan drew closer to the cot, studying the once handsome face. Frederick's breathing was very shallow, and it appeared he had lost consciousness.

The captain seemed to have the same thought. With a callousness born of practice, he grabbed a bucket of cold water near the cot and threw it in the prisoner's face.

Frederick gasped, his body jerking spasmodically. His eyelids were so swollen and puffy, he could not open them. He turned his head, his lips cracked and bloodied, his rasping voice barely above a whisper.

"H-has he come? Count von . . . Furstenberg. Has he come?"

Stefan knelt on one knee next to the cot, the captain hovering over his shoulder. He glanced up, annoyed. "I can assure you, Captain, if the prisoner says anything of importance, you will soon know it. For now, stand back."

The captain's eyes widened in surprise, but he quickly complied by retreating to the entrance to the tent.

Stefan turned once again to Frederick. "I am here, Count Althann," he murmured. "The captain says you want to speak with me."

"Kassandra . . ." Frederick moaned. "Kassandra . . ."

Stefan blanched. For a moment he said nothing

. . . could say nothing. His eyes bored into Frederick, the same unsettling chill he had felt earlier racing through his body.

What rantings were these? Had the man gone mad from the pain, his mind dredging up memories from the past as his life streaked before him? Why, Frederick had not seen Kassandra since . . . since Prince Eugene's gala. Had he been summoned only for these lunatic mutterings?

"Kassandra," Frederick repeated, his voice cracking and breaking, yet stronger this time.

Stefan reached out and gripped his shoulder, regretting his action when Frederick groaned hideously. He drew back, restraining himself, not knowing what to do, feeling as if he were the one going mad.

"Why do you say her name?" he asked, his breath jagged, his face taut and drawn. "Why?"

"First . . . you must promise me."

Stefan started. "Promise you . . . promise you what?"

Frederick tried to lean forward, struggling against his bonds, but he fell back, the wasted effort shattering his body with wrenching pain.

"Promise me . . . I will . . . die swiftly. N-not. . . impalement. Please . . . promise me, Count Stefan . . ." he whispered, tears oozing through his swollen eyelids and streaking down his ashen face. "S-swear it."

Stefan swallowed hard. He was certain this condemned man knew something about Kassandra. And he was bargaining, even now! He nodded quickly, his throat constricted, then remembered Frederick could not see his assent. "Yes. Yes, I swear it," he agreed. "I swear, on my life. Now tell me. What do you know of Kassandra?"

Frederick turned toward the tented ceiling, a great shuddering sigh expelling from his body. "She lives," he murmured simply. "She lives."

Stefan's heart stopped. God in heaven, what was this man saying? Kassandra was alive? He leaned closer to Frederick's ear, his voice a desperate plea. "Where?"

Frederick's parched lips began to move rapidly, whispered words spilling forth in rasping succession, punctuated by moans, sighs, curses, as he spun the sordid tale of treachery, deceit, and murder. Stefan listened silently, wracked by tumultuous emotions, one woman's name searing into his mind. Sophia. You have done this to me, to Kassandra. Sophia . . .

When Frederick could speak no more, his face twisted in agony, tears spilling down his cheeks, trailing through blood and sweat, Stefan laid his hand upon the tortured brow and stroked it gently, his hand shaking.

They remained so for a long time, until Stefan at last rose to his feet, swaying ever so slightly.

"You . . . have sworn," Frederick gasped, sensing his movement.

"I have sworn," Stefan murmured. "Your death shall be swift, Count Frederick Althann." He turned from the cot, the captain rushing over to him at once.

"What did he say—"

"Torture him no further," Stefan ordered as he strode toward the entrance. "And cut that other man down."

"But, Commander, I have my orders," the captain blurted. "Until they give me information—"

"The information has been given to me," Stefan shouted, his gray eyes ablaze as he wheeled sharply. "You will receive like orders from Prince Eugene within the quarter hour. Now, see that the prisoners are bathed. Make their last hours as comfortable as possible. Give them brandy to dull the pain, and warm broth. Do you understand?"

"Yes, Commander." The captain nodded, shrinking back from this outburst.

Stefan did not stop until he passed through the guarded entrance, drawing in great breaths of air as if he himself had just been released from prison. He set off toward Prince Eugene's tent, Frederick's words roiling in his mind.

Kassandra was alive! It was just as he had believed since the day she disappeared, just as his instincts had told him! And she was here, had been here, for weeks . . . so close, so close. Yet his incredible happiness was tempered by abject despair, the two emotions crashing together, leaving only the harsh light of cold reality.

Kassandra was in the hands of Halil Pasha, had been given to him as a gift that very night. God help her! It was not so much that she could be in the grand vizier's arms at that very moment, but that she faced certain death in the morning if Prince Eugene won the battle, as he must!

A ragged sigh tore from Stefan's throat as he recalled the previous summer's campaign, the decisive victory at Peterwardein, Hungary. He and his soldiers had been among the first to enter the slain grand vizier's tent after the battle.

They were greeted by a gruesome sight, a sight that haunted him still. The women in the harem had been brutally murdered for fear they would fall into the hands of the infidels. He had never seen such a slaughter of innocents . . . They had been beheaded or strangled, their silk-clad bodies lying where they had fallen in pools of blood.

Stefan broke into a run, his lungs burning with exertion. Somehow, somehow, Prince Eugene must position the cavalry so that the attack against the Ottoman lines would not only be swift and deadly, but also so that he might make it to the grand vizier's tent in time to stop the senseless massacre. It was Kassandra's only chance . . .

# Chapter 42

Prince Eugene sat astride his white stallion, his dark gaze piercing the swiftly receding fog. His army was spread out before him, poised just to the south of the Ottoman camp, farther than he could see in the murky predawn light.

But he knew they were there. The Imperial forces had silently crossed the Danube in ordered precision to assemble on the immense eastern plateau overlooking Belgrade. Row upon row they stood bravely, infantry at the center, bayonets fixed and ready, flanked by the cavalry, colors flying and drums silent, all hushed and waiting for the signal that would strike up the cadence and sound the march.

Prince Eugene drew in a long, steady breath. He knew that the moment he gave the command to advance, the Turks would hear their drums. Suddenly alerted to their position and the imminent attack, they would swing their heavy cannon to the south, and the bombardment would begin.

So be it, he thought grimly. The moment had come.

"Sound the advance!" Prince Eugene shouted, his words echoed by other voices as his commanders took up the chorus, the drums beating fiercely in measured response, the great army moving forward. "To the glory of the emperor, and the Holy Roman Empire!"

"To the emperor!" Stefan cried, wheeling Brand in front of the left flank of cavalry, his hands firm on the reins. Prince Eugene's words of last night rang in his ears, burning like a firebrand into his mind.

"Use your best judgment, Count Stefan. As soon as you sense the enemy is routed and in retreat, take your men and make straight for the grand vizier's tent. If you're in time to save your lady, only God may determine."

Please, let it be so, Stefan prayed fervently, Brand lunging forward beneath him. Let it be so . . .

Kassandra lay huddled on a soft mattress spread upon the silk-carpeted floor, her hands tucked under her chin, her gaze fixed in front of her. She took little notice of the oriental luxury of the small ante-chamber, strewn with brocade pillows embroidered in gold thread, a carved chest inlaid with ivory set near the tented wall, the fringed carpets three deep beneath her mattress. It could have been a rat-infested prison, damp and dark, for all she cared.

Her shimmering silk-gauze chemise and trousers of vivid rose might as well have been cut from coarse woolen cloth. They seemed to chafe at her skin, the transparent fabric clinging to her nakedness.

The Chief Eunuch had forced her to put them on the night before in place of her torn garments, then had allowed the ladies of the harem to peek in on her. They had laughed, pointed, and tittered, babbling in many different languages, none of which she understood. She had merely ignored them. Finally the Chief Eunuch had sent the curious women scurrying away with a simple gesture, his amusement thwarted by her silent indifference.

Kassandra sighed deeply, rolling onto her back. It

seemed that indifference had become her last defense against whatever her fate might be.

For some reason, Halil Pasha had spared her life, and she could well imagine why. Her attack had obviously not daunted him. More likely, she thought, shuddering as she recalled his black gaze upon her when she had been dragged away, it had encouraged him. If she was to survive, she would have to seal off her inner self, her emotions, in a layer of feigned passivity. He might ravage her body, but she would never allow him to break her spirit. No matter what happened, she must sustain her will to escape.

Escape. A brave thought, yet how distant it seemed, she thought dully. She had never felt so desolate, so devoid of hope.

Even the numbing comfort of sleep had evaded her through much of the night. She had dozed fitfully, perhaps five minutes here, or a quarter hour there, always waking whenever the Chief Eunuch silently entered the antechamber to check on her. The artillery fire, which had suddenly increased tenfold less than an hour ago, had not helped either. The ground was shaking from the constant barrage. She could feel it through her mattress.

Kassandra closed her eyes, her head drifting to one side as sheer exhaustion overwhelmed her. Perhaps finally she could sleep, despite the rumbling. She needed her strength, and sharpened wits, to endure what lay ahead . . .

A thunderous explosion suddenly shattered her fleeting slumber, its violent force rocking the ground. Then came another, and another, five explosions in rapid succession, each one closer than the last.

"What?" Kassandra gasped, sitting bolt upright, clutching a pillow to her breast. She had slept only a moment, but she was completely dazed, as if she had been sleeping for hours. Another explosion rocked the earth, and she jumped up with a startled cry, dropping the pillow and clapping her hands over her ears.

What was happening? It sounded like the Turks had turned their own cannon upon themselves!

Her eyes widened, her breath catching in her throat. No, that was absurd. There could only be one explanation. The Ottoman camp was under attack . . . Yes, that had to be it! The Imperialists were attacking! Stefan!

Renewed hope flaring brightly within her, she drew fresh courage at the thought that Stefan might be close by, perhaps even in the camp. She ran over to the tented wall and pressed her ear against it. She knew the antechamber was within a larger tent, but she could swear she heard the muffled sounds of running feet, men shouting, muskets firing, the ring of sword against sword—hand-to-hand combat!—and the screams . . . horrid, agonizing screams of wounded and dying men.

Fully awake, Kassandra willed herself to be calm, despite the excited thoughts that were skittering about in her mind. She had to think clearly, carefully.

Perhaps in the confusion she could attempt an escape. She would have to flee through the harem, but this might be her only chance. There was no other way out, at least not that she knew. Sweet Lord, it was worth a try!

She crept quietly toward the entrance, her hand trembling as she gently moved aside the swaying brocade curtains. She was surprised that the eunuch guard who had been keeping a constant vigil in the short corridor leading to the vast outer chamber was not there. She couldn't believe her good fortune!

Kassandra stole into the corridor, her heart beating so hard against her ribs that she thought for sure

it would give her away. She was almost to the outer
set of curtains, reaching out to draw them apart,
when she heard a high, piercing scream of sheer terror, unlike anything she had ever heard before. It
was coming from the harem.

It raised the hair on her scalp, sent flickers of fear
streaking through her body. Her hand froze in midair.

What was happening? she wondered wildly, as a
keening wail broke just beyond the curtains, a
mourning lament, followed by wild, terrified shrieks
from a chorus of female voices.

Kassandra braced herself against the tented wall,
afraid to move, yet afraid to linger. The unnatural
voices of eunuch guards sounded above the terrible
cacophony, like lunatic ravings. She heard the unmistakable swoosh of scimitars slicing the air, dull
thuds striking the carpeted floor, pitiful pleas in a
dizzying array of languages, punctuated by tearful
sobbing, rising to a fever pitch, then suddenly cut
off . . . dead silence, until another female voice
screamed in hysterical supplication, chilling desperation . . . silence.

Whatever is happening, you can't stay here, Kassandra's inner voice warned her. You can't stay
here! She moved once again toward the curtains,
her hands shaking as she drew them aside, her
knees quaking in fear. She nearly fainted from the
horror that greeted her, her eyes wide, uncomprehending.

There was blood . . . pools of bright red blood everywhere, splashed on the tented walls of the harem,
streaming from beheaded bodies lying where they
fell on the silk carpets, staining the flashing scimitars wielded by eunuch guards.

And there was motion . . . women running in
desperate, futile flight, screaming, crying, being cut
down, one by one, while others fought, and clawed

at their own necks, crumpling to the floor as silken cords quickly strangled the life from their bodies.

As will happen to you, Kassandra, if you stand here. Run . . . run! She lurched forward as if shoved by an invisible hand, one thought in her mind: flee, or die in this place.

She skipped over blood-soaked torsos, barely evading eunuch guards who lunged for her, her eyes fixed upon the unguarded entrance to the tent as she dashed across the vast chamber. Her breaths tore at her throat, her lungs were on fire, but she ran as she had never run before, every fiber in her body straining with the effort.

Heaven protect her, she was almost there! She could almost reach out and touch the swaying curtains—

Suddenly a massive form stepped in her way, blocking the entrance. She ran right into him, headlong, a silken cord whipping about her neck as she fell heavily to her knees.

Kassandra gasped in disbelief, the breath wrung from her body as the cord tightened cruelly across her throat. She looked up, tears stinging her eyes, straight into the broad face of the Chief Eunuch. He bent over her, smiling, a twisted smile, a grimace of death . . .

She shook her head, her mouth gaping in a silent scream, her fingers prying frantically at the cord. Wheezing and gasping for air, she dropped her hands limply to her sides. Her eyes closed, blackness swirled around her . . .

A deafening roar sounded in her ears, twice, three times. An immense weight crumpled on top of her. But she felt nothing, only a strange peace settling over her . . . It was so restful, so quiet. No more struggle, no more heartrending pain . . . no thoughts. Only peace.

"You there, help me! We have to get him off her!"

Stefan shouted to several of the soldiers who had accompanied him to the harem tent, while the others moved swiftly through the vast interior, rounding up the eunuch guards at bayonet point and saving what women they could.

The two men threw aside their pistols, heaving together with Stefan to shove the black eunuch from Kassandra's prostrate form. Yet even as they rolled him to one side, the corpse clung tightly the twisted cord around her neck, his huge, clawlike hands frozen in death.

Stefan sank to his knees beside her, gritting his teeth as he forced open the eunuch's lifeless hands, loosening the cord from her throat. Dear God, if he was too late! He gathered her in his arms, stroking her fiery hair. She was so deathly pale, scarcely breathing . . . Surely she would not be taken from him after what they had both suffered!

Stefan held her against his heart, kissing her as if he could breathe life back into her body. "Kassandra . . ." he whispered against her lips, his voice jagged, breaking. "Kassandra, my love . . . my love."

Kassandra heard a familiar voice, deep, rough-edged, calling her name, echoing to her from some distant place, calling her back from her nether sleep.

It sounded so much like Stefan . . . What a cruel trick for someone to play on her. But it grew louder, more insistent, demanding she answer . . . demanding she return. And she wanted to answer. Oh, how she wanted to answer!

Stefan sharply drew in his breath as Kassandra's eyelids quivered and fluttered open, her amethyst eyes staring up at him. But there was no expression reflected there, no recognition, only a glassy emptiness. He bent and kissed her again, desperately, yet so tenderly, drawing her back to him, pulling away at last to search her eyes, his heart thundering in his chest.

Kassandra blinked, her body convulsing in a single spasm as sensation flooded her limbs, sweet breath filling her lungs, chasing away the darkness, the swirling mists. She looked up, her gaze full of wonder.

It was Stefan's face, haunted, drawn, beloved . . . so beloved, hovering above her own! She could feel the strength of his arms about her, strong, safe, holding her fiercely, as if he would never let her go . . .

Her hand trembled as she raised it to his cheek, touching him gently, as if to assure herself he wasn't a dream.

She smiled.

# Epilogue

⌒◯◯⌒

*Vienna, Austria*

**B**rilliant sunlight splashed across the great bed, a glorious October morning beckoning to the couple nestled beneath the rumpled sheets and shimmering brocade bedspread. Yet they seemed in no hurry to rouse themselves, as if they had all the time in the world.

"Good morning, Countess," Stefan murmured in Kassandra's ear, nudging her awake with gentle kisses along her silken shoulder.

Kassandra stretched luxuriously, her skin tingling from his touch. She leaned back against him, her fingers playfully entwining in his thick black hair.

"Good morning, husband," she breathed, testing the word upon her tongue. Husband. She loved the sound of it, as she loved him, more than she could ever express. Love seemed to fill the room, like the golden sunlight, vibrant, alive, so full of promise. This was their first morning as husband and wife . . . her first morning as Countess von Furstenberg. She laughed softly. She loved the sound of that, too!

As Stefan drew her closer, his arm wrapping about her slim waist, Kassandra fell contentedly silent, remembering the beauty of their wedding the night before in the domed grandeur of the Karls-Kirche.

There had been candles, thousands of flickering candles to light their way to the high altar, and resplendent music, the Court Orchestra, choirs, and chiming bells merging in joyous song and celebration. But most memorable of all, the recitation of their vows before God and man . . . and their kiss, sealing their eternal pledge.

Then as husband and wife, she and Stefan had shared in the wonder of watching her father take Isabel for his wedded wife during the same ceremony, attended by the emperor and empress, Prince Eugene, and the entire Viennese court.

Save for two, Kassandra amended with little enmity. Archduchess Sophia von Starenberg had not attended, nor had Count Frederick Althann . . .

Her expression grew pensive. So much had happened since Stefan had rescued her from Halil Pasha's harem. The Imperialists had won a decisive victory that day, the fortress surrendering soon after. Many men had lost their lives on both sides, the grand vizier counted among the slain. And Count Frederick had lost his life, executed as a traitor, yet swiftly by the sword, as Stefan had promised. Prince Eugene and his army had returned to Vienna a month later in triumph.

Archduchess Sophia von Starenberg had been tried before a high court and sentenced to live out the rest of her days in penitential solitude, imprisoned within a strict Benedictine convent in the foothills of the Alps. And Adolph, her accomplice, was now a jester at the prince-bishop's palace in Salzburg. The high court took pity on him and merely banished him from Vienna, as he was forced to perform Sophia's evil deeds in fear for his life. His confession was instrumental in implicating the archduchess not only for her vile plot against Kassandra, but for the death of her husband.

Happier events had occurred as well. Her father had recently been appointed court minister to King George; he and Isabel would be returning to England within the month. Isabel could hardly wait to begin her new role as a court minister's wife, and eagerly anticipated the whirl of social duties that would accompany it. They would be sorely missed, but visits to Wyndham Court would soothe the parting for all of them.

Stefan had retired from military service to devote himself to his burgeoning estate . . . and most important, he had added when he told her the news, his gray eyes tinged with laughter, his new wife.

Kassandra blushed at that happy memory, sighing faintly. Yes, so much had brought them to this day. So much good, so much bad, a bittersweet collage of piercing joy, unfathomable sorrow, heartbreak, tears, laughter, and hope.

"What are you thinking, my love?" Stefan asked, sensing her thoughts. He nuzzled her nape, inhaling the jasmine fragrance of her fire-gold hair. "If not of me, I shall be very jealous."

His teasing drew a smile to her lips once again and she rolled onto her back, looking up at him.

"I was thinking how fortunate we are, Stefan," she murmured. "How fortunate that we found each other as we did." She flushed warmly, remembering that afternoon of stolen splendor, so long ago. Their chance encounter, ordained by fate, had set into motion the events that had forged this fierce love between them, a great love, a love that would endure whatever life brought to them.

Stefan traced his finger along her cheek, pausing at the lush curve of her mouth. His heart ached with love for this beautiful woman . . . his wife, a love that was woven into the very fabric of his soul.

"Yes, I'm a very lucky man," he breathed husk-

ily, drawing her into his arms. He bent over and
kissed her smiling lips, hungrily, passionately,
greeting this special day with a splendor all its own.